Otter Coast

A Medical Marijuana Mystery

Maia Kumari Bree Chowdhury

ASEI Arts
Coquitlam, BC, Canada
2026

Copyright ©2023
Maia Kumari Bree Chowdhury

email: admin@aseiarts.com

Published by ASEI Arts, Coquitlam, BC, Canada

Distributed by Ingram

Name: Chowdhury, Maia Kumari Bree, author

Title: Otter Coast | Maia Kumari Bree Chowdhury

Description: First edition
First published Chatham, NJ, USA (2023)
Current printing: ASEI Arts, Coquitlam, BC, Canada (2026)

First US Print Edition 2023 Identifier:
ISBN 979-8-9861854-1-5; Second Printing, 2026

First US Digital Edition 2023 Identifier:
ISBN 979-8-9861854-2-2; Second Release, 2026

Designer: Laurie Landry (2026); Lori Dalvi (2023)

Editor: Jillian Magalaner-Stone

www.aseiarts.com

By the Author

Fiction [series]

The Erenwine Agenda: A Hydraulic Fracturing Love Story
Otter Coast: A Medical Marijuana Mystery
Rail: A High Speed Adventure

Non-fiction [manual]

Reiki: A Manual

Anthologies [contributor and curator]

Anthology House: A Visionary Ecology Project
Anthology House 2

Doctoral Work [scholar-practitioner]

From Design Thinking To Leadership: A Qualitative Study

Dedication

To the Ocean

A Note about the Novel

This is a story a decade in the making, begun partway through writing my first novel, The Erenwine Agenda. Influences in my life as a writer during this time were many, including moving house more than once, experiencing with you all a global pandemic, raising two children, creating a new household for myself, and expanding on the creative front.

It is with this revitalized focus on well-being and finding one's inner compass that I now share with you the second in the Erenwine series, Otter Coast, a story about medical marijuana, an ancient artifact, and a journey to illuminate a long-buried mystery that I hope will delight and entertain you, dear reader.

Be well, read on, and enjoy.

—Maia

Part I: The Medicine

~ 1 ~

Creation

She counted the weave on her fingers:
wove weft, wove warp, wove weft, wove warp—the covering
took shape, and as she held the fibers in the midafternoon light,
the piece warmed in her hands.

It was a small square,
then a rectangle, and then, an oblong.
When it became long enough, she wrapped it around the gourd
from which she'd carved eyes and added seashells.

The wrapping molded in a fibrous weave around the gourd's
shell, solidified, and anatomized with hot wax which cooled fast
on her fingers.

It gave her the pleasure of its embodiment.
She felt it as a real-thing, and as she picked it up, she felt a
momentary lack of stability in her fingers, hands, arms, and seat.
She took a long breath in.

Putting the gourd down with an audible exhalation,
she next brought a bundle of smoking herbs, barks, and roots
well-tied, to her forehead, then to her throat. Blessed them with
her out-breath.

As she breathed in and out, she whispered in her language,
"Grandmother Spirit, Otter Spirit, Grandmother Otter, come
through the mask before me. Bring your playfulness to bear."

Then, she stood and leaned, dipped the mask in the amber
that pooled before her where she'd crushed and melted the
honeyish resin to a liquid, keeping care of her hands, and using
her cupped flints to lift and lower, lift, and lower. The blaze
would be seen for distances farther than the eye could know, and
she danced around the hottest center of the work, keeping care
of her long hair, braided back, and her woolen garments, pulled

tight. She held the gourd high until it hardened, her arms tiring, and when it was no longer soft, she set it to rest in sunlight.

Sunlight turned to moonlight, and the mask was whole and golden in its full creation. The wax inside lay suspended as if captured in a liquid moment; the fibers, shells, herbs, barks, and roots, caught as if askew to the wind, all kissing the gourd's surface. In the morning, she painted it with an oily, resinous mixture she'd prepared, and lowered the mask into the still-hot coals of before. Once cool, she inserted, with chewed wax for bonding, more small amberish flints.

It was done. It told her so with a shimmying rush of energy up her forearms. For a time, she would pick it up and put it down, whisper and listen, whisper, and listen.

"Welcome

Welcome Grandmother Otter Spirit

Welcome playful one

You reside in this mask

But you are not bound by it

When one who carries this mask

Connects with you

They will see through your eyes

They will feel through your essence

They will play in the waves

The way you know

Brings joy."

This, she said

This, she knew.

One day, the mask quivered and shook, leapt from her hands, and danced across the ground, danced up into the tree, danced into the air, and danced across the land.

It danced all the way to the coast, where it took its station in the ship-bay, and as it did, she saw it go in her vision and in her mind's eye, and soon it was beyond her vision and only in her mind, with the ancestors; the ancestors with her.

The mask went west with the wind, alert and on point at the
leading edge of the current.

It dove in and out and played with the waves, always
attentive to the ship—the many ships—on the ocean, with
cargo, human cargo, this cargo shivering and displaced, terrified,
and angry, desolate, and uprooted.

Always, the mask sang its song of home, and rivers of this
home reverberated through the wind, to the sea, and through to
the souls who would always have connection, and through to
those who thought they had lost it.

The mask found its new home in a house,
in a tree-sheltered clearing.

In the clearing was a glow, and in this glow the mask
came to rest.

From the glowing home, Grandmother Spirit rose out and
beyond, connected still yet expanding, and through both eras of
atmosphere and strata of time, she tapped down on the land that
shone out from beyond, and her essence came to rest on a stone
cap of a tall parapet on the top of a towering brick building in a
busy city, many days, years, and centuries, many oars, lengths,
and reaches, from the moment of her journey's origin.

At this parapet, in this city, above this river, at the ocean's
meeting, stood a young woman with her back to a flock of birds.
The birds clustered on the parapet, perched and ready to fly. The
young woman fiddled and focused her thoughts, able to see a
great distance in the other direction, on that clear, winter's day.

~ 2 ~

Rooftop ~ December

"Almost done up here," she said to no one. Amalia Sengupta Erenwine flipped to the next page of her work notebook and realized it was the last. For the time being, from where she stood on an old Manhattan rooftop behind a crumbling parapet wall, the last page of her notebook would have to do. She was well-back from the edge, yet she wanted to peer over. Instead of taking notes, she'd take pictures. Her cell phone's camera was handy and small enough to maneuver. Could she reach out over the edge of the parapet to snap a picture of the façade below?

Notebook on parapet, she slipped off her gloves, stretched out her arm and snapped a picture. The phone's camera did not respond. Either the chill of winter or the angle of her hand must have made it unresponsive. She dug out the stylus Betsy had given her on the ground floor of the building, to be used during the cold weather inspection with her work tablet. She used it to take a picture of her feet. That worked, but could she reach out over the parapet to do the same, capturing the condition of the brick wall from above? She began to lean out, phone in one hand and stylus at the ready in the other. Felt a warm glow on the back of one hand, and then on the other. The warmth moved up her arms as if embracing from behind, from within, from above. It soothed her, brought her back into the moment. The reach beyond was too far. "Not worth it!" She'd heard of architects falling from rooftops during inspections. "Not me!"

She stepped back and shook out her hands, jiggling the phone, and in the cold, her rings began to slip off. She pocketed them. The warmth receded into the chill of the day. Instead of continuing her inspection, she'd take a break to photograph the view of water towers in TriBeCa beyond. The city and region were in the slow process of recovery, two months after the hurricane, or superstorm, as it had been named by meteorologists and the media. Power was restored and water had receded; sand still filled the ground-floor spaces of homes up and down the New York–New Jersey coastline. From up there on the roof, all Amalia saw was beauty.

The phone was cold yet functioning; she'd be able to make a call if she wanted. Didn't want. Didn't need. Felt no pull toward anyone at all. Things had cooled between her and Mark since the events of the previous month, and she'd be leaving soon in any case, to visit India for her grandfather's funeral. She should reach out to someone. Being alone in the shadow of all that had transpired was not good. She'd be better off if she had someone to confide in. Jen? Sandra was still far away, and a video chat was not the same as a hug. Mark had let the notion of her possible miscarriage roll right over him. Her tummy felt tight. Could not quite take a full breath.

Maybe the Reverend Mildred? Amalia typed in a text to Mildred, who'd been agitating for a new panel discussion, this time on medical marijuana. She popped her gloves back on. Of course, she'd go to Mildred's panel. There were no telltale dots coming in response to her message, no indication that Mildred was on it and typing back. They were more than generationally separated in that respect. Mildred, for all her wit and vitality, was not going to get into a text chat with Amalia. Of this, Amalia was certain.

Didn't matter. Too cold for more gloveless texting. The eraser-like end of her stylus, which had worked well enough for the photography, was unsatisfying when it came to conveying any emotion in a message. "Little phone, hang in there, it's cold I know. You can do it!" She put the phone and the stylus back into her jacket pocket where it was warmer between her body and the wool. She'd scribble out on the last page of the notebook. What did she need to capture? What had Boss Lady asked her to note? Betsy was downstairs. Amalia didn't want to ask her again, letting on that she hadn't been paying attention the first time she'd been given instructions.

"Document," she wrote and said to a grey city pigeon that perched on the parapet. It hopped away and flew north. "Direction." The bitter chill of the winter's air made her lips feel slow. "Details." She buried her chin deeper into the scarf wrapped twice around her neck. Who did she need to connect with on the direction of the details?

"Sunil." She'd been connecting with Sunil over structural engineering. He was both easy and fun. She and Sunil had become neighbors once she had moved to Hamilton Heights from the Upper West Side, out of Sandra's great aunt's rent-controlled apartment and into her own sparse quarters, shared with Mark. Sunil, the uptown condo conversion project, and she, were within a few blocks of each other, and while she didn't run into him too often going to and from the office downtown (she could never make the early trains, and she would often work late), she did run into him every Saturday morning at the laundromat on Amsterdam Avenue when Mark was out for a run. A run, or some other thing. Some time they spent apart. What did Mark do, then, when she was laundering?

It was their deal: Mark did the dinners, had food ready when she came home, and Amalia did the laundry. Mark worked from the tiny one-bedroom apartment all day, except for the times he parked himself in a coffee shop or went to meet his former colleagues at Atlantia. She guessed they were still colleagues since they worked on the same projects. Mark consulted to the industry—no longer in it, and able to provide what he called constructive criticism of media and public outreach from within the industry. He wasn't a lobbyist, but he hadn't given up. Some days, she wished he would. He was a gas-evangelist, and she'd grown used to it—and accepting of the transition fuel—but hated the fracking it still involved, and despised Mark's continual defense of it.

The environmental center project in Binghamton was threatening to come undone because of her fight over fracking—and gas companies weren't even fracking in New York; Atlantia Actuaris, underwriter-on-the-fence, had simply salivated to start fracking in New York. Of course, the theater project in Scranton, Pennsylvania, was funded by the natural gas industry. She'd be back there in days, to meet up with her parents and to fly to India for her grandfather's funeral. No time to look at projects while she was there. Family first. She had a sideways feeling of offness about the theater project that she could not quite put a finger on. It was the natural gas connection, she knew, of which fracking was a part. She'd known going in. Told herself it was okay, it was a bridge to a new energy path, but it wasn't seeming so. It was seeming permanent, and not at all transitory.

Mark said it could go either way.

She'd tried to talk with him about it more, and yet every time she did, they ended up in a fight. And it wasn't just about fracking. Ever since the Reverend Mildred had announced the upcoming discussion panel, they'd been arguing over that, too. Amalia was tired of it.

She turned from one water tower view to another, 180 degrees behind her. As she took a step forward, a flock of grey pigeons lifted up and swooped in an arc around the roof and landed on the adjacent building. How long had she been up there, daydreaming? Betsy Polson was a floor below, surveying the inside of the old warehouse, a potential new adaptive reuse project that had come to Polson Grohman Architects and Engineers in the past week, as the building transferred to new owners. Amalia had slipped away and upstairs through the bulkhead door, ejecting herself from the top of the main set of stairs in the underserved building, and up to the roof, when Betsy had been paying half attention. She'd been curious to see the view of the city. And a beauty it was.

The bulkhead door was locked. Hadn't she left it resting open behind her? A rush of anxiety overtook her warm, daydreamy, bird-ringed moment. Tried the handle again and banged on the metal face of the door. She felt her hands sweaty within her gloves, her abdomen lurching. "Firetruck!" she said, repeating her father's oft-muttered curse. A firetruck might be what she needed if she didn't get the door open.

It was cold and bone-dry there, with patches of ice-crusted snow in areas untouched, smooth, and unbroken expanses of arctic polar vortex–spun crystals. "Think, Amalia!" A flush of heat popped up her scarf and to her face, and not the gentle warmth of the earlier moments. This was full-on panic. She stood where the snow had been cleared, out as far as the cable trays back from the parapets where the building's departing owner decided to install an out-of-season renovation Betsy did not think was code compliant. The cable tray installation had halted before Betsy Polson and PGAE—not just Betsy, but Max

Grohman too—had been brought into the work to convert the warehouse into a mixed use, TriBeCa-based facility.

She needed to get down. Warm, and down. Banged hard on the door again. "Betsy!" No answer. Had she gone down to the street to look for her wayward intern? Amalia fiddled with her phone, camera still open from when she'd decided to take the last water tower picture, and threw herself against the door. Oh, dummy she was. Her phone. Took off her gloves again and called Betsy's cell.

"Where are you? I told you to wait, not to head back to the office."

"I'm on the roof." Amalia could hear traffic sounds beyond Betsy's cell.

"Roof? What roof?"

"Of the warehouse. In TriBeCa." And it was getting colder. Her hands and face numbed in a gust of wind. The gentle warmth that had pulsated up her arms and encouraged her back from the edge would be welcome if she could figure out how to find it. The hot panic had subsided, leaving her on the verge of freezing.

"I'm in a cab on the way back to the office, Amalia. What are you doing on the roof in TriBeCa? I thought I heard you say you were going."

"Going—to the roof—I'm locked out up here."

"Holy crap. Hang on. I'll call the building super. Are you okay? Hopefully, he picks up and lets you back down. I'm going to hang up now to call him. No wait, stay on the line. I'll call him from another line."

"I'm okay. I'm sorry." Always sorry, always apologizing to Betsy.

Moments later, Betsy was back: she'd reached the building superintendent, who was in a meeting with Sunil, who'd arrived in the meantime with an intern from his engineering firm. The building super would be right up, no doubt with Sunil and the intern close behind. Amalia could only wait. She put her gloves back on and her phone in her pocket.

Sunil stood on the other side of the door. "They're trying again," he said, his voice muffled. The door was stuck, and the super couldn't unstick it. "You okay there?"

"As okay as ever, couldn't be better." Why wasn't there a window in the bulkhead so she could see him? She should call Mark. Pulled her phone back out, but it would not turn back on. "Dammit." At least she'd got help before it froze up. Phone hadn't been right since it had got all wet back at the environmental center site in Binghamton. Quirky with powering on and off, freezing up—now, freezing up and not turning back on.

It was back then in Upstate New York she'd temporarily lost her phone, and later connected further with Mark, en route to the fracking panel discussion the Reverend Mildred held the following weekend. Without the first trip to Binghamton, she'd never have seen the flyer for the fracking discussion.

Mildred, who'd performed an impromptu marriage ceremony of sorts, didn't yet know Amalia and Mark had not completed their marriage paperwork. Betsy didn't know either. Who knew, and who didn't know? Her parents thought she was living with her boyfriend, who they liked. Betsy, Max, and Jen thought she was legally married—or at least, had no reason to think otherwise, since they'd observed the goings-on the previous month. Amalia had never told her parents since their focus was on her grandfather's passing. She'd tell them in time.

Amalia stomped her feet to get warmer, jumped up and down. Hoped the superintendent would be back soon with whatever means he found to open the door.

Later, sirens wailed, a group of FDNY firefighters broke down the bulkhead door, and Amalia, soon wrapped in an emergency blanket by an attending police officer, shivered and with thanks accepted a hug from Sunil.

"We've got to stop meeting like this," he said.

"We've never met quite like this before." She shivered. He hugged her tighter, and the strength in her returning hug surprised her. The intimacy of the moment restored a measure of calm within her, and the warmth she remembered from the rooftop's edge returned. A flush filled her from within. She wanted to find a way to stabilize on her own between vacillations of warm and cold, security and anxiety. Didn't need this man; didn't want to need.

It was only back at the office she realized the tablet and stylus were not with her. The inspection report would be incomplete, at least, for the moment.

~ 3 ~

Reverberation

"I'm sorry," Amalia said. "I'll go back."

"You're frozen," Betsy said. "Go home and have a hot shower, warm up. You're not going to feel better just wrapping your hands around that hot coffee. We'll get the tablet next time we go." Betsy was right. Amalia did not need to stay with the office crew, apologizing and shivering. Who was that helping? She'd go home.

One subway ride later, up the west side of Manhattan, Amalia was in her neighborhood, walking past the cemetery, by the bodega, and up the four flights of stairs in the once-upon-a-tenement building. It was a friendly, if noisy, apartment block. Mark would be home, she assumed, but when she'd texted (from her warmed-up phone), he had not responded. Maybe he was heading downtown on the subway to his favorite Chelsea café, nearer to her office, and close to the Flower District that they both loved. If so, they'd been ships passing in the night. Subway cars sliding past each other in the darkened tunnels underneath New York.

Inside, she took off her coat, peeked around, and saw that he'd been in the middle of a paper-sorting exercise. They'd both be leaving on different trips within days. Hers was more somber, his more exploratory. She shivered from the transition from outside cold to inside heat. He'd left a mess of sheaves of paper sticking out the recycling bin. Unlike him. He must have been in a hurry to clear things out before taking them downstairs to the street bins and rushed to complete the task before she got home.

A different kind of edge caught her eye, and she pulled at a thickness of paper. A photo. She held it between her forefingers and thumbs as if it was a piece of ID she'd found on the ground: peering into the image, seeking the identity of the person in the picture, she held the photo by its edges, tattered from having been moved from place to place.

Unfamiliar writing on the backside. The papers must have slid down around it after he'd jammed them in. He was too private—even with Amalia—to let something personal be so apparent. "I'm getting rid of a lot of stuff," he'd said that morning before work, as he had begun to empty binder after binder of geology printouts and class teaching materials into the recycling. "Not going to need these in Iceland," he'd said. He had sounded final in his tone. Amalia wondered if he was forcing it, as if trying to convince himself, or her.

The writing on the back of the photo was curvy, and Amalia wondered if the woman was, too. A shot of jealousy reverberated through her bones as she pieced together handwriting and facial features. The woman had dark, long, and wavy hair that blew across her cheeks as if dancing in the wind. She was tanned and seemed to have dark eyes. She might have been curvy, but Amalia couldn't tell: the image was cropped at the shoulders. On the back, in the curvy writing, Amalia read aloud: "To Mark, with all my love, Helene." The woman looked like she could be a sister of Amalia, but she was not. Of this, Amalia was certain. "No sister, no friend."

Amalia stuffed it back in between the papers for recycling and exhaled with puffed cheeks to the room. Pulled at the buttons on her sweater, yanked off her tall boots, peeled off her underlayers, and stood, naked, before the room, then turned to the bathroom. She needed to do more than warm up. She needed to wash away the feeling that there was more in Mark's world than she wanted to know.

A shower restored her. Mark had not texted. It was four o'clock in the afternoon. Boss Lady expected her back at work. She texted Betsy:

I'm not feeling well.
Staying home.

Restlessness ran through her veins and gave her a jolt. Needed to keep her hands busy. She'd pack for her own trip. What would she need in India? Warm weather clothes. The aunties would have new outfits for her, and jewelry. She'd take books. Her gut twisted in a knot. Should she bring her exam prep materials? Her first architectural registration test section was scheduled for when she'd return. Sure. She could study on the plane. The soft-covered books, large and flopping, borrowed from the office and heavy as bricks, along with tidy box after box of flash cards, went soldier-like into her large suitcase. She'd have time, time among the ashes and ruins of her life, time to take that step forward from a place only she could inhabit. Her gut released its tension a little and for a moment she had a flash to it all being over: she, a licensed architect, and he, a sanctimonious geology professor and petrochemical rep. The thought of it brought her no relief, and the bitterness returned.

If only she could find a way to sweeten the feeling; she hated to leave on her trip to India with such sourness.

~ 4 ~

Company

"There's no reason for you to feel rattled," Mildred said to Amalia on the phone. The girl had called in the early evening in a huff of energy. "It's very normal to have mixed feelings."

"I can't get over this sense Mark is hiding something," Amalia said. "Every time I try to talk with him, he shies."

"He's in the middle of a lawsuit, you said so yourself."

"Not the right time, never the right time," Amalia said. "I don't know when is. I don't seem to have my timing right. I can't wait until his deal with the fracking company is figured out. I'm not having cold feet. He's completely distracted by his work."

"Can't blame yourself or anyone else for bad timing, or for someone else's focus. That's their business. Just got to open to the winds of opportunity to sniff out better alignment."

"How do I do that?"

"It's an age-old question," Mildred said. "You'll know it. You'll find it."

"Tell the girl," she heard in the foreground of the room. "Breathe, Amalia."

"I don't know what you're talking about."

"Focus on your breath. Meditate on your breath."

"Mildred, I do love you, but that is not what I'm talking about."

"Change gears," she heard in and around her temples. "I have faith in you, Amalia." She sensed the girl's breath release in a gentle exhalation over the phone. Imagined her shoulders dropping, and her carriage settling into a soft chair. Mildred held the image.

"It's not just the fracking thing, Mildred. It's the medical marijuana thing, too."

The girl was determined, she'd give her that. "He's pro-fracking and pro-medical marijuana? And you're not?" Mildred continued to hold the image of Amalia, relaxing.

"No, he's pro-fracking and I'm pro-medical marijuana."

"At least you both know what you stand up for. That's more than a lot of young people can say." Mildred took in a deep inhale and focused on relaxing within herself.

"Don't know about that. I think most people of my generation have a lot they want to stand up for."

"And you two don't agree on what that is. An age-old problem." Mildred paused. How much did Amalia want to hear? "My advice? Take it to a tree."

"I had a feeling you'd say something like that. I'm as much of a tree hugger as you, Mildred, but I don't think talking to trees is going to get me and Mark any closer."

"Tell you what, next time I'm with a tree, I'll have some special words," Mildred said. "Me and the tree."

Mildred McCaine stood behind the cold, stone bench in the small cemetery behind her church in Upstate New York. Amalia's doubts settled in front of her, pooled in a state awaiting release. There was nothing to be done save to see the girl as whole, well, and worthy. It was easy because that was the girl's true state. Nothing doing.

A large oak tree's branches graced the cemetery, bare to the winter sky. "I had a question for you, but I cannot remember it." Maybe Raymond would nudge her. Knowing Raymond's ashes were there, buried and marked, brought her peace. Out of this sheltered peace rose a sense of reaching for more answers. Mildred saw an acorn on the ground next to the stone grave marker. She slipped off a mitten to pick it up, and held it in her palm, cupped. Slipped her mitten back on over it. The acorn sat there like a little bump on a log. A frog on a log. A bump on a frog. She smiled at the feeling she had a little friend with her, hidden away in her mitt.

She'd been asking questions for years. Her Reiki practice gave her a sense of soothing. Sometimes, came answers. For the life of her, though, as she stood there behind Raymond's memorial bench, bundled down in her coat, scarf, and hat, she could not remember the question she'd been asking. Her mind was a blank, a calm blank. As she stared into the stone of Raymond's plaque, she held the acorn between two palms, the acorn thickly padded in a prayerful pose. An image emerged in her periphery. It moved, and with its movement, her head moved. Nothing there. She shook it off, felt a grumble from within her buried tum, and stuffed her mitted hands deep into her coat pockets. "Almost dinnertime," she said. She wriggled the acorn out with her fingers, let it lodge deep into her coat pocket, and stuffed her hand back into her mitt.

The walk of a few blocks between church and home was a treacherous one at that time of year, icy, and so, she'd driven. Parked close. Always got her good spot, labeled for her! The Reverend Mildred McCaine. And she had a blue 'Handicapped' tag, too, not that she felt she needed it. Her eyes were just fine, thank you very much. "Eggs," she said as she started the car. "Shall we have eggs for dinner, Raymond?" He didn't respond. Didn't usually. Suited her just fine. She had a busy evening ahead, planning for the next panel discussion. An errant oak leaf floated down, dry from autumn and stuck all winter, and hit her windshield. "Eggs it is." Didn't need Raymond chiming in with his from-the-grave opinions. She was fine sorting it out on her own.

Mildred peered at the email on her computer screen. Knew there would be consequences. She refocused on the task in front of her, shifted her glasses back up the bridge of her nose. Father Jasper, instigator of many great works of social charity and kin to boot, had written with a new idea. Instead of holding another community forum—medical marijuana had been Mildred's idea—why not hold it on a double header set of issues, to double the attendance? He himself would be pleased to suggest ideas that his own congregants would travel to discuss. Veterans Affairs? PTSD? Side effects—children's use of prescription drugs? He listed several possibilities. Mildred saw them all as relevant to be sure, but none grabbed her.

What intrigued her more was why people were up in arms about medical marijuana in the first place. She didn't understand it. Used it, didn't understand how others could be against something helpful.

"Prohibition," she said. There was a role there for the voices involved with the early 1900s Prohibition movement, a keen influence on her early years growing up in Maine, before they'd traveled across the continent to the West Coast. She'd grown up in the shadow of it, as had her whole family.

She knew just who to contact. She picked up her phone to call her sister in Canada. From where Mildred sat in her own home in Binghamton, New York, she could picture how Muriel would stand when she answered the call. Her sister would be in their mother's condo on Salt Spring Island, tended with love since Mother's death, and she would be by the kitchen window where the old phone coiled itself from the wall. Muriel would be looking at the ocean, the Pacific Ocean. She would be staring out at the view Mildred knew well and had not seen since the previous autumn.

There was no answer on the other end of the line.

"Fine," Mildred said to the room, and hung up without leaving a message. She turned to compose a new email.

"Reminder!" she said aloud as she wrote. "Our Medical Marijuana panel discussion is expanded! We will embrace new issues! Bring your questions. Bring your loved ones." She backspaced over the last few words. Her fingers ached as she typed, stiffening as they sometimes did. "Bring your—best ideas." She backspaced again. "Bring your—open minds." She smiled. That was it. She shook out her hands, wrists allowing a slow release.

Later, she tried Muriel again. Mildred fiddled with the acorn she'd picked up off the ground. Muriel, stationed well inside the Salt Spring Island condo, had much to share. She recalled scant details but had many thoughts to contribute: the documents of Papa, she said, were all still in the Vesuvius house on the other side of the island, as she had not done the big purge since Mother—Mama, to Muriel—had died. Mildred rolled the acorn between thumb and middle finger as she listened to her sister's recounting. The condo hadn't had room for Mama's things, Muriel explained, and since they'd decided to keep the Vesuvius house for Muriel's grown daughters and their girls, there had been no rush to empty it after Mama moved out to the other side of Salt Spring Island. "Come," Muriel said. "The island misses you. And I'm all alone in Mama's now, and the girls have all taken over Vesuvius. I could use the company."

"I will come." Acorn smoothed, Mildred balanced it on the windowsill next to her. She'd lost a husband and her own mother in a short space of time. To reconnect every few months with her sister was a good thing. She felt it all the way down to the shins. Mildred looked down to see the littlest kitty brush up against her leg, nuzzling for a snuggle.

~ 5 ~

City Lights

Dear Amalia,

The view outside my hotel window in Reykjavik is stunning. The people here have been extremely warm, in contrast to the cold of winter. The sky is dark all the time and the city is lit brightly. It feels cheery. The people here have figured it out.

By now you will be on your way to India via your parents in Scranton. I hope all is well with your family there and with your grandfather's funeral ceremony. I know you were a little nervous about it all, or excited. Both? You were very buzzy when we said goodbye at the apartment. Please give my best to your parents. Tell Sou I'd love some more of her excellent cooking when she is back. And to your dad, please tell him I called his colleague at the University of Scranton like he suggested. It was a helpful link in the case. Joseph would like to know, I am sure.

I can't provide too much more information about the case at this point. I seem to have the information I need to represent myself, outside of Atlantia Actuaris. The missing piece was a legal bit that your dad's colleague helped with. Fracking regs sure are a mess in the US. You were right about that. Not that I'm saying hydraulic fracturing is all bad! Not saying that. Just that the legislation needs to catch up. I am sure we could go on for days about that once you return.

The Icelandic geothermal meetings are going well, and the sites I'm investigating will take some time to sort out in terms of who-owns-what. I seem to be on track to being able to provide some good geology public relations consulting worldwide, at least with Iceland as a start. It was a lucky break to have connected outside of Atlantia's range, at a time when I am happy for the independent cash flow. Making a go of it on my own just might work. I know you're busy with your own work in architecture, and rising too, especially as you are leaping into your licensing exams. I need to figure out how to do this on my own and not depend on your free time to help me with the environmental consulting.

Signing off now from the hotel-above-parking-lot spectacular view—aurora coming into sight—must grab pictures while it is bright. City lights tend to dim the aurora a little but right now it is great!

Yours ever more,

Mark

P.S. When you're back it will be the New Year already—since we will have missed Christmas together, let's do something celebratory. I'm thinking snowshoeing? Do you like that? You let me know. We can go anywhere. I'm open. It will be fun to be with you no matter what we do.

P.P.S. You know the café I've been working out of in Chelsea, the one that maintained its power after the hurricane? The server there put me onto something good, taking a drawing class. I was getting stuck drawing the figures for our comic book project. I think this will be a good thing. Maybe even before you return. Timing is an issue though. With the consulting, and the class time, there is not much left in the middle, and I want to spend time with you when you're not studying for your architecture exams. And did I tell you? Timmy and Candace are coming into Manhattan to see a specialist. Something about the baby's heart. I'm sure it will be fine. The best pregnancy specialists are in New York. I told them they could stay with us. Hope that's OK. We can sleep on the kitchen floor in sleeping bags and give them the bed. Candace will be better in a bed. Sorry if I forgot to mention that earlier. It came up same day as you were leaving. That is a lot for a P.S. No, for a P.P.S. OK. Sending email now!

P.P.P.S. Wait, one more thing. Did you end up deciding to go to the Reverend Mildred's panel discussion on medical marijuana?

~ 6 ~
Energy

Dear Mildred,

As I sit in the warmed interior my hotel in Reykjavik, on my own, I think of you and all you did to assist me and Amalia in finding our way. You are a blessing in a human bundle of energy, and we love you very much.

Hope you had a good Thanksgiving holiday and wishing you a big early Merry Christmas (they are already preparing festive lights here!),

Mark Redd Stone

P.S. Hope to see you and Bert again once I am back. He is quite the charmer! Is he staying in Binghamton with you, or did he go back to Canada? Either way, I am looking forward to seeing at least you, when you hold your next panel discussion—marijuana, I don't know why you chose that for a topic, but I am sure you will run a good meeting. And speaking (writing!) of Canada, I plan to spend some more time with my grandmother in Quebec. You and Bert could drive up from Binghamton to see us. The land is beautiful.

P.P.S. All is well with the fracking case. Thank you for your help, so to speak, with the files. I have returned them to their original location. I hope I did not cause you any trouble. I'm tying up loose ends with the old company. Might even swing by Wales on the way back to put the last details to bed.

P.P.P.S. I hope you were able to resolve everything with your parishioner Frankie, too.

~ 7 ~

Cookbooks

Fresh inside after an abrupt taxi ride from the bus station to her parents' house (the fare a luxury inspired by not wanting to lug her suitcase), Amalia found herself digging into her mother's old cookbooks to look for the perfect and most satisfying treat: homemade custard. What called her to this comfort was not a desire for its light sweetness or its creamy texture, nor its malty richness. And she was not called to it for its carbohydrate-sugar-feeding alleviation of feelings of suffering or loss in the face of her grandfather's passing, for whom she was heading to India to mourn. It was the color she sought, and she felt the color in the house as much as she desired to absorb it by making and eating the custard.

The hurricane-turned-nor'easter of the previous month had spared her parents' warm home in Scranton. She'd given it a quick once-over on arrival. The house was fine. It would all be closed up, in any case, as they would soon fly to Kolkata—forever known to her family as the Calcutta of her mother's childhood—for the funeral there; they would travel together as a family. Amalia had suggested she fly on her own from New York, because wouldn't it be simpler? She'd been overruled, and since her parents were making the bookings and paying for the tickets and, in fact, the whole trip, she was not flying from the better-serviced New York but was transferring from Pennsylvania.

The cookbook fell open to the custard recipe. She looked at the relative proportions of wet to dry ingredients and wondered if she would find what was needed in the kitchen, or if she'd have to go out. In the fridge, she found a container of milk, but no eggs. She would improvise if needed. It was not the taste she was after, it was the nourishing vibrancy of the hue. She'd had a sense of it on the bus ride over: golden, halfway between butter and crème caramel, and oh, so delicate. The words for its nutty lightness escaped her, and although she whispered the possible combinations as she had looked out the window: "butter cream, butter yellow, custard cream," none came close. It frustrated her sense of order that something as simple as the color of custard would elude her ability to be pinned down. She would need to see it to establish a correct answer.

The recipe called for a lot of sugar, more than she had realized. Mark would have something to say about it. He'd wanted to come on the family pilgrimage, since they were married in all but the formalities of paperwork. It was because she'd had a freak out that they hadn't completed the marriage. It wasn't a freak out about Mark. She'd had a tiny little miscarriage after their trip to City Hall, or maybe a heavy and short period, she couldn't be sure, and even though it was a while ago, she still felt tender from the event. He had not understood. Her mind rolled over the events as her finger trailed the recipe page. She'd call him. He'd be busy with work. She'd wait.

A crush of gravel in the driveway alerted Amalia to her parents' arrival. She danced to the front door to greet them, knowing they would not expect her to be home. She swung open the door and leaned on the doorframe. "Do you have any custard powder? Because we're making custard!"

"Amalia! How did you get here so fast? Where's Mark's car?" Her mother ran up to hug her. A smell of cinnamon on her mother's breath rushed at Amalia as she was enveloped in her mom's arms. They must have stopped at the mall and had the cinnamon buns; a not-so-secret treat they'd all enjoyed on big shopping days.

"Come help me with this," her father said. He opened the trunk of the car. Amalia and her mom walked arms around each other to join him. Amalia nestled into her mother's breast for warmth outside as Joseph stepped back from the car to embrace them both.

"Hi Dad. Hey, you cleaned out the mall!" The olive Subaru trunk, with Republican and Democrat signs propped to the side, was full of bags from the mall: small appliances, bed sheets, cushion covers. "Please say this isn't for me and Mark," she said, looking at the frilled edges of the fabrics. "And no, he didn't drive me. He's in Iceland. I took the bus." She pulled out two bags.

"I forgot he'd mentioned the possibility of Iceland." Her dad straightened up. "It's the new suitcases behind we need to get to first. We might as well pack them all up here." He squeezed her and landed a kiss on her cheek. "This is all coming with us to India."

"Thanks for organizing," Amalia said. "I'm just glad I was able to get time off work."

"Your boss Betsy would have to let you off for a funeral, wouldn't she? What's Mark doing in Iceland? I never did hear," her mom said. "It's too bad he didn't bring his car, because we wanted to give you the tent and the sleeping bags from the basement."

"Who knows what Betsy would or wouldn't do. Mark's there for work. And the sleeping bags would be lovely, thank you." Amalia paused. "You didn't get a Christmas tree, I noticed." She reached into the Subaru for the suitcases, new, black, and sturdy, and as large as were sold. "Planning to shop much in Calcutta?"

"We're taking all of this, and we might as well fill up on the way back." Her mom took one suitcase and extended its handle all the way up. "It's not like we're going sightseeing. And no, we didn't get a Christmas tree. Why would we when we'll be missing most of the holiday here?" Amalia caught a hurt tone in her mom's voice.

"I'm sorry about your Bapi," Amalia said. She put her hand over her mother's on the suitcase handle. "I know how much you wanted to be there."

"Let's just go inside, shall we? Let's hear all about how you and Mark are settling into that crazy city of yours. How are his brother and the girl?"

"They got married," Amalia said. She herself had taken off the ring Mark had put on her finger the same night. Wasn't ready to share with her parents, and it wasn't official. Why put her toe into dangerous waters? They loved Mark. It was enough they'd supported the moving in together. Amalia was not ready for the marriage conversation. "I guess they thought it was a good idea to do it before the baby comes."

"Always a good idea to be married before babies," her mother said. "You keep it in mind, Amalia."

Amalia felt a rush to her cheeks and a simultaneous churning in her belly. Did her mother know? Intuition did run in the family. Had she spotted through her clothes on the long bus ride over? The bleeding had been heavy, enough for it to have been more than a period. Could it be continuing, so long after? She ran her hands behind her back and smoothed her hips. "Let's help Dad pack the suitcases in the driveway," Amalia said. She'd moved from car to house and stood astride the door threshold, unsure if she should follow her mother inside or go back to her father.

"You said something about custard when we pulled up? We just had cinnamon buns," her mother said. "And we brought two, one for you and one for Mark."

"More for me," Amalia said. She followed her mom inside, drawn by an uneasy desire to come clean. "Mark and I almost got married." She hadn't meant for such a fast delivery.

"Amalia. A little soon, don't you think?" Her mother closed the door behind them both. "Don't think you should let your father hear."

"I thought he loved Mark. He was supportive of us living together."

"He's a complicated man, Amalia." Her mom looked to the door. "They all are."

"Are you okay, Mom? I mean about Grandpa's passing?"

"It's a relief, to be honest," she said. "Of course, I wish I could have seen him. Or talked to him. It's good he isn't suffering anymore. His lungs could only take so much, they said." Her mother exhaled through open lips, and as she did, her jaw softened. "I don't know how much more news I can take. I'm fine, but this is my max."

"Now's not the right time to tell you I might have had a miscarriage." Amalia bit her bottom lip. Had not meant to tell at all. It had come out. It was out.

"Amalia." Her mom's brow furrowed, and she seemed to freeze in place for a moment, then she held out her hand. "Hug?" She pulled Amalia in, and rocked her back and forth in a strong, exaggerated, and silent embrace.

The warmth of her mother's arms and the smell of cinnamon buns, combined with the rhythmic movement of her mother's body against hers opened Amalia into a gush of tears and shudders, shudders and tears, and her mom held her up. The pressure in her belly subsided as the tears released, and she felt the spasms cease. When she stopped crying, her mother held her at arm's length, smiled, and said, "Custard? Let's make custard." She held Amalia by the hand and drew her into the kitchen. "Do you need to see a doctor? Or did you already?"

"I did before I came. I went to a clinic in Manhattan. They said they thought it could be either a miscarriage or a period, but since it was early, they didn't know, and said it would pass. There's nothing wrong, you know? My body is fine. It's my mind I'm not sure of."

"You're not sure you and Mark are ready to be parents." It was not a question.

"I'm not even sure why Mark and I are together."

"Other than you love each other."

"We do."

"And maybe that's enough right now. You don't have to figure out the future. Not right now. What does Mark say?"

"I don't know. I can't think." Amalia sat on a kitchen chair. "I looked for a custard recipe." Wiped her cheeks with both hands.

"It's on the container." Her mom brought down a box of Bird's Custard Powder from the back of a high cupboard. "A classic." She smiled. "It'll do us both good. And it doesn't need eggs, which we used up because we're leaving."

The door opened behind them, and Amalia's father called, "help me with the suitcases, Sou, I need to know which appliances are staying and which we're taking."

"They're all going. All the appliances."

"Mom, they have appliances in Calcutta, they don't need appliances from Pennsylvania."

"They don't have these appliances!" Her mom made a fist and pounded the counter. "It's the demonstration of gift giving, Amalia."

"But appliances? Do they even work on the same power?"

"They have converters!"

"I'm going to feel silly when they open these. Couldn't we just bring a coffee table book of photos of Pennsylvania?"

"We have a book, too," her dad said. "We have everything!" He came into the kitchen. "Mmm, custard! Are we having some?" He kissed her mom on the lips, ever demonstrative and ready to show affection. "Some sweetness for my sweet love," he said.

Amalia shook her head. Cute. Did they even know how lucky they were? Her phone buzzed in her pocket, and she ignored it. Buzzed again, must have been a text or two coming in from Mark. She pulled out her phone. It was from Sunil.

Left the condo conversion survey in my office, and I'm away for the weekend.
Do you have it handy? Need to check something.

Why was he checking the survey on a weekend?

No sorry. I'm away too.

Where are you?

Pennsylvania. Where are you?

Upstate New York. Surveying some property damage here after the hurricane.

Why do you need the condo survey?

"Who are you busy texting with? Can you hand me a mixing spoon?"

Had an idea I want to check about the depth for geothermal. Like we were talking about when we met.

She remembered. And the bad fateful date afterward.

Can it wait? Jen can get it to you on Monday.

Why not you on Monday?

I'm going to India tomorrow. With my parents.

Cool, why? You didn't mention it.

Funeral.

She passed her mother the large spoon from the drawer. Sunil hadn't written back. "How long does it take for the custard to be ready?"

"Long enough you can finish texting with Mark. Why don't you just call him? What time is it in Iceland?"

"It's not Mark, Mom." She felt her cheeks get hot. Dammit! She didn't even like Sunil anymore. Why the guilty blush on her face in front of her mom? Her phone on the counter buzzed.

I'm sorry. Call me when you're back if you want to talk.

He ended it with a heart emoji. Amalia felt the tips of her ears get hot.

"You all right, Amalia?" Her dad motioned. "Come help me with the suitcases."

"And the appliances." She shook her head. "Fine, let's pack the appliances. Mom, you good finishing here?"

"Good as ever, sweetheart," she said, and gave Amalia a kiss on the cheek. "We'll be okay." She turned back to the custard and a small drop of liquid fell from her mom's cheek into the mixed pudding, leaving a little concentric depression of cratered, golden cream.

~ 8 ~

Firewatchers

Mildred canned the lights in favor of the candles over the darkened fireplace. Raymond would have had the hearth lit, but not her, not alone, and not with the cats as firewatchers. The candles would do. In a recognition of her love of a good, warm hearth, however, she put a candle down low in front of the fireplace. Eliza came close, sniffed, and turned her back, swishing her long tail high and away from the flame. "It's us for Christmas," Mildred said. She had no Christmas ritual of her own to speak of, at least not since Raymond. She put it all into Mercy Church. She'd often thought of sleeping there, and with the onset of Christmas blues, thought of it again. There was purpose for her there. There were people who needed her there. It made the idea of a parsonage make sense. Why had she chosen to continue living blocks away, after Raymond's passing? Maybe she was clinging to him. Maybe it was time to go. She could try it for a night. Christmas night, of all nights, would be a good night. She didn't even have to sleep. She could stay there and stay up, see the sun rise, and roll right into services.

Mildred felt alive at the prospect, and with that, blew out the candles, picked up her bag and keys, petted Eliza and the others, and walked out the front door.

"Goodbye, Raymond." She felt no sadness, just the optimism of the moment, and despite the goodbye in her words, felt that Raymond was with her in her heart, guiding her with grace down the front steps.

~ 9 ~

Saraswati

The trip to Kolkata (for it was Kolkata when it came to travel, not the Calcutta of the past) was long—first a taxi ride from Scranton, then three flights, and another taxi from Dum Dum airport through Lake City and to Park Circus—but uneventful. The cousins, aunties, and uncles who met them at the airport were happy and tired, it being middle of the night, and the house helpers who met them—Amalia couldn't help but think of them as servants—were beaming and interested. The heat of outside at night was quickly supplanted by the air-conditioning inside. The appliances were unpacked with glee, and each admired, then set upon the long counter in the kitchen wing. The photo album of Pennsylvania was laid on the dining table, and pictures of Amish farm country discussed in detail over chai and biscuits in the middle of the night.

Amalia felt as if in a dream, her fatigue and the murmur of shock at the change of physical and cultural environs provoking her into a kind of walled-off state from the family, in which she felt like a mime clown, motioning, and acting and presenting as if everything was normal, when in fact it was not. The numbness did not wear off, and when the next day they went in the cooler winter morning air by taxi to the Ganges, to Kali Ma Temple, and later back to the burning ghats, she was quite untethered, to the point of feeling her cells had come undone; she could, if dipped in water, dissolve into nothing.

The Ganges provided the opportunity. At its banks, she stepped in, barefoot, her chappal sandals set aside with the others, and the length of her borrowed sari—draped around her by a loving auntie—trailed in the water, its wet length along her leg, and she hiked it up above her knees. The group had stopped at the river to see the cremation site before the ceremony was to begin and end at the temple. The funeral pyre was ready, and her grandfather's body would soon be delivered. He would have a traditional ceremony, her mother said. Whatever that meant. Sari dripping along her legs, Amalia slipped her wet and gritty feet back into her chappals and followed the group back to the waiting taxis, where they drove a short distance to Kali Ma Temple and spent much longer looking for a place to stop. The driver dropped off Amalia and her parents near the temple and he waved them on, showing them where to go.

A fog of color, hibiscus, and incense, chai stands, and icon sellers laid the way from taxi to temple. Amalia followed her mother and held her father's hand, aware of the rings she'd left behind in New York.

Her mother knew where to go. They followed.

Inside, the temple was thronging with visitors, devotees, tourists, and, like Amalia and her family, those paying funeral respects. Not that Amalia could tell them apart. She followed her mother in a line of patrons and before long she stood before a holy man who said a prayer and pasted sandalwood onto her forehead in blessing. The crowd pushed against her, and she followed her mother to the other side of the temple.

"We go, now," her mother said. "To the river," her mother spoke louder, over the din. "For the cremation." Amalia could not tell if her mother's voice was happy or sad, yet her eyes spoke what her tone could not: bright, elevated, and connected, Amalia's mother was in her natural element. For years, Amalia had seen her as a small woman who had held back in expressing her talents in favor of supporting her husband's academic career and the moves it required: Vancouver, Scranton. Scranton, and where next? There was another position coming, and home would shift once again. Soumya Sengupta Erenwine stood, all of five feet tall, in the mass of worshippers, and radiated.

"I'm happy, Ma," said Amalia. "So happy to see you like this. Happy to do this with you." She squeezed her mother's hand.

"I'm happy, too," Sou said. "Do you feel him with us? I feel him with us." She motioned her head toward the exit. "Come, let's say our goodbyes, which are not true goodbyes, and we will move on." Her mother smiled, ducked her head, and with a squeeze of Amalia's hand, drew the family forward into the enveloping heat of the day.

For the remainder of the ten-day trip, Amalia ate, walked, slept, and felt the fog come and go, and she was reminded of the veil of culture shock and its influencing protection. It was best to let in a little at a time of the environment around her, or her senses would overload, and she'd become sleepy again, and need to lie down. It could have been the time difference, too, of course, or the shock of the loss of her grandfather, or the striking relief she felt at being away from Mark. She loved Mark. He didn't fit into this portion of her life, and as much as she wanted to be with him, she could not see him joining her on this part of the journey. And he had not. With his business trip to Iceland, he could not have come even if she had insisted.

In New Market, she looked for something to give to him, a token of her trip, and a memento to take forward in their life together. She imagined him in the apartment: its autumnal colored walls, soft and spicy, with its sari silk curtains, hung by the two of them on a day early in their short courtship. He would be working, sitting at their little kitchen table in their tiny common space, adjacent to the tiny bedroom and next to the tall light shaft, the common ventilation stack for the whole building. He would have the window ajar, and he would be hearing the music of the neighborhood, Dominican, Cuban, Haitian, Puerto Rican—and he would be tapping his feet, enjoying the rhythm, picking up his pen to make a note on some papers next to him, looking up, thinking of her.

Maybe he didn't think of her in her absence, but thought of others: maybe Helene, his ex, or maybe his brother, Timmy. Maybe his parents, deceased, or his grandmother, alive in Quebec. Maybe he wondered if he and Amalia had been right to want to elope, and maybe he was glad they'd never signed the papers. Maybe he was glad she'd had a miscarriage. Maybe he was glad she'd got her period; whatever it was, maybe he was glad he wasn't going to be a dad. She imagined him looking down at the floor where they'd sat with roses, and she imagined him looking up at the wall, bare and rust colored, awaiting some adornment from her trip. She'd get a Ganesh, or a Durga, some godly remembrance of her trip. In the end she chose a weaving of Saraswati. She and Mark were always learning, always searching, and always aiming to breach the gap of the wisdom they sought but could not reach. On their walls, they would share Saraswati of New Market, Goddess of Learning.

The vendor rolled the image of Saraswati, made of stiff woven fabric, into a tube and capped each end with a rubber band, snapped twice as if for good effect, Amalia thought, as a justification of its value in the monetary exchange. When he passed it to her, he murmured something kindly. A blessing for her and Mark? She smiled and stood before the man.

"You must pay, Miss." He pointed to the price.

Amalia's father handed rupees to the man and thanked him with pressed palms. "Your mother will like this," he said.

"It's for me and Mark, Dad," she said. "For our apartment." She felt her face get hot.

"Your mother told me," he said. "About almost getting married."

She wondered if he knew the other thing.

"You know, if you want to get married, we can help you. Have a party. Bring your cousins from here and England. Make it something special."

"All the cousins from all the continents." Saraswati scraped the underside of her arm. "It could be fun," she said. "But I don't think we're ready."

"It sure seemed like you were ready," her dad said, "at least from what I heard."

"I don't think I'm ready to take the last step. The formal step. Making it official. Not yet."

"Okay, Pumpkin. You'll know when you're ready. Maybe you just need to live together for a while. Under your new Saraswati."

"May she guide me."

"You're more like your mother than you know."

"Could be good for you, if you're talking about her sweet tooth," she said, as they passed a Bengali sweet shop vendor, with air conditioning blasting out from the little stall into nowhere. She steered her father toward the glass case of desserts. "I need to cool off!" The air conditioning that flew to nowhere swirled. The sweets—round and curved, pressed, and smooth: gold-leafed and plain, pistachio-crusted and white—laid out before them like a palatial treasure trove of delights. Amalia breathed it all in. She and her father selected confections and had them wrapped to take home, a treat for the family to share. Walking, she leaned a little on him.

"They didn't have sweets like this in England," her dad said. "Not when I was growing up there, nothing so delicate or sweet. Delicious, yes, and heartily loved, but nothing as pristine as Bengali sweets."

"There must be a lot of Bengalis living in England by now, wouldn't you think? There must have been when you were there, too."

"Sure, maybe, but not where I lived. We were grown of our own soil, my ma used to say, of those in our village. Stock of the soil. What we grew, we ate, and what we didn't have, we bought or traded from other villages, and they were of their soil, too. Not a Bengali among us." He smiled. "I think that's why, when I met her, I found your mother entrancing. Enlightening. Lively. So unlike me. I found her and she found me, and we made you." He put his arm around Amalia. "And one day, you'll make your own little ones, and you'll understand just how bright the world can be." He stepped outside the edge of New Market to the street. "Now, we run." He pulled Amalia by the hand to the curb. "Ready?" Looking both ways, they ran into a gap in the traffic and dashed across the busy street, between the honking horns and pulled carts and orderly trams and taxi lines, all the way home, sweets and Saraswati with them.

One day, the fog in Amalia's brain lifted, and she went for a walk alone. She traipsed up and down the curbs, watching for traffic and people and dogs, and found her way to Shakespeare Sarani, of which she had a dim recollection from her last (and only other) visit to the city. The street of booksellers had entranced her then, and it did again. She felt like she was in a movie, watching herself walk along the street edge: above, not quite there, and without such tethering, allowed herself to daydream in a new direction. The street beckoned her in ways both illusory and creative, and a warm wind brought smells of cooking, spicy, and baking, sweet.

The scent brought her back to her feet. She stood in front of a book-vendor's stall and passed her hand over a volume. Odin: A Norse Story, said the title, and she paused there. Her fingertip traced the letters O, d, i, n. Odin. The wind brought her to the moment, and when the bookwallah asked her for her selections, she shook her head and said no. She would not buy. She backed up to the curb. Odin, Norse god, whispered on the wind and called her to the next stall, where she bought a blank sketchbook and charcoal.

"Your English ancestors," Amalia said at dinner. "They were also Scandinavian, weren't they, before?"

"If you believe the ancestry charts, yes," her father said.

"When would they have been, I mean, do you know how they went from Scandinavia to England?"

"They traveled all up and down those coasts for centuries, I think, millennia, didn't they? There were battles and marriages and trading."

"And babies, of course," her mother said. "Mixed babies, just like you."

"Except not at all like me," she said. "They had white parents, European parents, it would have just been different language."

"Back then, though, it must have seemed they were worlds apart, no?" Her mother looked dreamy. She sipped a lassi drink before her.

"Back then," her father said, "there was so much intermarriage in the villages they'd have benefitted from the genetic diversity. They'd have been stronger for it."

"Hybrid vigor, I know, Dad."

"Vigor, yes," her mom said, and giggled, sipping her drink. She blushed.

"Mom! What are you drinking?"

"This? A little bhang lassi your cousin whipped up for me," she said. "He said it would take the edge off my jet lag and grief." She laughed and sipped some more.

"Mom!"

"It's fine, Amalia, it's fine. You should try some. It might help you relax. Chill out, you know?"

Amalia could not believe what she was hearing coming from her own mother. "How many have you had?"

"Me? I think this is my second." She looked at the glass. "Yes, it looks like the second." She smiled. "Don't look at me shocked, Amalia. Your Ma needs to cut loose too, you know, sometimes."

Amalia shook her head. "I don't have a problem with it, I just have a problem with you with it," she said. "I'm just—not—" Her head hurt. "I'm going to bed," she said.

In her room, Amalia texted Mark. She was not sure of the time difference, but it did not matter.

My mother is high on bhang lassi. I can't wait to come home to see you.

She looked for a sign of his reply.

Bhang as in pot

He was awake.

Yes

Don't you have it

I didn't.

"Why not?"

Why not, she wrote.

"Seriously?"

It's not like it's all bad, she wrote.

I don't condone drugs, he wrote back.

It's not drugs, Amalia wrote.

"Not hard drugs. Just bhang. It was even in my grandfather's ceremony," she said to the room. She looked at the phone. No telltale sign of typing or receiving. Put the phone down and went to get herself ready for bed. Pulled off the salwar kameez she'd worn for the day and changed into another one for sleep, wiped off her makeup with a cloth. She'd been wearing a lot more makeup since arriving there; her fresh-faced New York appearance looked blank and unready for the day in Calcutta, and she'd taken to applying more makeup like her cousins, in a careful display of outward attention. She brushed her teeth, and her hair. She spent a long time on her hair and wondered if he had finished composing his thoughts, writing back to her.

She went to turn off the light for sleep, and before she did, she checked her phone. He had not written.

~ 10 ~

Aurora Borealis

Dear Amalia,

This is a quick note to say—Aurora Borealis is amazing! Wish you could see it. Even with city lights you get a bit of it. I am booking a Northern Lights tour. Not that I need it. The sites themselves have a good dose of magnetic play all about them, too. Just depends on timing, one's timing, when one arrives. I feel like they've been avoiding me, at least on sites. Or maybe I'm too focused on work and just not noticing. That must be it.

Love,

Mark

P.S. Hope Sou is feeling better. I have been out with people from the town, didn't have a chance to check in before.

P.P.S. You didn't mention if you decided to go to the medical marijuana discussion. Count me out.

~ 11 ~

Odin's Wind ~ January

The vision came through her like a forceful wind as she sat there in the middle seat row on the Air India flight, five rows back from her parents, after her grandfather's funeral. She had wanted time alone, with her parents, with her grandfather's memory, and with India. Calcutta. Kolkata. The place called them all home, and in going home, she'd unfolded another aspect of herself, her soul, and her calling. The vision was a swirl and she, in it.

She would paint it; it was a strong and clear image. A strong wind with color, captured on canvas. A very, very big canvas. At first, she'd seen it as Kali, or Calcutta's incarnation, Durga, but then as she had investigated the face of her Anglo father as he stood on the banks of the Ganges with her grandfather's ashes, it became as much from his English and Norse background that this wind came, and she called it Odin. Now on the plane, the image formed clear as wind. Palpable yet hard to pin down, clarifying and mesmerizing in its flow.

Excited, she reached forward in the spirit of this new vision for the pens and paper shoved into the side of her carry-on bag and bumping her head on the seat in front of her, giggled. Hadn't felt such power from the pulse of a creative work—not since she had sketched the form of the environmental center on paper with Jen, a short time ago.

The tray table was large enough to hold her sketchbook, filled with little vignettes from her trip. She flipped to a new page and let the pen flow across the whiteness, its blue ink capturing the bare essence of a large work in her mind forming as Odin's Wind.

~ 12 ~

Weeds

Stony-faced, Mildred pulled at the errant weed from between the wooden steps, but it didn't come up. Couldn't imagine how it had found its way in the cold and survived the storms and rock salt laid to make the path more walkable. "Tenacious thing." She let it be. "Any weed so hardy is worthy of being called a plant. You've earned your place." The ice on the pavers had melted off in the last heavy rain, and the weeds—plants—were growing, too. She salted the path for the second time that day, and up the old wooden stairs, with the plastic pot of salt she'd brought from the house. Rested on the sturdy handrail. "Raymond," she said, "thank you for insisting on getting this handrail fixed." She'd long since removed the temporary ramp up the front to their Binghamton home, packed off by the medical rental company along with Raymond's bed that had held him in those precious last days at home, in the front living room, the place he'd inhabited for the last decade of his life. The Reverend Mildred pulled herself up to the porch and set down the plastic salt bucket.

"Reverend!" A familiar voice from behind sounded, and she turned with care, not wanting to lose her balance on the still-slippery porch, aware of patches unsalted.

Mildred squinted, the caller coming into focus. "Frankie, my boy." He stood next to her car, parked in the handicapped spot in front of her home.

"Need to borrow your car, Reverend." He stuffed his hands deep in his pockets. "If you want your stuff."

"Frankie!" She hurried as fast as she could safely go, back down the steps, over the weed-turned plant, across the salted stone path, and to her car. "Shh! Are you crazy? Frankie." She shook her head. "If you need to get somewhere, fine. But don't go yelling about our private business all up and down the block, now, you hear? No. Just—don't do it."

"If you want your stuff, I need a car," he said.

"What happened to your car?"

"I got—" He sputtered out an incomprehensible word. "Need your car."

"Fine. Come inside and I'll get you the key. And for goodness' sake, let me rest on your arm."

Frankie propped her up along the path. "You fix this up yourself, Reverend? Keep off all the ice?"

She nodded, leaning harder onto his side. His warmth pervaded and she felt a kinship with this man, this unpredictable man who'd shown up to her congregation a year before, introduced by the inimitable Father Jasper. "Just me, Frankie." He'd arrived with all the spirit and wind of a wave come crashing to shore. Much like Jasper himself.

"I can help you, Reverend. For some money like." He helped her up the stairs. "How are your eyes today, Reverend?"

"You are kindly," she said. "They're so-so. Better with. Your stuff." She opened the front door, exhaled, and stood at the entrance. "You can come in." He stepped over the threshold behind her, standing on the doormat in his winter boots. She reached for the key on the hook by the front door, ever-ready for her daily drive—a short one of a few blocks—to the church. "Here you go. When you come back, just leave the Alero in the spot out front."

"What should I do with the key?"

"I'll be here, unless I'm asleep, in which case—leave it in the mailbox here." She pointed to the red box, painted by Raymond, attached to the yellow-painted wall. He'd joked she would never lose sight of the mailbox. Had he known? The glaucoma set in after he died. "You mind the ice, now, Frankie. And don't go leaving my package in the mailbox, you give it to me directly. When you see me." He gave her a blank look. "You give me the package the next time you see me. Not when you drop off the car key, because I might be out somewhere."

"Or asleep," he said.

"Or asleep."

Frankie departed down the wooden steps, stepping on the plant she'd saved. "No matter," she said to herself.

Mildred settled inside, petted the cats hello, put on the kettle for tea, and watched the cats meander away. The temperature of the house was steady despite the cold outside; old steam radiators chugged overtime to keep the home toasty warm. Still, she shuddered. That Frankie. She was distracted when the phone rang and answered it without expectation. Bert. He was in a talkative mood. The head cat, as she liked to call Eliza, strutted back into the room.

"Claudia and me, you see, she and me we had a thing going back then," Bert said. "And we got in touch again a while back, see?"

She held the handset with one hand and felt for the container of cat food in the lower cabinet, poured some out for Eliza who strolled around Mildred's legs like they were there for the cat's pleasure alone. Eliza partook.

"She's back in Vancouver and I go to see her sometimes. And she's been to see me."

Mildred's entire midsection lurched with a plunging feeling, but she said nothing. Let the phone slip a little from her grasp and let the handset down a few inches from her ear, her elbow propped on the kitchen counter near the landline's base. The male heart was susceptible to women the likes of Claudia. Mildred had been married, been around the block more than once. Her first husband, at age eighteen, left her after a year. Mikey. Her second, Carl, drifted away when she couldn't get pregnant—not her fault, she knew. Her third, Raymond, now he was a keeper—though she couldn't keep him from dying. Every time her love had met a Claudia, he'd been charmed. Even Raymond, who had in fact met Claudia at the same time as he'd met Mildred; Mildred considered this a coup of sorts, marrying Raymond when Claudia had not. But maybe Claudia was not the marrying type. Bert was still yammering on about something. Her phone was still away from her ear. Brought the receiver back to listen.

"I wanted you to tell you myself, directly I mean," he said. "Not via the invitation in the mail."

"Aha."

"You'll come?"

"To what, Bert?"

"To the wedding—didn't you listen?"

At age eighty-three, Mildred expected more maturity of herself, and yet proved herself youthful to the core. "Bert, you two-timing son-of-a-bitch," she said. "You got no right marrying her behind my back. You have no feelings. No decency. When were you going to tell me?" Her hand shook on the phone. Her jaw twitched. She and Bert had never even discussed if they were dating long distance, or what they might do once they'd gone back to their separate coasts. It had been an affair back then, in the early 1990s, and it had been an affair this past season, too. She opened her mouth and snapped it shut, biting the inside of her cheek. "Ow!"

"I'm sorry, Mill."

"Don't sorry me! I don't need you!" She slammed down the phone. In her anger, the handset missed the base and hit the counter. Mildred soothed her cheek inside with her tongue.

"Mill? You there?" His voice came from the phone.

She exhaled and turned to lean with her back to the counter. She shook her head. Had to get a grip. Picked up the handset. "You had to break up with me over the phone? You couldn't have the decency to fly out here and tell me in person?" Her cheek smarted from the inside out, and she put a hand on her jaw, soothing it from the outside in. Her Reiki could not flow in her anger or frustration. It would not run. It had its own engine, or battery, or power—although she could allow a good run of Reiki, she often felt it bounce off her if she was in a state of despair. It didn't join her in that place of sorrow. She could look for soothing instead. She ran her tongue around the inside of her mouth. It did soothe. "Soothing is welcome."

"Mill, I'm sorry. I didn't know."

She wanted to get off the phone. Couldn't figure a way to end it and hanging up hadn't even worked. Her hand moved to her forehead. A headache formed.

"Why don't we talk later," he said. "When you've calmed down."

"I am calm!" She yelled into the phone.

The phone line went dead.

"Argh! Eliza!" Eliza, crunching her kitty kibbles so hard the sound vibrated through Mildred's slippers to her toes, looked mildly at Mildred from her bowl in the corner. "I should've got a dog," Mildred said.

~ 13 ~
Attrition

Amalia sat back, resting on pillows, and put her feet up on her bed to look out the window to the rear at the old and improbable urban tree, a tall, aging beauty, sprung up from the concrete behind the Manhattan apartment. It had lost branches in the storms. The clear blue January sky set off its silhouetted branches in a dramatic appeal to her senses. Wondered if she could bring contrast into the painting she had in mind. Hopped up to find her large sketchbook, still nestled down the backside of her large new tote bag, a gift from Jen after the Christmas break. They had not exchanged gifts. Jen had said, "you need this," and handed it over like it was charity. "Give up your old string bag," she added. Amalia didn't mind. She wasn't one to turn down a gift, and she didn't have a head for shopping; input from Jen was welcome.

The tote bag had come after the trip to India, and Amalia had readily adapted to carrying it on the subway, her large sketchbook in it. It was a lot to lug; she wanted to have the book with her in case an idea hit for the painting. She felt a bit defensive about carrying it back and forth, like she needed to explain it to someone, and in fact Mark had asked once and pointed out a second time: she needn't carry a large sketchbook back and forth in a large tote bag, if it was to merely capture a small idea. "They make smaller sketchbooks," he'd said. Annoyance at the memory scratched at her throat.

She sat with the large sketchbook across her lap and tried to push him away. He wasn't home, so what was she doing letting him float into her thoughts when she wanted to draw? He would be out at least another hour, having gone to his favorite café, down by her office, and a long subway journey away. He had a case to put together.

Back in the small sketchbook from India, she'd covered several pages in a single, dancing line connecting from page to page. Looked to her phone for time. How long had she been drawing? Her pencil dotted and made little squiggles along the line as she found her way back to the beginning of the sequence. Mark was creating a comic book of the two of them. He was good at that kind of thing. She could do architectural sketches. The drawings she did for work were functional, pretty, and conveyed meaning. They were mechanical, structured, and showed a mastery of form. It wasn't what she wanted. What she wanted was to flow with color across the page.

Mark seemed to be able to do it with ease, in the thumbnail sketches he was doing for the comic book. The ecological mystery comic book had come from both of their minds and shared inspirations. It was as much hers as his, he said, and he invited her to be a part of it. She could not. Their multiple fights over environmental issues wearied her, and although she felt she was right, it didn't make her happy to feel it. Made her feel— worn down. It was like a war of attrition between them, and it was not sustaining. Didn't help their relationship. They would then agree, though, finding some small nugget of common ground, and when they did, they'd both light up like Fourth of July fireworks, and she'd think all was well and good in their world.

Amalia picked up her phone to text him, wondering when he'd be back. Maybe they could work on the drawings together. Leave her painting idea aside.

Was she procrastinating? Every weekend and evening she'd committed to studying for her architecture exams. Lunchtimes too if she wanted to push through. A challenging time to have entered a new relationship, one with its own demands and needs of time and shared space, intimacy, and connection. Mark understood, even if he didn't like her repeated absences, her departures into books and calculations and online quizzes.

Staying a little longer, he wrote. On a roll. OK?

OK, she wrote. "Okay."

She'd order a pizza on her own, then, or go out for some. Laid the small sketchbook from India atop the large one, little canvas next to the books on the floor, found her tall boots and coat, wrapped her scarf long around her neck, pulled her wooly toque down over her ears, and set out, half-empty tote bag on her shoulder.

Outside, the blue cold met her face with a slap as if to say, "you wanted some, here you go!" The day had already turned dark. Even in its sharpness, the temperature agreed with her. Bundled up as she was, eyes peering out between the bottom of her hat and the top of her scarf, she felt safe.

She would bring pizza home for both of them, for dinner. Mark, as he'd said, was on a roll and needed to focus. "Stupid fracking dispute case." Amalia shook her head inside her warm layers and crossed the street to the new pizzeria up the block. It wasn't hers to say, but even though she was pleased he'd left the company, she kind of understood why his former colleagues thought he should stick with them for the class action suit. He was too vulnerable on his own. Had no power as an individual named in the suit, representing himself outside the bounds of Atlantia Actuarius. If it had been up to Amalia, she would have told him not to quit, to stick with it because he believed in the work, even though she didn't, and to see the changes through from the inside. But he hadn't, had instead made the big gesture of quitting, consulting on his own, and roping her into being his eco-sidekick. "I am not your fucking eco-sidekick," she said to no one.

The pizzeria looked warm and inviting as it radiated into the cold. Swung open the doors, two-handed, and even the door handles felt cold through her thick gloves. Who was she kidding? They weren't on the same page, and never had been. "I'll take a large cheese pizza," she said when she got to the counter. "Pepperoni on half."

"The spicy pepperoni's great here." She heard a familiar voice behind her in line. Sunil stood, bundled and smiling.

"Shit," she said, wondering how much of her inner monologue she had spewed out loud, under her breath. His face remained in the same smile, not giving away any hints of her possible utterances aloud. She inhaled. Exhaled. "Sunil."

"You're back," he said.

"Kind of," she said. "Think I have reverse culture shock."

He nodded. "Spicy pepperoni, large," he said at the counter. "Happy to talk about it sometime," he said, and looked quite genuinely kind, his brown eyes soft.

"Just cheese, she said to the server. "I'll take whatever you have ready."

Amalia took the box as it was handed, nodded to Sunil, and left a wad of cash on the counter. "Have a good night," she said to the air, and left without so much as a smile to Sunil.

"What the fuck?" Why couldn't she have stayed and responded? She ran across the street to home, agitated, and ran up all four flights of stairs to the small apartment. Unlocked the front door, angled off the hallway, and pushed in, slamming the door behind her. Mark sat on a chair in the main space. "Mark! I thought you were taking more time." She hadn't even been gone twenty minutes.

"I lied," he said. "I was already off the train and walking around the block when you texted me."

"You said you wanted more time." She put down the pizza box on the edge of the table, avoiding Mark's papers. "I would have got the pepperoni."

"I did. I do. It's too cold to walk around thinking. I figured I could work here, since you're studying." He frowned.

"It's fine." She exhaled. "What are you doing? How's the case going?"

"It's complicated. Do you want to hear?" He pressed on before she could answer. "They're going down a rabbit hole saying because of the family's evidence not being stored at headquarters, it was in the field office and not transcribed into the system—the originals, handwritten reports, and the medical receipts—they're not admissible. There's no date stamp on them, no way to say when they were created or submitted. You know when Mildred picked them up."

"Bullshit." Her own language surprised her, and she laughed at herself since she'd already been on a swearing streak since before he got home.

"They're saying I tampered with evidence. Why are you laughing?"

"I'm not laughing at you. And you didn't. Didn't tamper with evidence."

"I returned the documents."

"You didn't steal them."

"I didn't stop them being stolen."

"Mark. You didn't ask Mildred to take them. You didn't even know she and Bert were going there, or that they'd even know how to find their way to your site office. You need to get back with Atlantia so they can represent you properly. You're like the lone wolf in this, and you're not stronger for it. You're—I don't know. You need the pack, right now."

"Can't believe you're saying this. You're anti-natural gas. And now you want me to go back to them."

"Not back to gas, back to the people who will represent your interests in the case. It's different. They have the power to pull in the attorneys who can put the case together properly. Not you."

"Not me, just a geologist."

"You're more than a geologist," she said. "You're an artist, and you're an amazing human." She smiled. It was true, he was an amazing human. Just the thought of it made her glow inside.

"You and me, we can do this together," he said.

She shook her head. "I'm not an attorney. I'm not even an architect yet."

"They're saying the frack fluid came up through the groundwater around the houses. And the cows drank from the ponds, polluted, and the people drank the milk."

"I thought it got into the household water supply."

"It did."

Shook her head again. "It's too big for me. I'm not a lawyer, and neither are you." Opened the pizza box. "Want a slice of cheese pizza?"

"Kind of lost my appetite," he said. "We can do this together."

"But what, exactly? Represent you in this case? Draw a comic book about environmental issues? Eat pizza together? We can't even eat a fucking pizza together."

"Amalia, this isn't like you."

"What, swearing? Maybe it is." Her phone buzzed with an incoming message which she tried to ignore. She put her hand on the phone.

"Being so discouraged."

"What?" She wanted to turn over the phone but suspected it was not the right time. "Maybe I have good reason to be discouraged." She felt herself coiling up inside. The phone buzzed again under her hand.

"I don't think so."

"What would you know? You're never even here. You don't know how I feel. You don't know what I want. You don't even know which exam I'm taking!" She flipped over the phone; Sunil had texted twice.

"Yes I do, it's the one about construction. Construction sites. Something about that." Mark sounded as wound up as she felt.

"Not the point!" She yelled at the ceiling, shaking the phone in her hand. "What are we doing? Why are we even doing this? We're shoved into this tiny apartment together, but we never see each other, never talk about anything important, and never even finished getting married," she said, feeling herself uncoiling. Dropped the phone in her anger, and it tumbled into the pizza box.

She sat down next to him and took the phone out of the pizza. It slipped, greasily, from her hand. "Can't even do this right," she said, and wiped the phone on her pants, leaving it on the table. Reached in for a slice of pizza, which she felt a sudden and urgent need to eat.

He put a hand over hers and she let the pizza drop to the cardboard box below. "I—" The box fell to the floor, pizza flipped upside down. "I see," he said. Mark jumped up to pick up the box.

Amalia picked her phone up off the floor, went into the bedroom, flung herself down onto the bed, and sucked air through her pillow's fabric edges. The phone buzzed again in her hand, and she flipped over onto her back, holding the phone over her, arms as straight and wavering as saplings. Her stacked canvas and sketchbooks still lay next to her, a reminder of what had irked her earlier. The inability to communicate was a constant annoyance, and one her efforts did not seem to improve.

You left fast. Felt bad I didn't get to ask about your trip. And the funeral.

The next text was less weighty: a simple pizza emoji with a smile. She rolled away from the door, lying on her side with a view of the old tree. Started to type back to him, then heard Mark come in behind her. The smell of cheese pizza wafted in.

"I saved some of it." She felt him sit down on the bed next to her. Put a warm hand on her lower back. "I'm sorry."

She rolled over, knowing her face was a mess, tear streaked, long hair strung across like a web. She still had on the long scarf from outside, and it pushed up into her chin. He pulled it down to reveal her lips, and he gave her a kiss, a little one. Amalia let the phone drop to the bedcovers next to her.

"You didn't do anything," she said. "It's me." Pushed the phone with her elbow and it fell to the floor.

"I'll hire an attorney," he said. "I won't do it alone."

She nodded. Sat up a little and reached for her pizza. "Still smells good," she said. Amalia was hungry. The pizza was good. "Still fresh," she said. "A little crispy on the edges."

He took a piece. "Mmm. And soft in the middle, cheesy."

"The sauce is good."

"The cheese is good," he said. "This is so good."

She laughed. "We are ridiculous, you know." Shook her head. "So good. I'm sorry, too." She pointed to the sketchbooks. "I was trying to draw." She reached for the little one and opened it with a clean finger. "I got this far," she said, indicating the line.

"Intriguing," he said. And laughed.

"It's a friggin' line," she said. Pushed him back on the bed and kissed him, pizza grease and all. Kisses soon turned to more, and before long, clothes had come off and they rolled in the bed beneath the warm covers, and all was forgiven.

Must have fallen asleep. She sat up fast, in the dark. Mark lay next to her, and her sketchbooks and pizza box lay on the floor next to them. The silk sari curtains remained open to the night sky; her tree was silhouetted against the golden glow of the sodium street lights from the block beyond. Mark snored lightly next to her. It was okay. They would be okay.

Mark rolled over. Stretched out a hand to put on her bare shoulder. "Come back," he said. "Warm in here." He wrapped her into a hug. "I'm sorry about before. There was something else. I didn't know how to tell you."

Amalia rolled into his warm embrace. "What?"

"Timmy's selling pot. To get money for him and Candace and the baby."

"What?" Amalia sat up. "How do you know?"

"He told me."

"What, just like, 'I'm selling pot to get money for me and Candace and the baby?'"

"Pretty much. We were on the phone, and I was trying to drill down on how he was going to cover their costs, where they are going to live when the baby comes. And he said it, all defiant-like, as if it would put me in my place. Shut me up."

"Wow. And did it."

"Pretty much. I hung up on him."

"You hung up on your baby brother. And then you came home?"

"Yeah."

"And I yelled at you."

"Mmm hmm."

"I'm sorry, babe. What do you want to tell him?"

"I just want to help him," he said, running his fingers through his hair. "I don't want to tell him anything."

"Understandable."

"If Mom and Dad were alive, none of this would be happening."

"If your mom and dad were alive, would we even have met?" She sat up. "You would not have moved Timmy to Pennsylvania from New Hampshire, would you?"

"No, I'd still be teaching at the college."

"And still dating Helene."

He laughed. "Wow, you're right. I'm glad I'm with you." He kissed the top of her head. "I don't know what to tell him."

"You don't have to say anything right now," she said, trailing a finger down his chest. "You're home, we're fine, and you can figure it out tomorrow."

"He's selling medical marijuana."

"You could speak on Mildred's panel."

"No way, never again."

"That's how we got to know each other." She sat up. "At a Mildred panel."

"I have nothing to offer on medical marijuana."

"You do, you just expressed strong opinions."

"Strong, unformed, emotional opinions."

"Perfect for a Mildred panel."

He shook his head. "I'm against it. I have nothing to offer her."

"You're against medical marijuana? I know you don't like it recreationally."

"Of course, aren't you?"

"Why—" She stood up. Felt another fight coming on. Couldn't do it. She smiled and extended a hand to him. "Come have a quick shower with me." There were better ways to pass the time than to fight about medical marijuana.

~ 14 ~

Lay It Out

A big canvas. Such a big canvas. It had seemed doable when she was back in the store, and even when she had lugged the thing home to the Hamilton Heights apartment on the bus and up the blocks she'd had to walk from the stop. When she'd moved in, it had been tricky with the bed mattress, which took two people to move it. She wanted to do this one herself. It was not until she had carved out space for herself that she flowed toward the art supply store, into the canvas aisle, and then to the cash register, and then onto the street, with the big, big canvas. Such a big canvas.

Amalia stepped back from it in the hallway and realized that although she had room to store the canvas in their apartment, she did not have room to paint it. Not in the way she wanted, by stepping back and then diving in. She could lay it across the kitchen counter and across to the dining table, but then she would be able to neither cook standing nor eat sitting. Put her hands in her hair and rubbed her scalp. It would take some time. She could take the canvas off the frame and cut it up and stitch it back together, hang it back on.

What had she got herself into? It had seemed right in the store, a natural extension of her desire to paint, and now she could not do it. She exhaled with great emphasis for no one and decided it would have to wait for another day. The canvas could stay in the hallway until she figured out the next step in the crazy constellation of Odin's Wind.

~ 15 ~

Snarky Knee Jerky

"I need you to fill in for me this week," Jen said. "I'm supposed to go down the Shore for a site visit. I'm not sure I'd make it back in time for my doctor's appointment."

"I could. I'm not sure I'll know what to do."

"It's easy. It's for the pro bono work we started after the storm last fall. We're inspecting, stabilizing, and raising some of the homes that took the brunt of it. Take pictures and bring the questions back to me. Don't answer any," Jen said.

"Why are we doing pro bono work? I thought Betsy and Max were concerned about cash flow."

"It's a group effort between a lot of firms. And maybe it called them, in some way. Besides, Amalia, we don't take all our money from the natural gas industry, sometimes we give back."

"No need to get snarky," Amalia said, her brow furrowing at the recollection of her past misdeeds at the firm. The way she'd handled natural gas involvement in PGAE's projects seemed to follow her no matter how she explained, unexplained, and tried to turn it around. "I understand." She could concede. Hadn't tried that in a while. "The Pennsylvania project is on hold right now anyway until Betsy and Max meet with the Board of Directors of the theater complex. It's fine. I'm all about pro bono. Can I call you from down there?"

"I won't be free. You won't need to call. The contractor's sharp, and we have a good relationship. If he has questions, he'll be fine having you bring them to me. Tell him it will be a couple of days before I can get the answers."

"I thought you had a doctor's visit."

"And—I'm going in overnight. It's okay. Betsy knows."

"Are you okay? I mean, is there anything I can do?"

"It's fine. I'm fine."

"Are you coming home after? I mean, do you need someone to help you after?"

"Maybe, yeah. Are you offering?"

"I could. It would be good to get out of my apartment. I definitely could." She hesitated. "I've been meaning to ask you, how's it been going since you and Suky split up? Or Paige, for that matter."

"Suky would not have taken care of me after this." Jen shook her head. "She would have said she'd do it, but it would have been all about her, and what she needed. And Paige and I are just friends, now."

"Suky's not bad, I saw her. She's still working with Sunil." It was true; as mechanical engineer on the majority of Polson Grohman's projects, Suky was heavily involved. Amalia didn't like to say this out loud to Jen, who had an apparent knee jerk reaction. "I have no problem with Suky, Jen."

"I have no problem with her either, other than she voted Republican!" Jen hit her keyboard with emphasis and stood up. "I am printing you the list of what you need to look for down at the Jersey Shore houses."

"Have they all been inspected? I don't even know what you're doing down there other than what I started right after the hurricane."

"It's the same. Everyone's waiting for their FEMA money. We're completing the first round of inspections. Some of the properties weren't accessible before, and now they are." Jen walked to the printer. "This will be a good guide." She paused. "It's a hysterectomy, by the way."

"Okay—uh—you want to go over the list first?"

"And then what?"

"I don't know, maybe talk about why you're having a hysterectomy?" Amalia looked around the office. "It's you and me. Betsy won't be back for a while."

"And Max is as MIA as ever."

"I don't think he's part of this anymore. I think he's in Florida for good. My point is, we are alone here and it's okay to talk. And even if Betsy were here—I'm sure she wouldn't mind. Does she know?"

"She knows I'm out for a medical procedure and I need a few weeks of downtime after."

"After as in, you weren't planning to come back, and you didn't tell me?"

"Why would I tell you? It's not like we're best friends."

"Ouch."

"No pain intended." She gave the printed lists to Amalia. "You let me know when you're ready to go over these. And Amalia, I am thankful you'll stay. I appreciate it."

At home, Amalia felt icky from the thoughts that persisted. Wanted a different path to open before her. How could she get there? And to where? It was not a place or a concept she had in mind to land like a perfect gymnastic vault. Wasn't even sure she'd recognize it when it arrived. What was it, that elusive feeling? It had something to do with happiness, but it was even more general than that. She took a deep breath in. It was like the feeling of relief from full inhalation, and exhalation. Inhalation, exhalation. Like drinking cool water when overheated. It was a sense of refreshment. Generalized, feel-better renewal. Just thinking of it brought a small smile to the corner of her lips. Hopped up from the edge of the bed where she'd perched, looking at her clothes for the next day, and took a sip of water from the glass at her bedside. Began to gulp it down, felt it pour through her. Stood, closed the curtains, and stretched up toward the top of the window. "Tomorrow is going to be a better day," she said to the tree outside. "Because I said so!" From within, she felt her tummy rumble in agreement.

She looked out toward the tree through the parted curtains. It seemed to wave, its branches like a multi-armed goddess, not Durga, not Kali; a goddess who assembled and reassembled before her, for her, in the branches that moved in the wind. The clouds beyond moved with a flow that corresponded to the larger arc of the tree's movements, light against a dark sky.

What had she been thinking before she'd gone to the window? Couldn't remember. Could not put a finger on it. Mark was still out. The apartment was quiet. It had been a long time since she'd felt friendly and close with a female friend, and although Jen had both pushed her away and brought her closer with her comments, Amalia knew they leaned on one another. For so long, she and her old friend Sandra corresponded long distance, and Amalia had even taken up residence in Sandra's great aunt's rent-controlled apartment on the Upper West Side, but somehow after Mark had appeared, Sandra's presence in

Amalia's life had faded, especially after she moved, and Mark moved in with her. Was she being a bad friend to Sandra, ignoring her for Mark? Didn't want to be that kind of friend.

The apartment was quiet. She had time to kill before Mark got home. Didn't feel like studying. Where Sandra was in Italy, it was midnight.

The video call was quick and most satisfying; a connection made and solidified, and although Sandra was woken from her sleep, they planned to connect weekly.

It was something to look forward to. Amalia looked out toward the tree while she finished undressing from work. Clouds moved fast beyond, and the branches appeared to dance. In this dance, Amalia saw a rhythm that she felt click into a connection at her core, and as she took off her earrings, she undulated a little from the feet up, and smiled. Tomorrow would be a better day. Because she said so. "Thank you, tree," she said. "Thank you for watching over me, watching over Mark. For watching over this space, and for being the perfect grandmother tree that you are."

~ 16 ~

Down the Shore

Amalia faced the storm-trashed building with the ocean behind it, wind strong at her side. Bundled into her winter coat and layers, mitts thick and insensitive, she struggled to hold and read the pages Jen had printed for her. Wished she'd let Jen review them in person together instead of having swept the discomfort of the conversation away in a hurry of needing to leave the office. Her eyes watered in the chilly sea breeze. Jen would be okay. And Amalia would have to improvise.

First, she'd find the contractor. Mark's blue Saab had taken her this far. She could do the rest on foot. The contractor's van was parked in the sand-covered driveway; he had to be close. He'd know what to look at. Easy enough. She peered through the glass of what remained of the front door. "Hey!"

"'Round back," she heard from outside. He was on the ocean-facing rear deck, unscrewing plywood boards that closed off the house from wind and ocean ferocity.

"What you got?"

"Turned to mold since you were last here."

"I haven't been here before. I'm Amalia Erenwine. From PGAE. I'm here in place of Jen Savin."

"Keith." He gave her a squinty look. "What I have here is mold to deal with." He pulled off the plywood panel and threw it to the side. "Step over." He indicated the new wooden sill that lay at the threshold. "At least you got the right boots."

"Whose house is this?" The steel-toed work boots had been a last-minute purchase on the way down to the Jersey Shore, and they pinched where they were not broken in. She'd strapped herself into them in the car at a rest stop. "I can't imagine they're living here in this house."

"Jacob's."

"Where are the Jacobs now?" Amalia scanned the deteriorated kitchen. Cupboard doors hung from broken hinges and a smell of mold permeated the space, filling her nose and throat with what she hoped was the good kind of mold. She saw some white fuzz on the edge of the counters. Was that the good kind or the bad kind? White, grey, black, brown? If she had ever known, she'd forgotten the categories as she stood there with the contractor.

"Got a cell phone number, that's all."

"For Mr. Jacobs? Or Mrs. Jacobs?"

"Jacob." He looked at her with a strange glance. "You here for the building or social services?"

"The building. The people matter, too, right?" She kicked at the tile, and it came off in a puff of sandy dust. "Oops."

"Wouldn't do that. Haven't tested those for asbestos."

"That would be bad."

"It's one tile. It's not bad. But with FEMA coming and doing their own inspections—"

"No red flags?"

He smiled. "You got it. You go on in, I'll be back when you're done. Call me any time." He scribbled his number on the back of a piece of paper, a receipt dug out of his pocket.

Two hours later, Amalia was cold and beat. The boots cramped her legs and the list from Jen was half-checked. Keith had left her there after assuring her of the building's structural stability, said he had other properties to visit, and was off. At least he'd given her his cell number. She could call him with questions.

Truth was, she didn't know what she was looking for, and she didn't know who to ask. Didn't want to look foolish in front of the contractor. Didn't want to call Jen, who had given Amalia increased responsibilities at a time when Jen was faced with her own difficulties. Jen was an intern, like her; with years' more experience, Jen was tasked with project management work by Betsy, who was too busy for it all. She could call Betsy. Amalia's job was already on the line since having written that stupid pros and cons list about hydraulic fracturing the previous fall. She didn't want to jeopardize her job. Not like there were a lot of other jobs for her, and as much as she loved them, she sure wasn't going back to live with her parents for good. The city would keep her. Mark would keep her. Betsy would keep her.

Thud. Amalia spun on her boot heels at the dull noise that came from within the structure. "Hello?" Hoped it was the wind and not a broken bit of building that Keith had missed. Thud, thud. "Anyone there?" No reply. She peeked around the corner of the bedroom door, still shattered by hurricane debris from the previous month. "Keith?" She'd call him. If there was a person there—one who was not responding—would she want that person to hear her voice? She switched her phone to silent mode and began to tap a message to Keith.

Beams OK here?

Yeah why.

Creaking.

Just expansion and contraction in the weather.

And that's OK?

Seems fine to me. You're the architect. You tell me.

Fine. He wanted it that way.

What else do you need me to follow up on?

She'd been able to consult Jen's list once she was out of the wind. She had not found every condition and didn't know how to find some of them in the first place. No answer from Keith. She was the architect. Oh, not so. She was the intern. Representing the architect. And she'd been told by Jen to take pictures and bring back questions. She could do that, even if she could not find everything on Jen's list.

There were no more creaks or thuds from the building. Amalia felt certain she was alone. She set about photographing what she saw in each room, careful to show context and direction and to make notes in her book about each location. Her phone took good enough pictures, not great. Why hadn't she brought the camera from the office, as Jen suggested? Why had she run away? Was the conversation so hard? For her, it had been. She didn't want to think of Jen suffering. And she was hurt that Jen had said they were not close. Yet, she had accepted Amalia's offer of help at home. There was that. They could build a friendship. For the time being, it was work. She'd focus on that.

Jen was a good mentor, even if still an intern herself. Amalia wasn't sure why Jen had stalled out on taking her licensing exams over the winter break. Jen had shared architectural registration study guide materials, flash cards and books, saying she didn't need them for a while. Amalia absorbed them with an eagerness that bordered on hunger. It was something she wanted, even if Jen was on the fence. Maybe it was Suky. Or the recent hurricane. Or the federal election. All seemed to have taken a chunk of Jen's energy, even with the Democratic win Jen had helped with by canvassing. Amalia would find a way to fill the gap. The least she could do was to give Jen a complete survey of the building, as she'd been asked to do in the first place.

What constituted a full survey? They didn't have drawings of the building. Did they need them? Amalia had come down for the photos and the contractor questions. She could do a little more. She had a tape measure in her bag from her last work meeting. No decent camera other than her phone, which needed replacing. She could do a set of measured drawings of the rambling, beachfront structure and could tag her phone's photos to the drawings. That would be helpful. Helpful to Jen. Helpful to Betsy and Max. Helpful to the firm, and, she hoped, helpful to Mr. Jacob, whoever he was.

She trotted down the sandy interior staircase to the main floor and back out the loosely boarded exterior at the rear, to Mark's car down the block. Hadn't she left a roll of drawing paper in there? She put her bag down as she rifled through Mark's possessions on the back seat—unpacked after his move from Pennsylvania and into her little city apartment.

Amalia was thirsty for more of the trajectory on her path to becoming a registered architect, and for her passion for design. She was in it for the long haul. Found the roll of tracing paper along with a partially frozen bottle of water, which she brought with her in case. Back out behind the building, too cold to stay out long, and she was in the moldering kitchen with the trace rolled out on the counter, frozen water holding the sheet in place. She had a pen in her pocket; began to draw the outline of the kitchen floor plan, but the grittiness of the sand on the counter popped little holes through the thin trace, and she looked around for a better way. Needed a book to lean on. A thick, dry, sturdy book. Didn't look like Mr. Jacob was much of a reader. Maybe a cookbook? A phone book. "Come on, Mr. Jacob! Must have something." She went into the living room, which up to that moment she had avoided due to the putrid smell of the sofa, still damp at its core. What color of mold was that?

She heard herself scream then gasp as she saw a man's body lying on the sofa. How had she missed it before? How had Keith missed it? Amalia backed up into the kitchen, heart pounding. Fingered her phone in her pocket and wished for enough stability to remember what one was to do in such a situation, if she had ever known. Was it Mr. Jacob, dead and forgotten? Pulled out the phone and began to dial 9 1 1. "I'm in a house. And there's a body." Her heart rose.

"There's no body! I live here, you fool!" A tall, aged man in a heavy lumberman's-style flannel jacket came toward the doorway. "And you'll get out of my house!"

"There's a man!" She gave the operator the address of the house. Swallowed hard. Didn't know where to look.

"Ma'am, do you need help?" The smooth voice of the emergency line operator confused Amalia in the sensory crush that came with the odor coming off the man. He must have been sleeping on that moldy sofa since the storm.

"I—no, I'm with the homeowner."

"Give me that." The man extended a shaky hand and grabbed the phone. "Hello? I'm the homeowner and there is an intruder. Please come right away." He hung up and handed the phone back to Amalia. "That'll take care of it!"

"I'm not an intruder! I'm the architect! And you can't call 9 1 1 on me!" She stuffed the phone in her pocket. Would clean it later.

"You called 9 1 1 on yourself, missy. And there ain't nothing called a female architect. You're nothing but an intruder, and I know why you're here."

"Hey!" Amalia felt the rile inside. "I'm an architect!"

"Really." He crossed his arms in the doorway.

"I'm not an architect yet. I'm an intern. Intern in architecture."

"Like I said."

"You don't have any right! I'm here to do a job. I'm here to help you. Are you Mr. Jacob?" She wanted to call Keith for backup. Didn't want to look foolish in front of both client and contractor. She could sort it out herself if her heart slowed down.

"Jacob." He turned and went back into the living room.

Amalia stepped forward but was stopped by the smell that followed him and emerged from the room at the same time. "You sleep here, Jacob?"

"When I have to." He shuffled to the end of the sofa to pick up a pack of cigarettes.

"There's no heat. And there's no power."

"There's power. Just not when anyone's around." Jacob lit up a cigarette and drew long on it, gazing toward the sea through the dirty glass. "But you should know that, since that's why you're here."

"For the building."

"If you like to call it that."

"It's a building. A home."

"What I meant was if you like to call the stuff a building. What are you building? What are we building? It's downstairs. I moved it from the top floor before FEMA came. Storm spared most of the crop. Generator runs overnight and I keep it quiet by day when the inspectors are here. But you must know all of that already. Neighbors don't say much because I supply them, too." He drew again on the cigarette and offered up a deep, chesty cough.

"You should get that cough looked at, Jacob." She ventured a little closer to him in the room. "Not good to sleep in the cold."

"You're not listening. It's not that cold. Generator's on. All night. Gotta keep the crops going. Keep the generator going on and off in between inspectors, too. Seems okay. How much you want?"

It was not as cold as she might have expected an abandoned house to be in the middle of winter, that was true. She hadn't noticed until he mentioned it. The plywood panel over the rear door at the kitchen kept things tightly sealed, and she noticed from the inside that the front door had clear plastic mounted around its frame. She must have peered through it from outside when she'd first arrived. "You sleeping downstairs, Jacob, or here? In the living room?" She hadn't noticed a downstairs despite examining the entire structure, inside and out.

"Mostly downstairs. Basement." He took another long drag on the cigarette and barked out a deep cough.

Amalia hoped he wasn't contagious. She pressed on. "Anything you need me to see down there? I'm here for the building."

"Suit yourself. Building." He snickered. "Follow me." Jacob left the cigarette lit on the edge of an ashtray at the end of the sofa and bent down to rest on both knees at the end of the room. He moved slowly. Looked like he was about to pray where he knelt, but then lifted a loose plywood board that had been covered with sand. The grains scattered into two neat piles on either end of the board as he lifted it, removing the single panel from the living room floor in a reverse puzzle-like move.

She hadn't noticed the panel until that moment. The whole floor appeared to have been covered in plywood after the storm and more sand had blown in, or maybe been brought in. Amalia wondered where the carpet was, or if it had ever been carpeted before. Didn't like to ask. She fingered the phone in her pocket, remembering that 9 1 1 had been the last call placed, and Keith, the last person texted. She could reach out to either again.

Jacob let the panel fall, and he got up, swung his legs down into a shaft, and with a grunt, moved with difficulty down a newly revealed staircase. His head remained above floor level. "You coming? Regular staircase here, handrails and everything." He continued, and Amalia heard the pull and click of a cord from a ceiling lightbulb below. "How much you want?"

"When you call 9 1 1 and hang up, don't they show up?"

"Did you give them the address of the house?"

"Uh-huh."

"They're not coming."

"Why?" She hadn't approached the hole in the floor and spoke without seeing him below.

"Why? You ask too many questions. You coming or not?"

What was she afraid of? She was there for the building. And she had nothing to lose. This guy was slow to move. "Hang on." Pulled her out phone again and tapped Keith's name.

This guy Jacob, he's here.

OK.

He legit?

Never met him face to face.

You coming back?

I can if you want.

Yes please. Soon.

Ok be there in ten.

Thank you!

You OK?

A-OK. Just come.

Keith seemed to have a genuine concern. He'd be there soon enough. "Yeah, Jacob, I'm coming." Her heart rate had slowed to almost normal. She could do it. Curiosity overcame her nerves. As she approached the open shaft to the basement, she heard the drumming sound of a generator starting up deep within the house. "You ventilating that, Jacob?" She approached the top of the stair, and true to his word, there was a new wooden staircase and a comfortable handrail installed on each side. She assessed the top step. Sturdy. The handrails. Steady. Built by someone who knew how to build something strong. The foot of the stair was lit with the bulb, but she could not see Jacob, or the generator, beyond a full-height plywood wall at the bottom landing. Jacob's cigarette ash hung, about to fall into the basin of the old glass ashtray at the end of the sofa. She took a deep breath, tobacco and all, and descended. "Jacob?" She banged on the plywood.

"This way." Jacob popped his head out from behind another panel, beneath the head of the stair. A deep magenta glow emerged around his head. The smell of generator gas and something else, earthy and sharp, caught the senses of her nose and throat. "One kilo or two?"

"Jacob. That's not what I am here for."

"I don't have other stuff."

"I'm here for the building."

He looked confused. "Hang on." The magenta light went out and he emerged, generator grumbling behind him. "Up." He pushed her toward the stairs and turned to screw the wooden panel back in place behind him.

Amalia moved, pressing beyond the feel of his hands on her back from where he stood behind her. She took the stairs two at a time. Coming to the top of the gap in the floor and pulling herself up and through the wooden opening to the living room, she let out a deep exhale. "All good here, sir!" She saw the ash from the cigarette give way in the current of her movement. Back out through the kitchen. Heart pounded. Slipped on the sand at the back, rounded the corner to the side, out front. Looked up and down the street; no sign of Keith or anyone else. No neighbors. No activity. Some partially demolished houses, and that one, standing, degraded, large, functioning, and loud.

Jacob had not caught up. He moved too slow. She broke out into a run for Mark's little car. Her throat hurt by the time she got in, from cold or smoke, mold, or what; it didn't matter.

She had her phone.

She'd left her bag and the roll of tracing paper with the start of the kitchen sketch.

"Dammit."

Car keys were in her pocket, rattling against her dirty cell phone. She beat a fast path back to Manhattan.

"We have no jurisdiction down there," the New York City police officer said, standing in the doorway of PGAE. "And medical marijuana's been legal in Jersey for a while now. Not much we can do."

"But that man is suffering!" Amalia's jaw tightened. "He can't be ignored. His house is trashed from the hurricane and he's inhaling all those—what—I don't know what he's inhaling, but it's not good. Mold and stuff. Marijuana plant fibers."

"I can see you care about this gentleman. If he was offering you more than a kilo, that might go beyond a New Jersey limit. And to be honest I'm not up on Jersey. I'm not sure how it would work with a home grow op."

"I don't care about him!" Amalia didn't want to care about him. Truth was, she worried for him. "Okay, maybe I care a little."

"Best you can do is call the police there, give them the address, ask them to do a drive-by."

"I did call the police there. And I gave them the address."

"He got anyone else looking out for him?"

"A contractor? One he hasn't met in person? Maybe a rep from FEMA? I'm not sure."

"Amalia," Jen said over the phone on speaker, her voice cast to the room from the hospital, "let's let Betsy handle this. It's way beyond our job descriptions."

"No. Betsy isn't even going to hear about this until we get it resolved."

"You supposed to be working on that property?"

"We're supposed to be inspecting it," Jen said. "Making some recommendations for repair."

"My advice is, write up your report, turn it over to the town, let the town know it's a grow op, and let their building department oversee it."

"Building department? For a drug issue?"

"Building departments handle grow ops all the time these days. They'll coordinate with the health department down there. It's a local issue. If they decide to shut it down, it'll be done fast. You don't have to do that yourself. Let them know that you think there may be an issue and they'll follow up."

"That sounds pretty good, Amalia," Jen said. "You got enough photos and notes we can put it together?"

"I think so." Amalia felt a tug in her gut. "I want to do the right thing, but I don't know what that is."

"He just told you," Jen said. "Sir, thank you very much for your time. I think she's got this."

"You should go back," Mark said over the phone. "Get your bag at least, and you can get the rest of the photos you need."

"I don't know. I beat it out of there."

"The cop told you it's legal. And you were concerned about him. The guy. I could go with you."

"I don't need you to go with me. I can take care of my work on my own. At the very least, Sunil could come."

"Sunil?"

"You remember. Our structural engineer."

"Right. And you'd need a structural engineer."

"Maybe."

"You and Sunil could go."

"Except it's supposed to be pro bono and not take much time."

"You and I could go."

"No. I already said I can take care of it."

"Fine, be stubborn. The offer stands. Go with Sunil at least."

"Why, because I need a man to protect me?"

"Come on. I never said that."

"I'll manage it."

Amalia pulled out of the street parking first thing the next morning away from their apartment, aware her wallet was in the bag she'd left at Jacob's, thankful she had her keys. Damn straight she'd manage it. She'd go first thing down the Shore and try to catch up with Keith while he did his rounds, and he could escort her in. Not that she needed a bodyguard. He had the tools to remove the plywood panels, and he would lend legitimacy to her presence, should Jacob appear. She didn't get the sense that Jacob had anything untoward going on. Other than the sealed-up basement, after two hours of scouring the inside and outside of the place, she'd found no evidence of any fishy business and nothing like weapons or stashes of cash.

She suspected Jacob was a pensioner trying to make do. She imagined he'd raised his family in that house, was a widower, and was too proud to ask his kids for help; he must have turned to the valid and legal practice of providing medical marijuana in the State of New Jersey.

She thought so. And she didn't know if one could grow the stuff just like that, or if one needed permits (she presumed he had them), or if there were limits. There must be limits, that would make sense. She'd suggest to Jacob that he investigate them, for his own well-being.

She did care about his well-being. He was a client, and he reminded her of people: the man at the voting booth the previous fall; her grandfather in their video calls at the end of his life; even reminded her a little of Max, crusty on the edges and sweet inside. She smiled. This would be fine.

~ 17 ~

Art Students ~ February

Amalia stood at the solid doors of The Art Students League the following month, sheltered from snow by a scaffolded sidewalk bridge above. Much of the city had a shuttered-in feeling from rampant safety scaffolding, protecting pedestrians from falling debris of crumbling buildings. It bothered her—the debris, not the scaffolding—and she hoped in her work she could address it. The doors felt heavy in her grasp as she pulled, and the brightness and wonder of the student-focused art space inside came as a shock to her chilled senses. Jen had said to meet there. She had spent the past weeks after her hysterectomy in a gentle recovery and hoped to return with deliberate slowness to yoga. In the meantime, she'd taken to hanging out with her usual yoga teacher, after the classes she had yet to resume.

Her yoga teacher was part of an exhibition that included his own work. One piece, Jen said, to be celebrated. They would meet to celebrate him; it was a chance for Jen to get out of her apartment and to process the news Betsy shared earlier in the day, the implications not yet understood. Amalia felt foggy in her head amidst the chatter of students but soon felt the friendliness of a familiar warm hand on her shoulder: Jen, smiling, next to her yoga teacher.

"Jeremy, meet Amalia."

"Nice to meet you." He extended a congenial hand and pulled her in for a cheek kiss. "Thank you for coming."

"Not at all. Congratulations on having a piece in the show!"

"It's a test run; we're not even open to the public for another month. But thanks. It does feel good. Let me show you around?"

Jen gave Amalia a push on the back. "Go! Explore."

What was the hurry? Jen was up to something. Jeremy was as gracious as she might have expected a yoga-teacher-turned-art-exhibitor to be, and he guided her through the whole mocked-up exhibition space and out to the hallway too, hand resting on her lower back. She didn't mind.

"Don't be bothered by Jen. She thinks I should ask you out."

"Oh really!" He was forward if nothing else. "You know I'm living with someone, right?"

"And?"

Amalia shook her head. "I'm sorry. Jen misspoke."

"It's Jen, really," said Jeremy.

Amalia looked up at the wall of art. "It's Jen you want to ask out."

"She's single."

"She's gay."

"She's open."

"Oh?"

"She told me," Jeremy said.

"I didn't know that." Amalia looked back at him, then up again at the wall. Could she ever see her own artwork displayed in a gallery? "Why don't you try asking her out?" It made sense, Jen foisting her on Jeremy, or Jeremy on her. Maybe she had mixed feelings.

"I'm with you right now," he said.

"You're an in-the-moment kind of guy." She smiled and they walked back up the hallway into the main exhibition space.

"Jen said you were in India."

"I was."

"Must have been amazing. I've always wanted to go. Yoga and everything."

"Mmm." Amalia stood in front of one art student's collected pieces.

"I'm running a yoga hike retreat up at Bear Mountain soon. You should come."

"Why did this student get this spot and so many pieces?"

"Do you like them?" He went with her divergence, and Amalia felt the relief in her abdomen.

"They go together."

"There you are. They go together. And you should come to Bear Mountain. It's Jen's favorite place."

"Is everything that simple to you?"

"Simple, no. Fluid, yes." Jeremy let go of her lower back. "And there's Jen."

Jen, flushed from Amalia didn't know what, gave a fangirl wave toward Jeremy from across the open space.

"Oh, my." Amalia stared at Jen. Maybe she did have a thing for him. She felt a buzz in her back pocket, a text. It was Mark.

Hi A, running late, back about 10.

"Sorry, just a minute, it's my boyfriend."

OK, I'm out with Jen still, back about 11. BTW big news from work today!

~ 18 ~
Words

Dear Amalia,

I'm writing sitting in the hall of The Art Students League, and I saw you. I don't think you saw me, but I saw you, and who you were with. Who was that guy? Why did you tell me you'd be out late with Jen? What the heck is going on?

I guess we'll talk when I get home, assuming you are home too. I hope so.

I don't think I can put this all in an email.

Mark: Are they sending you to Scranton?

Amalia: No! They put me on a partnership track!

Mark: Super for you. Did you see my email? Just ignore it. See you about 11. Catch up then.

Amalia: :-)

~ 19 ~

Straphangers

"I'm home!" Amalia called out to the kitchen, and not seeing Mark, peeked her head around the corner in the one-bedroom apartment. He lay asleep, or seemed to be, beneath the heap of covers they'd piled on for late winter: her comforter, his quilts, and the still-borrowed quilt from Sandra's Great Aunt Joan. "Mark?"

"Hey." He rolled over, groggy. "What time is it?"

"I have news! What do you mean, it's 11 PM. I said I'd be home by eleven." She sat on the edge of the bed and unzipped her tall boots and began to unwind the scarf from around her neck. "You want to hear, or you want to go back to sleep?" She propped her bag up next to where she'd left her large sketchbook on the bedroom floor.

"Sleep sounds good." He sat up. "What's your news? You got a promotion? Partner track?"

"Betsy said Jen and I are well poised to take over the firm from her and Max when we're ready. And when they're ready." The glow of the memory returned to her belly and lit her cells from within. "So good!"

"Did you get a raise?"

"No, just that." She patted him on the leg through the quilts. "It's so good!"

"Did you get a promotion? Did they make you an associate?"

"No, silly, I'm still an intern. This is like a bookmark for the future."

"No promotion." He flipped back the covers.

"Where are you going?"

"Water. Bathroom. Water."

"It's amazing! Jen and I can take over the firm! When we're ready. When they're ready. They're going to write it up with an attorney to say that once our licensing is completed, that when they're ready, they will begin the transition."

"Betsy's not that old. Max might be."

"Max is already out. He's never there. And I don't think Betsy will want to do it on her own."

"Or with you?"

"Maybe that's the point of the transition. Maybe it would be the three of us, me, Jen, and Betsy."

"Did she say so?"

"What is wrong with you? Why are you being contrary?"

"I'm not being contrary. I'm getting water. It's a logical question to ask."

"I don't want you to be logical, I want you to be happy for me!" She felt tears begin to sting the corners of her eyes and bit them back. How had happiness—giddiness—turned? "I don't want to do this again."

"Do what again?" Mark stood with his back to the kitchen sink and sipped a tall glass of water.

"Don't act all deadpan with me."

"Deadpan is for humor. I see no humor in this."

"You're telling me." She pulled the wooly cap from her head and unbuttoned her coat; winter layers were suffocating inside. Dropped the coat on the back of the chair.

"You going to hang that up?"

"No!" She went into the bedroom and slammed the door behind her. "What the hell!"

"Amalia." She heard him through the door, speaking with a new softness. "I'm sorry."

"For what."

"For being a goof. Of course, I'm excited for you." He scratched the door. "Let me in?"

"There is no lock, dummy, you can come in." She swung open the door.

Mark extended the glass of water to her. "Peace?"

"In a glass of water?" She accepted it, took a sip, and put it down on the floor next to the foot of the bed.

"Or in this." He pulled her to the edge of the bed and pushed back the quilts, kissed her on the top of the nose, on the cheek, then the other one.

"That could work." Amalia giggled when he kissed her neck and pulled him up to meet her lips. "Or this," she said.

"This works." The kisses soon turned into a struggle with quilt layers and clothing, both of which were cast aside in favor of bare skin.

"That's better. But it's cold."

"I have a solution," he said, and flipped the quilt sandwich over them in a colossal mound of warmth, muffling them from the receptive ears of the neighbors whose music wafted in through the shafted window in the kitchen beyond.

They snuggled and slept, and although Amalia hoped they would, no love was made. He fell asleep, as advertised, and as sensual as it was to lie naked next to his warmth beneath the covers, Amalia shivered, and she got up to dress. Her foot knocked something hard and there was a cold splash across her foot—the forgotten water glass—and as she shrieked, she kicked it without meaning to, and the glass smashed against the corner of the wall, sending shards along the floor in a wet, slick layer of tiny, sharp fragments scattered across the little canvas and sketchbooks. They cleaned it up together naked, throwing on sweats after, then went back to bed without discussion.

Amalia rose from a restless sleep. It was well before her alarm was to wake her for work, and she rolled slowly out of bed to not rouse Mark. They'd cleaned the glass and water together; all was still. Could she slip out of the apartment while he slept? The old door of the walkup building creaked at the most inopportune times, and the other doors on the same shared hallway did the same, often vibrating through the apartment. It was a noisy home, even before the music came on in the neighbors' apartments, a happy cacophonic buzz with a life all its own.

But it was quiet: no doors, no music, just snowfall outside the window offering a soft icy whoosh when it blew against the glass.

A momentary snore from Mark gave her a jump and she stood up from the bed when he rolled over. Tiptoed to the door and into the bathroom, with her phone. Looked at herself in the mirror, down at her phone, back at herself—then scrolled through the text messages.

A noise from outside the bathroom reminded her Mark slept. It was a hallway noise, a neighbor. Grabbed her toothbrush, opened the bathroom door, gathered her work outfit, bag, and warm coat in one armload, tall winter boots in the other hand, and let herself out the apartment's front door.

The hallway was quiet. Any rustling from her would transmit back into the apartment, so she tiptoed down the flights in her socks. Layered up at the bottom and set out to find an open coffee shop at dawn. Turned out not to be easy, and it was cold in the snow; it would be easier to hop onto the subway and get coffee near the office.

Early commuters gathered on the subway platform and for a minute or two she looked for Sunil. She soon gave up.

At the office, she cleaned herself up for the day, sipped coffee from Starbucks, put on some music over the speakers on her computer, and set up flash cards on her desk to study for her first Architectural Registration Exam test section. If she kept her head in it, she'd get through, early mornings, late nights, studying, focused, and challenged.

She'd felt numb since India. Dim awareness of something not right rose in her as she read each flash card in turn, flipping over one for the next answer, looking at them as they came in succession. It didn't have anything to do with Mark, or her grandfather, or the baby that wasn't—she could not put a finger on it. Maybe Mildred would have a good perspective. A missed call had come through on Amalia's screen the day before, and with it a brief message from Mildred. She'd return the call later. For the moment, she had flash cards, coffee, and a quiet office, snow beyond the window, and an opportunity to ignore everything else. The numbness blanketed her and wove into the cards, and when she flipped to the next answer, she felt her eyes well with tears.

~ 20 ~
Ganga

Retying her shoelaces with one hand while squatting next to her office desk was not working. Amalia put the cell phone next to her computer—texting Mark would have to wait. She bent forward with both hands free and tied one lace, then as she reached for the next shoe, noticed a little flake of dried mud—a vestige of the fateful visit to Mark's frack site in Pennsylvania. Mark's company's hydraulic fracturing site. Not Mark's frack site. She ought to separate the two. And he'd quit that job to focus on consulting to the industry—she needed to remember the strides they had taken together.

She scratched off the mud with her fingernails and picked up the phone and typed,

Home late, catching up here.

To which he replied,

I'll keep dinner.

She sighed, knowing she had it rather good with this not-quite-legally married live-in boyfriend. Pulled her warm cardigan around her, layered up with jacket, hat, mitts, and scarf, and left the office—quiet, everyone gone—to meet Sunil at Andrews Coffee Shop.

The chill dusk gave her a moment's pause as her breathing adjusted. She'd forgotten her work notebook. Didn't need it—she could remember what Sunil would tell her and she'd write it down after. Could put it in her phone but didn't want to be rude with her phone, recalling their failed date in the fall. In any case, she could cross-check it with him later via email. She turned up the street toward the corner. He hadn't arrived, which gave her time to check her phone for messages and news. Mom and Dad continued to pepper her with invitations to move back to Pennsylvania ("you can't be enjoying the city now it's been hit by a hurricane," to which she replied, "the city is recovering—and my work is helping"). Her and Jen's work assisting Betsy and Max on post-storm recovery efforts for homeowners and business owners along the Shore was a vast undertaking, shared between offices. But although she and Jen supported it, they hadn't seen much in the way of full recovery. Too early, too hard to know what resources were available through grants or loans for rebuilding.

"Hey—good to see you." Sunil stood in front of her, equally bundled, twinkly eyed. "How was your trip?" He kissed her on the cheek in greeting; a surprise, and she returned his hello with a handshake he accepted with some awkwardness. Sunil stood back a step.

"Good trip." She took off her hat and scarf, aware of how overdressed she was for the warm coffee shop. "Strange, though. Have you ever been to a Hindu cremation?" Should she go there? He was the only person who might share the experience, outside of her immediate family.

He nodded. "I have."

Amalia leaned toward him where they stood, perched against high stools. "This might take two rounds of coffee."

The counter server put two hot cups in front of them, and Amalia put her phone away—wanted to show she could break the habit of texting Mark when Sunil was nearby. She took the coffee. The scent of it traveled through her with ease, bringing a smile to her lips. "It was amazing and light and kind of happy, almost dispassionate. Nobody seemed sad, at least not how I would have expected here," she said. Her hands wrapped the ceramic mug, fingers warming fast.

"Was there ganga?"

"Yeah. Is that a thing? Ganga-infused cremations?"

"It was when we went to my grandmother's," he said. "The flowers were in with the herbs they burned."

"Cool." Amalia didn't know what to say; she took a sip of the hot coffee. She'd be up late with all the caffeine, evening already. Would Mark be up when she got home? "Did you know before I went away, I almost got married?"

"What?" he sipped back his coffee hard. "Ow. Hot. What?"

"I kind of got engaged and almost fully married to my boyfriend Mark."

"You never mentioned it." He put his mug down. "And you're wearing rings I never noticed."

"It all happened pretty fast," she said. "He moved in with me up in Hamilton Heights, after I moved into your neighborhood last fall." She looked at Sunil, who looked back with some concern between the eyebrows. "To be honest, I'm not quite sure where we're going."

"Maybe it was too fast." He sat up straighter on the stool.

"Mmm." She patted her bag. "I forgot my notebook back at the office. Tell me about the probe locations for the geothermal." She sat up taller, aware of how close they sat. And later, when she bundled up to leave, she promised herself she'd return to study. The place had a good vibe.

In Andrews Coffee Shop the next day and alone, Amalia studied in a booth all to herself.

"What is the difference between a contractor and a subcontractor?"

Amalia flipped over the index card on the table.

"A contractor holds the primary contract for construction and hires the subcontractor directly. The owner does not hire the subcontractor."

She figured that was good enough for a basic answer, although she suspected there was a lot more to it.

"What is the benefit of using a stipulated sum contract?"

She wrote as she whispered, "the owner knows what they are getting into, except for change orders." More or less. She'd have to research that one a little more.

"What is substantial completion?"

She flipped her index card over.

"It is when the construction project is complete and ready to be inhabited although there might be some punch list items left. And it is a milestone for payment of the contractor."

"What is a punch list?" She read to the server, "I'll have a refill of coffee. And do you know what a punch list is?"

The server laughed. "I can tell you who's on my punch list!" She refilled Amalia's mug. "What you got there?"

"I'm studying for my architecture exams. But you know, can I ask you something?" She rifled through the papers in her bag.

"I don't know much about architecture, sorry."

"No, this is about medical marijuana."

"For real." The server shifted on her feet and looked around. "My aunt uses it."

"Okay. That's good." Amalia held her pen poised over a new and blank index card. "Number one: what do you think of medical marijuana?"

"I don't think I can answer this while I'm working. But maybe we can talk later after my shift. I'm off in half an hour. I'll come back? You'll be here?"

"Sure. Until you guys kick me out, I'm studying."

"What's this for, by the way? The medical marijuana thing?"

"It's for a panel discussion I'm involved with."

"Wow, cool. You architects are the coolest. I always wanted to be an architect."

"Me too," Amalia said. "Me, too." She hoped she'd fulfill that mission. Her mind went out the window to the cars on the street. She'd have to find a way to get through the exam prep while doing what she needed to do for the medical marijuana panel. She didn't want to let Mildred down.

The Reverend Mildred and Father Jasper had suggested making the panel less about marijuana and more about medication, to draw a larger audience. Amalia had an inner, unspoken hope that it would draw less heated debate. A heated debate was not going to help her swim through her architecture exams.

While it was fresh in her mind, she wrote in her notebook. The words formed on her lips as they flowed from her pen. Whispering, she took it all down.

"Do you support the use of medications that can help people?

Do you support research to advance knowledge of those medications?

Are you concerned about legislation around that research?

Are you aware there is a medication that can help many different conditions that is not legal across the country?

If you had a loved one who could benefit from this medication, would you support research on it?

If you had a loved one who could benefit from this medication, would you support its legalization?

Are you aware of the history of Prohibition in this country?

Are you aware of the impact of legalizing substances in other countries that are illegal here?

Would you like to know more about research around these medications/substances?

Would you like to know more about legalization of these medications/substances?"

~ 21 ~

Laundering

The questions lolled about in her mind during the workweek, to be recounted on the weekend. Saturday. A day of reorganization. On Saturdays, Amalia did laundry for her and Mark, and while the laundering happened, Sunil often appeared at the laundromat at the same time.

His laundry bag, the same burgundy one he had the previous weekend, lay across the table between them, where she folded and Sunil sipped takeout coffee from the bodega across the street.

"Great structural you reported last week," she said. Heat rose fast up her neck. "Great report you wrote structurally, I mean. Dammit." She shook her head and laughed. "Coffee looks good."

"I would have brought you one if I'd known you'd be here," he said. "They make it good there, you know? Everything is better in Hamilton Heights."

"I meant, you wrote a great structural report last week. There."

"You're saying you don't want me to bring you a coffee next time?"

"I'm just saying, you did a good job on it."

"Suky did most of it. I just did the structural part. She did the mechanical part, which is what it's about."

"This is convenient! We can discuss the report while the towels tumble." She felt herself blush. "I mean. I have been thinking. Your report didn't mention the stairs. If the stairs are poured concrete in a steel stringer, how are we going to refinish them? I'm thinking of it as I look out at these fire escapes across the street—these fire escapes—thinking of the condo work."

"Chip out the concrete and set new treads," Sunil said. He loaded up the machine next to hers.

"Labor intensive."

"Maybe they're not poured, maybe they're precast."

"And then we could lift them out?"

"No, you'd still have to chip them to lift them. And they'd likely have a mortar bed they'd have been laid in. I'd have to look at my field notes."

"I think we might have to leave them."

"Are you keeping the whole stair?"

"I was assuming so." Her gaze drifted across the street. "It's not up to me. I'm not the architect. Betsy's the architect. I'm the intern." She looked at him. "But I can pass on the message. Tell me? What are our options?"

"If it's an open stair like you say, then it's not going to be tied into the load bearing structure of the space, and you could remove the whole thing and put in a new stair. If it's important."

"I'm sure it's simple enough, I just haven't done it. I remember learning it in school. And Betsy showed me on another project. It's something I need to know how to do."

"You're in luck because I can help you."

"I am in luck, yes."

"Two heads are greater than one."

"We didn't hire you to design an open staircase."

"No, but before you remove the existing one you should have it assessed structurally. And as your structural engineer, I would be the person to help."

"I thought you said if it's open it wouldn't be load bearing."

"I should check it."

"You should check it."

"I could go with you. Next time you're there." He smiled.

"Because that would be fun?" The heat in her cheeks intensified and she stared into the center of the washing machine.

"No, Amalia, because it would be the right thing to do." He sounded quite serious.

"Structurally speaking."

"Absolutely. We could go now; it won't take long. I'll show you."

Amalia moved closer to Sunil on the sidewalk, closer to hear, closer to move through the crowd of Saturday shoppers on Amsterdam Avenue. He pointed out some of the old metal fire escapes and they walked past a distinct smell of skunk—not the animal kind. "Whew, that's some strong weed," she said.

"That's the good stuff," he said.

"And you'd know how, exactly?"

Another week, he brought her a coffee and she sipped it as she folded.

"My grandfather died of mesothelioma."

"I'm sorry. Were you close?"

"I felt close. We were far away. But I felt we were close."

"Then you were."

How open a book did she want to be? "When we went over it was December, you know?"

"Good time of year there in Kolkata?"

"Pretty nice. The air was good. Have you been?" She doubted he had; he called the city Kolkata, belying a lack of family ancestry there.

"Me? No. We're on the other side."

As she suspected. Something relaxed in her belly, and a sense of interest rose. Felt a prompting to tell him more, to ask. "You know when you said they had a ganga-infused ceremony for your grandmother?"

"I do."

"And you know when you said you have a preference for the good stuff?"

He smiled. "I do." He nodded.

"You know I'm going to this medical marijuana panel, right? I was wondering if you'd like to speak on it." Mildred had been asking around and had asked Amalia and Mark outright if they would do it.

"What? No. I have nothing to say on the matter."

"More than me."

"Look, I have no interest in being a spokesperson for or against medical marijuana. I'm not interested."

"All right. Say you could help someone? By your presence."

"You mean, I could help you?"

"No, I mean you could be helping someone in the audience." She felt her grasp slip. "Like, you could be a great help somehow." She laughed. "Okay. I hear what you're saying. You don't want to do it." Her laughter turned to a big exhalation. "I guess I have to do it. I thought you might do it instead of me." She gave him a sidelong look.

"You are too much! Ask Jen if you need some help. Or Suky."

"They're not speaking to each other anymore."

"I don't mean they have to do it together. They might have something to say."

"One Democratic and one Republican lesbian opinion on medical marijuana?"

"I heard that was why they split up."

"Because they had differing opinions on medical marijuana?"

"No, because Jen couldn't stand that Suky voted Republican in the last election."

"There are worse things to disagree on."

"You're saying you would split up with someone who had a different political opinion than you? Or that you wouldn't date in the first place?"

"Not at all. In fact, I'm already doing that. Mark and I vote differently."

"And how's that going for you?"

"Well, pretty good, considering my guy won the last election."

Sunil smiled. "Good for you."

"And good for the Democrats."

"Good for the country."

"Mark voted for him, too. He came around in the end."

"But what if he voted Republican?"

"I did."

"What?"

"I voted Republican. Not because I'm a Republican, mind you, but because this old man in front of me in line voted wrong and I swapped his vote for him."

"Can you do that?"

"Of course. You can do whatever you want in the voting booth. Vote however you want. It's just between you and the curtain."

"And your conscience."

"That's why I did it. My conscience." She paused, aware of a tightening in her chest. "I did something else." She'd wanted to blurt it out before she could decide to take it back.

"You two again." The voice came from behind. Mark.

The following week he was not there, and she sighed, but after the washing machine had begun to spin, she looked away from the center of the drum, knowing he was behind her.

He was, of course. He smiled and waved from the door, where, as she predicted, he had his burgundy laundry bag slung over his shoulder. Amalia swallowed and reached for her phone to call Jen. Times like these called for a wingman.

"Hey!" He loaded his laundry into the machine next to hers. "We have neighbor machines today." He was just so happy about it. Jen wasn't picking up. "Maybe we can grab a coffee together, this time, outside."

Amalia slipped the phone back into her pocket, a small smile cracked out from her inside, and she heard herself say, "I'd love that." The smile inside grew, and one part of her screamed "what are you doing?" while the other part was content to keep smiling and nodding like a mechanical wind-up toy. Her phone buzzed with an incoming call. "Excuse me for a moment." She had a quick look, didn't want him to have reason to continue thinking she was phone obsessed. Mildred.

She'd ignore the call from Mildred. She felt a slight pang of guilt at the thought of the woman who had performed Amalia and Mark's almost-wedding, and the words of encouragement she'd offered over the phone. Amalia sighed. "Yes, let's go for coffee, and I'll call Mark to see if he can join us."

"Okay, but I was hoping we could talk about work. He might not feel included, you know?"

She moved her head up and down, up, and down. "I would hate for him to feel like a third wheel."

"We wouldn't be long."

"It doesn't matter, now that I think of it. He's busy until dinner."

The machine next to her took off at full rotational speed, and as she leaned on it, she caught its vibration.

At work the following week, Amalia arranged a bouquet of roses for the meeting table, a continuing trend since the previous fall. They smelled heavenly. "I put Sunil's name down for the medical marijuana panel."

"That was nice of him."

"He doesn't know."

"That wasn't nice of you."

"And he does not want to do it."

"Why would you do that then?" Jen brought the drawings to the table. "These are ready for Betsy's meeting. And those are nice, they smell nice."

"They do." Amalia twiddled the stems around until they sat well in the vase. "Is she going on her own or is Max going too?"

"I have not seen Max in forever."

"He's still down South, I think. This was his project, wasn't it? About Sunil. I must take his name off. The posters have already been printed."

"Amalia! That's wrong. You didn't even ask first?"

"I didn't know the posters would be printed. I just suggested his name."

"Suggested or put his name down as a speaker?"

"Kind of open to interpretation."

Jen shook her head. "Does he know?"

"No! And you are not going to tell him. I will handle it." She turned each print over in front of her on the conference table. "I'm glad I got these roses before the meeting. You know how Betsy took to that."

"That was weird. Weird and nice."

"We started doing it after the fracking meeting. Bringing in roses to meetings."

"Amalia, whatever magic you work, you go, girl. Just don't sign me up for any panel discussions without my permission first, you hear?"

~ 22 ~

State of Grace ~ March

Amalia stood squished between the straphangers on the way home, uptown, alone, with a wandering mind. The warmth of the woman next to her, pressed against her arm, passed through her thick coat. She liked it. She'd noticed something since her return from India after having to land back in the old way of doing things at work—after having to reconcile the parts of her recent experience.

Noticed it was easier to be in a state of grace when she opened herself up to the idea of it to begin with. She felt it as she appreciated the warmth of the woman next to her on the train.

Noticed it was much easier to be in the receiving of good ideas when she was relaxed and feeling nonconfrontational. She'd felt it with Sunil. Wasn't sure where it would go; she liked it.

Noticed when it was already better to begin with, the more good stuff occurred. Which came first, feeling good or experiencing good things? Did it matter? If it was all good in the end, what did it matter which came first? She'd felt it with Mildred, before. The woman next to her had a similar vibe. And as Amalia had that thought, the woman shifted and squished herself through the sardine-tin of passengers to get off the train at the next stop. The absence of the woman left an ineffable gap next to her, the gap soon filled by other passengers and distractions.

Amalia tried to go back into the good feeling. It was easier, though, when she felt good to begin with, sometimes for no reason at all. Sunrise, sunset, warm and cozy older women like Mildred—it didn't matter what put her into the state of grace. She called the feeling her sweet spot. Mark laughed when she told him and she tried to explain, but it didn't matter. He didn't get it and he did not want to go down that road with her.

His reluctance to engage with her was explained to her the following week, in Mark's own words. "I am through," Mark said. "I am through it. I am looking at a new passage. I have booked a ticket back to Iceland, and I am moving through it. To Iceland. On my own. I've been offered a job by the geothermal company."

"In Iceland? Wait, when were you going to tell me about this? It's not like I can just up and move to Iceland." Nice thought, though. She imagined setting up a little cottage for the two of them near the coast somewhere. Maybe she could see design clients there. A separate entrance for her home business? Should she get an architectural license in Iceland—or could she, even?

She noticed Mark's soft gaze on the tree through the back window. His back looked relaxed, a gentle curve. He stood up. She hadn't seen him like this in a long time. Maybe never. Something new was emerging, and she found herself interested.

Mark went to the window. "I'm going on my own, Amalia. Just me." He didn't turn around. The good feeling Amalia had cuddled within her with such clarity eluded her.

She made dinner for both of them, even though it was awkward. Amalia dumped the leftover vegetable peelings from their dinner into the worm bin and poked at the countertop compost with a fork. It had been a good experiment, but in the move from Great Aunt Joan's temporary lodgings to her apartment now shared with Mark, the compost had fallen into some neglect. The worms seemed happy, though, still receiving a constant dose of food scraps. Amalia had not thought the design through all the way when she built it with her dad's tools in the garage in Scranton. She looked more closely. At over one year old, the bin's unfinished wood edges and interior were beginning to show some rot. She had taken out the new soil when needed and dumped it in Central Park when she lived nearer. In Hamilton Heights, there was no park close to her. "Cemetery across the street" was all she could come up with. As for the rotting wood, she was at a loss. She had a whole kitchen ecology center in her hands that needed care and tending. "What the hell am I going to do with this worm bin?"

"I need some advice, Mildred." Amalia walked outside in the bright early spring air, anticipating that Mildred would find some kind words. She gulped in the breeze, greedy for its refreshment. "Mark and I seem to be splitting up."

"Dear." She heard Mildred shuffle and shift, as if the phone had dropped in her lap. "That is tremendously disruptive news. I have only just settled myself down for a cup of tea and a read, and no sooner do I get myself ready to enjoy, I hear this."

"I thought maybe you'd have some advice. Because you're good that way. And you know Mark. And me." She watched a small bird pip its way along a branch on a tall tree that graced the road near their apartment. It had something in its beak. Nest-making season in New York was coming soon, but the ground was still frozen. Maybe it was hungry. "Something to feed the soul."

"I'm too invested," Mildred said. "I love you both too much to see you fail."

"You think we're failing?" Amalia felt tightness rise from her midsection. "You're our champion!"

"I don't mean you're failing, Amalia, you are fine. But if the marriage breaks down, then that could be considered—an abruption."

"We never finished the marriage paperwork after your ceremony, Mildred. I didn't want to tell you but there seems to be no reason to keep it from you now."

"Not married." The phone fell silent.

"Mildred? I'm sorry."

"Goodness, child, stop apologizing right now! There is nothing you have done wrong. Nothing! You hear me? You are a perfect child of all that is, and you have done nothing wrong. Now. Why don't you come up here for a bit? Take a break. Nothing like a few days away to get one's head sorted."

~ 23 ~

Color and Ashes

Dear Amalia,

I'm at a loss for what to say. I don't know how we came to this. I am sorry for my role in our falling apart.

Which brings me to the next. I want to turn the comic book with the two characters over to you. It was inspired by you, and I wouldn't continue it without you. So—here I present the pages. You can do with them as you see fit, including a cremation to ashes if that is best.

What is done is done, and there is no going back. We are likely better for having known each other, even if we are now apart.

Yours,
Mark

~ 24 ~

Before the House

Before the house, was the land.

And before the house, the land and the people had a knowing, a mutual knowing of how to be: give and receive, receive, and give.

The house knew none of this, having been borne of hands from different soil.

The house and its earliest foundations and walls—walls mimicking cut peat blocks, no easy substitute to be found in this new land—these foundations and walls took on water.

For the house dwellers, this was a trouble.

And with this trouble that came with the rains, came another trouble: what to do with the stores in the cellar.

Too much lost on the ship's journey.

Not enough to sustain in the new land.

The stores in the cellar, preserved by those in the motherland and sent with the house dwellers by ship, those stores were all they had, and this troubled the house dwellers with every rain.

To appease the local gods of weather and soil, the house dwellers took to ceremony, but not to sacrifice.

Even to the gods, they wanted not to sacrifice a sole precious morsel of nourishing life.

Over this they fought, for some of the house dwellers begged to continue the old ways and to sacrifice.

The conflict tore through the house, and when it did, the girl upon a waking dream brought out her talisman of sorts from pieces found by her elder.

She whispered it back into being, this mask of home, and when the mask became enlivened in her space, she knew exactly what to do. Years of observation had prepared her.

She coaxed it to come to her, cradled it in her hands, and whispered, "What is your name?" Felt its reply in a shiver: "Otter." She took it to the river and said, "Otter, I release you from this gourd," and as it shimmied away she saw its coat of fur shine in the moonlight.

For the pieces then, she took a strong box, her promise box for betrothal, a later and as yet unknown-to-her betrothal, and in this promise box she laid this mask's elements, formed of pieces found, and buried it in the shallows of the house to await its next animation.

Part II: The Mask

~ 25 ~

On the Table ~ April

Mildred touched each piece of paper on the table, laid just as she'd set them out the day before. A night's sleep had provided clarity after the hubbub of Easter preparations, service, and takedown at the church, but she'd still not sorted a solution. Muriel helped to provide nuggets of information that almost provided an understanding of how they all worked together.

She held up the first piece of paper to the light; she'd put them in chronological order, best she could. It was the top of a waybill of sorts, or a receipt. 1800s? She couldn't make out the rest of the date. There had to have been something earlier, too. Muriel said she had some pieces.

The first two numbers were easier to read: 1 8. Didn't help. There was still a piece or two missing.

She knew the trail connected to the rum running. That was no mystery. She'd lived that in her early years, a kid in Georgetown, Maine, speaking the language and inheriting the legacy of Prohibition: Moorehouse, Poorhouse, Roughhouse, Rum. It was a rhyme the locals made up to track the way to the booze. First, pass the old Moore Homestead, easy to spot, then the house with the poor folk—poorer, they were all poor in that corner—then the rough 'uns—and then her house. Her house with the fresh hung laundry, extra on the side where Mama took in the far neighbors' sheets, and downstairs, peeping through the colored glass block and out to the dirt road, ever-wary of the booze-man's motor vehicle, come to tax, come to collect, come to arrest.

They never knew which it would be. Arrest, it was meant to be. Collect, it was most often. Tax, just another word for a bribe. The booze-man would come. That was known by all.

It was the wonder about medical marijuana that got her thinking. She'd seen, or thought she'd seen, evidence of other trade, beyond the rum; had it been then, when she was a kid, before they'd gone to New Jersey, or earlier? And what had it been? Opium came to mind. The medical marijuana made her think so. Not the using of it, because she had no discernable mental effect from it, but the thought of it. Remembering the whispers and the uncertainty around any open discussion.

Moorehouse, Poorhouse, Roughhouse, Rum. Who had lived those few houses away, at the old Moore Homestead? Not the Moores, not when she'd been there with her family in the 1930s. She'd been just a girl. Went and gone in there once. It had been shuttered, the family away, although where they'd gone, she didn't recall. Maybe hadn't known then, either. Mildred remembered the creak of the back door on its hinges, unlatched, open and providing an easy passage for her and little Muriel to enter.

Muriel had liked to touch things, and to collect them. Muriel, the librarian, the early categorizer of little things found and stolen. She'd taken something that day at the old Moore Homestead, and Mama found out later and made her return it when the family came back. It left a hole in Muriel's collection, this gap of the stolen thing, since returned. Was it a little thing or a big thing?

It was a hook. Muriel had taken a hook. Not a fishhook, not a meat hook. Bigger. Something like a meat hook, maybe. It had weight to it, Mildred remembered. Not a meat hook. What was like a meat hook? Something to do with whaling? A whaling hook? That was possible. There was whaling then, off the coast. She remembered the blood on the beach. Yes, there was whaling. Or was it the blood of another? A whaling hook would have been too big for little Muriel's hands.

No matter what it had been, it felt connected. She picked up the receipt from the 1800s. How old was the Moore Homestead? And what had been going on in the 1800s?

Mildred looked at the prescription before her. She'd been feeling good, seeing better, and the Reiki helped. Her own Reiki-hands on her own eyes brought her soothing. She'd learned it during Raymond's transition months, and it helped.

Couldn't quite say how or why. She trusted it. Knew in theory how it worked, even taught in theory how it worked. Was it any different from the other healing modalities she'd been introduced to over the years? They were all soothing, they all brought different aspects of light or sound through the body, and they all came from the same source. Didn't that make them similar enough to consider eliminating their boundaries, and seeing them all as one?

No—it was tradition, practice, and repetition that kept them apart; a basic cultural liturgy attached to each. Reiki, for better or for worse, stuck to her. It was her learned tradition. And lately she'd been feeling she wanted it more, and any drugs, less.

This left her in a bit of a conundrum because she'd already announced the medical marijuana panel discussion. Not that she needed to be a user to host the discussion, but she'd noticed for certain that her feelings about it were changing. She was less attached. Maybe this would make her more impartial, a good thing.

She picked up a third piece of paper from the table. A photo of Mother and Papa and the first house they'd boxed for shipping, next to the tracks. Who had taken the photograph? They'd left that day. Had a neighbor mailed it to them later? She squinted in. Moved her head from side to side to try to see all the pieces on the table at once, but her peripheral vision wasn't good.

She needed to talk to someone. Rattling around wasn't doing her any good. Bert, back on Salt Spring Island, would be busy at his lavender farm, setting up his workers for the next season, maybe even preparing for his marriage to Claudia. There was that. She'd not call him. Muriel would be setting up for story time where she still volunteered at the library that she'd once called her day job. Mildred hadn't made many local friends after Raymond died, and his colleagues from Binghamton University fell away a few months after the condolences and the moving on. Oh, she could call on them anytime, and they'd come   they invited her every few months—but it wasn't a regular thing.

She wondered about Amalia and Mark, and how they were doing. She had their cell phone numbers. Amalia would be at work, and Mark was working from home. She tried Mark first. And he didn't answer. She tried Amalia—and it went straight to voice mail. She left a brief "Hello." Fine. She put on the kettle for tea.

~ 26 ~
Sketching

"I need to take some time off, Betsy. A couple of days."

"Everything okay at home? Your parents all right?"

"They're fine. I need to visit an old friend."

"Something's come up?" Betsy shook her head. "Never mind. None of my business. If you need to take two days off, you do it. When were you thinking?"

"Soon, this week or next."

"Not this week unless you have to. We have too much happening with the condo deadline. And your work on the performing arts center has to move ahead."

"Next week is your environmental center meeting and I'm supposed to be getting your drawings ready for the potential project sponsors, right?" Amalia hesitated. "If it ends up not being Atlantia, I mean."

"I meant to ask you—I was going to do the meeting in Binghamton, but I might not be able to make it because of this conflict with Landmarks here. I wonder if you could do the meeting."

"In Binghamton? I'd love to. I have a friend in Binghamton." She hesitated to add it was the Reverend Mildred, who Betsy would remember, and whose memory might trigger recollections of Amalia's wayward participation in the fracking meeting Mildred hosted.

"Works out well. I'll need to prep you for the meeting. It's Wednesday. It's to get Susan and Jeffrey ready for their open house the next weekend."

"Could I take Thursday and Friday off then, too, and stay up there? It's near my friend's."

"You could. Take Monday if you need, too."

"Generous of you. Don't you need to confirm with Max?"

"We're not paying you for taking the time off. You don't have any vacation time left."

"It's generous of you to allow me to take the time off."

"Even if we are not paying you."

"Exactly." She smiled. "Thank you for the meeting arrangement. I'll do right by the company."

"I know you will. No more surreptitious spreadsheets."

"No ma'am. I have no agenda."

"You are the embodiment of the Erenwine Agenda, Amalia."

"Not anymore. I've changed. I'm not making pros and cons lists anymore."

"No? What then?"

"I've started painting environmental visions."

"I'd like to see."

"So would I. They're in my head, to be honest."

"This time away might help move them out."

"Maybe. I hope so. It's not comfortable being congested, you know, creatively congested."

"You make it sound like a head cold!"

"It kind of is."

After lunch, Amalia watched Jen sort through papers from a disorganized file cabinet. Even with all of Betsy's fastidious diligence during the move to the new space, some files had arrived out of sequence, grabbed in a hurry when the post-superstorm move happened without preplanning. Amalia laughed. "Post-superstorm-preplanning," she said aloud.

"An oxymoron if I ever heard one," Jen said. "There was no preplanning here. I mean, look, whatever even is this?" She held up a diagram of colored squiggly lines.

"That's the frack diagram we were looking at. Must be some other environmental center project stuff there, too."

"Like this?" Jen held up a sheath of ripped-edge tracing paper sheets with grey and black hatching, overlaid page on page like a bundle of slate.

"That's them—my earlier sketches." Amalia jumped up to take the bundle back to her desk and laid them out one by one. She'd felt a stirring when she did them. To look at them brought it right back. She found a pencil on her desk and rolled out a curl of tracing paper and pressed it flat over the sketches with the side of one hand, smoothing the paper again, and again. The repetition of the movement was soothing, and she continued until she was aware of a shift within her to which her automatic response was to draw. The lines came fast across the page, as verticals, horizontals, diagonals; hatching and cross-hatching next, and in a flurry of new torn paper edges and quick pencil strokes, she amassed a new stack of about twenty images within a few minutes. She sat back, dropped the pencil atop the sketches, and massaged her right hand. "Done."

"Whoa, what were you thinking?"

"I wasn't. Drawing."

"Lots of thinking here—these are logical," Jen said. "May I?" She took each sketch in hand, one after another. "You have all the ideas here that we've been talking about. And these are all drawn proportionally to scale." She looked at Amalia. "You're amazing. Freehand, no less!"

"It flows. And I go with it."

"And that is why Betsy and Max haven't fired you!"

"Come on, not fair."

"They know you have talent. Amalia, what you're doing here, this can't be taught. You're a natural."

"Anyone can do this."

"Not anyone. You can do it. You are uniquely qualified to design this environmental center. Everyone sees it. For whatever reason, you're tapped into the project. To the land."

"The land they want to frack up as soon as they can."

"They, being—"

"Mark's old natural gas company. They don't own it. They're just the investors. Potential investors. If I didn't screw it all up last fall. It's public land with the easement in trust for the environmental center. But yeah—I do care about it. I wish they'd trust me more around it."

"Looks to me like they're trusting you plenty. You're even going to the open house presentation."

"Opposite. Betsy told me before, not to go to the open house while representing Polson Grohman."

"But that's not what she meant. Read between the lines, Amalia: she trusts you to generate the material, trusts you to hand deliver it to the client and to explain it to them, and even said that you can go to the open house, she just can't pay you to go because she can't bill for Polson Grohman's attendance." Jen looked bright-eyed as she crossed her arms.

"Are you challenging me to go to the open house?"

"Maybe. And maybe to trust yourself a little more. You're not going to screw anything up. You learned your lesson with the spreadsheet last fall. You care about this project and you're good at explaining the vision behind it."

"I need you to rally me along."

"That's my point, Amalia, you don't need anyone to rally you. You've got this handled."

"All right." Amalia walked to the window and let her gaze float out toward the distant Chrysler Building spire. "Say I do have this managed. How do I not speak the truth about fracking that site?"

"No one is asking you to weigh in with an opinion on fracking."

"Exactly. If I don't bring it up, who will?"

"Okay, bring it up, but make light of it."

"Make light of fracking? Yeah, right."

"You could say, 'I've been asked to keep my opinions on fracking to myself; these comments are off the record and don't represent my employer's views.' And then on the open house day, when you're not on company time, you can say whatever you want to say."

"I could, I suppose."

"You most definitely could. And you will. Because it's the only way you're going to move ahead with a clear conscience. And honestly, Amalia, it's right for the project. And for the client."

"This should come from Betsy, not from you," Amalia said.

"Betsy's not in a position to say it. As Assistant Project Manager," Jen said, "I am."

"As Assistant Project Manager," Amalia said, "you're in the dangerous position of knowing too much and having no power."

"I have authority to make some project decisions."

"If you run them through Betsy first."

"I can read between the lines. I've collaborated with her for a while, now."

Amalia felt seasick. She could not abide by the feeling of wobble that passed through her core. "The sketches are good. I can stand by the sketches." For the moment, that would have to do.

The worm bin was listed on Facebook for sale as

"Lightly used; happy worms and fresh soil included. Free to a good home!"

"I'll take it," Sunil said. He hadn't seen the post online but jumped at the opportunity when she told him about it over laundry. "Assuming your partner is okay with that."

"'Partner' is a bit of a strong word. We've been more roommates lately. And that roommate would be happy to see it go." She had a momentary flashback to the fireplace ash and bucket Mark had used on his own compost back in Pennsylvania and her whole abdomen shifted into a slow knot. She felt it come on, the wave of uncertainty, and she focused on her breathing. It released. "Amazing what the breath can do," she said.

"Breath of soil and water," he said, staring without focus into the center of the laundry drum that spun before them. He turned to her and smiled, gaze broken. "I'll give it a good home. Promise."

What Amalia wanted most to tell Sunil was that she loved him, and yet. It wasn't something she would ever say, she was most certain. At least not in the way that she wanted to. She could say, "Sunil, I love collaborating with you!" Or "Gee that was lovely, that thing there," or "Sunil, you could make a girl love you." None of those came close.

It was a blend of brother-love and lover-love, neither of which she had words to describe when it came to this man with whom she defined a large part of her budding career, now partway through her internship. Still. It was not a longing, but a loving. She looked forward to their encounters with an excitement that made her feel like a little jumping puppy dog.

No one else would understand, she was quite sure. Not Mark, and not her parents. Not Jen, who worked side by side with the two of them. Once when they'd been on a deadline Jen caught a whiff of Amalia's sentiments, and Amalia shut down the trajectory as fast as it had emerged. Didn't need that clouding the workspace. Wouldn't have been professional.

Did he know? She tried to push it away by immersing herself in work, but the feeling remained and expanded. Acknowledging confusion did not help her. It made her feel more helpless in the face of the situation, and an inner confrontation was born: one that wove in and out of their meetings over engineering details, and persisted over Saturday morning laundromat run-ins. It twisted her midsection like a bedsheet in a long-running clothes dryer.

~ 27 ~

Change

Amalia sat at the wheel of her rental car in Chelsea, preparing to drive up the Hudson, across New Jersey and back to New York, to deliver the work to Susan and Jeffrey for the open house. Map app ready. Snack, water bottle ready. Mildred's home address, to be her base camp for the weekend, also ready. She put on her sunglasses, turned up the tunes, and peeled out of the side street traffic to meet the flow of the West Side Highway.

The drive would be easy and fun, fun and easy, she told herself. All she had to do was drop off the boards, make a quick presentation of talking points to be shared at the open house, and then she'd be on her way to Mildred's for some real rest and relaxation. It could be both a work trip and a holiday. She was excited to see the solar panels that Mildred had made sure were installed at the church in the aftermath of the fracking panel (couldn't help but feel proud that she had inspired that change). She could decide about attending the open house later. Part of her was curious about what Jen had said and implied, yet a larger part of her wanted to be sure to preserve her job. Although no longer helping to pay her grandfather's medical bills at the hospice in Calcutta (which, truth be told, were not that much—a chance to feel connected and helpful), there were other debts. Her debt to Nadel, ex-boyfriend in Vancouver. And her student loan debt, a regular part of life she did not even regard in the same category as other debts, but as a monthly recurring transaction to be endured, like a utility bill required to keep the apartment lit.

The traffic thinned after the 79th Street Boat Basin, and her gaze wound its way up the river's tidal coast. Somewhere in there was a lighthouse, a little red lighthouse, memorialized in a story she'd had as a child back in Canada. Funny how a childhood story could function as a beacon for one's adult wayfinding.

From one coast to another, and from one country to the next, she continued to find beacons of light to guide her. At this, she laughed aloud. "I sound all greeting card," she said to the car. It was true, and she felt it with Mildred. There was a change ahead for her, and it connected to Mildred.

After tearing up the Palisades Parkway beyond the George Washington Bridge, she opened the windows—fast, fresh air blew her hair back and she tapped the wheel as she drove. It would be a good retreat.

The turn into Susan and Jeffrey's was easy to find, even though she'd not been there before. Their house, an old structure near the site, would be relocated to be part of the main welcoming center of the environmental center. It was integral to the new design that had emerged since Atlantia Actuaris had begun to get cold feet, and a new, anonymous group danced around the edges.

The house was dark, and no car greeted her in the driveway. Bikes and kayaks remained alongside the house. Hadn't they been expecting her? Had she forgotten to confirm?

At the front door, she was able to peer into the glass sidelite to see they'd left in the middle of a meal—the table was crowded with plates and food, coffee cups and half-finished juice glasses. The kitchen, at the end of the old hall, bore no signs of movement.

What should she do? What could she do? The sky had greyed during the drive north, and she hesitated to leave the presentation boards on the porch, even with their wrapping of tracing paper and the shelter of the overhang. Maybe she could tuck them behind the porch swing? "Doubt is a killer," she'd heard Mildred say, and she spoke the words aloud. She would leave the boards on the porch swing, where they would be both sheltered and visible to Susan and Jeffrey when they returned. Win-win. She sent a brief email to them from her phone and copied Betsy. Her work was done. Would she return? She would not attend the open house. She would keep her job.

Driving away, she felt a little hollow. She'd been looking forward to the exchange with Susan and Jeffrey. No matter. Mildred's next. They'd have extra time to play.

She took out her suitcase from the back and set it on the sidewalk next to her. The Air India tags remained on the handle, a visible reminder of her trip last winter. She tried to pull the labels off with one hand while she closed the trunk of the Nissan with her other hand, and in that moment felt a pull in her shoulder where she'd wrenched it while rock climbing with Mark the previous fall. "Let go the suitcase. Let go the trunk," she said to herself, and took a deep breath. The breath didn't come, and she frowned at herself, feeling tight in the chest. With a little effort she was able to close the trunk with two hands. Looked around to the street, which was devoid of people. Hoped she wasn't blocking anyone's house exit; it looked fine. Her breath felt tight and short, and she rubbed her shoulder, looked at the suitcase. Tried again to remove the labels, which appeared to be easy to unpeel. Their plasticky covering made it impossible. She yanked the label, which aggravated her shoulder, and she winced, bent forward at the waist, and put her hands on the suitcase. A tear escaped her eye and she brushed it away.

The onset of more tears stung her lower lids and she blinked hard to shut down the trajectory that threatened to erupt. Too late. A second tear escaped, growing larger at the edge then balling up into several in a chain reaction. She stood up and walked away from the suitcase. Leaned on a lamppost, then held it with one hand for steadiness. Its overpainted, enameled grooves made a ready handhold for her gripping fingers. Cold shocked her bare skin. She looked at her suitcase there on the sidewalk next to her and felt annoyed at the sight of its handle, tagged with its Air India labels. Could she not have found time to remove those stupid tags with a pair of scissors? Frustration welled in her eyes.

The momentum of tears shimmying out of her triggered a chain reaction of shudders. Shuddering traded up for shivers and the tears mixed with twitches in her jaw as she tried to suppress the stream. Stupid. What was she even doing out there with her suitcase?

For a second the feeling she had was released. She was watching a movie, a film of a girl with a suitcase, crying against a lamppost for no clear reason. The moment shifted as fast as it had come, and she was in the pit of her sad stomach, sobbing and rocking and then, without forewarning, she was laughing.

She could not believe there was room within her for laughter, but there it was. Belly laughs. Big, air-gasping belly laughs. A sequence of explosions within her, one emotion superseding the other.

A steady stream from her nose and eyes was easy to wipe in a single grand gesture with the sleeve of her grey coat. And when she looked at the smear of her goopy emotions on her clothing, she felt a bubble of giddiness within her. The tears that had come with the shift found no path to follow. She patted the lamppost. "Thank you, dear Lamppost, you were a most gracious host to my crying." She almost leant to kiss the post but thought better of getting a chill on her lips.

"Silly," she chided herself. Crying and laughing over suitcase labels. Her grandfather would have admonished her for it. She looked up at the lamppost behind her, and the light atop it in that moment flickered on and off, on and off. Maybe he would have said it was fine. Maybe it was fine to have bouncy emotions erupt in the middle of the day. Or maybe there was some way to get ahold of them, so they didn't get hold of her. The light flickered again and went dark. She waited a moment to see if it would go back on. "Grandfather," she whispered to the light.

"Such a vision of brightness on a cold day." An old man was down the block, coming up into the cul-de-sac, waving one arm and carrying a bouquet of flowers in the other. Who was he talking to? Was he waving at her? She turned round to see if anyone else stood behind her. There was no one. She turned back to watch him approach, and he'd turned into a house between them. Or had he? She couldn't see him. The crying must have made her lightheaded. Time to go to Mildred's.

The tall old house of the Reverend Mildred stood ahead, beaming out to her from the end of the cul-de-sac loop, an old wood-frame structure with chairs and a bench on the yellow painted porch; the kind of place she'd grown up with as a teen in Scranton, and as a child in Vancouver. Where was home? New York City, Hamilton Heights, to be specific, although she'd felt as much at ease in Calcutta as she did in any of these other cities. Was home a matter of heart-centeredness, or was it a matter of being comfortable and at ease wherever one was? One and the same? She'd ask Mildred.

As Amalia trod up the wooden steps, their creaks announced her. She looked up and down the long porch, her first glimpse of how Mildred arranged her life. The small seating area was inviting, and the front door heavy with stained glass set into leaded cames, further set into wood. She knocked. She listened. A car drove up into the dead end street, and she realized there was no car in Mildred's driveway. All quiet; maybe Mildred, too, had gone out or forgotten. To be fair, Amalia was a few hours early, having completed her environmental center drop off well ahead of schedule.

What to do? She'd hauled her suitcase from the little red Nissan rental. She tucked the suitcase behind one of the porch chairs and sat down with a large exhalation. The April day was cold in Binghamton, and she was glad she had worn extra layers. Checked her phone, looked up and down the road that met up with the cul-de-sac.

Mildred had said she could come for the weekend, and to come straight from her environmental center meeting. No meeting had happened, but Amalia's part of the transaction was done. She could leave her bag on the porch and walk around the neighborhood until Mildred returned. Sent her a brief text message, then set out for a springtime stroll through the streets of historic homes in various states of restoration.

She'd been alone all day, and her mind was blank from driving. Once she'd passed the Palisades and driven back into New York State, she found herself thinking back on her previous road trips, and how fun they could be. The favorite one she recounted was the bus trip back from Binghamton with Mark, after the fracking meeting.

This got her to wondering how far she was from Mildred's church, the place of the last community meeting. The neighborhood had a familiar feel. She continued along until she found an intersecting main street and followed the artery along and saw the big stone building, Mercy Church, rising from the houses. Mildred said she'd inherited it, moved her group in after another had moved out. How did that work? Did Mildred's congregation own the building? It didn't matter to Amalia. The concept of ownership of something communal intrigued her.

At the side of the church, aptly called by Mildred "Mercy Side," Amalia saw the Reverend's aqua-green car in its handicapped parking spot and displaying its coordinating blue handicap tag from the rearview mirror. The old Alero and its New York plates were joined by another car of similar age, a Camry with Vermont plates. Amalia had a sudden wish to not notice those details. She had a habit of latching on, and she wanted to latch less. "Latch less!" She trotted down the few concrete steps to the basement.

The door was unlocked, and she went in. The community room where they'd had the fracking meeting was empty and quiet. Chairs stacked up on the side. She went through to the kitchen and back up to the chapel where she and Mark had almost married, and where Mark's brother Tim married Candace with a certificate to prove it. For her and Mark, there had been no completed marriage certificate, only waylaid plans to seek its completion.

She heard a rustle in the hall beyond, and called out, "Mildred?"

~ 28 ~

Ladders

Mildred stood at the bottom of the tall, straight roof ladder and cleared her throat. "Coming up, Frankie," she called. Put a hand and a foot on at the same time, then backed off. At 83, was it a good idea to climb a straight shot up to the church's roof to counsel a wayward parishioner? But Frankie was no ordinary parishioner. In a short span of time, he had become as close as family. He sat at the near edge of the steep slope. "Fortunate," Mildred said aloud. "Thank God you didn't go all the way." She crawled from the top of the ladder, pulling herself over the hatch curb edge and onto the shingle roof, hands bearing scratches in the process. The solar panel repairs, begun the previous month, appeared stalled. They'd promised to return by the weekend, which meant power would be turned off, and there would be no Sunday services until the power was on.

He turned. "Go away, Mildred. You can't help me. I in this too far." He spoke in his typical stilted way.

"We'll talk, then." She remained in a crouching crawl, trying not to look out toward the edge of the steep roof. Not a recommended activity for a church reverend of her age, ability, and eyesight condition. She squinted. He looked a bit blurry in the near distance, and she blinked hard to get focus back, but it was no use. The glaucoma blur prevailed. "Come here." She lifted her hand to wave him over, and hoped he was as intent on looking out for her as she was on looking out for him. "Wow!" She feigned a fall, hoping the action would draw him nearer.

It worked. He was at her side within moments, scrambling up the steep slope, hands and feet akimbo, and was soon holding her by the ankles. "I gotta," he said.

"Got you," she corrected. "Have you, to be more exact." She was fine. Had his attention, though, which was what she had wanted. She sat back and fell a little into him, catching her hand on the top of the ladder. "Frankie," she said. He squinted into the spring sunlight, the rays beaming in low at the angle of four o'clock. Mildred wondered how long he had been up there before she'd noticed daylight streaming down the shaft and into the hallway broom closet, light spilling through the normally closed door and into the corridor next to her office. Wondered how often he came up without her knowing. He was silent, staring out, hand still on Mildred. "Nothing we can't sort out with a good talk," she said. "Now why don't you tell me what you've got going on. I'm sure I can be of some help, even if it's just to listen."

He looked back at her, wild in the eyes. "I in too far," he said. "They come after me," he said.

She wondered then if there was a diagnosis she might have missed, might never have been told, or that might never have been made. "You'll be fine, Frankie. We'll get you some help."

"I do not want the police," he said, enunciating with a kind of care that caught Mildred's attention. "Police will make it worse," he said.

"Who's after you?"

He squinted.

"You can tell me." She put a hand on his arm. "I'm safe, Frankie. I won't tell."

He shifted a little and wrapped his arms around his legs where he sat, cross-legged, knees up. "They—you know. The ones I get the pot from."

"The pot. The pot I got from you," she said.

"For your eyes," he said.

"Yes." She spoke slowly. "For my eyes. Frankie, you said you grew that yourself."

He looked down into his knees. "Some I did."

"And some you didn't." Mildred exhaled. He was part of a drug dealing ring. What she didn't need in the church. And who was she to criticize? She was one of his buyers. "Frankie, it helps my eyes," she said.

"I know," he said. "And for you, Reverend, I do the growing. But sometimes there isn't enough. The lights ran out. I ran out. When I lost my job over at the plant, I didn't have enough for the electric."

"When did you lose your job, Frankie? I didn't know." A wind was picking up on the roof, and the old oak tree at the back of the parking lot waved its budding branches to the sky. Mildred wanted to go down.

"Kirkwood Penguin laid me off," he said. "I was high." He bowed his head into his knees. "I miss the forklift, lifting all those books. Good work, for me."

"Maybe you can get your job back," she said. "Let's go down," she said. "Frankie, it's getting windy up here."

"You go," he said. "I stay."

"I'm not leaving you up here," she said. Wished she'd had the good sense to put her cell phone in her pocket before climbing the ladder. Wondered if she could go back for it and call for help but didn't want to leave Frankie alone. Father Jasper would know what to do with the boy. The wind kicked up a notch and gave her a little fright inside. She stilled herself, invoking a sweet and soft wave of Reiki to come into their meeting, and to give her the grace to continue the conversation. She would stay. "Father Jasper, you talked to him recently?"

He raised his head at the name. Smile curled up a little at the edges of his mouth. "Good Father."

"You talked to him about this?"

"He's the one who got me in on it."

"What—the pot buying?"

"My dealer."

"Father Jasper is your dealer?" Mildred couldn't believe it. Never in a million years. "I don't think so." The boy must be delusional.

"Met the dealer at Father Jasper's."

"In Vermont?"

"I go to Vermont."

She nodded. Knew they had a longer back connection. "You're from Maine, originally?"

"Maine, yes, I from Maine." He dropped the 'am' when he spoke. "I from Georgetown, Reverend Mildred, like you." He looked at her, unblinking.

"How did I not know you're from Georgetown?" Something tugged at her inside. Something wasn't right there.

"I—" she heard the 'am' drop—
"from your place, Reverend. I know you. I know your family. Long time." He squinted at her.

She felt it was too much. The tree seemed to agree, waving broadly in the wind. She would go down. And she'd get Frankie to lead the way. "Frankie, I have to go to the bathroom, and I need you to help me down," she said. "I got up, but I can't get back." She looked down the ladder shaft. A straight run ten feet down. Enough to break one's back with a misstep. If she could convince him to help her, he might go willingly.

"Hello? Reverend Mildred?" A young woman's voice floated up the ladder and the top of the metal shook as steps were taken up the rungs. Amalia. The girl wasn't coming until evening. Amalia's head popped up above the ladder opening. "And you have a friend!"

"Amalia." Mildred turned to give her a pointed look. "You remember Frankie from the fracking panel last fall. We are coming down," she said.

"We not going down now," Frankie said. "Not until we talk."

"Fine with me," Amalia said, hoisting herself over the edge and onto the old slate roof. "Beautiful up here. Look at that tree from above! Cold, though." She squatted on the steep slope next to Mildred, bracing herself on the top of the ladder. "I went to your house first, Mildred, but you weren't there. I came here, and I saw the light in the hallway by your office shining down from here."

Frankie looked sideways at the new visitor. "Don't like her here," he said. He made for the ladder, pushed Amalia to the side, and climbed down.

"Well would you look at that," Mildred said. "You did in a moment what I could not do on my own."

"What, get him to leave?"

"Get him to go, and now, Amalia, you can help me get down." The young woman led Mildred down, inch by inch, until they both stood on the flat floor of the broom closet. She went back up the ladder to close the hatch door at the top. "Don't forget to lock it," Mildred said.

Amalia climbed back down and wiped her hands on her pants. "All set. What were you doing up there?"

"Counseling a lost soul," Mildred said. "Now we must find him."

It was easy; he sat in Mildred's office, waiting for her, not going anywhere. "Could have made an appointment to see me here," she said to him, and inwardly she laughed. Didn't want to disturb the boy any further. Why had she called him a boy? He had to be at least fifty.

"Don't want her," he said, pointing at Amalia.

"Now, Frankie, she's with me. And she's trusted," she said. "No need to worry. What you say to me, you can say to her." And it was true; Mildred did trust Amalia. Ever since the honesty with which that girl had expressed herself and her doubts on the fracking panel, Mildred held her up as a sort of beacon of hope: Amalia, bright Amalia, Amalia would tell the truths, be a bearer of rightness, and bring balance to the larger whole. In her eyes, her glaucoma-unbalanced eyes, there was nothing that Amalia could not do if she put her mind to it. Amalia brought balance to Mildred's perspective. Amalia saw the future where Mildred could not.

Frankie was having none of it and pushed past the two women. "Maybe another time, Reverend," he said. And walked out of the room.

"I never," said Mildred, and sat down on her office chair. "That boy. He shakes me up something silly."

"Let's get you home, Mildred."

"I have my car," she said. "But I'll be happy to have you drive. I'm a bit wobbly. I don't know what's gotten into him." She didn't say the larger worry, of what he'd begun to allude to. She had to wonder. Father Jasper had introduced them. But in fact, had he followed her family's trail?

~ 29 ~
Tea

Amalia slept over at Mildred's. It had been a restful night. Downstairs, Amalia turned her attention to the sunrise through the back window. If she could capture it in a sketch, she might get closer to finding her way back into the painting she'd daydreamed. She had her small sketchbook with her and tiptoed to get it from her bag.

If she sketched the horizon first, she could get the grasp she sought, on color, on light, on the form that she wanted to bring into her larger work. This Emerging Day, she wrote atop the page. Mildred had left out the makings of tea, for an easy start to the morning. Amalia set about to boil the water, pouring it over the dry, loose leaves. The tea was too hot to drink. Amalia went back to the sketchbook, flipped back some pages to the vignettes she had sketched in India. There had been a tea vendor there, a little chai stall on the street edge, chaiwallah, and the tea had been good. Hot, sweet, spicy, and milky. She would have to make some for Mildred. Her host remained sleeping and the sunrise called.

She went outside onto Mildred's back porch, bright with flowers in pots. Looked for a space to put down her sketchbook, or to sit with it on her lap, but found everything covered in little drops of dewy condensation, in that mid-spring early morning way. She heard a noise behind her.

Mildred had opened an upper window and tapped on the insect screen. "Yoohoo! See me up here?"

"Good morning, I came out to sketch but it's too wet. Thank you for leaving out the tea."

"Ah." Mildred paused. "I didn't leave out any tea. Hang on there. I'll be down in a moment." She closed the window partway and then spoke through the open slot at the bottom. "Don't drink that tea!"

Amalia put down the sketchbook, aware of the brightening sky behind her. She'd not been able to grasp the sunrise in her drawing, and the essence of it eluding her felt like a slipping away.

"Good morning to the kitchen, good morning to the porch, good morning outside, good morning sun, and good morning, Amalia, my lovely house guest! Don't drink that tea! Don't drink that tea!"

Amalia had returned to the kitchen by the time Mildred reached downstairs. "I'm good, I didn't."

"It's my medicine. I am sorry, I should not have left it out. How are you feeling this morning, Amalia?"

"I'm okay, I'm fine. The tea—your medicine was on the counter, so I thought you had left it for me. Because you're sweet like that." Amalia gave her a hug.

Mildred welcomed her with open arms. "Lemonade. That'll be better for us. I'll bring it from the fridge. Meet me on the front porch."

The gracious front porch was welcome on an unseasonable morning, warm for the middle of the spring. "You come. Let me see you again. Beautiful. You're beautiful!"

Amalia put down her sketchbook on the step to embrace Mildred again. "Let's sit!"

"Come. Let me pour you some lemonade. I'm happy you're here!"

"What do you do out here?" Amalia accepted a glass, hoping for coffee eventually, and sat on the porch in one of the sun-bleached wooden chairs, still cold from the morning air, a contrast to the warmth on her face.

"I muse."

Amalia smiled at Mildred's generality. "And what do you muse about?" The lemonade was sweet and tangy; perfect. Maybe she didn't need the coffee.

"Whatever amuses me! Yesterday, it was stars and cells."

Amalia looked sideways at Mildred. "Oh?"

"Stars and cells, that's all we are," said Mildred. "And speaking of cells," she says, "did you know that there are trillions of them in the human body and they are all in communication? And we can talk to them! And we can use Reiki to direct them."

"I don't know about that. Big claims, Mildred. Don't think you should go as far as that." Amalia leaned forward to put her lemonade on the low table between them. The woman was a powerhouse of some kind, and while Amalia wanted a little bit of it, she didn't want the crazy.

"It's true. I know it." She huffed a breath out as she pushed up from the armchair on the porch. "Doesn't matter what you think, doesn't matter what I think." She paused. "It kind of does matter. If you don't think, you give up your power. Thinking is power, people!"

"Why did you become a Reiki Master?"

"There was no other way for me—it was inevitable. I'd begun to learn and practice after my husband got sick, and it continued. It was a natural flow. A next logical step."

"You got more into it for him?"

"Oh heck, no. I did it for me. It saved me!"

"How did it—save you?" Not that Amalia was in any doubt that it had; she'd experienced Mildred's hands at work and knew the soothing of her energy.

"I'd forgotten the space between the stars and the cells," she said. "It reminded me." She stood at the edge of the porch and pointed out across the street. "The church is over there. I bring that space between the stars and the cells to the people who come to the church. That's all I do. I remind them. They already know it."

"You're the Reverend Mildred McCaine as well as a Reiki Master."

"You better believe it! I have the sign over my parking space to prove it." She smiled. "Best thing that ever happened to me from getting glaucoma, that parking space."

"And you're originally from Canada? BC, like me?"

"No. Georgetown, Maine. We went to Canada after, and I met my husband there. All the husbands."

"And you came to Binghamton—"

Mildred smiled that coy smile of hers that let Amalia know Mildred was in charge. "Tell me how it's going with you and Mark." She sat down and refilled Amalia's lemonade from the pitcher and pushed it across the table. She was focused; Amalia felt a nice glow from her. Mildred was genuine. And lit on lemonade, apparently, as well.

"We were in conflict—we were fighting, arguing about something big and important to each of us, in different ways—marijuana—and then we turned to you. We began to talk about you, and what happened around the fracking meeting last fall."

"And you used the recollection of what you learned last fall to move through it."

"It was a catalyst, I think. It was not a quick fix. You shared a perspective of wellness. That came first. The perspective."

"Your process with Mark is a perspective."

"Tell me about what you saw when you met me and Mark."

"You two? Hotheads the two of you!"

"Come on now."

Mildred let out a "harrumph" and slapped her hand on the armrest of the chair. "You had your opinions, strong opinions, and you were letting your hot heads get in the way of seeing where you agreed. Not only where you agreed, but where you could make some real change. And not just that. You had a real spark."

"Like you could see love at first sight?"

"I wouldn't go as far. You were tightly wound. And Mark didn't know what to do with you." She took a deep breath and looked ready to launch. "Yes." She nodded. "I will say, through the grace of Reiki and all that connects the stars and the cells, you two made an impression on me. A big, shimmery impression."

"And we figured out our dispute over fracking?"

"Well now why are you asking me? You were there. It's your relationship."

"It is, Mildred." Amalia looked out at the street. A lot of new questions rose to the surface of her mind. "Okay. Here's the thing. Mark and I have different cultural backgrounds and religious backgrounds. You do Reiki, which has nothing to do with how we were raised. Your Reiki touched both of us and kind of connected us back then, despite our differences. Did you know? Have you seen it before?"

"I've seen it happen time and time again. It's not always. It happens if the people involved are open to it. If they're closed, closed minded, shut off from the possibility—then no. It turns off."

"Like a switch?"

"They're not receiving it. I can be flowing it but they're not receiving it."

"Were we receiving it? Is there an 'on/off' switch for Reiki?"

"My dear, Reiki is one of those energies in the universe we cannot explain with words. You have to trust it is present and working."

"And if you don't? What if you don't believe it?"

"It can still work, just not in a distinct or palpable way the person receiving it would know. It might be loosening the edges of some greater tension. If someone is closed to it, I don't offer it. I don't go where I am not wanted."

Amalia took a deep breath. "Did you feel Mark and I were open to Reiki when we were on the break at the fracking meeting?"

"I think you were. He was pretty upset at the time."

Amalia wondered if the question bubbling up in her mind was too far out there. But this was the woman who insisted they were all stars and cells; maybe it wasn't too much to consider. "Can the earth receive Reiki?"

"I think the earth is always in a state of giving and receiving. Whatever it is, rain, Reiki, you name it. It's all the same."

"And there isn't the same on/off switch as you were suggesting with people?"

"People think too much for their own good! Which is why they would do well to focus their thinking. With intent." Mildred squeezed her hands together and leaned forward, then pushed herself to the edge of the chair.

"I believe we're on the same page there." Amalia sat up straight, sensing the window closing on the opportunity to continue the conversation. "Do you think Reiki can help me connect with my grandfather?"

"Not in a pushing it way. Do it if it feels good to you. There is no agenda to it." Mildred stood up from the chair and picked up her empty glass. "I'll leave you the pitcher to refill your own."

~ 30 ~
Stick Shift

Mildred smiled. She did rather like having young company. Her nieces were far away, and she saw them on occasion, enough to feel connected but not often enough to sink in with them. She could sink in with Amalia in a satisfying way. A nice rhythm was establishing itself between them; maybe there would even be other visits. "Do you ever go to Maine?"

"You know, I've never been. Mark and I went to New Hampshire, and we talked about visiting Maine."

"I was thinking it would be fun to show you around where I grew up. I don't know what is coming over me right now, Amalia. I feel I'd rather like to go there with you. For fun. You and me."

"Okay. When were you thinking of doing this adventure? Maybe when it warms up?"

"Oh, no. Too many bugs. The colder weather is nice. We could go in the fall when it's still warm by day. The cold will have stopped the bugs in their tracks." Mildred looked wistful. "Fall seems way too far off. It's still cold now, you know; it's much colder still than here in Binghamton."

"I've heard that."

"Moorehouse, Poorhouse, Roughhouse, Rum!"

"I've never heard that!"

"We could go now." Mildred smiled. And stood up, ready to make a move for her car keys.

Amalia stood up as fast as her host. "It's a bit impulsive, don't you think, Mildred? And don't you need to be back for the church?"

"I need to do some church business on the way back in Vermont. We could go now and be there by evening. Church is closed this weekend 'cause the solar panels. And all." She felt the excitement rise and couldn't catch a full mouth of coherent words. "We divested from fossils like you said."

"This is crazy."

"But fun." Mildred picked up her car keys from the counter and shook them over her head. "We'll take my old car; leave your rental car here. Better that way! Could be deep mud tracks if the ground's thawed. You know how to drive stick shift?"

~ 31 ~
Road Trip

"I'll leave my little rental here. It's okay if I move it into your driveway here at your house, I assume. But not in your handicap parking spot."

"Spot's not for much, you know. I have the glaucoma, that's why I still have it. We had it for Raymond and his wheelchair before. But yes, park in the driveway instead of in my road spot." Mildred stood back to assess. "I haven't been back since we left in 1935," she said. "It was all stick shifts back then, you know. Fine if you drive. My hands get stiff when I grip for too long."

A tree branch creaked overhead in the stiff wind, and Amalia wondered if it was going to give out over them. She didn't know the telltale signs of what might be about to crack, and she wasn't going to wait around to find out. She'd driven a stick shift once or twice back in Canada. Couldn't be too hard.

The branches of the old tree swayed as if beckoning her into her little rental car, which she moved into Mildred's empty drive. The stick shift shouldn't be too much different, she reckoned, as she got in, remembering the clutch. Mildred's car shuddered to a stop. "I'll need a minute to remember," Amalia said, as Mildred got into the passenger-side door of the compact aqua-green car.

"It's an Oldsmobile Alero. Last model Oldsmobile ever made. Raymond was quite proud of it."

"How did he die, if you don't mind me asking. Was it recently?"

"You do like to jump into it don't you, Amalia. He, Raymond, years back, we moved here to Binghamton. We bought the house when he was at the university, after we moved from Vancouver. And this car." Mildred paused for breath and exhaled with an audible hiss. "You're from Vancouver, too, aren't you? We talked about it before."

"I was born in the US, grew up in Vancouver," Amalia said. "But we moved here in high school—moved to Pennsylvania, I mean."

"We were out there on the west side, out at the university. Raymond's job took him all over—we were in Vancouver, but we had a sabbatical in Jerusalem, then our time here in Binghamton. He was in Ithaca, too. All over."

Amalia steered the car out from the spot, into the cul-de-sac. The feel of her foot on the clutch was becoming familiar. "Like riding a bike. Which did you like best?"

"Which bike? I had a bike when I was a girl. When we were traveling up and down with Papa's houses, up and down to Delaware. Stayed there, doing that, going back and forth, until I was a teenager."

"I didn't mean which bike. Which place. That you lived. Which place that you lived did you like better." The clutch was a little trickier as she sped up, and the gears clunked into alignment as they moved out of the cul-de-sac, ahead to the emptying, post-rush-hour roads of the morning.

"I liked them all, but you know the one I like the best in retrospect? It was the time in between when we didn't know where we were going to go—when all the options were open, and we were looking at a whole map of the world, deciding where we might land." Mildred smiled out at Binghamton, as if it was the world.

"And you landed here."

"I did. I was married before, you know. Twice before Raymond. Those, they didn't last long." She shook her head. "You never know what life has in store. There's always something better around the corner."

"And your husband, the one who died—"

"Raymond."

"Yes, Raymond—he was your something better."

"I like to think so." Mildred rested her head back on the headrest. Closed her eyes. "Going to rest for a bit now. You drive and tell me when we're getting close to lunch."

Amalia drove following the route she'd come into Binghamton, back out, and soon had to pay attention to the map app's chirpy directions, which Mildred seemed to sleep through.

By the time they got to Connecticut, Amalia had to go to the bathroom, and she was downright hungry. She pulled in at a highway rest stop and had to shake Mildred to wake her. "Lunchtime," she said gently. The woman's head rolled to the side. "Mildred?"

The Reverend woke with a start. "We're here?"

"We're in Connecticut. It's lunchtime. Picnic?" Amalia reached to the backseat for the bag they'd packed in Mildred's kitchen. "When you said you knew," she asked, picking up on their previous conversation, "how did you know it was time to move on from those relationships?"

Mildred ran her fingers through her white curls, bobbing them into awakeness just like the rest of her. "Wasn't up to me, at least not as I saw it at the time. Those fellas, they went on their own way. Now I see I was part of it, too. Back then, I was fast and ready to blame them for everything."

"But what if it was their fault? What if they'd done something, been resistant?"

"They might well have been. It takes two to tango, you know? There are two people in every relationship. I was as in it as the rest of them."

"How did you know you were ready for Raymond, when you met him?"

"Didn't. Time told me. Time revealed everything."

"Nice," Amalia said. "You kind of grew on each other?"

"Something like." Mildred opened the lunch bag and spread it and its contents across her lap. "Now—tomato and egg sandwich?" She handed half to Amalia.

"And what about the church? How did you end up running a church in Binghamton?"

"I took it over from the former reverend before she moved away. She wanted to retire. She was a different denomination. I'm Universal Church. I am—not nearly as conservative as she was. She was a good money manager, and she handed me over a group that knew how to manage dollars, knew the tax incentives, and over time, we came to own the building outright. I like to think we came out ahead before we even started."

"When did you become a reverend?"

"Been a while, you know. Went together with me becoming a Reiki Master. I think it happened slowly over time, too. I have a bit of an imposter complex about it. I'm not a reverend, you know."

"You're not?"

"I have a piece of paper, says I am. But am I? I never went to divinity school."

"Do you think you might want to go? Who gave you the piece of paper?"

"I might." Mildred deflected the second question. "Put it this way," she said, "I'm a good manager of people and their moods, and my faith keeps me going every day. I believe in Reiki, and I believe what I do helps people. What more do I need to know?"

"But—" Amalia put her sandwich in her lap. She hardly liked to say it aloud. "What if people say you're a fraud? I don't think you are. But—don't you worry?"

"I didn't, not until Frankie last night." She shook her head. "He's got something. I don't know what it is. He nudged me on this trip, you know. Him and Raymond."

"Frankie—"

"Frankie put some doubts in my mind. I want to see what there is to see in Georgetown. My family left some traces, and I don't understand them entirely. I'm glad you're up for the journey. This requires friendly company." She smiled at Amalia.

"I'm always up for adventure," Amalia said. "I don't know what I can offer you, though, other than driving both ways." She smiled. "Listen, Mildred. You've helped me so much already. You let me know how I can help."

With lunch done, restroom attended, they were back on the road within a half an hour. Amalia put on some music, a new radio station, and Mildred bopped along, her curls bouncing along with the movement of the highway and the cars alongside it. The road was busy, early rush hour beginning as they passed from Connecticut into Massachusetts and drove along Route 90. Her mind wandered with the trees and cell phone towers as they passed quickly on her right, left, and from the front, moving fast behind them. "Do you believe in past lives?" The Alero was moving well in her hands, beneath her feet, the gear changing no problem.

"Sure," said Mildred, "but I don't think it pays to get too wrapped up in them. Why do you ask?"

"I've been working on this painting. An idea for a painting. And whenever I sit down to do it, I have this feeling like I've done it before, I've seen it before, I know it. But then it stops, and I can't go any further with it. Can't get it out."

"And you think it's something from a past life? Something you are remembering."

"I was in India a while ago. For my grandfather's funeral. Did I tell you? I wondered if it was connected. It was then I got the idea."

"A past life in India? Possible."

"No, it was more like a past life in something Scandinavian. I'm not sure exactly where it was. It felt Nordic and it was with a big sense of the gods once important, back in earlier times."

"Entirely possible. The question is, what did those feelings have to reflect on your current situation?"

"What do you mean—as in, what can they teach me?"

"Not even as large. Just, what is the feeling you have in them? In these visions and memories?"

"I guess I feel connected to a strong flow of creativity. And I feel good about it, and like I want to express it. Express it any way I can—which right now, is in this time."

"Forget the past lives. What happens now? Painting aside. Just the feeling."

Amalia changed lanes, responding to the map app's chirping to get ready to exit beyond Boston. "I feel it now, even. While we're talking about it, changing lanes. Getting ready."

"Getting ready for what, exactly?"

"Right now, I would say, it is getting ready to exit past Boston. I would say it's the feeling of getting ready to create something big. Almost like giving birth to something, except for not giving birth to anything." She hesitated, wondering if she should tell Mildred about the possible miscarriage. Her gut pulled together in a little knot. "It's like, you want to write a story, but you don't know where to start. Have you ever felt like that?" She exhaled and took a hand off the steering wheel to rub her belly, releasing tension.

"Sure," said Mildred.

"And what did you do about it?"

"I wrote, I wrote something like letters. Wrote letters until I felt ready to write something more."

"And in the end did you write your novel?"

"Me?" Mildred laughed. "Never! I'm still waiting for the great event."

"Doesn't leave you feeling unfulfilled?"

"There's always something more to do, you know. If there was nothing left to do, there would be no life left to want to live."

"As long as you don't write your novel, you have life left to live?" Amalia shifted to the lane on the left and laughed, then looked back at Mildred.

"Not exactly. Look, you're young, you have lots of time ahead of you. You can doodle, you can write letters, and when you're ready, you can put those doodles and those letters together into something great. Maybe it's a creation. Maybe it's more than one. Maybe it's neither—maybe for you, it's a building. I don't know."

"What does all of this have to do with past lives?"

"Oh." Mildred tapped on the window. "I thought I got you off the topic. Well. This is how I see it. Past lives—whether you believe or not they exist, and I do—don't come in as memories randomly. They come in when they have a match. With something we're working out in our real and current lives." Mildred sat forward into the seatbelt and adjusted it. "If the memory or the recollection is helpful to you, then great! You following? If not, then you're free to disregard it. It's your choice." She sat back into the seat. "I wouldn't get too hung up on it. There are life lessons everywhere, you know? A past life recollection is another source."

"For another life lesson. I should take it as input, kind of like a dream."

"That's a good way of thinking of it. Kind of like a dream," Mildred said. The exit peeled off ahead of them.

"I missed the turn. Dammit. Missed the turn to 290. I'll take the next one." A couple of miles up the highway she made a turn onto a quieter road. "This isn't the right one. One forty-six. I'm going to take the next exit off this one. Exit 8 to Millbury. I'll turn around there." At the roundabout she was confused. Which way should she peel off? Ended up on Main Street. That felt right.

Mildred sat up straighter and looked around, intent in her focus.

"You been here before?" Old houses, white with black shutters and gracious porches, lined the street. US flags wove up and down. "Very Americana," said Amalia. "You know, those flags used to freak me out a bit."

"What do you mean?"

"Growing up in Canada—even with high school in the US—it seems odd, you know, the degree to which the flag is flown here."

"We had Canadian flags all over, don't you remember? Or maybe it was different then. I don't know." Mildred shrugged. "Flags are flags. People fly them. Don't matter a hoot to me."

"Should be a place to turn around soon," Amalia said. "But that sure is pretty." A pond lay ahead on the right. They lost the pond and picked up another on the left. "Water everywhere." She followed the edge of the pond, keeping left. "I think we lost Main Street."

"But that sure is pretty," Mildred said, echoing Amalia's sentiment.

Newer houses packed together in the heavily wooded landscape. They passed an older house with a low stone wall out front. "Looks like where Mark took me in New Hampshire," Amalia said.

"Looks like the Moorehouse, as I recall," Mildred said. She turned to look as they passed. "I ever tell you about the Moorehouse?"

Amalia had a sudden whooshing feeling inside. Shook her head. "What's that?"

"You okay?"

"When you said Moorehouse, I felt it." She smiled. "No worries. Happens sometimes."

"Happens to the best of us," Mildred said.

Amalia blinked. "We lost the water on the left. Should find a way to get back to the highway."

"But this is pretty." A school bus stopped on the road ahead, letting out a student at a country road stop, thick in the budding trees. The child skipped across, backpack heavy, to meet her mother on the other side. "Never did that, did you? Take a school bus."

"Me, no." Amalia looked at the little girl and her mother. "Sweet, though." She looked down at the gas gauge while they paused. "Should stop for gas before too long. Maybe somewhere in this town." The bus pulled ahead, Amalia followed, and soon another beautiful pond came into view on the right. "Man, gorgeous." A scenic road sign popped up in view. "I'm taking it."

"Can't get more scenic than this," Mildred said. "Painters rested here," she said.

"You know that?"

"I feel that."

"You feel stuff too, then." Amalia nodded. "I feel it. Feel that—" She fumbled on the words. "Don't know how to describe it."

"Don't have to describe it." Mildred patted Amalia's thigh. "Feel it."

Amalia turned left to the scenic route, signed as Hutchinson Road. "Oh wow." The stretch narrowed to one lane, arched with trees coming into April leaf. An old farmhouse stood to the side, graced in front by a meandering stone wall. "Is this a private road?"

"No, look there are more houses ahead." Mildred pointed.

They drove in silence, taking in the old houses and stone walls, and then the trees opened a little and they came to the end of the road. "I'm turning left," she said. "I think that's the right way." The map app chirped, catching up. "We must have dropped the signal." She laughed. "But we seem to be on track, according to the app."

"Rerouting. Never understood those things. We need a road sign to set us straight." Mildred sat forward, hands on the dash.

Another school bus stood stationary on the road in front of them. "I can drop a pin in it," Amalia said, pulling over next to a school. "We can't go anywhere. Look at that. 'Boston Road.' We must be on the right path," she said.

"Boston Road? Boston Post Road?" Mildred leaned over to look at the phone. "Lookie there. I wonder if that Boston Road is the same as the Boston Post Road. You know."

Amalia didn't know but didn't like to say. "Sure." The school bus pulled ahead, and Amalia followed. "What do you know about the Boston Post Road?" At least she could deflect her lack of knowledge. Not that Mildred cared. Wasn't like it was a job interview or anything.

"These are old houses, Amalia!" Mildred pointed beyond the school. "I think this is the real deal. A little spur of the Boston Post Road." They passed another on the right. "I've got absolute chills," she said. "Look." She extended her arm and pushed her jacket up. Hair stood on end. "Absolutely electric!"

"I get that." Amalia felt a shiver, a ripple of knowing they were connecting to a powerful stream of energy, one that she felt unable to control, and that made her hand shake on the wheel. "I have to pull over."

"You okay?"

"Just—this is powerful. I don't know what this energy is." She took a deep breath.

"Call it what you will. Energy. Power, ancestors, flow. It's good, Amalia. Take some more deep breaths. This is yours to ride and to harness."

"Need to get out and stretch. Okay?" She pulled over to the side of the two-lane road and got out. They were in front of an old wooden farm building with barns behind. "Wooden roof, look." Amalia nodded. "You're right, old around here." She felt short of words.

"Breathe it out, Amalia. You're okay." Mildred rubbed her back, warmth pervading through the thickness of Amalia's jacket.

"Sometimes I get a wave, you know? Like a hit of energy. And I don't know what to do with it."

"And you just got it."

"Started back there when we came off the main highway. I get it even more." She looked at the old house.

"Is it like that past life feeling you mentioned before?"

"No, this is different. This is like, something happened here and I'm just knowing it."

"Something happened everywhere, Amalia. You can't go around in life letting the somethings of the world get to you. You have your own steering wheel," she said.

"Yes." Amalia looked at the house. "It's like, here we are on this road that leads to Boston, or maybe doesn't, but there's this house, and it's looking at me, I'm looking at it, and there's something for me to know."

"You want to go in? Go see the owners?"

"No." Amalia put her hand on Mildred's car. "I want to go." Opened the door. "I'm good." She let a ripple down her shoulders and was good, she felt clear and ready to move on. "Whatever it was, I'm good now."

She looked back at the old barn where the name 'Walton Thorns' was written. "Memorable."

"You know," Mildred said, getting back in. "There was a lot of Revolutionary War history around here. And native settlement. Could be anything you're picking up on."

Amalia drove ahead a few feet toward an intersection. "Crossroads. Now what? Looks like highway."

"If you cross over, you'll continue on this Boston Road," Mildred said.

"Do we have time?"

"Time! That's all we have! If you're fine driving when it gets dark, we have time. The hotel in Bath will be open late. And Amalia." She patted her pocket. "I brought cash for the hotel room, my treat."

"Thank you, Mildred—I'm in!" Amalia felt a ripple of excitement; all the better that Mildred was equipped to pay for it. She looked both ways along the highway and crossed over. "Boston Road, we're a-coming for you!"

The road, double wide, opened with fewer trees but was soon shrouded once again in old branches coming into leaf, gracing homes along the way, some newer, some more historic. She slowed for a pickup truck ahead, then another school bus.

Then, seemingly as soon as they'd begun their journey, the road ended in another highway intersection. "Now what. We're back at Route 146. 'Town of Sutton,'" she read. "At least we know where we were."

"Can you go straight ahead? It looks like you don't have to take 146. You can continue," Mildred said. "If you want to. You're the driver, I don't want to push."

"I'm going to continue." She waited for the light to change and pressed on ahead. "Seems like more busy roads," she said. "No, wait, here it's going charming again." She felt unable to string words together. "It gets kind of hard to talk when I get these waves."

"You don't have to apologize."

She drove a way down the road, past newer houses, an auto repair shop, and another school bus. "Wait, it ended." The Boston Road ended. "The sign, look," she pointed. "Says this one picks up the Providence Road."

"Providence, Rhode Island, I'll bet. Maybe we weren't on an old Post Road after all, but on some network that connected the towns before. Now I've got the shivers," Mildred said.

"Then the Providence Road it is," Amalia said. At the stop sign, she checked the map app. "It seems to be following us now," she said. "It's stopped chirping. No signal. I'll turn left."

"Feels right. Oooh, Amalia, I like this! Going on our internal radar. What an adventure. Thank you, dear." Mildred positively beamed.

Up until that moment Amalia had wondered if she was leaning too hard on Mildred for advice, then realized she was not—she saw in Mildred's eyes a sadness lift, and as a happy curl lifted at the corners of the Reverend's lips and eyes, Amalia caught another wave and realized the uplift was mutual.

"An old mill," Amalia said. "Dudley Mill. Reminds me of the New Hampshire places Mark took me."

"You and Mark. I didn't like to ask."

"We're fine," she sighed.

"After all that about energy flowing you're not going to bullshit me with 'we're fine,'" Mildred said. "Spill it. What's going on?" Mildred leaned back. "I mean, if you want to talk. Sorry, don't mean to push."

Up ahead, an old train bridge crossed. They passed through the walls of its stone footings, massive and shady on either side. "Think the underground railway came through here?"

"It wasn't a railway actual, Amalia. You know. Not just. There were all sorts of ways people got around. But could this area have been part of it? Sure, I'm sure."

"You know a bit about it."

"My gran told me some." Mildred frowned. "But she told me more about rum. Moorehouse, Poorhouse, Roughhouse, Rum. That was how they would find us."

"You know," Amalia sensed it was time to change the subject, fearing Mildred's good mood had vanished, and fast. "You know what you said about past lives? That we should focus on our present life?"

"Yes," Mildred was back in mentor-mode, sitting up.

"Back there I was feeling a past life connection—"

"Were you?"

"Maybe—but if that was the case, then what was it telling me about my present life? By your logic."

"It's not logic, and it's not mine. It just is."

"Okay." Amalia backed up the thought. Looked at the road ahead. Looked in the rearview mirror; the train bridge had disappeared behind the curve. She slowed to let a tow truck enter the road from a driveway, and as she slowed she noticed massive propane gas storage tanks, which reminded her of Mark and his gas company lawsuit, and up ahead, a sign for Millbury. They'd started this offline trek in Millbury. "We've come full circle," she said.

"In your life? Or on our road network?"

"I think, both," she said. She looked at Mildred. "If I'm trying to make amends with Mark, which I'm not by the way, because I didn't do anything wrong—but say I was—what does all this past life feeling have to do with it?"

"What were you thinking about when you had those feelings float in back there?"

"Honestly? Nothing. Not Mark." She hesitated and looked ahead. Millbury was pretty, and she spotted another old white-clad house with a large and gracious porch by the side of the road. "I was thinking about how you—or I—connect. Where we connect."

"You mean, if we're related?"

"Something like that. Our energy's obviously connected. I feel a resonance with you." Amalia shook her head. "I almost had it. It's gone now. The thought."

"It's you and me, then. Not you and Mark. If that's what you had on your mind when it floated in, I'd wager a bet it had something to do with our journey. Our stream of consciousness together."

Amalia nodded. Took the next curve in the road a little more slowly. "I've been working on this painting, the one I mentioned." Power lines were heavy where they drove. "Still haven't seen a gas station," she said, reminded of the need to keep powering on. "Maybe back here in Millbury."

"We could ask someone," Mildred said.

"And what fun would that be, when we could discover one on our own?" She smiled at Mildred.

"That's the spirit." The curling lips and eyes, smiling, were back.

"There we go! One right there!" Amalia pulled into the local gas station to fill up Mildred's vehicle.

Later, she pulled off when she had a moment, and they ended up on a road she had not expected. Her map app tripped insistently at her to return to the main route. "I caught a glimpse of the road sign: Boston Post Road. See that, Mildred? I had that flash again. Like recollection. And I haven't been here before."

By the time they reached the Marriott Hotel in Bath, Maine, it was dark outside. Amalia nudged Mildred, amazed that the constant chirping of the map app directing them to the hotel had not awoken her. "We're here, Mildred," she said. Pulled into the driveway, well lit, and shut off the engine. Mere miles from Mildred's childhood home, they would camp out at the nearby city's hotel overnight and investigate in the morning.

"Historic Maps of Maine," Amalia read on the hotel hallway wall on the way to their room. "Look, this one says Bath, where we are now."

"Do they have one for where I used to live?"

"So you can see the—what did you call it, that rhyme?"

"Moorehouse, Poorhouse, Roughhouse, Rum!" Mildred clapped her hands. "You never know, it would have a jagged coastline." They scanned the framed maps for landforms and water edges, all pale brown ink, faded into parchment over time.

"This?" Amalia pointed to one that had plots of land divided across the coastal waterfront. "The person who drew this had a steady hand," she said. "Look here." There were tiny letters. She peered into the map through the glass of the picture frame. "Oh! It says what job they had."

"I can't make it out," Mildred said.

"Baker. Tailor."

"Those are their names."

"Maybe." Amalia pulled back from the hallway wall. "Do you see your area?"

Mildred stood back and removed her glasses, leaning on the opposite wall for support. "If I look from a distance all I see is blurriness without my glasses," she let out a big exhalation. "That feels like about it." She pointed. "I remember the walk to the waterfront like this—the shoreline slope, the rocky beach like they've drawn it, and how we took out the boat." She put her glasses back on and walked up to it. "These houses, little squares. I can't see what it says."

Amalia looked more closely. "Judge, it says, at the big one."

"And what's that next to it toward the water?"

"Toward the water, there's a smaller house. Quite a bit smaller. And then there's dotted lines in a square. After that, there's just a long way to the water."

"But no other houses?"

"No, I'm sorry."

"What's up at the top? Up there nearer what looks like that road?"

"It looks like a bigger building. Maybe a church."

"What does it say?"

"Church."

"I think that's the Robinhood! I think we've found it!" Mildred jumped up and down, clapped her hands, white curls bobbing.

"You look like you're about five years old at a birthday party," Amalia said, smiling.

"I feel it! Oh, Amalia, I feel it! I've got shivers up my arms. Look! All the little hairs are standing on end!"

"Maybe your house was built after this map was drawn. There's no date on it, they've cut that part off out of the frame."

"It feels like it," Mildred said. She rubbed her eyes beneath her glasses. "I'll bet the Robinhood is still there," she said.

"Let's go first thing tomorrow, then, shall we?"

~ 32 ~

Robinhood

"Robinhood Free Meetinghouse," Mildred said, sitting at the wheel of the Oldsmobile Alero; it was logical she'd be the driver. "Put that in."

Amalia tapped in the words as Mildred said them, and sure enough, the Meetinghouse popped up.

"That's it. And from there, Moorehouse, Poorhouse, Roughhouse, Rum. That's how we called it."

"What's the address?"

"That is the address. That's how they found it when they came for hooch." Mildred looked surprised at Amalia's question.

"The Meetinghouse is the Moorehouse?"

"No! It's not. It's the place I remember was nearby. Remember walking that way. I'm sure I'll recognize it."

"When was the last time you visited?"

Mildred headed toward the bridge and followed the Arrowsic signs. Crossed the wide, old bridge that led from Bath over to the other side, closer to Mildred's childhood home. From the highest point on the bridge, they could see up and down the river for miles. "Kennebec River," Mildred said. She pointed to the Georgetown sign.

~ 33 ~
Moorehouse

There was gravel leading to a step up to a front door. There were two windows with broken purple bottle glass at ankle level on either side of the step, circling like eyes peering out at the feet of oncoming visitors. But what visitors? Mildred could not remember. The door was lidded by a heavy brow, a wooden lintel hewn by hand many decades before. The door lintel, held up by posts, came from an earlier time. She recalled a building within a building, and the front-door-lintel was the first signal that something stood there before the pretty, shingle-clad, wood-shuttered structure built by Mildred's ancestor, Mr. Bimson of Ontario.

Someone was living there. It looked tidy, with an addition of a screened porch on the side, visible to her from the road. Last time she'd seen it was the day they left on the train, Papa's kit house packed up in boxes, in the boxcar he'd commandeered for the long journey ahead.

She'd been all of five. Hadn't wanted to return, no reason, not until this mystery of a memory, this shadow of a thought, came back, poking at her in sleep, nudging at her when she was awake. Felt she couldn't do the next panel discussion until she'd got this sorted. If, as she suspected, her family had been dealing in opium, what would that say about her hosting a discussion about the ethics of legalizing or banning the use of medical marijuana?

Mildred pulled her car into the old driveway, silenced the engine, sent herself a quick shot of Reiki.

The house looked quiet, no one visible through the windows and no car in the driveway. A light was on inside, and Christmas lights wrapped the porch yet were turned off. Where did they plug them in?

"Can we have a look around?" Amalia's voice jolted her back to the interior of the car. Could she have a look around if no one was home? She could, but would she? Should she? Doubt slowed her for a moment and then she recalled a laundry-day of her mother's, a laundry-taking-in-day when she helped with the sheets on the line, and Muriel, two years younger, got tangled in them.

"Let's go." Mildred opened the Alero car door, hand at the ready to unbuckle herself from the driver's seat. The washing lines were in the back. Why did she connect that memory with the front? No. Muriel wasn't—couldn't have been—tangled in them. It was someone or something larger, shrouded in a sheet, gone out the cellar door and carried, a heavy thing, this shrouded thing. Closed the door without having even undone her seatbelt, not having moved a smidge.

She shivered; April in Maine was as cold as she remembered, from when she was a child. The shiver soon turned to a shudder. Looked at the house. Should she wait? Wait nearby for the new people to return, she introduce herself? "Let's go, Amalia. I'm going to head back to the first turn in the road that we took back there. I'll turn in the driveway." She revved the engine. The wheels would not go. A bone-cold stillness settled on them in the car, but with the wheels stuck, Mildred thought it best to not wait, and unclicked her seatbelt She bundled her layers around her and pointed to Amalia's door. "Out." The ground was solid, and the rife insects had not begun. Spring thaw had barely started, and the tracks in the ground, frozen, were not recent. Why, then, had the tires stuck in the mud? They'd followed them—the deep ruts had a solemnity about them. "It's a mystery," Mildred went on, "why anyone would drive out here without proper tires."

"We did." Amalia spoke for the first time in many minutes. "Put it in neutral and I'll give it a push. Mud shouldn't be too deep at this time of year."

"We had no choice." Up ahead, the tracks seemed to turn the bend. The old Porterhouse would be near. "Ground's frozen, seemed fine."

Mildred got back in. In the rearview mirror, Amalia coughed, her breath sending up a puff that blasted a clear patch through the developing frost on the window. She hoped to run into no one before reaching the old Moorehouse. Her own old house had been troublesome enough. "Give it a push!"

Mildred knocked on the Moorehouse's front door. It seemed there was a party, or some kind of large gathering, and her knocking could not be heard. Lots of cars in the driveway, and music coming from inside. Given the festooning of the porch, she suspected a family rite: a baby, a wedding, a shower. Not a funeral.

"Hellooo?" Mildred hoped she appeared friendly and part of things, not as an intruder. "I'm an old neighbor, come to say congratulations!" She was greeted by little girls who pulled her by the hand into the house. 'Kaitlin and Grisham' lettering festooned the mantle before them.

They didn't have room for her, said the woman who introduced herself as Kaitlin's mom, not with the wedding coming up, and they were sorry. Oh, yes, they would love to hear stories of the old Moorehouse, why not stay for a cup of tea and they'd learn all about it from one who knew its history. They'd found certain objects they didn't understand when they bought the house. Whaling hooks? They'd never guessed. And the rum running! A turn they'd suspected; now, hearing it from Mildred herself, it was too much fun.

"This used to be a judge's house, so they say," Kaitlin's mom said. They stood at the entrance to the living room.

"Was he called 'Moore,' I wonder?"

"Now, Amalia, don't go poking," Mildred said.

"Moores lived here, yes, but I don't know if they were the judge's family. This is an old house; foundations go back to the 1700s. You can see from the basement," Kaitlin's mom said. "Do you want to see?"

"Yes," Amalia said, "yes!"

"No," Mildred said, "no, no, no! We don't want to overburden your hospitality." She paused. "We'd be better off going for a walk, instead." She put a firm hand on Amalia's shoulder.

"You might as well take Whiskie with you, then. Whiskie!"

"We don't need whisky," Mildred said.

"I think we do," Amalia said, pointing to the German Shepherd who entered the room at the sound of Kaitlin's mom's voice. The dog came up to them and nuzzled.

"He's friendly. Former police dog, though, so knows how to follow commands, if you know what I mean."

"I can't think of anyone we'd rather have with us more than Whiskie," Mildred said. "I stand corrected. Whiskie it is."

"Leash?" Amalia noticed the dog had a collar.

"Never around here, but when we take him into town we leash him. Here, he's all right off leash. Follow me to the kitchen," she said. The mother of the bride took a treat from a jar on the counter, doggy lifting his nose to sniff. "Not now, Whiskie." She patted the dog's nose back down. "He's a German Shepherd–Husky mix." She handed the treat to Amalia. "Here you go. If you need to call him back."

"He can smell from far away, just like that? What—I hold out the treat and he catches the scent?"

"He has a strong sense of smell," said the mother of the bride. "He was a tracking dog." Whiskie approached Mildred, sniffing at her pockets. "See."

After discouraging Whiskie from investigating Mildred's pockets any further, and after receiving some more general guidance from Kaitlin's mom about the local area, they were off.

"What's her name, again?"

"Beats me," Mildred said. "Mother of the Bride!"

"I caught Kaitlin and Grisham, and that's written everywhere on the wedding swag."

"We can't ask her again now, can we?"

Mildred sighed. "We could call her 'Moore.'"

"Or 'Judge!'"

"The shed out back used to be Porters," said Kaitlin's mom, when they'd returned from their walk. "They lived there all small like, so we heard. It was before our time."

"We used to call it the Poorhouse," Mildred said.

"We never heard it like that. Just Porters."

Amalia leaned in on the conversation. "'Porters' could have been corrupted over time to become 'Poorhouse, couldn't it?"

Kaitlin's mom slapped Amalia on the back with exuberance. "Good for you, detective you are! You're on the scent of something, I'll say!"

"There was a family called Porter, I do remember that. They did live around us, but I don't remember where," Mildred said. "My grandma took in washing with them. Or from them. I don't remember. Maybe that was the same house as the shed." She frowned. "There was some big hook I remember there. Something my sister Muriel played with. I always remembered it as a whaling hook."

"When she was little? More like, something to do with the laundry, something for washing."

"Could have been." Mildred's brow furrowed. "We were with whaling families, then. We used to collect the whale unguent on the beaches."

"Now that's something you don't hear every day." Kaitlin's mom stood up. "For lanterns? Or perfume?"

"Soap, I think," Mildred said. I don't remember." She stood up. "Thank you so much for your hospitality. I think we should be going now."

"Now, no, no, you'll stay. Of course, you'll stay! We are all set up for guests. We normally run a bed and breakfast, you know? We have people here for the wedding, but you can stay in my room. We'll be happy to rearrange. Tell her, dear," she said, patting Amalia hard on the back again.

"Like she said, Mildred, they are happy to rearrange. It could be fun. What do you say?"

She would be the guest of honor, in the room of the mother of the bride. Amalia could bunk with Mildred. It was a small corner room, and it gave her a view toward the water, with a corner of the old shed peeping out, too. Amalia was set up with a mattress on the floor—oh yes, there was a lot of extra bedding, they said—they ran a proper B & B, and they were always prepared. They often turned away visitors when they were full in summer; it being the low season, they'd thought it a good time to book the whole house for Kaitlin and Grisham's wedding. They didn't expect a guest, now, did they? Could they turn Mildred back out into the cold, to sit in her car and drive to whatever motel she could find? No. She was a neighbor! And she came with all the history bits they'd been musing about! She was a treasure for the wedding party. Oh, she married people, too? They already had someone lined up for the ceremony. But it was nice to know, for next time, in case there was to be a next wedding at the house. It could happen.

~ 34 ~

Poorhouse

Mildred sat in the MOB's room—Mother of the Bride; Kaitlin had put a sign on the bedroom door that read MOB and it could not be forgotten. Mildred's sightline out the window ran past the shed toward the water. The room had a vague familiarity. The MOB was downstairs and had left Mildred to freshen up. Music wafted up through the floorboards, a live little band of three, a local trio—lively strings—and on those notes, Mildred's mind floated from her gaze on a little framed bit of antique patchwork on the wall right out the window from shed to coast. She turned away from the window and lay on the single bed, next to Amalia's bedroll on the floor. On her back, she mused at the ceiling, seeing a little shadow line of old wooden molding near the ceiling light. It was indeed an old house.

She'd told them there'd been rum running in the neighborhood, and rum for sure had been a part of it. But it was the medical marijuana panel discussion that had got her thinking: was there more? Was there marijuana, and was there opium? Her mother had made light of the medicines people traveled to them for, and her father took it seriously: there was taxation to avoid. Rum was the pleasure of the neighborhood, and there was no shame in rounding out with a little marijuana or opium's derivative, morphine, heroin, was there? That had been her mother's tone, way back when. People did not have the presence of mind to think otherwise, in a world where heroin was prescribed for pain by doctors, and marijuana was a regular part of the end of a long day's work. The issue, as her father explained it, was to avoid the taxation, otherwise it wasn't worth it. His Pap had set him up for it in an era of Prohibition, and Mildred's father had inherited the booze biz with the house.

She didn't have any evidence of marijuana or heroin; had the recollections of her parents' conversations. She did have that sudden and new memory, visceral, of her grandmother rolling someone in a bedsheet, though, and as she looked out at the coast from the MOB'S bedroom, she saw the roof of the Moorehouse sloping away from her toward the roofline of the Poorhouse, the cut in the trees at the road past where the Roughhouse might still stand, and the far peak of her old home, the place of Rum. They laid out in a new pattern she'd missed before. The posts for the laundry lines, still erected, formed a line. A gently weaving line all the way from the old mail road route to the coastline, across the four properties.

~ 35 ~

Roughhouse

"You can take him for a walk," said Mother of the Bride. "Just make sure he doesn't go chasing any geese. We still get them in between the migrations. He'll tackle them if he catches them and rip them to the bone. Forgot to mention that before!"

"Duly noted," said Amalia. She felt around in her pocket for more treats left from their previous walk.

The bag of treats was there. And something else. She pulled out a long skinny object from where it had jammed into the seam. Her old stylus! "I'd forgotten about this." She took the plastic bag of treats and stuffed it back down into her pocket. "Why's he called Whiskey? For the drink?" Whiskie's eyes followed the bag.

"Our Kaitlin named him. Whiskie, because he has these soft little whiskers. He's an old dog but he's still soft like that."

Whiskie nudged at Amalia's pocket. "Later dude," she said. "Let's go, you and me." She patted the dog atop his sleek head. "Mildred, I'll see you back. Going to go stretch my legs for a bit."

Whiskie led the way to the front door, down the front steps and along the path that led to the ocean. "If you go that way," said Mother of the Bride, "you'll see a couple old falling down houses. Maybe the ones that the Reverend Mildred remembers from her childhood. From the rhyme."

"Moorehouse, Poorhouse, Roughhouse, Rum," Amalia said. "Got it." Whiskie was already many paces ahead of her and she followed him down the steps to keep up. This dog knew the land and seemed friendly enough. He knew treats were coming at the end of the walk.

Amalia took in the overcast April day, chill in the air, frost at her feet. If there had been any morning dew, it had frozen solid into hoar frost. The roads were scraped dry, snow mounded at their sides. The small, paved area in front of the Moorehouse quickly changed back to gravel, and after not too long, the gravel filtered out into hard-packed dirt, snow mounded around a tire track line that ran two strips either side of center. The road dipped down.

"Hey Whiskie!" The dog stopped, tail suddenly between his back legs. Was that a good sign or not a good sign? Amalia did not know how to read this dog, or any dog for that matter. "Whiskie!" His ears perked up and he trotted toward her. Expecting a treat. They'd barely left home; she would not give it up until she needed to. "Whiskie, take me to a fun place. Take me to your favorite place." Could the dog understand? He turned, continued along the road ahead, and led her from the main path to a trail. The trail, she figured to be somewhere east of the Moorehouse, if her directions were still accurate from their arrival by car, and the path led through a thicket that then opened to an area with trees of thinner trunks. The weave of thick and thin entranced her. The thinner trunks ringed a shrubby area, and the dog jumped in. "Whiskie!" She couldn't see where he had gone. Walked downhill into a low valley to where he disappeared and investigated the deep shrubbery. She could see the ocean, peeking.

It seemed an old stone foundation had been laid, quite overgrown. Beyond the edges of the foundation she could see evidence of some old and rotted wood, earlier floorboards she presumed, and no apparent walls emerging from the nested wooden slats. "Whiskie. You found somebody's old cottage." Was it one of the two abandoned houses? It was small and looked more like something the size of the old outbuildings Mark had shown her in New Hampshire. Maybe somebody's old food storage or barn or shed. Her mind wandered. Shed. She felt knowing click into place. Awareness of familiarity came full into her mind, and, following Whiskie who now trod along the perimeter of the stone foundation, she pushed through the low bush and up to the wall where he walked.

It was a tall stone wall for a foundation. The frosted tips of last fall's low greenery gave way to dry stone at the intersection of nature and structure, the structure appearing about three feet high by her estimation. It banked into a slope, and where the top of the stone met the hill, she was able to walk onto it without difficulty. It continued below ground. For something so old, it would have to have remained intact through earth movements, hydrostatic pressure—she was remembering well from studying for architecture exams—and months and years if not centuries of frost heave. Someone who knew how to build in frost had created this long-lasting structure. Amalia looked across the foundation. Whiskie nosed in the ground behind her, distracted. She would be careful to avoid the wooden floorboards, which, no matter how old or new they might be, showed evidence of rot and would not support her weight. Suddenly, Whiskie bolted, a sound in the shrubs near him alerting both him and Amalia to the presence of a small squirrely animal—a squirrel or chipmunk, mink, or some other creature of Maine, common to the coast.

She flinched and swallowed hard as she lost her footing on a patch of slippery black ice along the top of one of the stones, as Whiskie lunged at the unseen tiny mammal. Amalia fell with a screaming, and with one leg following the other, landed squarely on the old wood planks. She split at least one of them between her hip and butt in falling into the cavern. Realized she must've fallen more than three feet beyond the level of the ground outside. Amalia looked around. The floor she'd fallen through was providing a complete cover for a root cellar of sorts. If there was a way in, there must be a way out, but she didn't see it. Light filtered from above, and Whiskie, alerted to present danger, quickly abandoned the small mammal hunt and jumped to the edge of the wood floor boards, testing their limits, peering in. "I'm okay, Whiskie. Good boy. It's okay, Whiskie." Her hip was sore, and she rolled to one side. Light cascaded from outside into the dark-bottomed space. She crawled on her hands and knees and felt around the rough wooden edges, feeling for splinters dimly illuminated, and for evidence of once upon a time human interaction. Someone had left a stack of old plates; they looked to be made of ceramic, but she couldn't tell. Felt the thick dust and grime and dirt on top of one and raised it to her nose. It had a dank smell. Whiskie was pawing at the floorboards above her. She looked up into the light and wondered how she would climb out. She'd fallen almost into the center of the small room, and from there she would not be able to climb the walls. Should she pull down some floorboards? The architectural preservationist in her hated to do this. Was there a way, instead, to fashion a ladder from the floorboards that had fallen beneath her? "There's no point in saving this past."

Whiskie looked in and growled, a growl of hope. If she and Whiskie were going to be friends for the duration, she'd have to figure out what he meant. "Whiskie, good boy." She patted her pocket and found the treats still inside. Wondered if she could entice him to help her, or if she should save them until later. She fell back onto her elbows, suddenly exhausted from the thinking. Closed her eyes, let the light and cold spring wind come down into the space to wash her in a refreshment that felt sublime. How she could feel good in that space, she did not know. She lay back, her hair touching the cold, damp earth. Her hat had gone astray in the journey. Without warning, a quick scrambling sound above was followed by the descent of Whiskie, who leapt down into the cavernous cellar and landed on top of her belly, expunging a great burst of air from her lungs, and causing her to grunt.

"Whiskie!" She sat up and he licked her face, panting. "Did you think I was dead?" She sat up and he pawed at her arm. She reached for the back of his head and scratched behind the ears. "It's okay, doggy." She reached into her pocket and gave him one treat. "Good doggy." He grabbed and crunched down on it, then immediately began to dig next to her. Amalia backed up, crab-walk style, to avoid being spread by the dirt that flew out from beneath.

"What you got there?" She sat back and perched up against her heels, then scooted back to the foundation wall where she leaned on the cold stone and watched from a safe distance. Whiskie dug with an intensity that told her he'd been trained for it. In her falling and his perceived rescue of her, was this somehow part of his next sequence of tasks? Maybe he was looking for a way out. Her mind drifted a little as she watched him move through layers—eons—of packed soil, hidden from above for who knows how long.

She heard a clink then, and Whiskie sat on his haunches and whined. He looked at her as if to say, now what? He went back to the hole he'd dug and sniffed around it, nosing in toward whatever had produced the sound. Amalia crouched forward. Couldn't see into the hole, now at least a foot deeper than the dirt of the cellar floor. She could reach him. It wasn't far. "Close your eyes and reach forward." She blinked. "Why eyes closed, silly? What are you expecting, bones?" She sat back.

Something had been discovered, and she did not know what. Whiskie stuck his nose into the hole and pushed her hands out of the way. "Fine. Have it your way." She moved back and lay down near the foundation wall. Whiskie continued to dig, and before long the dim light revealed the source, plink plink plink, his claws rapping on metal, and when Amalia sat forward to feel the edges of his discovery, she had a strong feeling of 'box.' She pushed with her fingers down the edges where he already dug, but the dirt pressed hard into her nails. Needed something to dig. Stylus. Pulled it from her pocket and used it as a small tool, moving dirt, one swipe at a time, away from where Whiskie had begun an unintended excavation. A metal face, dented but intact, revealed itself at the surface, and she used the stylus to scrape it out. Her sense of self began to float, and she saw herself as if from above.

Amalia stood in the foundation.

Whiskie sat back on haunches.

She held the box;

Whiskie jumped at it, almost lunging, and she fell to the side, losing contact with its cold edges.

The box tumbled to the ground next to her.

Whiskie nudged it.

It had given a deep thud from within when it fell, and the thud was heard again as Whiskie nosed and pawed the box over to its side.

Amalia felt dizzy as she knelt up, hand on Whiskie's back.

She wasn't sure if he was stabilizing her or shredding her sense of order, but the way he nosed the box over, and over and over again, thud, thud, thud—

brought her to realize that something deep inside, in her core, was connected, connected to this moment, connected to this place, connected to this box.

Amalia sensed something playful as she watched Whiskie nudge the box, thud, thud, thud, and she felt it within herself. Within her cells, like a tingle, like a ripple.

Wondered what was inside the box, put her hand on it to still its movement and to stop Whiskie's play. His nudging continued.

She brought the shallow metal box onto her lap.

It was rusted a little on the edges, and it was old, old. It had inscriptions and markings on the top.

Who had put it there, years ago?

Some Revolutionary War wife packing jewels or something else treasured, maybe a key to her house.

She shook it.

It felt solid inside, and she did feel something shift within it from one side to the other, as if what remained inside was a heavy and weighted object, padded within the box's dirty walls.

She held it in her hands and lifted herself up for the first time, her head poking above by just a few inches into the light of day, above the floorboards.

There would be time.

First, she had to get out of the pit.

Amalia shoved the stylus back into her pocket and wiped her hands down the front of her pants, feeling returned to her core. Looked around for something she could use and spotted the broken floorboards. She fashioned a ramp from them and pulled another length of wood from the edge, already loosened by her fall. She saw where she'd fallen, and the boards beneath her had pierced the clayey soil, softening in the April melt. Wondered why it was warmer there; maybe the stone foundation had something to do with it. Maybe an underground spring, cold still through the start of the new season. Didn't know. Didn't care. Whiskie had dug into part of the area he had pierced. She pulled up those boards too, the ones she'd fallen on and that he'd nosed aside. Laid them over the rest of the makeshift ramp.

Whiskie looked up its length at Amalia, then back at the ramp. She took a step toward the bottom of it, and he growled, tugged on the hem of her jacket, pulling her back with a firmness that surprised her. "Okay, buddy. You first." She patted him gently behind the ears. "You're a good doggy."

He bolted fast up the ramp, then turned in a circle at the top of it, barking to the sky, then nosing into the wind, toward her. She had the distinct sense he was attempting to make eye contact with her, and to keep it steady. "Okay, buddy. We'll do it your way." She held the metal box firmly in the crook of her arm and ran up the ramp, one, two, three, four five, six long steps, and jumped over the top end of it, over the stone foundation's edge, just as Whiskie had done. "Whew. We got this, Whiskie." She took out a treat from the bag and gave it to him. Wolfing it down, he then nosed and whined at the box, and she put it on the ground, squatting on her heels.

She was suddenly hungry, or thirsty, or both; she couldn't tell. Felt a little lightheaded. "Maybe we should take this back to Mildred." A chipmunk watched from a nearby log and cocked its head to one side. It sat still; even at a distance, she could see its heart beating inside its thinly furred chest, striped white and puffed up against the Maine spring cold. It felt distinctly chillier outside the foundation bottom, and the light was beginning to turn. She looked away from the chipmunk and down at the box lid. The metal was encrusted with dirt. The pattern she'd felt on its surface was distinctly prominent beneath her fingers. Couldn't make it out. She looked up at the chipmunk. "What would you do, little guy?" Whiskie was staring at the chipmunk, moving in slow motion toward it. Little guy caught sight of him and darted in between fallen trees. Whiskie dashed toward the sound of old leaves rustling, and past, following a scent, or a sound unheard by Amalia. "Whiskie!" He was out of sight, gone toward the road they'd traveled, and Amalia went that way, calling his name.

She was able to follow the sound of his rustling through the underbrush for some time and came to the dirt road. It wasn't a dirt road she remembered. She saw Whiskie ahead and he ran back to meet her when she called. Barked once and then ran away from her again. "What is it?" She walked ahead knowing that the roads must eventually intersect once again.

He delivered her back to Mildred's old house. Amalia took in all that was familiar from the day before. The lights were still off, but she caught a faint glow from the cellar windows, through old purple bottle glass. The light shifted slightly, as if someone had walked in front of a lamp, creating a refraction of rays as they passed by the antique glass that was set in at ankle height.

She saw no car in the driveway, nor one down the side. Whiskie growled low, no bark. He snuck up to the side of the house where there were no windows and sniffed. Was he still tracking the chipmunk?

Amalia wanted to call to the dog to have him come to her. She suspected a person was in the house, despite no car in the driveway. Didn't want to attract attention. Whiskie was in full stealth mode, sneaking up the corner of the house and nosing around the corner. Amalia considered moving forward toward him or backing into the woods. In the moment she hesitated, she heard a car approach on the gravel ahead. She dashed back into the bushes, the metal box still in the crook of her arm, beginning to be a heavy weight there. Whiskie looked up, and the oncoming car shone its headlights—now at dusk—into the driveway and toward the house. The beam missed Whiskie, and he skulked back into the bushes toward Amalia. "Whiskie," she said in a low voice. "Let's go home, boy. Home." She pointed to the road beyond, and walked deeper into the woods, hoping he would understand. She found the footpath they'd come on, overgrown and hard to follow in the dim forest light. She shivered in the dropping temperature, and trotted over dead branches and fallen logs, keeping up with him as he ran past her at a moderate pace, watching over his shoulder for her. They came back toward the stone foundation she'd fallen into, and he paused there, but she pressed on, and so did he, until they were back at the Moorehouse.

"What to do with you," she said to the box. Saw the old woodshed out back behind the house and tried the latch on the door. It was like a big old hook, not a typical latch. Something repurposed. It opened easily in her free hand, and inside she saw the remains of winter wood stacked, and a jacket hanging on a nail. The floor was bare. She stepped in; her foot caught on a floorboard. "Not twice in one day!" She took a step back. The board was loose enough; she put the box on the floor next to her, pried the end of the board up, and, peering in, assessed the depth of the crawl space below to be arm's length. She laid the box in the cavity and pressed the loose board back into place. Stood up, and as she brushed her hands off, Whiskie nosed at the floor where she'd laid the box. "It's our secret," she whispered. She'd figure out what next, after—she wasn't sure after what, but trusted that she'd know.

Back in the house, Amalia took a long, hot shower. Mildred chatted with Mother of the Bride in the kitchen, and other wedding guests milled around downstairs. No one had been out back; no one had asked her about her walk, other than to say she'd been out long, must be hungry, dinner was coming. She toweled her long hair and fingered some curls into place, framing her face with the twirls. Had to make herself a little wedding-decent. The rehearsal dinner would start in an hour.

How strange to be plunged into someone else's wedding. In her room, she dressed and looked around. A framed-out ceiling hatch had been set in next to the light that hung from the middle of the room. The hatch with its old wooden handle intrigued her, and she stood on an old, upholstered chair to reach the inset panel. Pulled on it, and the hatch opened, revealing a shiny and new metal attic ladder that telescoped out and down into the room. "Bingo!" She jumped back off the chair and moved it out of the way. The telescoping ladder came almost to the ground, running alongside the edge of the single bed and floor mattress toward the door. She tested the ladder, it was steady, and, as inquisitive as ever, she ascended it.

Someone had been packing to leave. Amalia fingered her cell phone out of her pocket and turned on its flashlight.

The little case in the attic was full and abandoned; a girl's nightdress, a change of small leather shoes, good ones, and a doll, one of the old dolls whose eyes rolled and blinked, but whose limbs moved with stiffness. A book; a child's book of prayer. Amalia opened it—the pages were dry and crisp, and with a fading inscription inside. She directed the light to the pages. Words formed on her lips: "To My Dearest Antonella, May you Find Peace, Always. Love, Your Papa. 1855."

She put the book back and looked around. Sunset glowed in; windows dusted with cobwebs. A beam of light directed her gaze across the floor, and she stood up to follow it. Stood up, felt the knock of her skull on the old wood ceiling joist that came at her angled, and fell. The light spun and then—

She awoke in darkness. Her head hurt like holy hell, and her mind wandered for several minutes as she pieced together where she was and how she came to be in the dark place that smelled like old wood. It reassured her, that smell, and she felt no fear, just wonder. A beam of light across the floor caught her eye. It was the flashlight from her cell phone, still on.

As she lay on the cold wood floor, something hard pressed into her shoulder. She moved a bit, and with a wince, felt around. It was the edge of the case, the suitcase, she remembered, and what was in the suitcase? Her fingers, stiff with cold, felt around through fabric and landed on the book. She picked it up as she sat up, a smooth motion, and with care she used one hand to balance herself upright. She didn't stand. She recalled a low ceiling and realized she must have hit her head. Explained the head bump and godawful throb.

Bending low, eyes adjusting, she made her way around boxes. By moonlight, she reached her cell phone and targeted the beam of light to the stairs; holding the railing with one hand and the book and cell phone with the other, she made her way down from the darkness. The old Moorehouse creaked with each step.

~ 36 ~

Mother of the Bride

"Haven't been over there in years, now," said Mother of the Bride. "Last I heard the house went up for sale but then it was taken off market. Empty for a long time, I think."

"We used to come over here," Mildred said. "Moores' shed out back. My little sister Muriel used to play in it."

"Shed's what we were calling Porter's and you were calling the Poorhouse" said Mother of the Bride. "We use it to store wood in, but we're almost done for the season. Shoulder season of cold and warm."

The shed was latched with a hook. A big arc of a metal hook. Mildred lifted it and entered the little one-room space.

In the dark, Mildred dug—clawed—at the edge of the floorboards in the Moorehouse's shed. What was she remembering? Something Muriel had buried? Hands felt tight. Fingers stiff. She couldn't get the boards unstuck, then recalled the whaling hook. She'd seen it in a dreamlike vision as she'd approached. It would be at the back of the shed, up high…and on a whim, she went back outside to the back of the shed, round about, and looked up high—and there was no whaling hook. There were hooks in the side of the wall, where whaling hooks might once have rested.

"Rested" seemed too gentle a word for so violent an object, violent in its association. She grunted to herself in the cold and returned to the front of the shed, where she hoped she would be sheltered from the worst of the wind, if not the cold. A motion over at the bed and breakfast caught her peripheral attention and, in that moment, she decided to not get caught—doing nothing, she would say—and she returned to her car. If anyone asked, she could say "just exploring!" and not have to lie about snooping for long hidden and recently remembered contraband.

It must have all been her imagination. There was no whaling hook, and there were no loose floorboards. And even if she'd been able to loosen them, her darned stiff fingers wouldn't let her lift them. No drugs, no forgotten liquor. An uncomfortable dissatisfaction wrapped itself around her like a long woolen scarf, wound a little too tight.

~ 37 ~

No Explanations

The next morning, Amalia ducked out the back door of the Moorehouse toward the shed, looking both ways. A wedding guest sat on an Adirondack-style chair out back. He drew on a cigarette in the cool morning air. "Out for a walk," she said, and looped back around to the front of the house and hit the gravel driveway, walking between the cars that still gathered for the pre-wedding festivities.

She would have to find an excuse to get back to the shed before she and Mildred left. Stood between the cars. Could she come back on her own to hit up the shed? Why had she not shared it in the first place? Mildred waved through the front windows of the old house and knocked. There was no way Amalia could pretend she hadn't seen or heard.

Mildred swung open the front door. She stood, dressed, coat on, and with her overnight bag in hand. "You beat me to the car! Thought you would be sleeping in, having a little breakfast downstairs with everyone. I'm almost ready. We should plan to get back tonight. Let's head over to my old house and not take too long. I know you must get back to work."

"Mildred, you know, I was thinking, we could take an extra day up here if you want. Betsy is giving me unpaid time off, and if I'm okay with that, she's okay with it. She already told me."

"Thought you were worried about money? You told me all about that ex-boyfriend of yours you owe money to."

"I'm not worried about it today. I'm having a lovely time with you, and I'd like us to enjoy it for one more day. There's no rush."

"I don't want to impose one more night on this nice family," Mildred said. "We could go back to the hotel again, I suppose."

"The pool did look good," Amalia said. "Wouldn't you like to get in the pool, Mildred?" What else she could do to convince the woman to stay one more night, to buy a little more time, to get back to the stupid shed? If only she had the forethought to share her discovery at the time. Now, she felt like a stealthy fool.

"I suppose we could go back to the hotel. It was a nice place. And the pool did look good," Mildred said. "We can decide as we drive. Let's go! I'm excited to show you my childhood hometown."

"I didn't eat breakfast, and my bag's still inside." Amalia pushed past Mildred, who followed. Three guests from the previous night gathered around the coffee in the dining room. "Mind if I join you?" She poured herself a cup of coffee and smiled back at Mildred, who stood at the kitchen door entrance.

"You're not from around here." It wasn't a question. The man with the coffee pot in his hand pointed at Amalia. "Where you from."

"New York," she said. "And some other places before that." Didn't feel like she owed him an explanation.

He leaned in towards her, peering and scanning up and down her face. Amalia took a small step back but wanted to hold her ground. All she had to do was get him to change direction in the conversation.

"You're not white," he said, "so what are you?"

She had not expected the impertinent question. Didn't even feel like answering it. She took a sip of coffee, strong and black, and she spat it out, realizing she had not put in the cream that she loved. "Sorry about that," she said.

"Cat got your tongue?" He put down the coffee pot.

"I can speak fine, thank you," she said. "And my ethnic background is none of your concern."

"I'm just saying."

She put her cup down on the table. "And what exactly are you just saying?" She bit the inside of her lip. She had spoken when she had not meant to. Wished she'd kept her mouth shut. He was in her face, wiggling a red finger at her nose.

"I am not trying to stir up trouble," he said. "I'm just saying, some folks are obviously white. Do you—what the hell are you?"

Amalia slammed down the cup, pushed past the man, past Mildred, and went into the kitchen. Put her hands on the old farmhouse sink. "Can we just go?"

"What's wrong, dear?"

"People aren't used to people like me around here. At least, not in this house."

"No offense, Amalia, but what are you talking about?"

"This is a really white community," Amalia said.

"They don't take well to outsiders, and it doesn't have anything to do with the color of their skin."

"Or so you say."

"I know," Mildred said.

"No, you don't, Mildred. You don't know what it's like to be a brown-skinned woman in a white community, or a black-skinned woman in a white community."

"Neither do you, you're white."

"I'm not white."

"You look white."

"Mildred, you are color blind. I'm a brown-skinned half Asian and half white woman."

"Whatever you are, my dear, you are lovely."

"That is not the point. Thank you. Not the point. You make assumptions about people based on what you see. They do. People do. Not just you."

"And what do they assume when they look at you?"

"That I don't belong here."

"You do belong here."

"I know, Mildred. It gets tiring fending off all that attitude."

"Fend less. You have so much inner fire, save it for you and for the things that matter."

"It sounds good in theory, Mildred. What do you know about it? I love you on many subjects. Not this one."

"Love on a subject." Mildred shook her head. The girl was troubled. "Conditional. You can't say you love fully, yet conditionally. It doesn't work that way. You can disagree, but that disagreement reflects your own misalignment. You would do well to meditate, my dear."

Amalia felt a roiling inside she hadn't felt in a while. "Screw that, Mildred."

"You can be uncomfortable with it, and it is still true," Mildred said.

She had to get out of the room. "I'm not uncomfortable meditating, I'm uncomfortable with you telling me what to do. Maybe I have my own way of doing things."

"Sure. And how's that working out for you?"

"Things are fine."

"They could be finer."

Amalia half-smiled. "They could." She departed with haste and slammed the screen behind her, leaving the heavy wooden door ajar. Maybe Mildred would stand up to close it. Why did it always have to be Amalia standing up?

The approach to the shed out back was chilly, despite the sun being near its peak in the sky. Now was as good a time as ever to escape into it.

Amalia opened the front door to the little building with its funny old metal hook—the door swung with a creak and jammed into the floorboards, angled off its hinges from the top. The metal hook seemed to weigh it right down.

"What does she know about me, anyway." Amalia stepped into the shed; more of a small cottage, she realized, on her new and riled-up glance around inside. What had gone on in there?

According to Mildred, her younger sister Muriel had some suspicion about the role of the shed in the family's rum running operations. By extension, Mildred thought there might be evidence of opium production there. What Amalia had hidden in the floor was nobody's business. And as within reach as it was, the box would have to stay hidden for a little longer until she could trust no one would see her with it.

It appeared to be more than a shed: along the back wall, inside, she saw a hole in the floor, patched over with a wooden circle of linoleum, and another hole in the wall above it, patched over with a wooden circle, overlaid with a pie plate, ceramic, supported on nails pegged out. They appeared to be evidence of some earlier industry, a stove, or a vent; maybe a chimney line had run through from the one-room shed to the outside.

What did Mildred understand about her life? Nothing. Amalia looked at the pie plate on the wall. Nothing.

"Amalia?" Mildred's voice carried from the back porch of the Moorehouse. Amalia ignored her.

A rat-a-tat woodpecker on the outside of the shed answered in reply, and Amalia stayed silent. Mildred could take that attitude and do what she wanted with it. The pie plate on the wall rattled under the vibration of the bird's hard rapping.

Minutes later, Amalia heard the crunch of gravel under tires, and she peeked out the front door of the shed, down the side of the house. Saw one of the guest's cars peel out the driveway, and best she could tell, the bobbing white curls of the person in the passenger seat belonged to none other than the Reverend Mildred.

Amalia began to wander the corners, peering through dirty glass at the woods outside. Cold, and no bears. There was that to appreciate; the bears had their own place to be. No bugs, either. Too cold. She would explore outside. Mildred would be back soon enough.

The shed door was left ajar behind her, metal hook hanging. She walked around the shed in circles, ever expanding, breaking brush, slender stalks cracking beneath her sturdy shoes. She would not get lost if she stayed in circles, rounding the trees with movements that kept the shed in constant view, even as the distance grew. The woods soothed her, and the birds joined in. It brought her a kind of easy pleasure to be in there, circling the shed. She went in it and dug into the corner of the loose floorboard with her fingers. Lifted out the box. "You are a marvel," she said, and took it with her outside.

After some time, sky darkened, and not with cloud cover. Simply the onset of evening through late afternoon. The sun had moved far in its arc.

She hoped Mildred would return soon. She was getting hungry. Didn't want to go back into the house, although her suitcase was still inside. Warm food was inside. Friendly people were inside. That guy was an outlier. She'd met men like him before. Didn't need to pay him a moment's more attention. It was Mildred she was more upset with. The loops around the shed unraveled her frustrations, one lap at a time. Didn't want to punish anyone, least of all Mildred. She'd talk with her. It would be fine.

She'd wait on the shed steps with the box where she could see the driveway and catch Mildred before she went back into the house. She'd show her the box and they'd talk about how to share it with the mother of the bride. Birds twittered in the early dusk in the trees at the front of the little building. It was a quiet place otherwise. An easy place to hide an opium operation, at the end of the long drive, deep in the woods. Mildred said the mud tracks in spring could get so deep they would lose a visitor every year. Her Papa would say it. Must have been true.

Amalia typed in her phone, playing with words while she sat on the step, box on her lap, waiting for Mildred. She'd alternated between hopping up and jumping to keep warm, and sitting, resting. Didn't like to keep jiggling the box. She sat. Words flowed well in the amber light.

"Sorrow and joy, joy, and sorrow.
Where do we play?"

~ 38 ~
Waves

At age five, Mildred was cast to sea with the men, and Mama didn't come. They sailed up and down the coast with the hooch barrels, and she was brave on the waves. Brave on the waves! That's what her Papa said, and he made it a rhyme they said together. She sat on his knee, and he paid attention. Papa was kind. Smelled of pipe.

She landed daily. These were short trips. She saw Mama on the way back. "It's just the summer, see," Papa said to Mama, "and then she'll be back. She'll start school. Kindergarten! This is her last hurrah of childhood," Papa said. "Let's let her go to sea."

There had been a cat. A black with white cat, a shy one, but she kept the mice away. Or ate them, as Mildred discovered down below one day.

It was rough-going at sea that summer. She told herself she was a fisher girl, and she'd ask the otters to bring her their catch. It wasn't about the hooch, her blind spot in it all, until later. It was the otters she'd come to see. The waves hurled her stomach about, churning, and she'd talk to the otters, even when she couldn't see them. She knew them. They loved her. She knew it.

These were the fun days, she recalled. Not fun for her Mama and Papa, who sat with knees touching and furrowed brow between them, furrowed and close they looked like one. "The hooch business is drying up," Papa said, "it's a pun."

"Now," he said, "we'll sell houses. The kits, the start up from the ground for a new family kind of kits, the kind Sears has plied for years. We'll sell houses, not hooch."

What did Mama say? Mildred didn't remember. But it was then that the boxes were packed, and the china given to cousins and aunts, and the train hurried into the station to pick them up on a Saturday at ten.

The cousins came to say goodbye that Saturday, and the aunts cried and pretended to not-cry. She was five, Mildred, that weekend. Still five. Not yet six. She remembered the faint yellow-grey stain of washed-away whale blood on the hem of her white dress. Or was it the blood of another?

They stopped in every state from Maine to Delaware for three years, and she didn't start kindergarten until they looped back up into New Jersey, their last East Coast stop after the southern spur.

When she was fourteen, they took a train west, and north, and then a boat, and had a new home: Salt Spring Island.

~ 39 ~

Delusions

She stood when she heard wheels on the gravel, a signal of Mildred's approach. Walked out toward the car sound, box tucked under her arm, and as she rounded the bend to the front of the Moorehouse, realized it wasn't the same car she'd seen leave. Shoot. Amalia squinted. "Frankie!" She hadn't seen him since back in Mildred's church. And he drove the old Camry with Vermont plates, the one she'd seen parked next to Mildred's car in Binghamton.

"I thought I might find you here, Miss Amalia." His head out the window, elbow pointing to her. A faint smell of deep woods bug spray mixed with pot came off him, and it almost made Amalia laugh—he must have put on the bug dope first. And why? There were no bugs yet. A well-trained ritualist in survival, he must be. That almost-laughter shut right down when she saw Mildred, slumped in the backseat.

"Mildred!" She ran forward and slammed her free hand on the hood of his car. "What have you done?" Under her hand, the momentum of the car stopped.

"She's just sleeping!" He turned off the ignition. "You not going to shoot or anything?" He came out with his hands up.

"No. Frankie." She pushed him aside with her hand and opened the unlocked back door, dropping the box to the floor. "Mildred." Her face was flushed, and she was breathing hard. "Frankie—what's going on?"

"Miss Amalia, I had nothing to do with it, I swear." He backed away from the Camry. Then, without leaving time for Amalia to react, he ran down the driveway. He'd left his bag in the car next to Mildred. Keys in the ignition.

A current of panic fluttered through her core. She didn't want to move Mildred, not until she had a clearer idea of what was going on. All was quiet in the main house, and the rest of the guests' cars were gone. Fished for her cell phone in her jacket pocket. Did she even have enough juice? She had battery but no signal. No service. Mildred looked calm, not contorted or injured. Amalia ran up the front steps of the Moorehouse and banged on the front door. Seemed they'd all gone for the day, and the only light that remained on inside leaked out from the kitchen beyond. Even the porch light was off.

Amalia turned fast on her heels and flew down the front steps, jumped into the driver's seat, still warm from Frankie's body, and pulled a fast turn in the driveway. Frankie was near the road. "Get in!" It seemed the best way. Only he knew what had happened.

"You're a witch, Miss Amalia, and I am not getting in with you."

He must be paranoid. She drove alongside him, at his pace. "Frankie, what happened to Mildred? I need to get her help. I need you to help me help the Reverend Mildred, Frankie."

"I can't." His footsteps faltered.

"She loves you, Frankie."

"I can't." He started to cry.

"Frankie, please get in the car. I'm sure we can work it out."

"You're a witch, Miss Amalia, and you're making her one too!" He blurted it through a veil of tears.

Over her shoulder, Mildred snored.

"What are you doing here, Frankie? Did you follow us to Maine?"

"I found you. I found her." He slurred his words.

Amalia wondered if he was drunk as well as high. "Just tell me what happened to Mildred."

He was walking faster—almost a run—and without warning, he veered off into the deep woods on the side. For a few moments she saw him in that liminal light, in the gap left by deer grazing on whatever could be found in the cold. He became smaller in the distance of the underbrush, and then he dipped fast, out of sight—he'd either fallen or run down a hill. Amalia could not tell. Should she run after him? There was no sound. Must have gone down a hill.

She didn't know whether to scream or cry. Stopped the Camry and looked back at Mildred, reached a hand out to pat her knee.

Mildred woke up at Amalia's touch, or at the sudden stop of the car which had lurched her into a new position where she sat, unbuckled, on the seat. She mumbled beneath her breath.

Amalia caught a whiff of marijuana on her. "Mildred." It was not intended to be admonishing yet she felt it.

Blinking, Mildred sat up. "I don't know what happened." She opened and closed her mouth. "Thirsty."

"You were with Frankie."

"Boy's in trouble."

"He is in trouble. With me."

"No, in real trouble. He's in it. He's bringing it. He's—" Mildred stumbled on the words. "He's in the middle of what we know."

"What do we know, Mildred? We're in the middle of nowhere. That's the only middle there is. What did you and Frankie do?"

The Reverend Mildred sat up. She didn't look reverendly to Amalia in that moment. She pulled herself up on the seat in front. "There is something I'm figuring out."

"Figuring out what? Mildred, are you okay? Did you get bopped on the head?"

"I'm fine. Never better. Let's drive. Maybe we can find Frankie."

"He's in the woods."

"You saw him?"

"He came here, Mildred, he brought you, in his car, and left his bag, left the keys, and ran into the woods. Said I was a witch or something."

"What are you smoking? Frankie's not here and he didn't bring me. You and me, we came together. And this is Father Jasper's car, I think."

"You think?"

"Vermont plates, I'll bet." Mildred spoke with her eyes closed and hands outstretched.

"Hang on." Amalia got out of the car. Sure enough, Vermont plates hung on the front of the car.

"Vermont. Where's Father Jasper?"

"Back at his house in Vermont, of course. He sent Frankie."

"Sent Frankie why?"

"Because Frankie knows, and he needed to tell us."

"Mildred, this is crazy. You're not talking straight."

"Damn straight." Mildred sat back.

"I'm going to take you to the hospital to get checked out."

"No hospitals. Not since Raymond."

"I need to know you're okay."

"I'm okay. It's no big deal. We vaped something. And then we smoked something. It was all okay, okay? We're okay. Okay?"

Amalia felt like she was mentally herding a flock of baby sheep. "Let's go into town and get a cup of coffee, all right? We'll clear our heads, you and me. Both of us. We need to."

Half an hour later, installed in a booth in a diner in Georgetown, Mildred owned up.

"We sold some stuff."

"Why do you say 'we' sold some stuff, then?"

"He's a good boy. Don't want to see him get into trouble."

"But you're covering for him! If he's selling contraband, that leaves you exposed! It leaves your church open, too."

"Can't touch the church, they can't."

"You're saying the church sold this stuff?"

"Nothing wrong with selling stuff. It technically is mine. On my family's old property. No one saying when it left the property." Mildred snorted. "Could have left with us in 1938."

"I thought you said you left in 1935." Amalia felt a little dizzy. Needed some cold water.

"I am FAN TAS TIC!" Mildred wrote it on a napkin and spelled it out. "This is going well."

"Nothing is going well! Where's Frankie? What are you two hiding? And where's Father Jasper?"

"Call him." Mildred pushed her cell phone across the table. "Last call I received was from him."

"Okay—" Amalia hit the number and within moments, Father Jasper answered.

"Mildred. Everything going according to plan?"

"This is Amalia. Don't tell me you're in on it, too?"

"Is the dear Reverend with you, Amalia?"

"Yes, she's here." Amalia listened to Mildred's half of the conversation and leaned in to hear Father Jasper's replies in the background buzz of the cell phone. Was it possible she was the only crazy one?

She seemed unconcerned about Frankie's disappearance. Father Jasper agreed Amalia should drive his car.

Their voices—Mildred's before and Father Jasper's in the distant cell phone transmittance—merged to static and she stared out the diner window, half expecting Frankie to walk by.

Mildred put the phone down on the table. Her eyes were bright. "It's all set."

"What, exactly?"

"Our pickup. Of Frankie. He's back at the house, Father Jasper had already spoken to him."

It appeared Frankie had kept his cell phone on him, despite having abandoned everything and everyone else.

"He knows where to go."

"Of course."

"And—how—?" Amalia's voice trailed off.

"He's from these parts."

"Ahh."

"But you left, so—"

"I had cousins who stayed. Aunts and uncles."

"And he's a relative?"

"Something like that." Mildred's voice was soothing.

"Is he your son?" She had to ask.

"Good god, no. No. He's not my boy." Mildred seemed clearer. "But whose son is he, you might ask."

Amalia did not want to ask.

"He's Father Jasper's nephew. Of sorts. Not biological."

"Father Jasper is looking out for him. Kind of like a guardian?"

"Sort of." Mildred looked uncertain as to how much to say. "Father Jasper is from Vermont."

"I know." This was getting painful, and Amalia didn't know how long to pursue the line of conversation. "At least you got the confirmation that Frankie is fine. And I'll drive." She motioned to the server that they were ready.

"I need to use the toilet," Mildred said, standing.

"I'll come with you." Amalia followed.

"You don't need to."

"I'm coming."

"Suit yourself."

"When we go back, it's along that road there, then make a right?" Amalia motioned outside as they passed the bay window.

"No. You can't get there from here. Don't you remember how we came?"

"Mildred, it's okay, I'll put the map app on."

"It's not on the map. No address."

"But that road has a name, or the crossroad?"

"Moorehouse, Poorhouse, Roughhouse, Rum."

"Every house has a street address."

Mildred washed up in the bathroom. "Not here. We had sayings. Little sayings. To find the way. Like I told you before."

"And Frankie knows this too? And Father Jasper?"

"No, Frankie's too young. He'd use the map."

"But you said there's no street shown on the map."

"Could be. I don't know."

"How do you even know—" Amalia followed Mildred out of the bathroom. "How do you even know we were on the right road? Maybe that wasn't even the right house."

Mildred snorted. "It's the right house." She sounded like her awake self again. Maybe the coffee had helped, or whatever she and Frankie had imbibed was wearing off. Either way, Amalia heard the change in her voice. "I'll take three of these," Mildred said at the cashier's desk, and grabbed an armload of potato chips.

Amalia put most of them back. "We'll take two." Frankie would want some. "Three," Amalia said, "we'll take three." Was she looking out for Frankie now, too?

"I can see your concern. Three packets of chips might be unreasonable for one person to eat. But I believe we'll each have one on the long drive back to Binghamton."

Mildred was forever reasonable, even in her apparent lack of reason.

~ 40 ~
Responsibility

Amalia,

Are you OK? Your voice message sounded oddly calm despite what you said was going on. Do you want me to come out there? You don't have to deal with Mildred on your own. I feel responsible. I shouldn't have pressed you about going. And Mildred should be a shared responsibility, don't you think? I left you voice mails after I got yours. Call me back. Or email me. Or text. I'm here. I'm here for now, I should say. I just got word they want me back in Iceland.

Yours,

Mark

~ 41 ~

Conductors

"Play, play with me says the otter, rolling and bowling, togging, and sloshing!"

"You can't say togging, Grandma," Millie said.

"But why not?"

"It's not a real word! And otters don't tog."

"If they don't tog, I don't know what does," said Grandma. "What's tog, then?"

Grandma put down the bed sheet in the barrel and stopped her body's rocking by stabilizing herself on the sides of the big vat of rinse water. "Togging is serious business, Millie. Come with me." She dried her hands.

"See over there? Past the stationmaster's house and past the conductor's house. See there?" She pointed to the chimney of Mrs. Moore's house. "See that?"

Mildred looked beyond. "I see only a bit of white. White with a bit of black."

"Yes, Millie. It's a sign." Grandma looked serious.

"Grandma, what's a tog?"

"It's an old word for dressing, or hiding, or encasing, or enclosing."

"You sound like Papa's dictionary!"

"Maybe I am." Grandma turned the other way. "See the shore, well, beyond the trees you know is the shore." She smiled. "They came that way. To and from, depending on whose business it was."

"Grandma, otters don't get dressed up. They don't!"

Grandma took her up a tree. The view was wide. The houses looked all roofy and the laundry all like blowing flags. From where she perched, beyond Grandma's pointing arm, was the ocean. It had a sparkle that morning, wasn't full of grey and solid.

"See that there, Millie? That there they used to call the stationmaster's house. They called that one there the conductor's house. And from here they could see the water."

"I can see the water. But I don't see the train."

"See, Millie, it wasn't a train actual."

"Was it the wagons for boxes for hooch?"

"Who told you that?"

"Papa has boxes for hooch."

"Oh, yes." Grandma nodded. "Let's go, Millie. I've said enough." Grandma's face closed, and she shimmied down the tree, pulling her skirt behind her where it had caught.

~ 42 ~

Rum

Back at the hotel, Amalia pulled Father Jasper's old Camry to a stop, right next to where Mildred had parked her Alero. She opened the trunk of the Camry to retrieve her bag, took a quick look for the box where it remained in the corner, nestled under Frankie's bag, and slammed the trunk shut. She'd done a good job of moving the box to the trunk, unnoticed. She'd be back for it as soon as she got the car keys from Mildred for the Alero and could transfer it without anyone seeing. Wasn't sure she should have taken it off the Moore's property, but it seemed more connected to Mildred, though Amalia couldn't say why she felt it. She'd deal with it all once she had Mildred's keys.

Mildred had wanted Frankie to stay with them; he insisted he did not need a place to stay. That he would return Father Jasper's car himself and stay overnight in Vermont. Amalia had serious doubts and insisted he come to the hotel with them. And in turn, he insisted on bringing the Father's car, insisted he would drive it himself, proclaiming himself to be completely sober and responsible. It didn't turn out that way. Amalia drove the Camry. Mildred drove Frankie in her Alero. Inside the hotel, Amalia found Mildred at the check-in desk. "Frankie's at the bar," Mildred said, nodding her head in the opposite direction. "I booked him his own room."

"Mildred. I did something."

"I know," Mildred said. It's okay. We all get rattled. That man was out of line." She twisted the keychain on her hand.

"What? No, that's not what I mean," Amalia said.

"You mean about driving Father Jasper's car. He said he didn't mind. You were doing a good deed. Anyone can see that. And I appreciate it, too." She handed Amalia the Alero keys.

Amalia pocketed them, relieved, and reached for the keys to the Camry. They weren't there.

"I don't have the keys to the Camry, Mildred." She felt around in her pockets. "Dammit! Must have locked them in the trunk." Amalia felt a familiar heat flush around her cheeks.

"Don't worry. I have Triple A." Mildred looked as if she might fall asleep on her feet. "Whatever you need, dear, I'm sure they can help fix." She yawned. "I must sleep, Amalia. To the room we go. I'll give you my Triple A card. Then you sort the car."

In the hotel room, Mildred put her head on the pillow, on the left side of the double bed. "I just need to rest now, dear." She closed her eyes and spoke through mumbling lips. "You have a good night's sleep there now, dear. It will all be okay in the morning. Card's in my wallet."

Before long, Amalia heard Mildred begin to snore, first a light snore, then, as loud as a train. She hadn't noticed it when they shared the wedding space, nor the previous night at the hotel, and she assumed this new cadence had something to do with Mildred's previously inebriated state that day. Amalia sank into the desk chair and fiddled with the remote. Turned the volume on low, and flipped channels, listening to Mildred snore, and wondering how the heck she was going to get that box.

Jumped up and peeked inside Mildred's bag for her wallet, and inside that wallet found the AAA service card. Mildred's wallet was more organized than Amalia had expected. Took a peek at her driver's license. New York State. Binghamton address. Born 1930. Older than Amalia had thought. Amalia put the wallet back, and the AAA card in her pocket. Smiled at Mildred as she slept, white curls bobbed up on the pillow in a face-frame that looked sweet.

Amalia had an idea to look for Frankie downstairs, and slipped out with her door card, whispering to sleeping Mildred that she would return. She found Frankie downstairs at the bar. He wasn't drinking, just sitting, watching some sports on the big-screen TV. Amalia wondered if he'd gotten high outside. He looked a little zoned out.

"Hey, Frankie," she said. He looked up, his eyes bloodshot red. He'd been crying.

"Miss Amalia." He reverted to the formality. "Don't have my stuff. Need the keys."

"Frankie." Her insides did a sudden drop. "I'm sorry. I locked the car keys in the trunk. I'm going to deal with it though."

"Miss Amalia," he said, his voice rising, "my stuff is in that car!"

Poor Frankie. Amalia sensed an opening, and felt urgency to help the man, aware of her self-serving interests. "I can help you," she said.

"You can break into Father Jasper's car."

"No, I'm going to make a call and get someone to come help."

"No."

"No?"

"No calls."

Was he paranoid? He must have stashed drugs in the car and wanted to keep people away. "Okay, fine. We'll do it your way. But you need to trust me, okay?"

"Okay." He looked hesitant.

"You just wait here, and I'll be right back," she said. As soon as she was out of his sight, she slipped her cell phone out of her pocket and dialed Mildred's AAA number for help.

"Expired," was the answer she received to her pleading question. "Dues not paid; do you want to reopen your membership to Triple A for the roadside service?"

"I'll call a local tow truck," Amalia said, and pocketed Mildred's card. Something to talk to Mildred about later, no time for dilly dallying with Mildred's personal finances.

The tow truck arrived within minutes. It had to have been nearby. She'd have to convince the driver to let her into an old car with out-of-state plates that wasn't hers. For that matter, it wasn't Frankie's, either.

She gave the driver a big and sweet smile, and before he could ask her any questions or confirm ownership of the car, she slipped him the hundred dollars in twenties that she had in her back pocket. "Help a girl out," she said. She smiled, knowing the falseness of her tone, yet unable to stop the put-on sweetness.

The man smiled back. Within minutes, he had the Camry unlocked, and she had retrieved both Frankie's satchel and the old box. As soon as the tow truck had pulled out of the hotel parking lot, she made a quick pitstop at Mildred's Alero, tossing the box into the back seat. It landed with a clunk and rolled to the floor. "Dammit, Amalia, be gentler!"

Went back inside. It had been a matter of minutes she'd been gone. Frankie was nowhere to be seen. She slumped down into a lounge chair, resting her bag on one foot and Frankie's satchel on the other, a makeshift blanket of sorts; she closed her eyes, and before long, felt her shoulders begin to relax into the thick, supportive, upholstered chair back.

Frankie came back around 2 AM, waking her from a shallow sleep. Without a word, she handed him his bag; without a word, he nodded, making eye contact, and left out the front door of the hotel.

He was shifty, that one. Amalia had her own business to focus on. She thought to leave Mildred a note on the dresser of the hotel room they shared. She didn't want to risk waking her; left her a note at the front desk. Trusted that Mildred, having still a drug-induced haze to sleep off, would not rise anytime soon. The drive back to Georgetown was quick, on a Monday morning and going against the end of rush-hour traffic into Bath. Well past sunrise, but not so far into the day that anyone should be around and about down near the old foundations she'd fallen into.

She wasn't sure what she was going back for. It had something to do with the box. It rested safely behind her on the back seat of the car; wanted to see more of where it came from, to take some pictures. She hoped Whiskie wasn't roaming and would give her up.

"Better not go past the Moorehouse's driveway to get there." Better the other way. She went toward Mildred's old house at the fork in the road instead of up the driveway where wedding guests might have returned or gathered. Didn't want to park at Mildred's old house either, parked along the road in between all the houses and their driveways, and since they were spaced a good half mile apart, she would have to walk no matter which way she chose.

Mist rose from the early morning Maine ground, cold and bright, a brisk wind coming from oceanside. She couldn't see a way into the old stone foundations. She'd have to pass by

Mildred's old house to find her way. She'd keep to the wooded edges and no one would see her.

She wanted to be back before Mildred awoke and began calling, wanting to get back to New York. Amalia would be quick. Up ahead, her paces took her closer to Mildred's old place. The Rum house, Mildred had called it.

She didn't want to have to get too close, wanted to miss whoever might have been inside when Whiskie popped his nose up to the window—but she needed the house to find her bearings to the old stone foundations.

There was no car in the driveway. The house, at least at a distance, appeared quiet, and there was no sign of movement. As she got closer, there was a faint glow of purple light through the old glass bottle panes at the side of the front steps. No shut-up past, no light flickering. There appeared to just be a steady glow. She went the way Whiskie had gone, along the side, and she dashed through the long grass tips to the wooded edge, along the scrubby side of the old garden. It had been cut at some point in the previous months, from the length of the grass. Someone had tended to it.

She was nearer to the house than she'd imagined she would be. Beyond the structure, grown with little saplings, stood an old birdbath. The back garden was silent and still, save the gentle swinging of an old washing line that moved in the light morning breeze, shifting the light in the tips of the long grass. She took the moment and ran straight up to the edge of the house, a wash of green stems dampening the legs of her jeans. Heart pounding. Something drew her closer.

At the corner of the old house, where the brick stood proud and crumbly below the wood cladding, was a small wooden board, laid crossways with other boards, and not at all grown over with the tall grasses that surrounded it. Someone had painted it green in what she assumed was an attempt to conceal it. Looked like a covering into the cellar, no different from any other cellar hatch door, except that this one was rough cut, and still smelled of new paint. It was a strong smell. But was it paint, or something else? She couldn't be sure.

"Probably unoccupied," Mother of the Bride had said. "Tended by an absentee landlord," she said. "Passed the lawn maintenance truck on the road more than once. Don't know many folks in the area who use a hired lawn crew." The lawn was grown over. Painting the cellar hatch doors while they were ignoring the lawn maintenance? No big deal. Amalia itched to get back to find the old stone house foundation, yet something pulled her further forward. She dropped to her knees into the grass when she heard a sound. Could have been a squirrel, or a deer. From inside? Maybe a mouse.

What was she doing? Half-lying in icy, dew-wetted, cold grass. Catching errant sounds on the wind, or from the groans of the old house. Chasing a mystery that had no reason for being. She just wanted to get some photos of where she'd found the metal box. Reminded herself she was on private property. Thought of what Mark would say about the gun-toting culture he'd grown up with in the neighboring state, wondered if she should get out while she could. She'd have to stand up if she was going to get out, and she didn't want to stand up while something was still rustling on the other side of the wall. She'd wait. Hoped her cell phone ringer had been turned off, felt for it in her pocket. Wasn't there. Uh-oh. Had it fallen out along the edge of the house when she'd dropped to her knees? She looked over her shoulder to see if it was visible behind her, and then over the other shoulder.

Something glinted in the rising sun, and it did not appear to be her cell phone. Closer to the wall of the house and just out of her reach, at the edge of the wooden cellar hatch door, was a metal handle of something lying flat. She wanted to know what it was, but afraid to move, she scanned the grasses around her, still looking for her cell phone from a distance. A huge disturbance at the edge of the grassy garden pulled her deeper into the grass, and her heart beat fast. Uh-oh. Before she could make a move or a next decision, a large German Shepherd Huskie was upon her, licking her face, panting, nosing, and nudging her to get up.

"Whiskie," she said in a raspy voice. "Good boy." She spoke with low tones to soothe him and to not alert anyone to their presence. "I'm okay, Whiskie, you don't need to rescue me." Was that true, in fact? Whiskie was both a blessing and a curse. Amalia put a hand over his nose and mouth and kissed the bridge of his forehead, and he let out a whimper, pawing her shoulder. He grasped the fabric of her jacket in his teeth and pulled. "Shh." Inside, voices. And nearing the driveway, she heard the distinct sound of heavy wheels traveling slowly over gravel. "Whiskie." She grabbed him by the collar, stood up in a half-stand, and began to dart across the open garden, letting Whiskie go as soon as he got the drift of where she was headed, which as far as she was concerned, was the hell out of there.

He stopped ahead of her behind a stand of trees at the edge of the clearing, looking back to her and the house. Amalia caught up to him and rested on the tree, concealed for the moment from view. Or she hoped.

A white truck pulled into the driveway. Amalia stayed behind the tree, didn't look. She couldn't see who got out the driver's side, or if the driver was alone. Heard footfall shift from gravel to softness and wondered if the footsteps' owner had traveled over the grass instead of up the wooden steps at the front of the house. The foot-faller seemed to be rustling in the grass, and she hoped Whiskie would remain still, and not give chase. She patted him on the head, stroking deeply between the eyes. He yawned in a stretched-out mouth as if to say, "nothing going on here." He looked up at her, and she crouched next to him, behind the tree. Wished she had some treats for him. Who needed reassurance, though, him or her? The sound from the house grew, and voices, male voices, conducted across the long grass.

If she could hear them, then they'd be able to hear her and Whiskie, too. More rustling, bumping, and what must have been the wooden hatch being moved off or moved back. She wasn't sure how much time had passed. Amalia heard an electric tool, kind of like a drill. She peeked out from behind the tree and saw a man in a hunting jacket and hood, packing a handheld screwdriver back into his rear pocket. He tested the wooden platform with a foot, then reached into the grass and laid something heavy and metal across the top of it. Must be the metal she'd seen glinting in the grass. The man reached for the screwdriver again and appeared to screw the metal bar down into the wooden panel, securing it from the outside.

She pulled back behind the tree before she could be seen. At least he didn't have a dog, or the dog would have scented out her and Whiskie in a flash. Amalia peeked toward the van, whose rear end she could still see from where she hid. Truly hoped there was no dog in the back. They should just go while they could, but she didn't want to risk her movements—or Whiskie's unpredictability—as triggers to bring on a confrontation. The back of the van was closed. No markings from what she could see. Couldn't make out the license plate; seemed greenish. Presumably from Vermont.

Vermont. Wasn't Frankie driving with Father Jasper's Vermont-plated car? But this was a different vehicle. Just a coincidence. Must have been.

"Stay, Whiskie." With a whimper of regretful compliance, he did.

She'd at least have to find her phone, even if she didn't figure out who was inside. She was a coward, not a detective. Instead of hanging around, she skittered herself right out of there, back into the woods with Whiskie in the lead.

The stone foundations should be easy to find from there, and since she didn't want to be seen on the road or near the houses, she'd stay in the woods until the coast was clear. Her car, she hoped, would appear only as a hiker's vehicle parked for a nearby jaunt. Whiskie balked. He trotted ahead of her, then nudged her back in the direction of Mildred's old house. "What is it, boy?" Her voice was low. "Don't have any treats for you, sorry. Is that what you're smelling in my pocket?" She fiddled deep into the lining. The old stylus lay pressed into the hem, dirt encrusted. Wouldn't be any use to her then and there. Just wanted her cell phone. She could wait it out. Wait in the woods until the men had left; but when they left, they'd see her car on the road. "Dammit." She'd have to go back for the car and move it, before they saw her and got suspicious, suspicious of her suspicions. "Whiskie. Stay here. Sit." She pressed her palm into the air toward his nose. He sat back, with an abruptness that startled her. "They trained you well, Whiskie. I'll be back."

She decided to track herself just inside the edge of the woods that ringed Mildred's old house to get back to her car. If Whiskie stayed put, as he appeared inclined to do, she'd be fine.

She had to get the phone. It had hundreds, no thousands of photos on it, and she'd never been careful about creating a backup. With the forgetfulness around the tablet at work, she'd taken to using only her cell phone for site notes and photos for office projects. No phone, no material for the reports she was to write. Why hadn't she downloaded the photos before the trip? No material, nothing to show. Nothing to show would mean only one thing at her upcoming six-month review at Polson Grohman Architects and Engineers: termination. And termination? With her student loans and the prospect of losing Mark's half of the rent? She'd be back with her parents in Scranton. And as much as she loved them, and knew they'd take her—if only temporarily—it was not what she wanted. She'd moved to New York City to make a go of it, and she had opportunities, so many bright paths opening, and a future she'd dreamt of for years, ever since she'd finished architecture school in Canada. By hell or high water, she was getting that cell phone.

The Oldsmobile Alero was untouched. No one around. Thank god she still had the car keys in her pocket. Her bag, with her wallet, remained where she'd left it on the front seat. She trusted the metal box was still in the back. No reason to doubt it was so. The car seemed fine. No sign of other vehicles coming or going.

She spun the car on the gravel road, and hightailed it back in the direction of Bath, not wanting to go all the way, but needing to be out of the zone of suspicion. She'd go just far enough to think through her next move.

The old Meetinghouse came up fast. Didn't want to stop there but it had people outside, and a sign out front that caught her eye. Not a Meetinghouse. It had been turned into a restaurant. And she hadn't eaten since the day before. Coffee would be welcome, too. Hadn't even paused at the hotel for caffeine before dashing away from the sleeping Mildred.

Everyone was very dressed up at the restaurant and gathered outside. Maybe it was in fact still a church. She patted down her jeans and jacket, wet and muddy still from the encounter at Mildred's old house.

"Amalia!" It was Mother of the Bride. Oh, god. She'd just walked into Kaitlin and Grisham's wedding.

Amalia waved back and walked back around the car. "Just stopped to check something rattling!" It was a lie, but it would do. She did not need or want a wedding interaction. Wanted the damn phone.

"Need some help? I'm sure one of the boys could help you." The MOB swatted at the air toward the groomsmen, all in tuxes and tails. A fancier affair than she might have expected from what she'd seen of the area, but plenty like the Pinterest and magazine weddings she'd once admired. No longer. "That ship has sailed, no worries!" Amalia banged on the trunk. "All good here." Hopped into the front seat and peeled out the driveway, down the road. Turned so fast, she left a streak visible behind her in the rearview mirror. The load on the back seat had shifted, too, and she heard the metal box bang to one side of the Alero. "Dammit." She looked up ahead on the road, and not recognizing where she was, decided to home in on her instincts to find her way back to Bath.

Five Islands Road. It was familiar to her from before, and she didn't need to stop to adjust for the map app's chirpy directions. She followed an old dump truck, its back flap flipping. Empty. As she felt. The truck turned right on Arrowsic Road. She followed the truck down the road, over a low, concrete bridge that afforded a long view down waterways in both directions. Dropped down the gear of the old stick shift, feeling the clutch beneath her foot. Shifting gears had come with ease, with practice, on the journey. She hadn't forgotten how. Like riding a bike.

She wondered if the river froze; was it ocean, salt, and freshwater mixed? If it ever froze, it wasn't that day. Spring was well underway in this part of Maine. Mildred had assured her that the bugs would be out in a flash, but they hadn't shown up yet. Shoulder season, the MOB had said. Amalia's shoulder twinged at the recollection, and she rubbed it, recalling her fall while climbing the previous autumn. "Dammit," she said for what must have been the millionth time that morning. Didn't want her thoughts to go there but didn't seem to have control over which way they went. She needed to shift. Needed something to break the rhythm. Didn't want to start thinking about what might have been, with Mark. "Dammit, Mark!" He was back in her thoughts. She changed gears again, letting the dump truck go its own way ahead on the road. She continued down along the two-lane concrete bridge. Drove at half the speed limit for some time, no cars behind her to urge her on. After a time, looking out at the sparse trees, a body of water opened on the right, and she pulled off into a little gravel parking lot, turning into the direction of the sun, well into the beginning of its day's march across the sky.

The bare trees above her left a striated pattern across the front windshield and dashboard. She squinted to look out over the water. A lone cloud, pretty and puffy, sauntered across the April sky. Amalia turned off the engine and got out, stood overlooking the pond's edge. She inhaled. Exhaled. Inhaled. "I'm alone." For the first time in a long time, alone in every sense: no human, no dog, and goddammit, no cell phone. She kicked the gravel beneath her feet and traipsed through the dead grasses from the previous fall to the pond's edge. Some sun-bleached tree branches lay at an angle to the rocky beach, as if left by a wind that had created a wave across the pond. The water was still, reflecting the blueness of sky, and capturing the pretty, puffy white cloud in the surface. She breathed in. And out. Breathed it in again. Out again. In and out, and again. Needed to not panic. Not about the phone, or the box, or the drive back with a mentally wandering Mildred. Not about the apartment, or the architecture exam preparations she needed to see through. No need to panic. No need. Just needed to breathe. She felt a shimmer down the sides of her arms, as if her body was saying, "It's okay, let it go," and she shook her arms out toward the water's surface, flicking her wrists and fingers as she did. Hoped no one was watching from behind. Didn't turn around to see. It felt better to be as she was, facing the water, beneath the sky, planted between the branches and standing on solid ground. Heard a truck pull in over the gravel. For that, she turned. It was the white pickup truck. And Frankie got out the passenger-side door.

The driver, faceless to Amalia, stayed put. Frankie hadn't noticed her yet and had not seemed to put it together that Mildred's car was parked next to the truck. A cell phone rang in his hand.

Amalia hid behind a cluster of scrubby trees, aware she needed to keep her footing below. He didn't answer the phone, just looked at it as it rang.

He knocked on the passenger side window and yelled, "It says it's someone called Mark calling. Should I answer it?" The faceless driver appeared to indicate yes, thumbs up, and Amalia leapt forward in that moment from behind the trees. It had to be hers. It had to be her Mark.

"Frankie! How are you! Isn't it a great day for a walk? So beautiful!" Amalia ran up to him and hugged him. The phone fell to the ground, and she kicked it away.

Frankie stood, arms dropping, uncertain of how to respond. "I found a phone," he said, nodding to it as she hugged him tighter.

"Don't you worry about that, Frankie. I'll take care of it." She held on tight to the side of his flannel jacket with one hand and bobbed down to reach the phone. Didn't want to let him go but had to let her hand slide down his jacket so she could touch the ground. "Got it!"

He pulled her up to her feet just as she pocketed the phone. "I'll find the owner. You don't worry about a thing, Frankie. I've got this." To prove her point, she kissed him on the cheek.

"Miss Amalia," he said. looking into her eyes. "I thought you were a witch, but now I think I love and appreciate you." He hugged her, and if Amalia could have, she would have hugged back—she was no idiot, though, and she pulled away.

"Thank you, Frankie!" She backed away to Mildred's car and beat a fast path down the road back to the hotel. What they hell was all that about? She wasn't a witch. And if she was, who would care anyway? That'd be her business. Not Frankie's! She had the phone. She had the box. She had the Alero. Now all she needed was Mildred. Didn't need to know what was happening at the old house. Didn't need to see the old foundations. And as much as she liked to think that she and Whiskie had become friends, she had to admit they were temporary companions on the road of life.

Only thing left was, what was in that box? She'd have to drive far to lose Frankie and his buddy, and there was no way of knowing which way they'd go. She could think of only one place they might avoid on purpose: a fancy wedding. Could not go back there looking as she looked. Hadn't brought anything wedding worthy, and her luggage was at the hotel, so even if she had an outfit, she'd have to go back and risk running into Mildred to get it. Mildred would want to know what she was doing, would want to come, and she'd have no opportunity to see what was inside the box. She could show Mildred. But deep inside, a feeling told her that it was for her eyes alone, at least for the first opening.

She could find a place to get a dress. Unlikely. Or she could go back, make an excuse about the car, and ask for help. More plausible. How would she find time and separation to look inside the box? If she wanted to open it, she'd have to try.

The road back to the Robinhood Meetinghouse was easy to find. Arrowsic back to Five Islands and turn. There she was. Had to have been all of five minutes' drive, but it was long enough to give her time to formulate a plan.

She pulled up next to the guests' cars. Everyone appeared to have moved inside the building. She went around the back, to the service entrance. The door was open a crack, even with the cold air. She saw a server pick up a flower arrangement and leave to go back into the main hall. Music floated out; live violin, sounded like. Nice. Classy. She and Mark never had anything like that. But then, it hadn't been a real marriage.

She'd take a chance. Went back to the car, opened the side door, and brought out the metal box, which had lodged itself into a corner of the floor.

It was a dull metal, with a dirt-encrusted engraving on the top. Pitted. It did not have any hinge that she could see, but it was closed. It looked like it had been sealed with wax around the edges of the box lid. Amalia closed the car's trunk with a quiet click and walked with deliberateness back to the step behind the Meetinghouse. Peeked inside. No one there. She sat back down on the step with the box. Perched it on her knees. Took a deep breath.

It was the first time she'd looked at it up close and without interruption. Couldn't tell how old it was. Just old. Dented and pitted, dirty and even a little sticky. The seal around the perimeter of the lid was interesting. Waxy. Didn't want to break the seal, but so wanted to know what was inside. The music was revving up inside, the violins reaching high notes that suggested they wanted to signal the guests to gather for the ceremony. There would not be much time before people began to emerge. Good thing was, no way would Frankie or his friend come near. She'd be able to make something up if the guests saw her and asked. With Frankie, not so much. And she'd kissed him on the cheek, which must have given him the wrong idea altogether. Bought her time, did that kiss. She took another deep breath.

Time must have been looking upon the box with grace because it had lasted well; the surface was marred, but the box was intact. The wax suggested that someone had intended it to stay waterproof underground where she'd found it. Where Whiskie had found it. Amalia closed her eyes and felt its edges. It had a weight to it, and when she tilted it between her two hands, something shifted inside. Like something padded. She looked at the seal. It was very consistent around the edge. If she had something sharp, she could make a long cut along the wax. Maybe even seal it up again. Amalia looked back into the kitchen. No one had returned. She put the box on the step, hopped up, ducked into the kitchen, and grabbed a large knife from the gadgets on the wall. For good measure, she also took one of the candles ready for the wedding dinner tables, and a box of wooden matches next to them that read Kaitlin & Grisham.

Back outside, she worked fast to make a long, swift cut along one side of the wax seal, then another, and another, and another. Flakes of wax and dirt fell on her lap where she worked, deep breaths rhythmic. "Keep it going. Keep the pressure." The lid was free. She put the knife down, and with care, lifted the lid from its base.

She stopped before it was all the way off. What if what was in there didn't want to be found? What if by opening it, she unleashed a torrent of responsibility for what was inside? Who had put it there, and why? Amalia took a deep breath. If she was going to do it, she'd have to do it then, and fast, or not at all. She'd begun to feel dizzy. Looked up at the trees that ringed the back of the Meetinghouse. Felt a familiar rush of energy, a connection to the broader flow of creative energy that had formed whatever was in the box. She thought for a moment she'd tip over where she sat, so great was the force of the rush. "Stabilize, Amalia," she whispered. What would Mildred say?

"Get the hell off this step, girlfriend!" Mother of the Bride stood over her, looking down from the kitchen side. "Get yourself in here, the wedding ceremony's about to begin!"

~ 43 ~

Swimming Pool

Mildred walked into the pool room at the hotel, not needing to sneak since it was open, yet aware of the 'No Lifeguard' sign and still water. Not having a lifeguard made her feel a little dangerous. She set her towel on a poolside deck chair, slipped off her running shoes, and climbed into the warmth in her long sleep shirt and lady underwear, white hair pulled back tight from her face, so her cheeks felt taut to the surface of the water. It felt exciting—how easily she was pleased! Stepping into the humid, chlorinated pool zone was shocking, and she felt her pores open to the relative moisture.

She had clues to assemble and track. A quick dip—Amalia would not mind, because Amalia would not know—it would help to open Mildred's mind to the possibility of connecting clues. She believed it. Amalia would not understand. Amalia had gone for a drive and a walk, or so said the note left at the front desk, and since she wouldn't be back anytime soon, Mildred had time to immerse herself in all of it. Frankie was with Amalia, too, or so it seemed, since he was nowhere Mildred had looked in the hotel. This was time for Mildred. Mildred in the pool.

~ 44 ~

For Good Measure

How to get out of the impromptu wedding invitation with grace?

"I got my period," she whispered to Mother of the Bride.

At Kaitlin and Grisham's wedding for a few minutes, back soon!

Amalia hoped Mildred would get the message and would not ask too many questions upon her return. Amalia had time to see what there was to see. And she realized it was the perfect opportunity to go back to the foundations where she'd discovered the box. Everyone who was anyone was at the wedding. She could go straight from the old Moorehouse past the shed and out to the foundations without having to risk passing Frankie and his friend if they were back and forth on the road.

And that was it. She was off, unsealed box in hand, and a wedding candle and matches along with it. For good measure, she brought the knife.

She fell into the driver's side as much as she put herself in the seat, ripples of jumpy butterflies pulsing from her core, up and down, and pulled the seatbelt around her. All the objects sat next to her on the passenger seat of the Alero. She gave the box a little pat on top. "We'll find you out," she said. "Whatever there is to find, we'll find it." For good measure, she put a seatbelt on the passenger side too, but it didn't even touch the box. She tucked in the candle, still in its candlestick holder, behind the seatbelt, and giggled to the windshield, to the trees, to the sky beyond. "We're doing it," she said to the box. "Let's find out what we can."

The road back to the Moorehouse was easy to find, having traveled it so many times over the past couple of days with and without Mildred in the car. No vehicles were parked in the driveway and the lights were off in the house. She assumed the reception would be held at the Meetinghouse. No sign of Whiskie. She felt—safe about her approach. Safe to leave the Alero there. She could always say she forgot something after their stay, and had returned, and not finding anyone home had decided to go for a walk. They knew she'd enjoyed the woods. That was enough.

Should she take the box? "Take you or leave you?" She unbuckled the candlestick. "Take you." On her few steps from the driver's side to the passenger side, she said a small wish to the sky, "Please guide me. Guide me." She smiled. The guidance was already there. She could feel it. And it emanated from the box.

In the woods, fast on her feet to find the old foundations, she saw the trees light up around her with sunbeams, strong in mid-morning. Dawn's misty rise from the frozen ground had evaporated in the sun. The shimmer in the woods intrigued her. "Come on," she said to no one. "Why am I here?"

"Why indeed," she heard the woods whisper back. "Why are any of us here?"

"Why did I find this, and what is it?" She soon found herself at the stone foundations, her board-ramp still in place. "Don't trust that ramp," she said to the box. There it was, just as she'd left it. Didn't want to invite Whiskie to travel down it alone, only to get stuck.

What if no one was near to find her if she fell? She perched the things she'd brought on the edge of the low remnants of the old stone foundation from where it rose to meet her shins. Lifted the board-ramp up and out, and a little salamander, new to the season and curled up underneath the top of the board, scampered out. "You're awake early," she said. "Did you have a good hibernation? Didn't see you before." The image of the little creature riveted her. Had she come just to see a salamander in spring? No. she had a bigger purpose. "Little box, what have you inside?"

She took a deep breath. Picked up the knife.

Picked up the candle and the matches.

Put down the matches. Put down the knife. Held the candle and brought the box to eye level.

Looked up to see the mist dance around her where she stood, cresting at the top of the trees as if dancing. A dancing wave of mist.

She was ready.

~ 45 ~

The Father

Mildred pulled herself up the pool's ladder to the slippery edge of the pool deck. Didn't want to lose her balance there. The swim had been a good chance to clear her mind. Why had she come? For some distant recollection of a whaling hook, blood on the beach, hooch in the woods?

And what of her encounter with Frankie, that had left her more clear in her mind than she had felt in a long time, not of what she wanted more of, but less? Even her vision felt better. Was it the drugs, or was it the feeling that she no longer needed them?

"Doesn't matter," she said to the pool room wall, tiled, white and shiny.

What she knew was that she'd seen her old home. The laundering image had come back with such vividness in her mind. Mama had been laundering and it had something to do with hooch. She had no recollection of drugs at the house, but why would she? Had they grown opium poppies? Mama always tended a nice garden. She could go back to that house and see if there were any remnants of poppy gardens. Would they have lasted, so many years later? And if Frankie had been truthful and clear when he spoke the day before of sourcing drugs from Maine, did that have anything to do with her own family's home?

She didn't want to get involved with illegal drugs—and Frankie seemed to be up to his elbows in them.

Wondered if Father Jasper knew about the illegal stuff. He was blind to Frankie's wayward tendencies. A good man, but so focused on his flock's brightness that he could not see when members of the flock diverged from a well path.

Mildred realized she'd been standing, dripping in her sleep shirt and lady undies, staring at the white tile wall. A family, led by a toddler, pushed open the pool room door. They babbled with happy family noises. Mildred waved, grabbed her towel, shoved her wet feet into her running shoes, and tied the towel around her waist. "All yours," she said. "I have a mission!"

~ 46 ~
Mists

Amalia lifted the lid. Put it on the stone next to her. The mists around her continued to shimmer and shift. Color revealed itself inside. Faded, stitched color. She lifted the little bundle from the box. It was a folded, wrapped quilt, with hand stitching. Could have been part of a quilt. Reminded her of the quilts she'd seen in her mother's collection: fragments, remnants, pinned patches, weavings of memory and soldiering on. The quilt held something inside.

She unwrapped it.

Looked up at the top treetops. "Is this okay, am I okay." It was not a question.

"You're okay," she heard. She squinted at the trees, feeling their presence closer.

A hum of wind, or a vehicle, couldn't tell which, permeated her little bubble. If it was a vehicle, she'd have to be quick.

She pulled with care at each corner of the quilt and turned it over to reveal what was inside.

All she found was a darkened, heavy, melon-sized half-shell shape, with some holes. It might have once had more on it or in it. The coloration of it varied around the surface and it was pitted, just as the metal box had been.

She took a deep breath.

"You're old." Much older than the quilt. She used the fabric of the quilt as a glove to her hands as she turned the melon-shape over, resting its rounded side face down on the inside of the quilt fabric.

The quilt fabric was interesting.

But what was on the back of the melon-shape was even more interesting. Her abdomen warmed with a glow of excitement.

It appeared that there were bones tied to the back of it, laces tied around the front. The odd thing was the laces did not look nearly as old as the melon-shaped thing.

She exhaled. It struck her as voodoo-like. What did she know of such things? Not much. And what was voodoo anyway? She didn't really mean voodoo; it was just the first word she could reach for that she felt had any semblance of connection to what she saw. Animist. It had spirit. It was connected. Someone—many people—had taken the time to imbue it with their thoughts and prayers and wishes.

She looked up again, and the mist had shifted back, up, and farther away, beyond the tops of the trees. She was with someone. It popped into her head as fleetingly as a flash of lightning, then disappeared.

"Grandfather, if you are near, please give me a sign that this is good. That this is a well thing. That I'm right to be here, and doing this, right now." The hum in the background had dissipated, too. Whoever or whatever was near had moved away.

It was just her in the wood with the box, the candle, and the knife.

She wrapped the melon-shape back into the quilt, replicating the folds and allowing the melon-shape to find its comfortable home back in the bundle. She put the quilt bundle back into the box. Put the lid on. Lit the candle.

Held the candle below the knife's blade to heat the surface of the metal, the dropped candle wax on top of it. Spread the wax all around the edge of the opening between box and lid.

Looked up, and Whiskie stood before her, head cocked to the side. He did not approach. "Dammit, Whiskie!" She dropped the knife, heart racing. In her focus on the small task of sealing the box lid, she'd closed her senses off to all that flowed around her. Her palms seemed to spring a leak, sweating, her brow sweating, despite the chill. "You shouldn't sneak up on people like that!" The knife, still hot and sticky, had collected all the debris of the forest floor. "Goddammit."

She threw the candle, the matches, and the knife into the pit of the old house foundation. Stood up, box in hand. "Let's go, Whiskie."

Wasn't sure what she'd tapped into. Didn't want to go a step further without the person she had come to trust, in a short space of time, with these matters of the invisible: invisible heart, invisible soul. A curling wave of sympathetic, compassionate love rose from her core as she stood back. It felt both unusual and inviting at the same time, and it unnerved her. If she squinted her eyes, she could almost see the energy around her dance.

She'd get Mildred, and she'd bring her back.
It wasn't just an inanimate object.
She'd felt it pulse.

Back at the car, Whiskie trailing, she decided. She'd tell Mildred she had left something at the house, something forgotten, and had to return. Something so vital that she could not live without it, could not go back to Binghamton or New York City without it. Her cell phone. Of course, she'd have to leave her cell phone behind to make it legit. She texted Mildred.

Coming back in a bit after I go for a short walk. Can you be ready to go in about a half hour?

Yes, came the reply, faster than expected. Mildred had her own current going. "Where should I put you?" Went for the trunk, opened it, then remembered that they'd be stashing their luggage. Back seat. Too visible. With the back door of Mildred's car open, she assessed the least visible option: underneath the passenger-side seat, accessed from the back. Mildred would not look there. And Amalia could put her own tote bag in front of it.

Windows ajar to the warming sky, Amalia hummed to keep her focus on the road and not on her new passenger.

~ 47 ~

Thoughts

"Tapping into old thought forms," said Mildred. "There's nothing scary going on here. You're picking up on what people may have thought, once upon a time." She held the box in her hands. Amalia sat in the driver's seat next to her. Fear had overtaken Amalia's better judgment and she'd pulled over before they had even reached the Moorehouse for her supposedly lost cell phone. Mildred's calm voice soothed her, and even in the car, seatbelt on, pulled over to the side of the wooded road, she felt her shoulders shift down. "Amalia, you get to choose. You get to choose what to look at. You get to choose which thoughts to focus on." Mildred held a remarkable calm about her, eyes bright.

"I could say the same for you. Why are you so obsessed with Frankie and his drug involved world? What's up with that?" She'd felt the object pulse. Couldn't tell Mildred until Mildred knew what was inside.

"Frankie is a good but wayward soul."

"You're awfully light on his drug involvement, Mildred." Amalia could not help the tone she knew must sound condescending.

"I thought you supported medical marijuana use."

"I don't think that's his use. And I don't think it's all marijuana."

"So what? Who are we to judge?" Mildred lifted the box into the air, gave it a little shake, and looked at Amalia. "There's something in here."

"I saw."

"You saw—what's inside?"

Amalia nodded. "I opened it. Back there. Where I found it. After. It's where I wanted to take you. Before we go. And my phone. I know where my phone is. It's underneath your seat.

And none of them are at the Moorehouse, they're all out at the wedding, I saw them. I talked to them."

"Amalia, my dear, you are making no sense. Are you saying you want to go to the Moorehouse or that we need to open this box?

"Neither. Both? I do need my cell phone," she said, leaning back to reach it.

"Let's open this box." Mildred peered at the neat seal Amalia had made around the edge.

"I did that. To protect it." Amalia reached into her pocket. We can try this. She handed Mildred the stylus.

"That does the trick," Mildred, said, pressing into the new wax seal. The stylus brought it out like a curling ribbon. She lifted the lid and put it on the dash in front of her. "My." She sat with both hands on the quilted bundle. Closed her eyes. "Have not seen this since I was a girl." She had a faint smile on her face.

"You've—seen this before?"

"This is it. This is what I've been trying to remember. What I was looking for. Why I came. Didn't remember what it was I was seeking." She opened her eyes. "Still inside, I am guessing. Gave you a fright like it did me, no doubt, when I was a child." It all came back in a rush. "Where did you find it? I looked in the shed, thought it was there."

"I put it in the shed for a bit, but I found it in the old stone foundations between the Moore's and your old house."

"Moorehouse, Poorhouse, Roughhouse, Rum."

"And so the foundations where I found the box, that was the Roughhouse?"

"They could all be one and the same as the rhyme. Or not at all. It was so long ago. How can I be sure of my memory?"

"Your memory got us this far, Mildred. Don't doubt yourself."

Mildred nodded again. "You've done a good thing, Amalia, but the box needs to go home. It needs to go back in the ground."

"I did a bad thing." Amalia leaned back into the driver's seat headrest. "I should have left it buried." She hadn't told Mildred of the strange waves of emotion and energy that had come with her discovery.

"You said Whiskie found it."

"I think so." If she accepted that Whiskie found it, then she could accept that the emotion and energy around it were valid. She wasn't sure why, but it felt to be true.

"If Whiskie found it, we should trust him. He's a tracking dog. Finds what needs to be found." Mildred nodded. "It will stay with us."

Mildred was a mind reader. "I could take it back to New York with me. Take it to the Met Museum. Get it evaluated." Amalia felt a little relieved at the thought.

"No way in hell," Mildred said. She put the lid back on. "This is coming back to Binghamton with me.

"I thought you said it needed to go back in the ground."

"But Whiskie was the finder, you said yourself. I'm rethinking." Mildred removed the lid again and lifted the quilted bundle from the box. "Oh, my!"

The salamander lay curled at the bottom. Peeped its head up. Mildred opened the car door, unbuckled herself, and took the box, the salamander, and herself out to the edge of the woods. Her back to Amalia, Mildred muttered some words and returned to the car. "All sorted," she said. "The little guy has a little pulse."

"You're not afraid of anything, are you?" Amalia's heart pounded and her belly glowed, all at once, and it was more than she thought any one body should have to experience at the same time. She giggled, the bubbles of laughter releasing her fears.

"You find the fun and the fun finds you," said Mildred. "It's not about what you're afraid of or not."

The giggles subsided. "That's what you call fun, what you and Frankie did yesterday?"

"No. I guess I'm speaking ironically in that case. Generally, yes."

"But not yesterday."

"Yesterday was valuable in so many ways. For example, it showed me what I don't want."

"Which is?"

"The edginess of the uncontrolled aspects of the drug trade. Who knows what Frankie had up his sleeve?"

"Mildred, there's something you should know."

"About this box. I know."

"How could you?"

"You don't have to say it out loud. It's enough to refocus, sometimes. Might not be fun, but if you know which direction you want to go, it helps. And so, about this thing. That you think I should know."

"Do you?"

"It's about Frankie. You think we have a funny connection."

"True. That's not it, but it's true."

"He's not my kin, if that's what you're thinking." Mildred closed her eyes.

"Who is he to you?"

Mildred looked out through the windshield. "He's my supplier. Of medical marijuana."

"I know, I already knew."

"It's for my eyes. Glaucoma. I have a prescription but it's easier to get from him. And it gives him a bit of cash, so why not?"

"He's one of your congregation members."

"He is now. Father Jasper brought him to me. Frankie was working for Penguin Books at the warehouse on the edge of Binghamton. Until recently."

The Alero pointed in the direction of the Moorehouse, yet Amalia didn't feel the pull to return. Her cell phone, though—

Amalia saw down the long Maine road toward the turnoff for the Meetinghouse, and the Moorehouse beyond. Mildred was right. There was no need to be fearful of an old object, of the woods, of a little salamander with a pulse, or of anything else.

"I didn't lose my cell under your seat. I left it there, but I was going to tell you it was at the Meetinghouse, so we'd have to go back."

Mildred frowned at the glove compartment as if it had something inside she could not see but wanted to reach.

"Because I want to show you something. Back there, that I found."

"Something where this was found."

"Yes. I found some things in the attic." Amalia cringed. "I don't want to you to think I've been snooping." She handed the aged paper to Mildred.

"You have." Mildred unfolded the scrap. "This might match up with what I have been trying to piece together."

"Okay, I have been snooping, but maybe it is good." Amalia took in a deep breath. It felt better to get it off her chest. "I want to show you where I found this." She nodded to the box, still in Mildred's lap. "I don't know why or how, but I think it connects to your old house, and something to do with Frankie and the drugs."

"Maybe. Maybe not."

"Do you want to see?"

"We've come this far. And it's why we've come, isn't it?' They drove toward the Moorehouse, past the Meetinghouse.

The gravel driveway at the Moore's was devoid of cars. "They're still at the wedding." Amalia parked at the edge of the lot. "In case they come back, I'll leave room."

She led Mildred, no sign of Whiskie, to the back of the house, past the shed, into the woods, following the thin rutted trail that she and Whiskie had traveled over the past days. It was just discernible to her: hollow reeds of early spring, crushed down by her boots, by Whiskie's paws. She knew where to go. Ten minutes, no more, and she and Mildred were back at the old foundations.

"It's three times you've been here, now," Mildred said.

"You're right. I have a theory of threes, you know."

"That good things come in threes? I hope so!"

"It's more like, that significant things happen in threes."

"If I might offer a different vantage on that," Mildred said, "I think it is more a matter of your expectation. When you expect something, the experience tends to show up, matching your expectations. So, if you expect significant experiences to happen in threes, you get more of them until—"

"I hit three and then nothing more happens? Clearly, I need to expand my expectations!"

"Amalia, my dear, you said it, not me!"

"This is where the salamander was," she said. "On the stone ledge. I fell in there."

"In there, how did you ever get out? And why is there a butcher knife in there? Amalia, this looks like a scene from a horror movie!"

"Not at all. I grabbed that lot from the wedding place kitchen this morning to open the wax seal on the box."

"Don't you think we'd better retrieve it?"

"I barely got out of there once I fell in. Do you really want to pull me out?"

"That would be an unequivocal No."

"I found the box in there. Or Whiskie found it."

"The dog revealed it, you said."

"Yes."

"And I think he led me to see that Frankie's been getting his supply from your old house, too."

"Frankie—and my old house? But there was no one there."

"Not when you saw it. I saw a whole operation going on. Could not tell exactly what, but I've investigated down the Jersey Shore and found a similar grow-op house for marijuana there. Got right into it. Looked the same. Basement operation, generator going, lights going, grow lights I mean. And the foot traffic, and car traffic—very similar. If I could get inside, I could probably identify some of the modifications they'd made to the house, too."

"Don't need to." Mildred peered. "The dog led you to this, and the dog led you to that?"

"Yes, does that mean anything to you?'

"I'd first trust a dog before I'd trust a human, I can tell you that. Especially one who was trained to lead and track and source, just like Whiskie."

"You think this dog, who isn't even here, but honestly could show up anytime, led us to these places because—because why?"

"That, I do not know. I might never know. But I can sense there are connections that go deeper than my conscious awareness, and that I trust will work themselves out."

"Connections, yes. First off—what about Frankie?"

"Frankie. He is Father Jasper's nephew. Sort of."

"And Father Jasper got him into pot."

"And Frankie has bills to pay."

"And needed to find other sources for his dealing."

"Which led him here."

"But why your house? Are you sure you're not related to him?"

"I am fairly sure, yes."

"Are you related to Father Jasper?"

Mildred looked pinched in the lips.

"Mildred?"

"He's my son." Her curls shook a little as she let out a breath.

"Why didn't you say so?"

"No one knows."

"What? Father Jasper—how can he not know?"

"He thinks he's my father's son—my younger brother. But only I know he's my son, no one else knows it."

"If Frankie is his nephew, then—who is Frankie?"

Mildred looked pained around the eyes. "He's my grandson."

"Frankie is your—your grandson? Whyever didn't you say so?"

"I only just found out. Jasper told me today that Frankie is his son. He told me on the phone. He wants to help Frankie get out of this pot mess. What a potty mess!"

"If Jasper doesn't know he's your son, then by extension, he doesn't know that Frankie is your grandson."

"No one knows. Not entirely true. My sister Muriel knows some. My parents knew some. Jasper is the son of a boy I met a long time ago. We had not yet moved to Salt Spring Island—in BC, you know it, you're from BC, too. Frankie is Jasper's son. My grandson. But Jasper doesn't know this. He knows Frankie is his son, though. But Frankie doesn't know."

"Go on." There would be time for explanations. Amalia wanted Mildred to stay focused.

"It was when we lived in New Jersey. I was just a girl. Fourteen."

"When did Jasper have Frankie, then? And how did they end up in Maine? You'd moved away? Wait—if Frankie doesn't know he's your grandson, then how come he is at your old house?"

"My father arranged it. We left the house with aunts and uncles when we moved away—when Papa went to sell kit houses. When he gave up the hooch business."

"And so, when you had the baby, he grew up here? In Maine? And then he inherited the house?"

"Yes."

"And then—"

"He raised Frankie, as his nephew."

"Not his sort-of-nephew, like you said. But his son."

"More or less. I guess that is how you would describe it." Mildred looked both relieved and pained.

The wind was picking up around them, clouds gathering over the treetops; rain would be on the way. Amalia felt a new pressure of time. "And he let Frankie live in the house."

"Father Jasper had sworn an oath to never have sex. Or children."

Amalia felt a raindrop. "If Father Jasper is your son, and if Frankie is your grandson—and neither of them know who you are to them—Mildred, this must have been decades of pain for you in keeping these secrets. Don't you want to tell someone? Other than me?"

Mildred nodded. While nodding, she said, "It's too late. I need to tell no one."

"But Frankie seems to think you're doing something bad, or that I am. This pot business, it could even shut you down, couldn't it? I can't tell you what to do, Mildred, but it seems to me, everyone would be better off if they knew a little more of the truth."

Mildred exhaled, hard. "Father Jasper first, then. But Amalia, what if he doesn't believe me?"

"So what?"

"Then what?"

"Do you need some proof? Do you have any?"

"Just stories. And DNA. We could do DNA tests." Rain fell in large, heavy drops through the tree branches above, scattered in where they fell, buffeted by the evergreen boughs that strung across the foundations above. "We need to go. They might be coming back soon, and they'll see the car. Is there anything else to do here?"

"I don't think so. Except deal with that." Amalia pointed to the knife, the candlestick, and the matches.

'Why a is there a candle in there, too?"

Amalia shook her head. "I'll get some branches to throw down. It'll be a mystery for the next person."

While she collected branches, Mildred said, "I don't want to go to the old house. My old house. I'm done with that. And I'll tell Frankie."

"Father Jasper first?"

Mildred nodded. "Yes. It is time."

The trip to Father Jasper's was easy. A long drive with a stop at a café first, and then they were in Burlington, Vermont. Amalia waited outside while Mildred did the deed of confronting the past. Amalia thought of her own family, and what it meant for Mildred, at age fourteen, to become a mother. Felt glad she had time to find her own path to motherhood, felt even a little glad for the miscarriage she might have had, and then, a little guilty. Timing and guilt. Guilt and timing. There was a relationship there she couldn't put a finger on. Seemed to her that feeling good or bad because of the timing of a thing that did or didn't happen was a huge waste of emotional energy. Knowing it didn't make the knot in her abdomen loosen any. Thinking she knew something—wanting to know it—and feeling it rooted in her body's knowing were very different things.

"It's done," Mildred said when she came back. "He knew. At least, he suspected. I've never said anything. And he had these—" she handed Amalia a folder, then pulled it back. "No, I need to see them first." The papers were assembled in an old-style accordion folder with a fabric ribbon. From the edges, Amalia could see what looked like ratty carbon copies and even some photographs. Mildred's eyes were red. "It was good. I am good. Let's go home."

"I think your mystery is solved."

"And yours? Have you decided about you and Mark?"

"I know I don't belong with Mark anymore. And that's okay. I'll figure out the rest in time. I am free to move in any direction, and it feels good." Amalia noticed a loosening in her midsection. "Good and right and timely."

"As my nieces say, Amalia, you've got this!"

Amalia reached to start the Alero, pressed the clutch as she turned the engine. It let out a sputter, and then—the engine made a grating sound, the clutch let out a thud beneath her foot—and the car fell silent. "Shit! Definitely don't got this."

"Out of gas?" Mildred looked over her shoulder toward Father Jasper's house. "He's still on the porch."

"Something different. That wasn't an out-of-gas sound. Maybe out of oil. Transmission fluid?"

"I have no idea," Mildred said. She unbuckled and put the folder on the passenger side floor in front of her atop the quilt box, balanced. "Got to catch him before he goes looking for Frankie."

~ 48 ~

Cars

Strange dreams followed Amalia through a restless night. The unfamiliar light of Father Jasper's kitchen clock, broadcasting into the room from the stove's control panel, reminded her of how many times she'd awoken. The Vermont stillness enveloped her in the room. Might have been the solidity of the old stone walls; whatever it was, the weave of dreams, blinking light, and stone stillness kept her suspended in a feeling of partial rest—of floating through—and of alertness. She was more than alert. She was intrigued.

Father had proven to be a steady character, much as Mildred had described him on the drive from Georgetown to Burlington. "It's on the way," she'd said, but it had taken them far out of their way and would add time to the journey. After all that had been seen, done, and shared, agreeing to the drive seemed the least Amalia could do. In many ways, it was the reason for the trip, although neither of them had known it going in. "We're not showing him the quilt box, though. That's just for us. Until we figure it out," Mildred had said.

Fine. Amalia was more concerned with getting Mildred home in one piece. Frankie was missing in action, but Father Jasper wasn't worried; the boy—grown man—had his own movements and responsibilities. If the Father wasn't concerned, why should the rest of them be? Frankie was his own person. An adult male! It could all be a ruse. She felt trusting of Mildred, though, as the secrets that spilled in the presence of the quilt box had seemed anything but rueful. A few decades late, maybe, but not spoken with any measure of distaste or disharmony. Amalia had felt Mildred to be true and felt it right down to the center of her gut. And that was as good enough a truth barometer as any. If the quilt box had any power at all, it was acting like a truth serum.

They took the Alero, fixed up by a local shop in Vermont the next morning while they waited, to New York. At Mildred's home in Binghamton, Amalia gave Mildred the box.

"I will put this special box next to Raymond's urn," Mildred said, patting the box lid where it came to stand on the mantel of the old fireplace.

"Raymond's ashes?"

"Raymond's once-upon-a-time ashes. I buried them at the church. But I can't get rid of the urn, can I now?"

It was a simple transaction punctuated by a very long hug. Once Amalia settled into her little red rental car, alone, she let out a whoop, opened the windows, and peeled out for New York City. Adventure delivered.

The drive back to Manhattan was simple, and she had a swinging-to-music feeling that stayed with her long after she returned the rental car and walked back home, the thirty blocks giving her an opportunity to clear her head, say thank you to the sky, and ready herself for a very good sleep.

~ 49 ~
Diaries

The day after her return from Maine, Mildred opened her old diaries and read them aloud to the room. This seemed to be the only way to make sense of it all. As she finished reading each one, she got up to add them to a growing stack on mantle shelf next to Raymond's urn, which sat next to the box from the house foundations in Georgetown. "In good company," she said to the box.

"Greenham Common, July 15, 1987

Am in the UK for first time since Gran's funeral in 1956. Can't say I remember much of it from back then, but I do recall the boy who lived next door to her, that he watched everyone go in and out of the house the day of her service. I came out with a sandwich for him and gave him one and he kissed me on the cheek. Cheeky boy.

Anyhoo. Toodeloo. I'm here with a group of women from Kent, they have a tent camp set up. They think it mighty funny that I 'defected' from my walking tour to be with them, and they have taken me under their wing. Yesterday I wove banners into the fence around the compound. Today, I tried to get the mud from my sleeping bag, but it seems to be all around. It's a great sisterhood here, unlike any I have experienced back home. I almost feel married to these women who I've just met.

I borrowed a magic marker from Ingrid and wrote on a t-shirt for myself, trying to fit in a bit. It helped. Maybe I'll give it to my daughter one day if I ever have one.

Which reminds me. Today was supposed to be the adoption finalization of Romana. It's not like I forgot, I just have not wanted to look at it. To Romana, wherever you are, I hope you find a family who loves you as much as I have. Your almost-mommy loves you still.

I got the final papers from D before I left. I hadn't wanted to write it until now, but I feel like I can now, or ought to. All these women processing all this crap—it's the least I can do. So today I bid adieu to D, and to Romana, and give myself to Greenham.

In time, Baby Jasper, in time.

It is you I remember.

Clayoquot Sound, August 29, 1993

Bert had me hanging on a tree today and I swear I will chain myself to it tomorrow if they come for it with the trucks. He is so very—lovely. Love, love, lovely.

Mom died this morning. January 15, 1995. Funeral in Victoria nursing home. Will stay at her place on Salt Spring, I think. Will have to clear out the stuff. Ugh. No more to write at the moment.

January 20, 1995

Muriel and I discussed it and we are keeping mom's condo on Salt Spring. Muriel says she'll use it as a vacation place. I think I might move there for a bit, and Muriel can stay with me. I am so rootless anyway, it doesn't matter. May quit Bentall Centre job and see what turns up on the island. I have some saved.

March 1, 1995

Officially moved to Salt Spring today! Boss was OK with quitting, and even offered to have me come in one day a week to check on past-due accounts. Might take him up on it. Only a what—five hour—commute to Vancouver?

Downtown Eastside Missing Women's March 16, 2005
Went to the DERA march today, sad, but good to be with a sisterhood of candle-holding women, walking through the streets of the downtown east side. Raymond joined us after work, and we went for dim sum. Kind of an odd way to celebrate our anniversary, but good, too. I said we should go to the Ovaltine for pie after, but he had to get back home to work on tomorrow's case. Oh well. I'll get back there another time."

Mildred's mind wandered back in time. Boyfriends. Lovers. Husbands. Men.

Get current. Current. She smoothed the fabric of her skirt against her hips. The print was up to date, and she gave her hips a little wiggle before she went into the shop on the main street of Chatham, New Jersey.

They'd settled a while back, and she'd begun kindergarten through books mother taught from, at the kitchen table. The kitchen table was her stable-place: it moved with them, and it was always the same. She was eight now, and they'd been to Delaware and back, selling the house kits. A local kid caught her calling mama "Mama" and had laughed, called Mildred "Babycakes," and from then on Mama was "Mother."

She went into the shop on the main street and waited for Doug to come from the back. He'd come. He must have seen her. An awkward boy, but handsome, and if he knew she was dropping by for only him, and not to buy, he kept it to himself. Handsome. He popped his head out from the back and gave her a grin.

Mother would be out for some time. She poured that boy Doug a lemonade from the fridge, and he grinned. He didn't talk, just grinned. That day, every day. She wondered if he was slow.

No, he had a quick wit and a sharp mind, she'd seen it that day. He'd done a fast calculation of change to give her on a dollar, and she was impressed.

Dougie looked out back. The yards were all connected and there was Papa's wooden layout. The plan was spread out on the kitchen table where they sat with lemonade.

"He lays it in pieces, see."

"He builds it in his head?"

"And then he lays it out."

"That's not what a carpenter does, not for a whole house, Millie. Not if he's shipping it up in a box."

"It's what Papa does. He said he's remembering what his Pa didn't teach to him."

"If it's what he does, then why isn't he very good at it?"

"My Papa's good at it! Just look at it. He's got a sunrise window and everything." Mildred pointed to the small cutout above what would be the porch.

"My father says you have to have economy in these things. I don't see what my father would say is economical about this and that sunrise window. And laying out like that, when's he even going to get it boxed up?"

It was a good point. Papa had been working on the layout for too long. But when it was done, they would move on to the next town. He'd built two in and around Chatham so far, only one per year, and she didn't want this next one done. It meant too many more goodbyes. "He's getting faster. It's a new trade. For him. And he's got a destination: Salt Spring Island. He's going to be an international builder." She smiled and poured Dougie some more lemonade.

She lay with him in the grass behind the house, hidden from view of the neighbors, that summer when she was fourteen, before Mother and Papa took them to Salt Spring Island, and years after Papa had found a boom time in his house-building business in and around Chatham. That summer, when she was fourteen, she lay with Dougie. In New Jersey, she conceived a baby. Before Mother and Papa took them to Salt Spring Island, she'd had the baby, in quiet like, and given him to the aunties in Maine to raise as one of their own. A baby boy.

Mildred was young when they'd inherited the land on Salt Spring Island. Papa wanted the family to branch out and struck it lucky: Mother had inherited property in the Gulf Islands from a distant and long-deceased great uncle shortly after leaving Maine (she had been the only heir of Mr. Bimson from Kingston, Ontario, who tried and relinquished his hand at farming in British Columbia; "a failure," her Mother said). It was not until Mildred was fourteen, and baby had come and gone, that they finally moved west. The market was unknown, and the Second War overshadowed them. To think of it. All that loss. Her Mother had chosen to focus on All That Hope.

The far horizon drew nearer to her, or so it seemed, as the train pulled itself around the bend. She sat up front, knowing her world's possessions tugged behind them in the boxcar bought by Papa, all kitted out with the kit house and their own possessions stacked in there, too. Empty of the kits they left behind: one car held one house, and Papa restocked the parts when they built one, found a field to assemble it in bits, to be sure it was right. He wanted the new kits to be just righter than the last.

Go where Papa took them. Which now was Out West and Up North.

"He's aiming for a demonstration in Victoria," Mother said. She'd insisted that since Mildred was now a mother herself—not that anyone in the family openly acknowledged Mildred's own maternal state—that she no longer use the babyish names of Mama and Papa when referring to her own parents. "He needs a delighted audience," she added, to which Mildred and Muriel had laughed. "He needs to speak up. We all need to speak up."

Mother often reminded them that she was (and they were, by extension) descended from a suffragette pioneer from Kingston, Ontario, the very same town from which Mr. Bimson—their ancestor of generations back—had come. Mother's Mama was the founder of the Kingston Quiet Suffragettes. "No more quiet, girls," Mother said. "We don't do quiet no more."

Her parents' marriage was indeed a quiet one, in which Mildred often felt the undercurrent of her mother's sentiments—and resentments. Grandma had been a quiet one, and Papa too. But not Mother, Mother who roused them at dawn with a wooden spoon on a metal bucket and sang them to sleep at night.

Speak up, her mother nudged. And speak up, she would.

She'd have a cup of her CBD tea, first. Goodness knew she could feel the pressure building, and she sought the sweet relief from it.

The otters emerged again, wet and lithe with motion forward.

They went to Salt Spring Island by train! Train, boat, and car.

The baby one was the cutest, she'd reckoned, and she befriended it.

Never came too close but she named it and held it in her mind's eye—only an atmospheric memory and no sentiment beyond the cuddling care—cuddling care.

That was her greatest recollection of the otters: cuddling care of one another, nourishing, nurturing, naturally.

She rolled the words around. Then out loud. "Nourishing, nurturing, naturally!" She laughed to herself alone. Alone in the room, she Googled "Otters" and she sipped her tea.

Sunny. Her favorite.

For its sun-loving belly and shiny wet head that soaked up the warming rays of the Maine morning. Little as its head was, that morning, warming.

Shivered then, in her gown, present time and place connecting her through diurnal temporal climatic memory. Or was it weather?

Couldn't remember the difference, climate, weather, weather, climate—

Mark would know. Mark would opine.

She called him. "I can't remember the difference between climate and weather, Mark."

"It's okay. Nice to hear from you. I'm glad you called. I need to ask you something."

Mildred took a very big sip of tea. "About your relationship?" She didn't mean to be leading, but sometimes it was the best way, the most direct path.

"Kind of. I'm working on a case, and I've been thinking back to the panel discussion. The fracking panel."

"And that is indeed where you and Amalia met." She would stick to her mission.

"Yes. But that's not quite what I'm getting at. Mildred, what occurred that made you want to host a forum on fracking?"

She didn't want to tell him it was all Father Jasper's idea to get her more people to attend the church. And besides, it was only half true. Truth was, Father Jasper's ideas had meshed perfectly well with her own experiences at that moment. "I will tell you, Mark. From my own perspective. I saw what was happening in the area—observation, not conversation—and in prayer, I saw a healing light come into the Church sanctuary and Mercy Side, a light magnet that drew people together to share their sides, bear witness. Not judge. I wanted to hold space for that sharing of sides. And I know a man, Father Jasper, who helped me to focus the idea."

"I like that. Nice vision, Mildred. Sharing sides."

"I saw it in a dream on waking."

"I get that sometimes. Moments of clarity when I wake up."

"And you should take note of that—that the moment of waking presents clarity. It might seem irrational, or not as expected, but it can take you in a greater leap outside of your expectations than you might otherwise go."

"Mildred, you are a balm for the wildly confused. A catalyst for conversion."

She laughed. "Conversion to what, exactly?"

"I'm Catholic, and I'm not changing."

"All right, Mark. That's not what I meant. And I don't think that is what you meant."

"I really wanted to ask you what you saw at the fracking meeting. What was the potential you saw?"

"In the event, or in you and Amalia?"

"Both. Either."

"I saw that you got together in spite of your differences. Who let go of what? To whom does one relinquish power and control? When and how does the pressure release? Who allows the other to save face?"

"I don't know, who does?"

"I'm not sure either of you found lasting relief from that pressure, to be honest. I wonder how much good or damage the panel discussion actually did. I can't hold space for good outcomes that other people aren't lined up to maintain or aren't equipped to move into on their own." Did she say that aloud?

"Mildred, that's very harsh. And harsh on yourself, too."

Ah. She had, indeed, said it aloud.

"I deal with that every day, too, in my own life. I decide what I can maintain, what I am aligned to maintain, or not aligned with and end up letting go." She'd been wondering about letting Bert go, and it was only on speaking it to Mark that she let herself realize it. A shiver jiggled her arm right through to her tea hand and the liquid spilled out the cup onto the table of papers. She put down the tea and wiped the wet with her sleeve. She had not, in fact, let Bert go.

"When does the pressure release, Mildred?"

"If I knew, I'd tell you, Mark. It's up to you." She paused. "Can I tell you something?" She decided to not wait for an answer. "I came of age in New Jersey. And when I was fourteen, I thought I was in love." She didn't tell him the rest; it wasn't important to him, not then. Too tender for her, still, to bring it up. "We moved across the continent then. I got a job at seventeen. Married at eighteen and again at twenty-eight. It wasn't until I took a break from it all and spent some time away, that I realized I needed a new perspective. Maybe that's what you need: a new perspective."

~ 50 ~
Time is Stretchy

"Time is stretchy," Mildred said, squatting with slow knees, her hand stroking the weed-turned-plant that continued to expand along the wooden steps. "It expands and contracts according to your allowance or resistance to the moment."

Frankie looked toward the old house. "If time is stretchy," he said, "and if I'm your grandson—" He took a deep breath. "And if Father Jasper is my dad—" He exhaled, looking back at Mildred. "Then are you my mom and my grandmother?" He blurted it out so hard that it sounded like "Mom and Grand," and all other syllables swallowed. He had big eyes, Frankie did, in that moment.

Mildred shuddered and felt she might tip over—she righted herself to center by leaning on Frankie where he perched, crouched next to her. "Help me up," she said. "I think we'd better have tea."

"What you said about time," Frankie spoke as he pulled her up, "if time really is stretchy like you say, then you could be both my mom and my grandmother."

"I'm not." She exhaled through her nose with a hard stop at the end. "Up." She stopped a moment to put a hand on the bottom post of the handrail.

"But you're like my mom," he said. He held her elbow as she mounted the stairs. "You even look like my mom."

Her extended family, his great aunties, had raised him in Maine. It was true, the family resemblance did transmit, generation to generation. "What are you getting at, Frankie?" She took off her light sweater and folded it down toward the hallway coat stand's lower shelf, tidy, ever a living-alone-tidier, she often thought, since Raymond died. It was easier to be tidier with one. She'd missed that of Jasper's growing up, and of Frankie's, too. No diapers. No toys. No messes.

"I took something." He looked sheepish as he pulled his wallet from his back pocket. Drew a very old, tattered photo from it. Held it out to her. It was a photo of a girl, a girl with bobbing curls—and it was her. Mildred as a teenager. She recognized it as of the time she'd lived in New Jersey, but she could not recall if it was before or after Dougie. Dougie, and Jasper's coming.

"Where did you—" She'd not sent a photo off with him when they'd taken Baby Jasper. Had one of the aunties confused the matter?

"I took it from the house. The house in Maine."

She turned it over, hoping for further evidence of Frankie's process of thought. She read aloud, "Baby Boy, this is your mom. Her name is Mildred McCaine, and one day you will meet her. Love, your Aunties." It wasn't dated. "Frankie, I'm not your mother." There. She'd said it. "I'm not your mother. I'm sorry. They wrote it in error. I don't know who wrote it, but it isn't true. And they don't even say who the baby is."

"You had other babies." He let out a guttural growl, deep from within his chest. "All this time," he said. "You've been lying to me." He pushed off from the kitchen counter. "Not right. Not right!"

So that was it. Frankie's mixed-up sense of order—stretchy time—came from a mistaken recounting of her Aunties, or a mistaken assumption by him, that he was the Baby Boy. And now he thought there might be others.

"It's what they called me," he said. "Baby Boy."

"It's what they called Father Jasper, too," she said. No wonder there had been a mistake.

"Then who?"

"Who?"

"My mother."

The truth was, Mildred didn't know. It had never been known. Jasper had, she learned later, returned home with a baby, its mother having told him she would have none of it. Abandoned, in fact, to the good and caring hands of its father. Father Jasper. Baby Boy, raising Baby Boy. And she'd missed all of it. She felt shaky all of a sudden and needed to lie down. "This is more than I can bear, Frankie." She waved toward the front door. "I need you to go."

He did go, and after she'd had a sip of water, she picked up the phone.

"He knows," she said.

And then, with all the grace of her kneeling to stroke the weed-turned-plant outside, and all the smoothness with which she'd folded her light sweater on coming in, she rolled in bed, eyes alight to the room, and realized she'd been sleeping.

There had been no kneeling by the front steps.

There had been no tidy folding.

And there had been no stretchy time with Frankie and a photo.

Mildred sat up, heart pounding. Something was not right with the boy. There was a kind of paranoia about him. A kind of trouble of the mind that followed him, that preceded him, that clouded him. She wasn't sure where it came from, but she suspected he had not always been that way, that fuzzy and neurotic way that made her feel ill at ease. She would shake it off. She would have some tea. She blinked hard, eyes coming into slow focus. She didn't want the usual tea. She wanted to find her way, playfully, with the otters who came in her vision, but not through the usual tea. She wanted to find her own pathway to stretchy time, to kneeling by the steps, and she wanted to do it in a way that made sense to her. No more deals with Frankie. No more furtive exchanges of packages and car keys. She had a medicine all within her that was open to her reaching, whenever she wanted it.

She called it Running Reiki, although she was never running when she did it. Simply put, it was her meditative practice of flowing the good energy of the universe through her when she called it, intentionally, and it felt good. That was it. It felt good. The medicines themselves could stay or go, and they could help or hinder, but either way, she knew that when she Ran the Reiki, she felt good, and it could be a partner to the medicines, or not. Either way. It made her feel good. Dreaming about Frankie's paranoia did not. She'd Run the Reiki. It would be her focus. And perhaps she would return to teaching others to Run the Reiki, too, just as she'd been doing before she took on the leadership of the Church.

She'd get up. She'd Run the Reiki and she'd see what happened next.

~ 51 ~
No Secrets

Later, she burned the diaries in the fireplace, page by page, sending up ash: every single one that had followed her around for her entire life, yes, and that held the secrets she'd been holding. Didn't matter anymore. Wasn't a secret. She was seen.

"We get lost in other people's sorrows," she said to Eliza. "And they magnify our own." She scratched the old cat behind the ears, eliciting an elegant purr. "In my life, I've helped people more when I've been less embedded in their sorrow. Less concerned about their expectations." Eliza padded around on the dining table, among the remaining covers of the torn and fire-spewed journals, moved by Mildred between mantle and table, and jumped down to the floor. She walked to the back door and turned to look at Mildred. "You're right, as usual, Eliza. A stroll outside will clear the way."

The brightness of the late day sun turned to the brightness of the week, and the following week, and the month, and the season, and she came to be comfortable in her companionship with the unearthed box, on the mantel, next to Raymond's empty urn.

~ 52 ~

Wax Work ~ July

In summer, she set out to do her seasonal dusting. A thick layer had built up around the curves and base of Raymond's urn, and around the corners of the box, where they sat, together. "You'll need a cleaning," she said to them both. The dusting took some time, and she enjoyed it. But when it came time to put the urn and the box back on the mantel, it was only the urn she moved into place.

It was time. Mildred wondered if she should call Muriel first, but thought against it, and decided to open the box by herself.

She covered the dining table in a clean white linen, and brought the box, still dirt encrusted, to the edge of the linen surface. The old tablecloth, the last vestige of her first marriage, a wedding gift she retained, proved to be a perfect face. She had thought the box had a lid but couldn't remember how the lid was attached. In her mind's eye, when she lifted the lid, the arc that it formed would look like a wheel. A wheel. Not a hook. But the hook, the big metal hook—the image of it persisted in her memory. There had been the hook on the shed. Not where she'd remembered seeing it, but what did it matter. Someone had repurposed an old hook, likely a whaling hook. This box had no hook.

She took a deep breath and broke the seal where it had reattached with residual stickiness from Amalia's wax work. Lifted the lid straight up. The quilt was as she and Amalia had left it. But wrapped inside: it was a lifetime ago that she'd seen inside. She had a flash in her mind of the object inside yet did not want to reveal it, fearing it would be degraded by the humidity in the room, if not also with more insistent power, the persistent nosing of her cats.

The nosing of the cats in the dusty air, Eliza and Kit and Kittie—the littlest still kittens and waiting to be named, so The Littles had become their collective name—made her thirsty for her own elixir. She wasn't due for the CBD tea, but she'd have some. She pushed away from the table and muttered to the object. Put on the kettle in the kitchen and turned on the radio there.

"The fire ripped through the town like a tornado," the newscaster said. "Our witness is okay; she was just outside of the town and the train tracks." It was a train fire in Quebec, north of her. The name of the town was familiar. Had Mark mentioned it? He must have. Yes.

Mildred shook her head. There was much trauma, all around. She listened further while the kettle came to a boil. A huge rail explosion had taken a chunk of the heart of Lac Mégantic in Quebec; this was Mark's grandmother's home. That's why Mark had mentioned it. It rang familiar from Mark. But what could she do?

Run Reiki. That was something she could do. She turned off the radio, closed her eyes, and summoned the violet light of Reiki to come through herself and to Quebec, a prayer in action.

She turned the radio back on and took the water off the boil. While she could see it and understand the elements of the dynamics, she didn't feel troubled. Not that it didn't affect her; it did, as it did everyone, of course. It was more that she felt a deep and overriding sense of compassion for all involved. Little did they know that such events, traumatic in their inception, might be transformative in their long run. Profound change came from small events, building over time. What was the change that would come? She didn't know and didn't feel the need to know. Whatever it was would come in time.

She didn't want the tea. The Reiki was doing it for her, relaxing her; she sipped a glass of water while she took some deep breaths. In time, after a more relaxed stretch during which she sat quietly with the cats, she returned to the object. She had to reach out to her sister. Although Mildred knew many things, she did not know what to do with the object or the box. Didn't know how to research the history of the thing. Her sister Muriel, a librarian to her core, would at least help to figure out a first step.

Turned out, Muriel was connected. Her "friend" Bob, who Mildred suspected was more than a friend, knew a thing or two. In fact, he was an archeologist at the University of Victoria on

Vancouver Island. Could he help to date Mildred's thing, without having seen it? And was it even Mildred's to date and identify? She felt it was hers. Hers in spirit.

She wrote to Muriel:

I want to know what this thing is. I want to know who put it there and why, before us. And how old it is, that might be interesting, too. It looks old. Very, very old. I remember that I saw it as a child, and that Grandma said it was ancient.

After a number of days, she heard back. Bob wrote notes about it—a tome, in fact—which Muriel copied into an email to Mildred. Mildred printed it, took it to the table, and pushed Eliza aside. The other cats nosed and noodled around but had enough sense to stay out of it. They'd come to know when to stay out of Mildred's way. "Have a listen to this, Littles," she said to the cats.

"Dear Mildred,
These are the notes from Bob. He says he can't do much without seeing it. Can we say what "it" is on email? I never know who is reading these things. Let me know what you want to do. Bob says if you can bring it over on the plane, he'll have a look. He also said you might not be able to.
Love,
Muriel"

It seemed feasible but she doubted she could do it. "Don't know about that, do you now, Eliza? Not taking this baby across the continent." She continued with the next sentences.

"Radiocarbon Dating Artifacts and Local Substrate
Carbon-14 isotope is formed by cosmic rays acting upon Nitrogen in the atmosphere, forcing normal Carbon-12 in surface soil to take up extra protons from the 'excited' Nitrogen.' "

Goodness. She was going to need a cup of strong, black tea. "Hang on, Eliza, hang on Muriel, hang on, Bob." She went to the kitchen. No more black tea! She'd have to go out. Her old

Alero was out front; Frankie didn't have it. "Be right back in a flash, Eliza; you keep them Littles in line!"

At the grocery store, Mildred mulled over her choices. She'd need something sturdy to drink, something up to the task. Held the first box: too sharp. Held the second box: too dull. Held another. "Not remotely up to the task, sorry!" She put it back on the shelf. Stood back. Let her eyes go a little glaucoma-fuzzy. A blue and red box caught her eye at the bottom of the shelf. Could it be? She bobbed down. "Red Rose! I thought you were 'Only in Canada!' and here you are! You've been holding out on me!" She grabbed a box. Looked over her shoulder. Grabbed another and went to the checkout. "I feel a little greedy with two," she said to the clerk. "But so happy to find you have this!" The clerk, unamused, rang her up and popped the purchase in an unceremonious white plastic bag.

The box of tea felt good in her possession, swinging from her hand from the store to the car. At home, she held the box and giggled to herself. Peeled the corner of the crinkly plastic wrapping and sniffed at the edge of the opening, inhaling the scent of the strong, black tea. "It's so good!" She put on the kettle and left the box on the counter next to it. There was time to read a little more while she waited for the water to boil. She put her reading glasses back on and read from the paper print, aloud and to the Littles. Eliza had gone away in Mildred's absence.

"Plants then take up this Carbon-14 along with stable carbon. Carbon-14 decays at a predictable rate back to Carbon-12, but not until the plant, or the animal that consumes those plants, has died."

Was the melon shape from an animal? It had animal characteristics, but it was covered in something tar-like. It didn't look like part of an animal. It looked like something that had pretended to be an animal. Like a shell. Shell of an animal? It wasn't like a turtle shell. And someone had made holes in it, once upon a time.

"Because of this, Carbon-14RCB dating works by measuring the ratio of Carbon-14 to Carbon-12 left in a sample by a previously living plant or animal and measuring it against the known ratio of Carbon-14 in the atmosphere (based upon climatic research.)"

If it was a shell, or a shape that was from an animal or a plant, then wouldn't it fit this profile?

"After 5,730 years, the amount Carbon-14 will have reduced by half. After another 5,730 years, another half will be decayed, and so on."
She got a bit of a shiver on reading this. Hadn't even thought the thing was over a hundred years old.

"This means that RCB dating is only statistically useful from between 5,730—60,000 years, after which time any detectable Carbon-14 will be negligible."

The water was coming to a boil. She pushed away from the table to check, printout in hand.

"Your melon shell–shaped object could be successfully RCB-dated by things like grains of sand or chipped-off tool spalls trapped in the grain, or trace minerals within tree rings from known volcanic activity, earth disturbances due to known floods, quakes etcetera."

Mildred finished unwrapping the Red Rose tea from the packaging. Wondered if there was a little treasure inside like she remembered: a little ceramic gift in every box. She'd once collected them. What had happened to all those porcelain goodies? Must be at Muriel's house in Burnaby, or Mother's condo in Ganges on Salt Spring Island. She couldn't imagine they were still in their old house on the other side of Salt Spring, in Vesuvius. They weren't there with her in Binghamton, that she knew for sure. The water was boiling. The teabags were revealed, fresh to the air. She dug her fingers in among them. Sure enough: a small ceramic house. Mildred smiled and set it on the counter next to the teapot. She'd have to find a special place for it. She brewed the tea in the boiling water, proper in its pot. The smell of home was strong. She reread the last sentence and caught the phrase at the end, volcanic activity, earth disturbances due to known floods, quakes etcetera.

Oh, the Great Flood, recorded in so many cultures' oral histories around the world. Had the melon seen this? She looked at it. Didn't seem possible. It couldn't be more than a couple hundred years old, could it? She continued to read to the room.

"This predictable-decay theory holds for other kinds of dating analysis, such as Potassium/Argon dating, which is useful for rocks and minerals (for example, the substrate in which your thing was dug up in Maine)."

The brewing tea was smelling good. Eliza was back in the room, interested in the printout and nipping at its corner. Mildred swatted her away. "Listen to this:

This method measures how much Potassium has decayed into Argon since the rocks were first formed in the mantle or by volcanic action.

I don't think this is for us," she said to Eliza. "We're not talking about anything that old." Eliza kept at the corner, and Mildred lifted her off the table and took her to the kitchen. "Let's have tea, shall we?" The printout remained on the table. Eliza twisted out of Mildred's arms and back to the floor in an elegant but determined kitty-leap. "Oh, Red Rose, come to me," Mildred said. She took a cup from the cupboard. Swirled the tea in its pot. Poured it almost to the brim. Went to the fridge for a spot of milk. There was no milk. None. She'd just been at the store. Silly! What was Red Rose tea without a spot of milk? She would enjoy the tea the way she knew it best. "Back in a flash," she said to Eliza and the Littles.

"I forgot this," she said to the clerk. "Can't have Red Rose tea without it!" The clerk was unamused once again but rang it up and put the milk into another unceremonious white plastic bag. This time, Mildred did not swing her purchase as she walked from store to car. She was thinking. Could the thing be as old as to warrant Bob's methods of inquiry? Maybe they'd need a different method. Something less archeological. Something more investigative of present-day methods. It could not be an old thing.

Back home, she poured the tea from the cup back into the pot and swirled it all around. Took a fresh cup from the shelf and poured a new cup of tea for herself. Opened the milk, added a bit. Inhaled the very strong tea, the milky addition, and smiled. "Tea the way it's meant to be," she said to the cats. Eliza had lost interest in the printout, and Mildred sat with it in the living room, tea in hand. She sipped. "Ahh, so good." Took a moment to let it settle into her cells. "Mmm, good!" She put it down next to her and returned her focus to the printout. She'd forgotten her reading glasses in the kitchen. Back up, glasses ready. She continued and read to Eliza who had returned.

"(Argon, being a noble gas, can escape liquid minerals, but re-binds to crystallized minerals over time). Because this is a much slower process, it can provide reliable date brackets older than 100,000 years.

Goodness," Mildred said, "I don't think it's over 100,000 years. Does anything even last that long? Dinosaur bones, maybe." Eliza looked unamused and left the room.

"For much younger plant humus and animal/insect proteins in soil, I suggest stable isotope ratio analysis."

That made more sense to Mildred. It was a younger object, for sure. She sipped her tea. Her delicious tea.

"Different base isotopes are measured depending on the sample retrieved."

Amalia had been the one to retrieve it. Who had taken it out when Mildred was young? All she knew was that her grandmother had it, that it had come from there, and that they had put it back in. They'd had a ladder. It came back to her then in a flash, the ladder, as she sipped the tea. Where had the ladder come from? The shed behind the Moores'? Or did her family have their own ladder? She continued.

"For soils and inorganic materials in soil, we can establish native and foreign provenance by measuring the ratio of the deuterium to hydrogen against known water samples."

Provenance. She knew that word. But deuterium? What was deuterium? She'd never heard of it. Okay, maybe she had once, but if she had ever known, it was long forgotten. Mildred continued.

The Littles came up to her and purred around her ankles. Food time, no doubt. Mildred swatted at her ankles then brought two of the cats to her lap. They sat on top of the print on her lap. "Fascinating stuff from this Bob, wouldn't you say?" The littlest Little, Kit, purred. Eliza came up and leapt onto her lap, and Mildred snuggled all three, and the print crinkled below them.

"Me oh my. I will have to have another cup of tea." She tried to stand with them all in her arms, but it was too much, so she let them jump to the floor, the printout falling with them.

On the way to the kitchen, teacup in hand, Mildred stopped at the computer. She looked up 'deuterium' online. And then, for good measure, she pulled her old dictionary from the bookshelf, and she looked up 'provenance.'

Two cups of tea in, and she was over her head in information. She realized it would require an expert analysis. Not her looking things up online and hoping to piece it together with words and phrases Bob had shared in Muriel's email. She wrote back to her sister.

Please thank Bob very much. And thank you too. This is clearly more than I can sort out on my own, and so I will consider Bob's suggestion to bring the thing, although I believe it may not be worth the trouble to explain it to Canada Customs.

I do have an idea though. Does Bob think I could bring just the bones? I could do that.

Tell me soon because I want to book a ticket. I will call Air Canada as soon as you say, and I'll have them set me up with a flight. I go through JFK Airport, as you will remember, but it's fine, I can go there for it. I'm just not sure about the security screening they have. It's worth a try. What can they suspect of little old me?

The email was received, and Muriel replied before Mildred had even got up to use the bathroom after her two cups of tea.

Bob says, to date the artifact he'd want to site-match (between other similar finds) any paint or inset elements on the artifact, and then examine the artistic styles of the culture, to find out if the artifact fits a known period.

He says that just because our grandma dug it up doesn't have to be a problem. Says he remembers someone in the UK dated specific fertilizer traces on an old handmade granite animal trough in a farmer's field, showing that the trough had to have been exposed sometime during the 1940s even if it had been reburied again. And 1940s—well, ours would have been dug up in the 1930s, so maybe that's a good parallel.

I don't know, Mildred, but I'll be happy to see you. I haven't been spending much time at the Burnaby house as you know. I'm in and out of Mother's condo in Ganges, and with the girls in Vesuvius. So, you could have the house to yourself, or come over right away and spend time with all of us here on Salt Spring.

By the way, did you know Bert Springer got married?

~ 53 ~

The Taster

She opened her throat-way when she put the last soil over the box, and the sounds that came brought her calm. Closed her throat to cease the song and flowed it in and out in little bits of vocal climb, until her master heard her below and called her back for cooking. Her in-breath and out-breath focus was not as practiced as the elders, and she was light-headed from the rhythm. Up the ladder from shelter bottom to the wooden floor above, she felt dizzy, and at the top, master pulled her and put her with the women for a time to settle with the cook pots. Light came through the open door and she could see beyond the draped flap to the ocean beyond, from their perch nestled into the edge of the lowly sloping hill, and there, she imagined otters played.

In the soup, was put bone. And in the soup, were added herbs, to which roots were stirred, and when it was boiled, she drank it into her, the steam carrying her high, better, stabler, and whole. The soup was for all, but she was the taster, and if she fell, then they would all fall, and none would drink the soup. This was her sacrifice: not of her choosing but of her destiny. The soup taster of the journey, the one who showed the open path. To her, they gave the herbs of the new land and the roots of the new soil; to her, they gave the new greens of the unfamiliar trees, and often she was ill. Her medicine tasting and food testing left her often drifting, and in this, she heard voices.

The medicine most favored by the seafarers was one brought from home, on the ship, and traded at a high rate of handing; the handing, from trader to trader, involved pelts when they were available, and swords when they were not. To be most safe with her store, she tucked some of the preciousness into the back of the creation in the shelter bottom, and when her master was in fury, she put a small sprig of it into his soup to soothe him. This she told no one, for to be shown as a medicine woman, she would have training of years, yet she had none. She hid her practice, and cultivated her skill, through experiment.

The otter voices spoke loudly in the new land, and they embraced her with the familiarity of home. And to the creation in the shelter bottom, she endowed Otter. When tired, or excited, she visited Otter, lifting him from his box, her promise box, in the soil. In those shallows, she put medicines, and she wished in this method of her self-devised ceremony, that they, she, and her people of home, would be well in this fierce new land.

Istania held the Otter mask from home and cradled it beneath her arms as if hiding it from being taken. It could in fact have been taken; none were intent on it at that moment: the ships in bay were the primary concern and securing them in the face of an overnight assault. She felt a draw to the ships, and solemn-like, she walked the trodden grasses to the shore. None noticed her, and she held the mask in her skirt-front, appearing—if any had noticed—as bread, or cloth, or even kindling. To the ships in bay, and to a bundle to be heaved up: she tucked the mask into the corner of it and bid it well. From those shores, she hoped to send it back to home, completing the journey that she would not.

Later, when fire broke out below deck, the mask was pushed off the ship along with the other bundles that might have caught the flame, and it came unbound from its hiding. Bobbing back to the shore in time, it found its resting place in the craggy rocks that ringed the unfamiliar coast, and when Istania came to retrieve her fish-traps in the morning, she cried not only for the lost ship, charred in the far distant horizon, and sinking below, but also for the finding of the mask, which had returned to a newfound sense of home.

She would not lose the mask, would not risk its separation from her once more. It had shown her home. She would protect it—it, and its grandmother-grandfather spirit within. She buried it. Below the space occupied by her bedding, and when all were out on forage, she dug: into the summer soil, soft and with no worms, she placed the mask, with food for winter (a leg of turkey she took from the table), and no cognition of what her grandmother-grandfather spirits would want or need underground other than the leg of turkey (which she tied to the back of the mask with one leather shoelace from her boot). This together she placed into the clay-like soil where worms did not travel. It would need some other casing: she lifted it back out, and worrying that the others would return from forage and see her bed asunder, she took a near garment, a wool fringe of her own creation, and wrapped the mask (and the bound turkey leg, sustenance for wintering spirits), several times, tying tightly with her other leather shoelace (for this she could think of no explanation to give the others), put the mass back into her promise box, and set the box with love and shaky hands into the hole she'd dug with bare hands beneath her bedding space. With no shoelaces to hold her footing steady, and with clay embedded deep into her fingernail moons, she would need a tale. It was only when the others entered and saw her bed asunder, boots askew, nails ragged, that their assumption she'd been taken, took her into the tale. She fought him off, she said, and he'd stolen her shoelaces. Nothing more. The men stood vigilant all night, and when no attacker returned, they let her about her days in a watchful state, although always, the men stood ready to defend. Istania knew there was no need for this, but to explain the lost shoelaces and the bed asunder, she floated along with their misunderstanding. It was home, this new land, and with its rocky shore and tumbled fish-trap crannies, she was content to watch for otters, and nothing more.

~ 54 ~
Catnip ~ August

Mildred sat in front of her old TV in the living room in Binghamton, comfortable with her ice water on the hot mid-August evening. Having learned of the upcoming documentary about marijuana by the Surgeon General, she was ready to watch, to weigh in.

Since scheduling the medical marijuana panel she'd been short on recent research to be included in the discussion's questions and answers. Didn't want to leave it all to chance, to the audience, or to Frankie. She hoped the Surgeon General would have something useful to say. Eliza and the other cats watched with feigned interest as she stood to adjust her seat cushions and raised the volume on the remote. They went back to skulking the corners. "You don't know what you're missing, Littles! This stuff is catnip!" And she giggled to herself.

Mr. Gupta—Dr. Gupta—started to talk about the "Green Rush" and legalization and asked if pot is good or bad for humans. The story turned to a family. A family? This was an unexpected turn. Dr. Gupta talked about a young man against drugs.

Aislinger, 1930s. She remembered him. Her father had talked about it, the loco weed. Reefer Madness, the film from her childhood, had left an imprint on people around her. Mildred shifted in her seat. She hadn't expected this to get personal. Dr. Gupta talked about how by 1937 marijuana had become illegal to use, and by 1970 was a Schedule I controlled substance with no medicinal value.

And then, the TV showed a darling baby girl, in the present, having a seizure. A perfectly healthy twin girl.

Mildred got a shiver up one side. Didn't feel good to see that.

The mother and father spoke with clarity about their daughter. Their daughter was slipping, as they watched. Epilepsy, damaging. The baby, by then a toddler, was having regular life-threatening seizures. Some of the medications she'd had could have killed her.

Mildred sounded for Eliza to come to her lap. Tears welled in her eyes. The father found an option to give the beautiful girl medical marijuana, even though he never would take it himself. The mother and father went back and forth in conflict; in the meantime, the child was having hundreds of seizures a week. Maybe they could consider marijuana. Would they be able to get it? Was there any protocol for gaining access to it? What would the parents do? The TV cut to commercial. "No!" Mildred shooed Eliza from her lap. How could they cut to commercial just then? She got up to go to the bathroom, then for a refill of ice water.

Mildred never had children to raise. Her first marriage ended before it ever started, the second was a nonstarter, and with Raymond, well, she was already sixty by the time they tied the knot. The process of adoption she'd hoped to pursue, the baby she'd hoped would be hers, spanned the years between the marriages and had not come to fruition. Sure, there could have been another baby after Jasper. Her sister Muriel had three beautiful daughters, and once the first was born, Mildred felt a tug of both wanting and of relief. She heard the TV shift back over to the parents' voices and Mildred shuffled into the living room with her refilled water glass. Dr. Gupta asked, what would you do if this were your child? God only knows, thought Mildred. Medical marijuana was fine for her, an adult; what about for a child? The parents decided to try medical marijuana when the girl was five. Mildred's heart went out in a thumping to the screen, and she pulled Eliza, who was keeping ever closer, back to her lap. The parents discussed getting a prescription for a child. Cannabis was considered by a doctor. Dr. Gupta talked about THC and the role of CBD in quieting excessive brain activity. They wanted low THC and high CBD. How could they get that? Some bright young men came on screen and talked about running a high-CBD medical marijuana dispensary with its own greenhouses. The camera showed inside a greenhouse that Dr G called the Garden of Eden. "Eliza, Bert will have to see this," she said. It looked just like his lavender farm greenhouse on Salt Spring Island. Bert swore he didn't grow pot. Liked it;

didn't sell it. The bright young men bred their own strains to help people's medical conditions. Mildred liked that. Another young man came on with a diaphragm condition and explained how well the medical marijuana worked to relieve his condition. "They do like the drama of it, don't they, Eliza," she said. She couldn't deny the obvious turnaround in both the little girl, and the young man. Not that she needed any convincing. She already knew from her own use of medical marijuana for her glaucoma that it could be soothing.

Mildred didn't know that so many people engaged in the research and development of new strains. That interested her. The TV story shifted back to a commercial which she muted on the remote. No need to clutter her brain. She stroked Eliza's fur and looked out the window at the onset of August's sunset. What would the story ending be for the little girl? She hoped it would be a good one. If it wasn't? Could she bear to keep watching? It was almost too much. Mildred closed her eyes and felt the flow of Reiki energy through her hands. With Eliza on her lap, receiving the warmth, Mildred mentally sent Reiki, distantly, to the little girl. She hoped the girl would be well. She hoped the mother and father would find peace. She sat like that for some time in the silence of the room, eyes closed, then remembered to turn the mute off and rejoin the TV show. Some people were smoking at a big party. Dr G wondered what the use of marijuana was doing to people's brains. What about the girl? Mildred felt invested in the family. She stroked Eliza's back. Dr G talked to another doctor about brain activity.

Reward, pleasure, hunger, well-being. All things that sounded good. What about the little girl? The documentary had gone on to talk about creativity and the high that some people would get with the release of dopamine. Sure, thought Mildred. Fine. What about the little girl? She could not imagine the anxiety of the parents. Less inhibition. Artists. High artists. That was not Mildred's top interest, although she was happy for the artist in the documentary. "A delicate balance" said the artist of imbibing with the creative work. The show shifted back to scientific studies.

To be sure, Mildred knew the studies were important. What about the little girl? She looked out the window; the TV show focused on driving and pot. Cannabis people had good control?

Non-cannabis people had less control when they smoked, or more? How impaired did people get? What happened to young brains? The show was getting to the pediatric interest. Maybe they would return to the little girl. They said to take the drugs early was not good for the younger developing brains. That made sense to Mildred. It wasn't something she'd want for her nieces. Oh! They indicated they would come back to the little girl. Mildred kept the sound on during the next round of commercials so that she wouldn't miss anything. When the broadcast came back on, it wasn't to tell the story of the girl, but of another user and his story. The young man they'd featured before became high on morphine. Another scared parent. They seemed much more comfortable with marijuana than with other drugs like morphine. Dr. G said there were almost no known fatal overdoses of marijuana. That was something to like, Mildred thought. Some users became dependent, although less than compared to other drugs or alcohol. The show focused on a teenage addict. Mildred was sure it was not addictive. Had she been wrong about that? The show described it as a compulsion rather than an addiction. Feel-good cannabinoids were naturally produced in the body. When a user smoked too much, the body stopped producing and looked for the introduction of the drug.

But how much was too much? And where was the little girl? Some of it was stronger in THC than other stashes of it. The Marijuana Potency Project—analyzing pot from drug busts—too strong, negative effects on someone who was not used to it. The potency of THC had gone up over the decades. That made sense to Mildred, seemed to match up with her observation of others. She'd never smoked recreationally; it wasn't until the glaucoma she'd even considered it. When others were partying with it, she'd been working. When others had offered it, she'd turned to light conversation instead. The parents of the girl were back on the screen, discussing their decisions to provide medical marijuana to their beautiful daughter. What a ride those parents must have been on. The father spoke on the screen about their viable options. Another commercial break! Mildred could not take another disruption in the story. She didn't give TV too much time and only kept it around for occasional use. It had been Raymond's thing. They'd brought it from Canada.

She turned on the mute and pushed Eliza off her lap. Out the window, sunset progressed. The air conditioner in the window, installed some months ago by a helpful Frankie, rattled on. Mildred went out to the front porch with her water to catch a breath of fresh air. What did Muriel think of it? They'd never discussed it, and Muriel did not know of Mildred's use of the stuff. Did it matter? Who knew? Since Mildred had announced the panel discussion, some must have figured out that she was a user. Frankie was her habitual supplier even though she could get a prescription filled; Frankie knew. Would it matter to any of her congregants? She could not imagine so. And where she lived, in New York State, it was legal for medical use with a prescription. She was out of bounds when it came to buying from Frankie, that was true. But she wouldn't let anyone know about that, and neither would he. Mildred went back inside to see if there was an update on the little girl, with whom she was finding a strong bond.

The littlest cat came to curl up in her lap. Eliza paced in front of the television and sat in Raymond's chair. The girl was receiving weed, with shocking results. In Afghanistan, the father watched a video of his daughter while he was away on a military tour of duty. They would try marijuana as a natural solution to her life-threatening seizures that were not responsive to other drugs. Finding a low-THC and high-CBD dose was key. They administered a dose. The girl went all day and night without a seizure. And the next day. No seizure. The mother's brightness was contagious, and the father's relief palpable. Mildred would have been happy for the show to end there, but it did not. It was a good conclusion. The girl was being helped. What more could happen? The family was running low on the right strain of medicine, the low-THC and high-CBD strain that helped their daughter. Mildred sat on the edge of Raymond's chair. Wasn't sure she liked where the story was going. "Better get that girl some more medicine, Eliza!" Too expensive. Not covered by insurance.

Aha! The parents connected with the bright young men with the dispensary and the greenhouse. Mildred felt a wave of relief for the family. Understandably, the bright young men were uncomfortable at first about providing high CBD marijuana for the family to give to the young girl. But they did, and it worked!

She was lifted from a catatonic state into wellness, high energy, and smiles. It was a remarkable—no, a miraculous—transformation. Dr. Gupta went to meet the little girl. Such a bright one, walking, talking, playing. Mildred relaxed a little. Before she got too comfortable though, large bold words in all caps flashed on the screen to state that there was no evidence of CBD treating epilepsy efficiently. "Bah to that, I say!" Eliza joined the other kit at Mildred's chair. Mildred leaned forward to bring her up. What was the point of showing that the CBD could help a little girl and then contradict the evidence in the next moment? Raymond would have had something to say about that. She could mention it in the panel discussion. Many large organizations said they did not support the use of CBD. The TV show veered to Israel.

Israel! Where she and Raymond had spent his late-career sabbatical, and she'd studied Aramaic during the days while he researched, wrote, rewrote, and taught. "Raymond, are you seeing this?" She smiled, feeling him nearby. Israel, a great innovator in medical marijuana. Hospitals and nursing homes in Israel were allowing patients to light up. The show went to commercials again. How many commercials would interrupt the story of Israel? She was curious to get back to it. Raymond had never gone into a home, not even at the end. She'd kept him in a rented hospital bed in the living room, right there, with the chairs pushed to the side. A home health aide came in. He died a quiet and peaceful death in his sleep, merciful, Mildred thought, although to remember it gave her sadness and a sapping of her strength that made her feel tired and hungry and irritated all at once.

She pushed up off the arms of the recliner and made her way to the kitchen, the commercials loud enough that she would hear when they transitioned back to the show. What would be a good snack? Maybe crackers. Toast. Tea and toast. She filled the kettle and put it to boil. No time for toast. The show was coming back on. Fixed herself a little plate of crackers and went back to the recliner where she positioned herself in front of the TV, half listening for the kettle. Jerusalem. The old streets, her once-home. Mildred nibbled the corner of a cracker, and her mind wandered down the old cobblestone streets of the filming. Days she'd spent wandering, listening, observing there. Israel's

Ministry of Health was ahead of the curve, with developments going back to the 1970s.

She recalled meeting someone from a government agency at one of the faculty parties but could not remember his department. "Raymond, do you remember?" He didn't answer, or if he did, she could not hear it. The show visited a state-run nursing home outside of Tel Aviv. A nice-looking older man smoked a pipe on screen. He had lost his wife, too. And once he'd lost his wife, memories of the Holocaust came back to him. Mildred heard the kettle and got back up for it. The Holocaust. It was too much, this show. All she'd wanted was a quick hit of information about medical marijuana, not all these triggers of family and sorrow. She made her tea, and from the kitchen heard the nice man say something about how he would dream, and fly. That was it. "Dream and fly. That's what we all want, no matter how we get there: to dream, and to fly." Over her shoulder she heard the show continue. Dr G went to a hospital in Israel and looked at marijuana use in recovery from chemotherapy side effects. Wait—Dr. Gupta said something about killing cancer cells. Could that be so? She took her tea back to the living room. It seemed too good to be true. The conversation had shifted already. Studies were being approved in the US, but the American focus was on preventing drug abuse, not researching marijuana use and its role in treatments of illnesses. That made sense, and she could understand why. The family with the little girl was back. They talked about how her brain function was building, not worsening, with the use of medical marijuana. Riding a bike, riding a horse. Other children were using the same strain, and the documentary ended on a hopeful note. Mildred sat back into Raymond's chair and turned off the TV, sipped her hot CBD tea. Had the documentary changed her mind about anything? No, it had confirmed it. She would consider how the information from the show might affect the upcoming panel discussion. "Eliza, what do you think?" To which Eliza, nestled with littlest Kit on the floor, purred in reply.

~ 55 ~

Transformation

Whiskie fell forward after her into the pit. He fell with something akin to a graceful plop, not giving away his weight or bulk, landing dancer-like with a lightness that, in the moment, made sense. He very nearly floated. What is it, Whiskie, she heard in her own head. "Transformation," she heard, in a voice that was not hers.

Amalia awoke with a start, aware of the late-morning light filtering through the apartment's sari curtains. She'd take them with her to Brooklyn. Mark would have to get something new to cover the windows after she left. She had not told him of her imminent departure, but he would not be surprised. He knew she was leaving. He knew he would be moving on. He knew, too, that Jen had offered a space to Amalia. He didn't know it was that day, planned hastily by Amalia and Jen the previous week. She'd meant to tell him, but he'd been away, and she'd not wanted to tell him by text.

Her eyes wandered over to the Saraswati wall hanging. It had been a gift to him. She'd leave it for him, but part of her wondered if he cared enough about it, or her, for it to matter. Still, it had been a gift.

A gift was what the new apartment was. Jen needed a roommate in her one-bedroom apartment, and Amalia would take up station in a corner of the living room. It would suit them both. And the sari curtains would help to divide the space in a gracious way.

She remembered a man named Gracious, from before. It seemed so long ago that she had been involved with that aspect of the condo conversion, doing a building façade inspection for which Gracious helped her navigate up and down the face of the old building in a lift, enjoying the view of the Hudson River and Palisades beyond. She wondered what had become of him.

The dream tugged at her mind. Whiskie felt present to her as she sat up in bed and looked at the old tree out back. "I'll miss you, Grandmother Tree. I'll miss you. I don't think I'll see you again. There will be more trees in Brooklyn."

Jen would be arriving within the next few minutes. Amalia, having slept late, was neither fed and watered as mother liked to say, nor packed and ready to go. Jen could wait.

She felt the nudging of the dog in her mind's eye.

Transformation.

She'd land with grace, this time, even if she didn't know how or even why. It would be without Mark, and she'd be fine.

She had a place to land. That was a start. And she knew who she wanted to reach out to next. It was time for the next Mildred panel, and Amalia would travel to Binghamton.

~ 56 ~
Talisman

"Come tomorrow. Stay with me." Mildred would be both anchor and host. She looked forward to seeing the girl again.

"I will. I'm hoping we can pick up a little where we left off, on our trip."

"Many threads for us to pick up on, yes? What did you have in mind?"

"Something along the creative vein. I liked how those conversations were going. I could use some advice about that."

"Write what comes," Mildred guided Amalia over the phone. "If it comes in a clear and loving stream, and it feels true and clear, then stay with it. Read it later. See what messages your subconscious mind has for you," Mildred hesitated. "Subconscious, or divine—one and the same."

"But how do I know what's clear and what's random? Fuzziness that's pretending to be insightful? I feel that insight when I'm painting. Clear is clear when I'm painting."

"Use this. Is it coming from a loving and unguarded part of your larger being? Trust that. Anything else—you're being driven by your own fears or anxieties. You get to decide. You decide which you prefer. You always have that choice." Mildred stirred the leaves in the pot. "Should be steeped enough now." She poured the hot tea through the strainer, into the cup. It created a curling wisp of steam that rose like a tendril. "What do you choose?"

"Steeped?"

"My tea, dear."

"I always thought I was an intuitive person. Serendipity finds me. I find it. But I don't know if that's coming from a what— what did you call it—a loving and unguarded place?"

"A loving and unguarded part of your larger being." Mildred picked up her CBD tea and blew across the tendril of steam to cool it; she brought it closer and imbibed. The medicine would soon relieve the pressure she felt behind her eyes. "It is like this," she said. "Like attracts like. Your serendipities follow your projections—like this tendril of steam follows my breath." She blew again, for effect. It made sense to her, but the girl couldn't see it. "Let's try something else." Mildred put down the tea and went to the front porch of her Binghamton home. The summer air was sweet and a little sticky; a haze settled outside in the far distance and a mirage of heat energy emerged from the pavement at the end of the street ahead. Mildred sat down. "This, that we found. That you found."

"The box. Whiskie found. Whiskie led me."

It had been moved outside to the front porch since Mildred had been unable to shake the dreams that came along with it after the intensive dusting—not bad dreams, but insistent ones—and while curious to her, she felt better not sleeping under the same roof as it. It didn't want to sit next to Raymond's urn—or rather, she didn't want that for it, or her. It would stay outside while she slept, and she would bring it in during the day if she wanted to have a look at it, or more likely, have a chat with it. Amalia didn't need to know any of that. She likely thought Mildred was crazy enough at it was.

"This that was found. You will recall, I had seen it before, as a child."

"And your grandmother put the thing in it again and wrapped it up."

"Talisman-like."

"The talisman is like a magnet?"

The girl had leapt ahead! "Oh, that's very good, Amalia!"

Mildred felt a ripple of excitement run up and down her legs. "So good!"

"Or a symbol, which is like a magnet."

"Reiki symbols do that, too."

"What's a Reiki symbol?"

"It's a—something that helps to amplify the energy that flows."

"The good and loving and unguarded energy."

"Yes! Oh, Amalia, you're getting this."

"I don't know what exactly I'm getting, but I do feel I understand. I can't put it into words, it's more of a feeling."

"A feeling of understanding."

"Of knowing that what you're saying about this loving and unguarded feeling makes a lot of sense to me. Keep going."

Mildred could not tell if it was sweat from summer sun or perspiration from her focus on the conversation, or energy moving, running high within them both. Running the Reiki. She'd keep going.

~ 57 ~

Panel Day ~ October

Mildred arrived at the church early.

"If today is panel day," Mildred mused, "then we will need guests. We will need panelists. We will need chairs." They had guests and chairs. "Roses, we need roses!" Mildred spun on her planted spot in the center of the community hall. "Last time, Mark brought them." She looked at Amalia.

"Not this time."

"He's not?"

"No."

"Not coming.

"I'm sorry, Mildred."

"Don't be sorry to me, there's no sorry there. You two. You grew together." She walked to Amalia and held her two empty hands. "You grew together and you're better for it."

Amalia withdrew her hands. "Roses. I can go out for roses."

"There's no time, they will all be here soon."

"We have the flower garlands from the weddings?"

"The silk ones. You're right. We could put them in a puddle here and make them look like an arrangement." Mildred motioned in a circle.

"It might look a bit like a funeral." A car pulled into the driveway outside, up the stairs, and parked in the lot where they could see it next to Mildred's blue tag spot. An old Camry. "That's okay. We don't need the silk flowers." The door of the car opened within view of the basement windows of Mercy Side, and Mildred saw Father Jasper's feet emerge from his car and plant themselves on the pavement. She gave a little clap. "Our guest of honor has arrived! Thank goodness, I thought it might be only you speaking on the panel! Father Jasper will round it out nicely."

"I thought you said you had a Registered Nurse and a local politician, too. Not just me." Amalia went to open the doors at the sound of Father Jasper's knock. "Hello and welcome!" She smiled at the white-haired gentleman who carried a leather briefcase and flowers. "Roses! Mildred, he brought roses."

"Miss Amalia. It is a pleasure to see you again. Mildred, I brought these for you in celebration of your great event." Amalia received the roses and took them to Mildred.

"The universe provides," she said, as she took the roses from Amalia. "And look, they're even in a vase this time." She put them in the middle of the three tables. "We are happy to have you join our panel, Father. This is your seat. And this is Amalia's seat."

"Who is the third one for?"

"We had a cancelation at the last minute. The nurse can't come."

"And the politician?" Amalia looked concerned.

"Never confirmed in the first place."

"You could sit there, Mildred."

"No, I want to be free to move around and take the questions."

"We could leave one seat empty for the people asking questions and they could come up."

"But they're not the panelists."

"We could pretend we have a medical authority sitting there! We could hold the space open for a medical opinion. Like 'we defer to the medical chair' on this."

"I like that. We could make a little sign. 'Medical chair'—it could be kind of fun, and you never know, maybe a doctor will show up in the audience and take the seat!"

"Mildred, how do you want to direct this, if we don't have a medical opinion?"

"I was thinking we could have each of you say what you think of medical marijuana and then take questions. And you can answer based on your perspective."

"I honestly don't have a perspective on it, Mildred. It's medicine, and it will keep getting tested and retested."

"Are we not also thinking of recreational marijuana and its legalization, Mildred?" Father Jasper walked to his designated seat and put his hands on the back of it. "I have many in my congregation who have asked about this topic."

"Yes, and Prohibition. That was my part, figuring out how prohibiting its use medically and recreationally can make more problems down the line."

"What you resist, persists, Mildred. It is a strong statement. We could open with that. You will say some words at the beginning? And in closing?" Father Jasper sat in his seat and folded his hands while he looked up at Mildred.

"Father, you are a picture of dignity." She smiled. "I hope we do right by you today. Yes, I will be offering words of opening and closing, and I will offer a Reiki blessing to the group as well."

"Perfectly appropriate."

"And Amalia has been researching the architectural implications of medical marijuana, which she can share, as they relate to buildings and communities."

"Perfectly relevant."

"And you can offer your view as they relate to your congregants' questions."

"Perfectly complementary."

"And we can defer to the Medical Chair for the medical answers."

"This will be more like a community-issues not a medical-issues discussion. Buildings, Communities, Legalization," Amalia said. "We need a legal expert."

"We have one! Father Jasper is an attorney."

"Not practicing. I am licensed in the state of Vermont, however. Just not currently practicing."

"You're fathering!" Amalia laughed.

Mildred glared at Amalia. "Not appropriate."

"I meant, he's Father Jasper, and he's fathering. I didn't mean he's fathering children."

Father Jasper covered his mouth in what appeared to be a large hiccup, and then he rolled out a huge belly laugh. "We will do just fine on this panel today!" And through his continuing laughter, they began to greet the guests as they arrived for the panel discussion and took their seats in the metal folding chairs in rows and aisles lit with the afternoon light of Mercy Side Church's basement Fellowship Hall, Mildred's Room of Real Life.

~ 58 ~
Fracking Revisited

Amalia recognized a woman from the fracking panel. She approached without haste, uncertain in her recollection of which perspective the woman had shared. As she looked, she remembered. She was the one who had wanted to report Mark to the authorities for something. Or was it to the media for something? Maybe she'd wanted to make a public statement about something his company was concealing. Amalia remembered. It was the woman with the sister who had the headaches after the frack fluid tainted her home's water supply in Pennsylvania.

"Hi. Remember me?"

The woman looked up from her bag on the floor. It was the woman who'd come loaded with printed information in preparation for the last panel. "I do remember you. You were the one who said we should all love the land." She frowned at Amalia. "How's that working out for you?"

Amalia took a step back. "How's your sister?"

The woman's jaw softened. "You remember." She nodded. "She's why I'm here."

"Okay, everyone! It's the starting time. Let's all sit, there will be more time to speak after. We have two guests today who've come from Vermont and New York City. Once you're ready, we'll begin. Please have a seat."

"Margaret," the woman said. "I'm Margaret."

The panel broke up at the halfway point for a breather. "So far, so good, Mildred." Father Jasper stood and shook out his legs. "Still stiff from the drive down."

"You'll stay at my house tonight, won't you? Like we discussed. No need to drive to and from Vermont in one day."

"I would be pleased to, and I thank you again for the invitation."

"We have Amalia staying, too."

"And her companion?" He nodded his head over to where Sunil stood at the back.

"She's not with him."

"I'm not with him. He's a friend."

"He drove all the way from New York City to see you on this panel and he's a friend. Isn't that nice."

"He is, he's sitting in the back laughing at everything I'm saying."

"That doesn't sound like a nice friend."

"He is. He's just—he has his own opinions on this stuff, and he thinks a little differently from me."

"Which he finds funny?" Father Jasper waved to Sunil. "Come on over, son."

Sunil saw the wave and responded with a nod. He pulled out his phone.

"He's ignoring me? Even in my own congregation that would not happen."

Amalia's phone buzzed with an incoming text. "Excuse me." She pulled it out; it was him texting from the back row.

I'm not going to sit in that empty chair and be on your panel.

Fine, you don't have to.

It's not up to you, is it?
You can do whatever you want.

The Father looks like he has other ideas.

Are you chickening out? Scared?

She looked up at him, and he put the phone on his lap.

"Fine." He got up and came to the front.

"Father Jasper, this is Sunil, Sunil, Father Jasper. Mildred, Sunil, Sunil, the Reverend Mildred. Sunil is a structural engineer I work with."

"I thought you were all great in the first half. The part about community growth and offering places for introspection was great. That's what many people need."

"And good ventilation!" Amalia laughed.

"That was a good point, Amalia. My own congregants have noticed an improvement in our common spaces where people can use medical marijuana, when ventilation is made the top priority. Not everyone wants to imbibe and why should they, just because a space is common."

"But it's not all smoked, right? It's tea, and capsules, and what have you?"

"We have those who choose to smoke. And we let them if it is medically necessary, with a prescription, in the church common room that we have designated for it."

"That's progressive of you, Father."

"We have those who have no other place."

"Homeless with medical marijuana prescriptions?"

"Or rather, with those at home who do not support its use."

"Even though medical marijuana is legal in your state?"

"Yes. We provide the space, which is legal."

"What about recreationally?" Sunil had become interested, Amalia noticed.

"The state is working on that. One day, it will be legal to use marijuana legally in Vermont. Right now, we have just passed a bill that makes it permissible to carry up to one ounce on one's person, and that is a big leap for us. A big leap."

"A big leap, yes, Father. People are gathering again from the restroom break. Shall we take our seats? Sunil, will you join us here?" Mildred indicated the Medical Chair.

"I'm not a doctor, I just play one on TV," he said, and pointed to his seat.

"You are a funny one," Father Jasper said. "A good friend to our Miss Amalia. You go on back to your seat, son, we'll be fine. 'I just play one on TV!' I will have to remember that."

The second half was more informal, the presentations and discussion having knocked off all the edges from the group, and an air of light chatter became the tone that bounced around the room and off its walls.

"I'd like to know more about what Amalia was sharing, about grow-op houses." Margaret stood at her seat.

"Okay, what specifically can I answer?"

"If you wanted to start growing, what would you need to do in your space?"

Amalia looked at Mildred and Father Jasper. "I don't think I should answer that," she whispered. "We're not supporting growing in houses, are we?"

"Just answer it like that," said the Father.

Amalia looked at Margaret. "I am not an expert on growing."

"Or using," said Sunil under his breath.

"What?" Margaret called out. "Who said that?"

"Never mind. What he means is, I'm not an expert in the use of recreational drugs. I'm an architectural designer, and I recently learned some more details about inspecting and renovating a house that has previously been used as a marijuana growing base. My answer to you would be opposite from what you're asking: not how to do it, but how to dismantle it. What to look for."

Mildred leaned forward to look at Amalia. "Why don't you tell us what to look for? It might be interesting."

"I don't want to single out any building or person. I will tell you generally. You might see a vent pipe that has been cut through the floorboards, to allow for ventilation from one room to another. It might be hidden under carpet. You must look for it. You might notice a smell, and there might be mold from all the humidity generated by the plants. You might notice that there are extra outlets around, at table height, that have been installed to power the grow lights. The windows might be blacked over to keep the light consistent with the grow lights. And the Drywall—you must remove the Drywall if there has been growing. The marijuana plant fibers can get into the paper surface. It can make it like an allergenic surface to people who are sensitive. It holds the fibers even after the growing operation has been moved or dismantled."

"How do you know all this?"

"I did building inspections. It came up. After the last hurricane our firm did building inspections as part of recovery work down on the Jersey Shore."

Mildred stood up. "If a house had been used as a growing base for anything, the wall surfaces might have become impregnated with the plant fibers."

"I would think."

"The walls inside should be replaced."

"Yes, I would think."

"Even if nice wallpaper was there. Old and nice wallpaper."

"I don't know, Mildred. I would say maybe. Yes. Even if there is nice wallpaper."

"Even if there is nice wallpaper that has been kept? For decades?"

"If it's been decades since the grow op then I don't know if the fibers would still be there. I don't know how that works."

"But to be sure?"

"To be sure, if you wanted certainty, you could rip out all the interior finishes."

"Even the old wooden cabinets?"

"I imagine you could wash those down with a TSP wash. I don't know. You'd have to consult an industrial hygienist. That's the person who would know for sure."

"Reverend Mildred, you're specific with your line of inquiry," said Father Jasper. "Do you have a specific property in mind?"

"Me? No. But you'd better watch out for that common room in your church, Father!"

Amalia looked at Mildred. She was quite sure to which property Mildred referred, and it wasn't in Vermont or New York; it was in Maine.

"Do drugs make people happy? Does it matter if people get happy from drugs instead of from something else?" Amalia posed the question to the Father, who sat across from her in Oliver's on Main Street. The panel had gone as well as could be expected, but Amalia was rattled by her own unanswered questions.

"Amalia, where do you feel most satisfied right now?" Father Jasper shook the sugar packet as he spoke, and his eyes twinkled when he tore the corner and the crystals spilled out onto his fingertips.

Amalia was entranced despite her earlier misgivings about this man: Mildred's son. A bit stiff. What Santa Claus–like figure hadn't earned a little stiffness over the years? Santa didn't always have it all together. She giggled at this when she realized that Father Jasper was licking the sugar crystals from his fingers, then dipping his fingers into his hot tea.

"The reason I ask, Amalia, is that it is often in our greatest satisfactions that we find the answers we thought were elsewhere." He folded the empty sugar paper around his fingers one by one, drying them. He sounded like Mildred in his tone.

"You look quite satisfied with your tea and sugar, Father." He did, and Amalia could not find anything more satisfying than watching him, in that moment.

"A good case, yes."

"A simple thing." She looked out the diner window at the rainy slickness on the sidewalks where the leaves had left their imprint. "I like that." She pointed. "The reflection in the wet pavement."

"Is it satisfying to you?"

"Not satisfying. Soothing."

"And why would you say those are different?"

"They feel different. Satisfying sounds more happy, soothing sounds more like I've been sad."

"Aha. And have you?"

"I have." She looked away from the Father and back out the window. A car splashed through a big puddle and sent a cold wave of water over a newspaper box. "Now that was satisfying!" She laughed.

"My dear. Whether you've been happy or sad is not the point. The point is to find some little nugget of gleefulness, no matter whether it comes from your happiness or your sadness. Just reach for the one that comes more naturally in the moment."

"Feeling soothed came first, but then I shifted pretty quickly into feeling a bit more   " She could not find the word.

"Alive?"

"That's rather dramatic, don't you think? It's not like I was feeling dead inside, Father. You still haven't answered my question."

"There you two are!" Mildred's voice rang from beyond the cash register, past the coat rack, near the front door. She shook a large umbrella and as she did, her head moved too, and the raindrops on her hood and umbrella flicked out and over the cashier's desk, landing on the laminated menus with a concordant splay. "Goodness!" She propped her umbrella in the corner and hung her coat. "Quite a soaker!" She looked for a way to wipe the wet raindrops from the menus and finding none, she walked toward the table where Amalia and Father Jasper waited.

"You must admit," Father Jasper said, "that was humorous!"

Mildred settled into the booth. "What are we having?"

"We haven't ordered food yet, just the tea," Amalia said. "Are you all right? You look like you got a chill out there."

"Mildred's hot blooded, I wouldn't worry about that!" Father said, then blushed at his own words.

"I am quite fine, Amalia, and the good Father is correct, I feel nothing. At least, not in the lack of warmth of my body. My eyes go funny. When it rains. All that splashing and reflecting." She squinted out the window. "Does something funny to the optics."

"The glaucoma."

"Mmm." Mildred picked up a sugar packet and shook it back and forth. "The medical marijuana helps. Lately, I've been finding I don't want it."

"I thought you liked it. Found it soothing."

"I do, Amalia. It's a funny thing, I seem to have found something I prefer even more."

"Please tell me it's not something from Frankie," the Father said.

"No; it was inspired by Frankie." Mildred shook her head, sending more little droplets to the table. "That time in Maine sent me right off the cliff, and I found I didn't want it anymore. Not just that I didn't want it anymore, but that I wanted my own Reiki more than anything else."

"You found your own alignment." Father Jasper nodded. "I thought as much. I saw it in your eyes after that."

"But it has not relieved the glaucoma in any significant way, it is just a preference."

"Do you think it might relieve your glaucoma?" Amalia was curious to know the power of Mildred's shift in thought. "Could it do that?"

"I think it could. Whether it will, I don't know."

"Father Jasper and I were talking before you came in. About whether something is soothing or not or satisfying. I forget exactly how he phrased it. Would you say the medical marijuana is soothing?"

"I definitely would. That's a good word for it, Amalia. But the Reiki feels different. It's more—soul satisfying."

"Maybe they can work together, for some people. Or in step, like with you. In a sequence. What I've found with my congregants, if I may interject, is that when they are relieved of some of the pressures of their circumstances by the medical marijuana, they are often able to find some ease in other and unexpected areas of their lives, and more ease is found on those edges. And overall, there is a great general sense of easing." The Father sat forward with an abruptness that startled Amalia. "I'm not seeing that they're particularly able to express it, though. It's like for many, that the marijuana, while giving a sense of ease— which is wonderful—also slows them down in their ability to express or shift into that more high-functioning place that they want to launch from."

"It slows them down?"

"Yes, Amalia, and that's not a bad thing, because for many, they've raced around for so long that they don't know what it is to find stillness. And when they find that stillness, it is soothing, and that is a good thing."

"But they need a bridge into something else?"

"I offer them prayer. They don't always see it as beneficial." The Father sat back.

"You could offer them Reiki," Amalia said to Mildred. "Or meditation."

"Or a walk in the woods," Mildred said. "That's what did it for me when I got lost in the woods in Maine. When I got high, with Frankie. On god knows what. Some mix he gave me, something from a little vial."

"Mildred!"

Amalia relaxed into the warm bath, a soothing place to let down her guard after the panel. Mildred's parting words to the audience had been "take care," and in the moment she heard them, Amalia took them to mean, "take care of you, Amalia, because no one else is going to." With Mildred and Father Jasper downstairs rattling pots and running water in preparation for dinner, Amalia took a few minutes to take stock, and to take care.

It had gone well. A few surprises, but none so great that they threw off the rest of the day. It had been handled; she'd handled it. Sunil's reaction had been funny, not funny ha-ha, but funny in a strange way, even though she'd laughed at the time. It didn't matter. It was done. She splashed the warm water over her belly.

What had Mildred said back there? That the resistance put up during Prohibition in Mildred's youth and before was akin to the resistance put up around drugs and marijuana legalization today. She insisted that the audience did not have to agree or disagree—yet wanted the group to see that active resistance could make it a larger issue, not a smaller issue.

And what about the recreational use? Amalia didn't care to do drugs, and that was her choice, her option, just as it was Sunil's. She preferred the floaty feeling she got from sketching. It made her feel free in her brain and outside of her body. It was the freedom she enjoyed, and that she imagined was a similar feeling that Sunil sought when he lit up. There were many paths to that floaty feeling. A meditative, nonmedicated path led to one type of journey; a medicated, marijuana path led to another type of journey. Each person to choose his or her own. Amalia sat up in the bath. "Everything in moderation!" She pulled up the drain release on the tub and watched the water begin its downward spiral.

And what about its appropriateness in medicine? "It is a medicine. And medicines have a valuable place in our lives," she said to the water as it drained. "Because sometimes the blocks we've thrown in our way are easier to overcome with a little medicine. And that's okay." She pulled herself up by the edges of the tub and got out, aware again of the noises of Mildred and Jasper making dinner downstairs. The pots rattled. "Cute," she said to the mirror. "Cute, cute, cute." They could not be a cuter family.

She realized then that she'd left the bath towel given to her by Mildred back in the guest bedroom. A small hand towel hung next to the sink. She could use it in a pinch, but, as she shivered with wet droplets running from her hair down her body, she had an immediate preference for a big, cozy towel. There must be some in there. She opened a latched cabinet opposite the toilet, presuming it to be storage for towels. No. Just boxes, and pushed-back boxes, with room for storage of old pill vials and ointments in front of them. What was in the boxes? Forget the boxes. What was in the pill vials? Picked up one, then another. They were all old clear plastic pots with white lids. They had little balls of green in them and weren't labeled. Curious, she opened one and sniffed. Smelled kind of sour and fresh at the same time. Wasn't marijuana, at least as far as her limited experience told her. That was more skunky, right? The next vial had a little more brown in there with the green, almost like a kind of bark ground up in it. What was it? She smelled it, with a tentativeness as she brought it to her nose. It smelled good, earthy, and pungent. Also not marijuana, she reckoned. Maybe there was marijuana in it? She was curious. Tapped a little into the palm of her hand. It sprung out of its tight ball once it hit the warmth and wetness of her palm, and too late, the steaminess of the room. She tried to put it back in, but it stuck to her hand, and expanded.

Amalia felt a little woozy. The nausea came in waves, and she sat down.

"Fresh cream," Mildred said. "Fresh off the top. It's like that when you get it right. But I'm not seeing that for you right now. I'm seeing the rings on the palms of your hands and I'm guessing, I'm guessing you put something there that left a mark, maybe a steamy mark."

Mildred was right. She'd put something there in her steaming palm and it had expanded, a little at first. The bud-shaped ball of whatever it had been had sprung to life in the steam and released its essence to her in its brightness, and she'd sniffed it close, tasted it, and then what? Mildred was sitting her down, no, she was already down. She was lying down on the floor. Mildred was sitting down next to her. The room was getting interesting. The ceiling above. Mildred looking down into her eyes, curls of white hair bobbing around round cheeks and the eyes in between winked at her.

"You're going to be okay. I'm going to get a cool wet cloth for you. Don't go anywhere."

Wasn't going anywhere. Leaned her head back on the floor. The ceiling came to her, and the corners of it curled up with little creatures at the edges, little animals, what were they? She watched them play there for a while. A cool cloth on her forehead.

"That'll do you better for now," Mildred said. "Which bottle was it, Amalia?"

She'd opened all of them, in that steamy bathroom.

"Which bottle did you tip into your palm? Was it the mix? I think it I was the mix."

Sure. The mix.
She heard a man's voice beyond Mildred's She coming down now?

"She's as high as a kite, Father."

Amalia stopped running. The floor felt good. Who was that man? Sunil?

"She wants Sunil."
"Do you have his number?"

"No, wasn't Sunil."
"Maybe he's still in Binghamton."
"Why didn't he come for dinner?"
"Sunil, yes, Sunil stayed over at the hotel on Main Street."
"Hotel on Main Street did she say?"
No wait, had she said that out loud? Sunil?
"I'll call over to there. Do you know his last name?"
"No. I'll just ask for a Mr. Sunil and see if they know."
"You can't say Mister, they'll get confused, Japser. Just Sunil."
"Sunil. Fine, I'll call over."

Amalia curled further into the side of the sofa, its legs hard against her back. It felt good, brought her closer back to the edge of her body. "Don't want that man there," she said.

"Sunil? Or Father Jasper?" Mildred sat closer to her, hand on Amalia's thigh. "I'm wondering if we should be taking you to the hospital. It's not normal to throw up as many times as you did."

The creatures at the corners of the ceiling beckoned, and she turned her gaze up to them. "See them? My friends."

"Oh, Amalia."

The underwater feeling was shifting, and the friends went back into the corners. Amalia sat up straight. Needed to go outside for air, fresh air. The taste in her mouth was sour. "Water."

"I can get you some, just wait here a moment." Mildred patted her thigh and with a grunt and a creak of the knees, pushed and pulled herself up against the sofa. "Can't remember the last time I sat on the floor."

Amalia leaned back on the sofa's edge. The room had stopped spinning. She was clear. All was fine. They'd have Sunil over as soon as anything, and maybe to the hospital too. Didn't need any of that. Didn't want the Father peering into her eyes, Mildred worrying. She pressed herself up against the sofa to standing, and with a wobble, she was upright. There was a window to the porch but the only doorway in and out of the room led to the hallway next to the kitchen. Mildred would be back in a flash. Amalia would be faster. She was fine. The window was easy, and she was through in a blink, landed one foot in a planter and the other on the wood boards of the old porch. Ankle twisted; she'd be fine. Kept going down the stairs, steadied herself on the railing. The air felt good. She breathed it in, happy to be alive for that moment of inhalation. So much to be thankful for.

Her hot cheeks burned in the cold air, and a tingle in her arms and legs reminded her that not all was normal. She should take some care. Some precautions. Right. She'd keep going, would not stop to talk to strangers. Main Street would be near enough, and she'd get to Sunil before they would. The breath was delightful, and it smiled within her, and her legs carried her fast with long paces. All was well with the world. Her midsection tingled with a coiling and uncoiling feeling, up her spine and into throat, and she pressed on toward Main Street.

Kalpana. His last name was Kalpana. She crossed over the street and wondered which way to Main. If she changed her name, what would that be? Amalia Sengupta Erenwine Kalpana: ASEK. She felt ace in that moment. Up ahead, the lights of Binghamton's Main Street twinkled. She could tell she wasn't all there when her foot missed the curb and she ended up in the gutter, lying with one leg bent beneath the other, between two parked cars and on top of a pile of leaves and debris. Oh well. She'd rest there for a little while.

On her back, hair rustling in old leaves, she looked up at the tree above. Pretty tree, in the light of dusk. Golden hour, they called it. Why hadn't Sunil come for dinner at Mildred's? Didn't matter. Then she heard the tree: "Why did you want him to come for dinner?"

Didn't, just thought it might have been interesting to continue the conversation.

"Then why did you push him away?"

She hadn't! Hadn't intended to. Hadn't known how to manage the intensifying reaction she was having and having with those peering eyes of Father Jasper watching on.

"Father Jasper doesn't matter to you," said the tree.

"You're a pretty tree," she said aloud.

She'd be back. Time would guide her. Time didn't lie. Time, not trying, would restore her.

"Sorrow and joy, joy, and sorrow. Where do we play? In the in-between? In the woods?" She sang the words to the tree. "All woods have the capacity to carry equal amounts of joy and sorrow." Words she'd mused before, came together with ease.

She felt out of herself, beyond her own skin. Imagined being wrapped in the old quilt of Great Aunt Joan. The thought soothed her, and she sat up. Brushed her cheeks of leaf debris. Pushed up to stand from the cold, stone curb and began to walk. She didn't need a new last name. The one she had was perfect and fine. Erenwine.

~ 59 ~

Bear Mountain

Amalia breathed in lungs full of clean mountain air, reminiscent of her time in New Hampshire with Mark. Unbalanced by the year's events, she'd come with Jen to the closest natural place she could find outside of New York City—Bear Mountain—to stabilize. It felt good, and she needed nothing more than this mountain and its crispness in the moment. She and Jen rented a car and made a weekend of it, camping in the tents they stopped to pick up from her parents' Pennsylvania basement. The air brought her to her senses and relieved the worries that had niggled at her, to the point where those worries could not be dredged at all. She couldn't remember what she'd been concerned about. Jen had suggested meditating in the mornings before work, and that had helped a lot. Yogi Jen with her yoga mat permanently attached to her, rolled up and bagged in a sleeve with a sling, a constant on the daily arrival at the office from the subway journey from Jen's home on Warren Street—a place Amalia was calling home, in lieu of Hamilton Heights. In turn, Amalia had nudged Jen to try doing yoga at home. It didn't have to be all out, out, out, in a studio, sweating it out with dozens of other people.

Jen told her of a retreat in the Catskills, a place where they could do yoga (or not), have meals provided, and sleep inside or out. Amalia wondered if it was a Jeremy thing. Maybe it didn't matter. It sounded accommodating, flexible, and easy. Just what Amalia was seeking.

But for the moment, it was Bear Mountain, Jen's favorite, with its bald rocky faces and rough-edged tree line. If it had been a person, she would have described it as ruggedly handsome. And if she could hear this person's thoughts, she would know them as soothing. Soothing and elevating, elevating and soothing. This person, this mountain, this being. This mountain and all it had seen, experienced, absorbed, and reflected. It stood north of New York City, alongside the Hudson River, a ready sentinel at the gateway to the regions north, south, west, and east.

Jen had offered her a joint—a hiker's balm of sorts, Jen said, and Amalia declined. She preferred a clearer head and connected experience. The one druggy time Amalia had was a bust; "a drug bust!" She laughed as she said it to Jen on the trail. Jen insisted it was the clearer experience. Amalia felt fluid with meditation and the visions present within her and didn't feel the need for something augmented. The drug explorations of Mildred— medical marijuana and whatever else the woman had in her bathroom closet, sampled by Amalia—those medical morsels of Mildred left her high and dry, and Sunil's preferences didn't touch her own, which was always for creative clarity.

Amalia stretched it out on the trail ahead—a tree-lined rocky stretch of stone steps and root ladders—and as she went, she looked for the light shafts she'd come to associate with expansive places. Light waves, light energy—neither daylight nor sun shafts—what she saw were the energy-tracks of trees, rocks, rivers and of the whole earth, she supposed. Didn't try to explain what she saw to Jen, who wouldn't get it, would suggest she get her eyes checked. Or maybe not. Jen was full of surprises.

As a roommate (and they were roommates, even though Amalia slept on the sofa of the one-bedroom apartment), Jen was predictable: she followed a chart of chores, did her laundry and grocery shopping at the same time every week, and studied for the architecture exams every night after work, except Friday nights, which she insisted they both take off. A break was necessary, Jen said, for the brain to catch up and to synthesize all the information that had been crammed in. And crammed, it was. Amalia studied nightly, even on the occasional Friday evening.

The light shifted as she moved through, and when the views opened, she lost track of the light and focused on the landscape as it rolled out in front of her: rocky and smooth, mossy below and blue above. Jen had gone ahead on the downhill, eager to get back, and Amalia wanted to hike. What she wanted most was to stay until sunset, but she'd be coming back on the trail in the dark at that point, and she did not want that for her weekend experience.

~ 60 ~
Devils' Cuts

Later, when Alleman went to find the wood for the fire, he tripped over an old log, buried under soft leaves. It appeared to be straight, as if cut by a man. Alleman pushed aside the leaves. The wood log had edges, sharp as if cut by an axe, and by a tall man with a long arm, wielding a short blade. He knew it from his own father's hand. The log had been there a long time, had not rotted, and had not been encountered by him the previous year. Alleman kicked into the leaves around and found other logs, some buried in part and some exposed.

It had been a cold and frosty winter, with many stones pushed up. He'd thought it the Devil's work, and others confirmed it. To make the soil untillable through the emergence of stones, as if overnight: it was only a sinful man who would experience sorrow. And these logs, thought Alleman, they taunted him with their straight cuts. Devil's cuts. Curious, though, he heaved one end of one log and looked it down. The length was good. It had the hand of Man. It could not be the Devil's work, not with a hand as had his father in the working of wood. He must have missed it in the previous treks. It could become part of the house he would build for Miriam when she came ashore on the next ship. He would tell no one but would return with a horse and a boy to claim these Man-hewn timbers as his own. Their clayishness suggested they had been buried for some time, and he could think of no other way they might have emerged, save the fast running of summer springs, washing away their overburden, and leaving the residue of their burial. A vision of his father's hand reached in the clearing, bright. Alleman would return for these gifts.

Later still, when Alleman returned to the clearing with a horse and a boy (the boy whom he had paid to remain in silence after), they clawed at the edges of the logs they found to be in some pattern, some with peg-holes and some with curves, some fallen and some laid. After a while and in the middle, Alleman sat: the boy stood with the horse, and Alleman poured whisky from his flask into the soil, as if in offering, as he had seen his native kinsmen do. Theirs was not a whisky offering; rather a tobacco one. Alleman would preserve his tobacco and offer his most sacred elixir instead. As he sat on that spot, he felt and saw the hand of his bright father in the clearing, once again. Could it be that his father was showing him a way? Alleman looked to the spot of the whisky on the soil, where he had pushed away the leaves. He'd told no one about his father's visitations, for surely they would call him wizard or witch, and for this he would be hung or burned, as had others already. Alleman knew this was not the Devil, but was, in clear vision, his father. And for this he was grateful and trusting. He looked again where his father shone, and with an inkling to stand, and to scratch down, Alleman scratched down into that earth, softened by the season's rains, until he had dug far down his elbows, and they were surpassed by the banks of the hole. He looked up to the light of his father, and with a whistle to the boy to come, he smiled. His father had led him to treasure. The boy came, and with four hands, they pulled the box from the cool and damp soil.

The boy screamed when the box was unsealed and opened, and Alleman, too, was startled, dropping the box where it lay. Inside, an amber, animal face looked back at them. He picked it up, and bones fell from the back of it, powdery dust coming from them as they landed. They looked to be a part of the whole, and Alleman was moved. He sat back and looked. Took out a long leather thong from his satchel. Tied the bones to the amber construction. It had been a wonder for someone, and they had left it here. They would return. They'd left it here as a marker. A marker for another, another who would come. It moved him further, and he felt a gentle nudge from within. Next to where the thong had been in his satchel, was his rough cloth. He brought it to the animal face and wiped its brow, seeing beneath the layers of darkness a brightness that revealed small plants inside. And shells. He did not recognize them as of that place, or of the place of his origin. Shells from another beach. He rubbed the surface with his rough cloth.

It flinted, and a spark flicked from the surface of amber, startling him.

With haste, he put the amber face in the box, pressing the lid back on. He felt for the candle in his pocket and broke off a piece, chewing and breaking the wax with his spittle. Pressed the wax mush into the edge between box and lid. He lowered the box and mounded the soil back over top of it.

The logs, they would stay. They were good logs, and he felt the certainty of a man who had been guided by the hand of God; he would accept the logs as the marital gift he knew them to be; he would build his house for Miriam, and he would finish it before her ship arrived. This would be the spot of it, and he would do nothing more than erect the timbers where they had fallen. The box in the ground would remain, and he would tell no one. Nor would the boy, because, Alleman discovered, the boy wanted only money, and more money was enough to buy his silence. The amber face had entranced and entrained him, and he'd been swayed, swayed by that thing, and although he believed the Devil to be a temptation everywhere, he felt it not with the amber thing itself. That was golden. That was good. Here, he would place his home. The face would grace the logs that God had given, guided by the Father. He would tell no one.

Part III: The Museum

~ 61 ~
Release

Antonella packed with haste, her slim fingers assembling small piles of what the family might need. Her logic told her: food and sleep, clothes, and books. Her piles were assembled thusly: dry flour in the sack (the most vulnerable of the items), straw bedding (clean) from the winter supply in the shed (it would not go bad inside, in the attic), buttons and thread for repairs to torn clothing (she wasn't sure what to gather for the cobbling so she set aside some goose grease hoping it would suffice for soaking into old leather), and the family bible. It had within it loose sheaths of paper, receipts and invoices of the transactions that proved her family's freedom. Should she take hers, the life-saving paper nugget of gold? If she lost it in the water crossing then she would lose evidence of her freedom, cast a full decade before. There was no time for second thought. It was safer to ensure its preservation, and it had been given long ago, almost ten years. She would not need the paper. She left it with the others. Instead, she took with her the colored fabric scraps not yet used in her latest quilt, tucked them into her boots, which became fat and tight against her ankles with the added pressure. The rest of the fabric lay deep in the ground where she and her mother had left it, wrapping the strange thing, putting it to rest where they'd found it, hoping it would watch over them.

The men at Portland Harbor said the Confederate action had been bad that day, and Papa urged them to go. Although they lived in a free state, the war beckoned, and Portland Harbor shook with the threat of its nearing. They would follow the old routes to Canada and would return after the troubles.

~ 62 ~

Bones

Mildred was up long before she needed to be, to get the bus to the Tsawwassen Ferry Terminal. Early to bed, early to rise. Her jet lag was silly; to be up at one o'clock in the morning West Coast time was going to throw off her whole day. Still, she was up and not a bit tired. She walked through Muriel's house in the dark, felt her way down the stairs and through the living room to the tall west-facing windows. The view, in the dark. Her favorite.

Burnaby lights twinkled below and blocked Vancouver lights beyond. A glow of city night light bounced off thin clouds, and although she couldn't see Bowen Island in the dark, by day it would be visible on her left. She looked right, to Seymour, Grouse, and Cypress, mountains lit twenty-four hours a day. She looked down at the road below. No traffic at this time, but there would be soon enough, with a shift change at the refinery at the end of the block.

She'd smelled it yesterday. But when she'd mentioned it to a neighbor, they said they smelled nothing and that they never smelled anything. In fact, he'd looked at her like she was a bit fou. She couldn't bring herself to think it in English. Crazy. There. Ah well. A difference of opinion. Or a difference of olfactory sensibilities. Same difference, in this case. She turned from the window and went to make a cup of tea, turned on the TV while the electric kettle heated up to a gentle boil.

She looked through Muriel's things while the TV chattered in the background. Not much new to see since last visit, except a pile of movie ticket stubs and her new library books. Why hadn't she returned them before she'd gone on vacation? Oh dear. Her sister, the delinquent librarian. Mildred recalled she'd kept her own library books out, too, before coming here. She put down her tea and thumbed through the top copy on Muriel's stack, a book about the life of artist Emily Carr. What a life it was. Those majestic trees. How did she get the light just like that? It seemed to Mildred that Emily Carr had painted spirit more than anything. She'd have to go to see them in real life. The paintings? The trees themselves? Maybe both. She took the book back to the TV, where she flipped its pages in the bright light of the screen.

Mildred hoped to hitch a ride from the ferry, a short walk up the road from the Long Harbour Terminal. She took her chances that someone would pick her up after the ferry traffic had begun to flow past. A young guy and his girlfriend stopped.

"Do you live on Salt Spring?"

"Yes, we do."

"What do you do?"

They looked at each other. "We weave. And we sell."

"You sell?"

This was an unexpected and well-timed encounter. She got into the Datsun on the side the fellow indicated. "I was going to go to the dispensary on Hastings Street when I go back to Vancouver, but if you're selling, I could get it from you, instead."

After a meandering island-time drive, they pulled into a lot at the end of a dirt road and Mildred got out of the old car. A spotted dog ran up to greet the young woman.

"I'll be right back," the man said. "One ounce okay?"

"Yes, thank you, dear."

"Would you like to see the weavings?"

"You have weavings? I thought that was a euphemism for drugs."

"No, we do. We weave." The woman led the way down a muddy path to a shed. "This is the studio." She opened the door. Gold-threaded silk strips woven with seaweed hung from the rafters. Light shone through the fibers and silk, and there was a faint smell of ocean and musk in the room.

"Oh, my."

"This is what we do."

"This is wonderful work. You sell these?"

"We do. We make more money on the pot, to be honest."

"What's this one?"

"It's an ocean tribute."

"It looks like a banner." She waved a hand over the letters sewn over the weave.

"It is. We took it to Victoria last year for the Defend Our Coast rally."

"You went? I got an email about that."

"You should have gone. It was amazing."

"I was in New York."

"Oh god, what were you doing there?"

"I live there. I'm visiting here. But I'm from Vancouver. Burnaby. My mother lived here. We lived on the other side, in Vesuvius, when I was growing up. And then we moved her, Mother, to a condo in Ganges."

"You've been all over."

"I come back and forth. I'm from Maine." Her mind floated to the year they'd lived in Israel for a year on her husband's sabbatical. "And Jerusalem."

The woman smiled that kind smile saved for those who make no sense. "I'm sure." She opened the door at a light rap, and her partner stepped in over the threshold. He handed Mildred the package.

"How much?"

"Nah, it's free."

"No, you can't do that."

"You remind me of my Gran." He kissed her on the cheek. "So yes, I can."

"Well at least let me buy one of these." Mildred pointed to the ocean tribute.

Mildred turned on the radio in Mother's condo and sat to listen to CBC's updates. The silk and seaweed ocean tribute banner lay across the table in front of her and she fingered it while she listened to the news.

She laid her hand on the quilt bundle, unopened since her intercontinental travel, having secreted the thing past Canada Customs. She'd passed it off as chicken bones, the quilt nestled deep inside her padded thermal lunch bag. Had the smarts to leave the metal box and gourd back home in Binghamton. The customs agent bought her lunch story and didn't open the package. The airport X-ray revealed what was inside: leftover bones from somebody's lunch.

She picked up Mother's old phone handset off the wall and called Muriel on the other side of the island. The quilt lay open on the kitchen table, and the bones sat, rune-like, Mildred thought, in the middle. She didn't fear the thing anymore. She'd made it this far; they had. It was time to get her sister, the perpetual librarian, to lay eyes on the bones.

Mildred sat at Muriel's kitchen table with the bones before them. Muriel's friend Bob the archeologist recognized the bones as of fowl.

"Ancient, by the looks of them, powdery here," he said, and turned them over in his hands. "They've been in something oily, waxy maybe, which has preserved them." He wore gloves, as did Mildred and Muriel. "You say you found them on the East Coast of the States?"

"Yes, in Maine. Buried near my family's home. Our family's home," Mildred said, nodding to Muriel. "And that bit fell off the gourd when I removed the bones. Just a sliver."

"I was little then," Muriel said. "Don't remember much."

"You've got something very, very old, you two. Very old. See this? This could be residual of bird bones." Bob gently turned over the bones with his gloved hands. "A forensic anthropologist with training in zoological anthropology could certainly identify a chicken-like bird from a few bones, but we'd need further testing to prove a match. The sliver of gourd might give us more."

"Could be something else, though, couldn't it," Mildred said. Chickens seemed so banal for such a mysterious object.

"You could indeed identify chicken bones from a very small fragment of mineralized bone, or even fireplace ash, with isotopic ratio analysis. DNA is also possible, with a bit of luck, especially if it's a chunk of heavier vertebrae or a thick drumstick."

"Hope it's not human," Muriel said.

"There are some studies that show you can date human burials from time-of-death by assessing mineral levels in bone and soil. If you had pig bones, now—plenty on them!"

"You think they're pig bones? They had pig bones in the Americas hundreds of years ago?"

"Who says it's from the Americas originally? And yes, there were pigs—brought over by colonists. Who knows, maybe even brought over by earlier explorers."

"Invaders, more like," said Muriel. "Vikings! Earlier European colonists? Chinese explorers?"

"The European colonists weren't invaders," Mildred said. "Quite the opposite!"

"Depends on who you ask," said Muriel. "Invaders they turned out to be!"

"There's something else," Bob said, putting the bones back down, lined up on the table. "For avian bones to survive more than a few years in earth-burial conditions, they'd need to be well buried, out of scavenger scenting. The larger, more mineralized bones, anyway. The smaller ones would first lose their collagen and become brittle, and then crumble."

"So, our bones are not old at all?"

"Far from it. They're likely quite old. I'm just saying that in an outdoor landfill you might find ten- or twenty-year-old thicker bones, but not ribs or wing bones."

"It's definitely more than twenty years old," Mildred said. If it made no sense to her, how could it make sense to them, the logical ones?

Bob continued. "We know of turkey farming and consumption patterns from hundreds of years ago because of these larger bones that were buried in alkaline middens that helped preserve them."

"Turkey bones are possible, aren't they Mildred?" Muriel circled the table to get a closer look, resting her gloved hands on Bob's shoulders

"Don't look at me, I'm not the expert here," Mildred said.

"It's a funny thing," Bob said, smiling and animated, "oddly, those preserved turkey bones lasted because the proteins were boiled out of them for stock first!"

"What, for eating, you mean? Mildred, that's possible, isn't it?" Muriel clapped her hands. She seemed happy to give Bob an audience. Were they a thing? Mildred would have to ask later.

"Could be eating, yes. With only the minerals remaining, the acids from protein and fat didn't degrade the bones any further.

There are examples of fine bird-bone needles surviving, or polished-bone tools, but in general, they've been carefully stored in dry conditions, or treated with pitch or beeswax or other things."

"Is that what the coating is, something like that? Beeswax?"

"That or something resinous. If you look here, it looks like there is something amberish embedded in this bit of the gourd. As if amber had encased part of it, actually. And the bones might have been boiled with extra animal fat if they were part of someone's meal."

Mildred thought of the areas that had been tapped for holes on the rounded side of the melon shape she'd left at home. She sighed. So much to know. Did it matter at all? Bob was only seeing part of the story, and she'd created the separation of the parts all on her own, having left the rest of the gourd itself on her linen-clad dining table in Binghamton. He'd been displeased with her about that, saying she was no archeologist in her treatment of the thing, its wrapping, and the box. But he was steadfast in his desire to help.

"If you leave these bones and this bit with me, I can have the lab run some studies on them." Bob sat back, took of his gloves. "What you got here, is a mystery."

"Hear the river?"

Mildred stood with Muriel on the back of Mount Tuam.

"I need to put these bones to rest, to stop carrying them across the continent."

"What's stopping you?"

Mildred, preparing to board the plane at YVR, was stopped this time by Canada Customs. "Have you been on a farm?"

Uh-oh—what now? "I—I've been on a lavender farm on Salt Spring Island." She'd visited Bert's place when he'd assured her Claudia was out at the bakery. "Why?"

"Possible transportation of agricultural bacteria across an international border. You'll need to quarantine your footwear for two weeks."

"It was a lavender farm."

"Any livestock?"

"He does have chickens."

"Ma'am," the officer said, "please step over here." He motioned to a holding area behind his booth.

"But I haven't done anything wrong!" She pulled her carry-on bag a little closer to her legs.

"Ma'am—" He looked at her bag, now as tight to her body as she could make it, ramrod straight against her thin fall coat. He waved to another officer. "We'll need to inspect her bag, too."

Nestled into a corner of the holding room, Mildred took a deep breath and looked around. Everyone in the room looked as perplexed as she felt, to varying degrees. She turned to the man next to her, a young, bearded gentleman with a leather case. "And what have they pulled you aside for?"

"They're interested in my video footage." He motioned to his bag. "I'm a filmmaker."

"Oooh, you must be a good filmmaker."

He laughed. "I don't know about that. I was doing a short documentary film about Canada Customs, and they wanted to see what I collected."

"Oh. And they might confiscate it?"

"No!" He smiled. "They want to see how they look on camera. I interviewed them and I'm waiting for their next break. They don't want to wait for the release date." The man unzipped his bag. "See?" He pointed to the camera equipment. "I'm a freelance videographer. I do work for PBS and that."

"Goodness me." Mildred straightened up. "They've got me in for lavender contraband. Or something." It occurred to her that she ought to shut up.

~ 63 ~
Freedom

The whistle in the wind reminded her of Maine. Mildred McCaine of Maine. How arcane! Mildred, three, not eighty-three; five, 1935. A beach. White stone, red-streaked. Tip of a ship.

She rolled over in bed. Blue luminosity bounced around the room, an effect of moonlight and streetlight, she supposed. It lulled her back into an old bed, a childhood bedroom. Blue light, white stone, red-streaked.

What was the red streak across the white stone? Whale's blood? Or of some other? In her bedroom, or in a dream?

Mildred held the piece of paper from Muriel in her hands. It was a third piece, matched with the first, and the second, found by Amalia. The tea sat next to her, and she put the paper down, sipped the tea. Was she ready? She was. The tea lifted her. She picked up the paper. Thought of her old otters. She matched the pieces, which fit together. Mildred inhaled.

"By the President of the United States of America: A Proclamation," she read aloud. Eliza jumped up on the table and Mildred pushed her away. "Not this one, darling.

Whereas, on the sixteenth day of October, in the year of our Lord one thousand eight hundred and fifty-four, a proclamation was issued."

She wasn't ready. Put down the paper. Picked up the tea. Smelled it at the rim. Closed her eyes and drifted in her mind to the other coast, to a day her father had taken her by rowboat to nearby Galiano Island.

The otters there, they delighted her. River otters turned to the sea.

In the morning shimmer and sheen of mist and glory they slipped in and out the cool air and cooler waters.

She felt the movement as her own.

Wanted it part of her day; she took off each shoe with care for their soles, laid them on the rocky shoreline while far enough back the tide wouldn't take them.

And she joined the otters, river otters in the ocean, sea otters born of river otters? She didn't know. Didn't care.

Plunged her head into the frigid, came up gasping and laughing.

Otters gone deep. Couldn't find them.

Too cold.

Too early.

Too salty.

Too slippery.

Too silly!

She knew she would be fine, all fine, warm, and dry. She chattered, teeth clattered, and she turned in sunlight to the shore. Fishing boats out, they'd get her if she needed. But the otters, where—

Splash! Behind her.

She turned to see not one, but three.

Mildred put down the tea, picked up the paper. It was time. The paper had been issued by a court. Her hand shook. She read to Eliza, who sat on the edge of the table with an obedient face.

"Know all men by these presents that I, John Jeremiah Moore, have manumitted and set free and by these presents do manumit Emancipate and set free from Slavery or servitude certain slaves belonging to me To wit Antonella Moore, a light coloured black Indian girl of the West Indies aged about 12 years and I do thereby give grant and release unto the said Antonella Moore all my right titles claim of in and to their personal services and labor and of in and to the Estates and property which they may hereafter acquire or which they may have heretofore acquired hereby releasing and forever freeing them from all claim that I may have had to their personal labor and services and by these presents do declare them free both from me and my heirs forever In Testimony whereof I the said John

Jeremiah Moore have hereunto subscribed my name and affixed my seal this the sixteenth day of October in the year of our Lord One thousand Eight hundred and fifty four."

It ended,

"Judge John Jeremiah Moore
October the 16th AD 1854"

~ 64 ~

Plaster

Plaster marks swooped over her head in the subway—someone had had fun creating the smoothed patterns once upon a time, and how long ago was that? A hundred years? The plasterwork and the feeling of its maker gave Amalia a feeling of resonance with that moment of creation. She could take it into Odin's Wind.

She intuited the hand of the maker. Felt she was hallucinating—or was it a vision? The feeling reminded her of the swooning energy and emotion she'd felt back at the foundations in Maine. Once upon a time, she'd have thought to tell Mark. He'd have only told her to see an eye doctor, or a neurologist. She felt the trick of the eye was connected to the box she'd found while away with Mildred, and to the object within it. She'd even had the same feeling walking around the fracking site in Pennsylvania with Mark, ages ago. Amalia realized she'd been seeing not only the energy of the earth and its disruption, as she'd felt pounded with it in Pennsylvania, but was also seeing the powerful force of creation, and all that was beautiful, serene, and profound. It was there before her, in the plaster swoops. Mark would say she was high. That she'd been smoking weed with Mildred.

No way. She wasn't one for drugs, and though he might have understood it, she hadn't told Mark about the accidental interlude with them at Mildred's.

She'd felt and seen so much then, but she'd been unable to translate the clear vision and feeling into her art, into words, and into concepts that she could share. It had left her both high, and sluggish. It wasn't a clean or clear feeling.

There, though, in the subway, as clear and clean as ever, she saw, felt, and connected with the arc of the plasterer's thought, form, and product of craft. The trajectory was clear. And she felt if she could see with that clarity, then she should be able to paint with equal clarity. She just could not figure out what was stopping her. One thing she did know for sure was that whatever was stopping her had nothing to do with Mark.

Once home, she prepared for Sunil's after-work arrival. Amalia heard him on the steps above before she heard the buzzer: Jen's old garden-level one-bedroom apartment in Brooklyn had become Amalia's de facto crash pad. Sunil was early and she spun once around the apartment and flashed a smile at the mirror, teeth clean, happy, and vibrant, ready for a date. This time she wouldn't post it anywhere or tell anyone. It was just her and Sunil. Jen was out, and Paige was nowhere to be found, having moved out some time ago.

But he wasn't interested—he had a business proposition. He wanted to create a new consulting company with her.

"I'm confused. I thought you wanted to go out on a date." Her cheeks got hot. She was over caring. She feigned fanning herself and added, "Silly me! Let's talk."

~ 65 ~

What It Takes

Amalia woke on a wave of a sunrise dream, one that beckoned her to look out the ground floor windows up to sky, to the tree-topped building horizon. She felt the essence of her Odin painting and in her half-awake state, a thought drifted in:

There is blue in the sky even at dawn; even in the grey to gold emergence of sun, and in a new day there is blue in blue sky—every color has within it an aspect of another. The spectrum is in every particle of light. It is the attunement or attention to one aspect that illuminates it, that illuminates the blueness.

The light stayed with her all day, and into the next weeks, fueling her, bridging to the next phase in her life.

It was only when she took some time off work and had some goofy fun that things began to come together. She hadn't realized how bound up she had been in her own thoughts and self-imposed pressures, caught up in studying for the exams. That one big, fat exam with its multiple parts, spread over days, weeks, months. What would it take to become an architect, honestly? Honestly. She could not remember when she had last had a good night's sleep, a good shag, a good haircut, a good anything.

~ 66 ~

Hunches

Muriel called Mildred in Binghamton.

"She told me it was secret," Muriel said. "I never told anyone. How come she didn't tell you?"

"I think she did tell me," Mildred said. "I just didn't realize it at the time."

"She said they buried a quilt there."

"I remember we buried something."

"She did tell you?"

"I was little, Muriel. We were still living there."

"She told you while we were living there? You must have been what, four or five?"

"Something. How old were you?"

"It was right before she died," Muriel said. "She said she told you."

"But I was so little. What did she tell you? What do you remember from before she died?"

"If I remember correctly," Muriel said, "the house was part of the Underground Railroad. And all the houses in the area were part of the same network, and it connected to the water, where Papa ran the boats. Moorehouse, Poorhouse, Roughhouse, Rum. It wasn't all hooch."

"When Papa did it," Mildred said, "it was all hooch." "But before?"

"It was Freedom," Muriel said.

"Path to it."

"Gives me the shivers."

"It's a good thing, why the shivers?"

"Shivers like goosebumps, Mildred. It's a good thing, you're right."

"Who was part of it, everyone? What did Mother say?"

"Not everyone. They had some to be wary of."

"In the Porter house," Mildred said.

"No, I think Porters was the center of it."

"In the tax man?"

"Somebody like that, yes."

"She told you?"

"She didn't have to. I saw it in her eyes."

"Eyes, that's not helpful, Muriel!" Mildred wiped her own with the back of her hand. "What did she tell you?"

"Why are you grilling me like this?"

"Because I saw something, Muriel, and I have to make sense of it. When I was little. I saw something or somebody carried out in a bedsheet."

"Somebody dead?"

"No."

"Somebody hurt?"

"No."

"Somebody hiding." Muriel murmured to herself. "That makes sense."

"How does this make any sense?" Mildred was distraught. "All this time I've had this awful feeling that somebody was murdered or something there."

"Somebody hiding. She told me."

"What?" Mildred couldn't believe it. "You knew? What do you know?"

"She said they'd acted it out for us once, but I didn't remember. Mildred, you remember. You are the one who does remember."

"I have no idea. Muriel, what is it? What did they act out for us? Who did?"

"The old Porter lady and Grandma. She said they'd seen it when they were kids. That their mothers would bundle the slaves out with the laundry and the bedsheets to go between the houses in a cart. When they were delivering the laundry."

"But Porters never did laundry! That was just Mama when the hooch wasn't paying."

"No, Mildred. Laundry was the thing when it was needed. It wasn't for the money only. It was for the shelter."

"Porters took in laundry, too?"

"They handled the business side of it. Set up the accounts, you know?"

Mildred remembered the room she'd stayed in with Mother of the Bride. "They had some quilt fragments on the wall of the Moores'. Maybe like the quilt that got buried?"

"Signals, they were, that's what Grandma said. Most were taken along but some were left as signals."

"Signals for us?"

"No, for the other slaves. They were signals on the Underground Railroad. The quilts. The patterns. They hung the quilts out as markers of what was safe, what wasn't, what to do, where to go. I'm not making this up, Mildred. It's written now. Oral history, written now. I thought you knew. She told me she told you."

"But we never talked about it, you and me. And I was young. How could I know." It wasn't a question.

"What else do you remember?"

"I remember blood on the beach, on the rocks. That's why I thought there was a murder."

"Maybe somebody got hurt."

"Maybe." Mildred looked up at the sky through her kitchen window. "Maybe I put the bedsheet roll and the blood on the beach together in my mind. Maybe I made it all up."

"What about the gourd-thing?"

"I don't know anymore."

"You said it was buried."

"It was hidden. Amalia hid it under the floorboards of the Moorehouse shed. I mean, Porters. The Porter house. The folks we stayed with at the Moorehouse told us that their old shed used to be the Porters' home, and Amalia figured out that Porters might've become 'Poorhouse.' It did seem big for a shed. But she found it buried in some old foundations nearby."

"Porters. But somebody left it there at the old foundations? Like maybe they were going to come back for it but then our Grandma found it?"

"I don't know. It was wrapped in quilt bits." Mildred paused. "I wasn't looking for quilts then. Maybe there were some extra pieces? I don't know."

"These old foundations, could they have been the Roughhouse from the rhyme?"

"Suppose so, yes."

"This gourd, you think it could be African?"

"How would an African gourd get here? They didn't bring anything. They were slaves brought over on ships against their will. They weren't exactly packing their mementos from home to bring on the trip because they'd be away for generations."

"Maybe someone else brought it," Muriel said.

"From Africa. Come on."

"Maybe one of the slave traders brought it."

"And it ended up in the old foundations near the Porters'? Behind our old house? The old Roughhouse."

"Anything is possible," Muriel said. "And maybe it's not African."

"It doesn't look Native American."

"Could it be Caribbean?"

"Caribbean of African origin?"

"I have no idea. I'm afraid I'm out of my area of expertise."

"I thought librarians knew everything." Mildred smiled out the window.

"Librarians know how to find answers." Muriel paused on the phone. "And this librarian knows just who to contact."

"Bob again?"

"Not Bob. He was great on ideas for carbon dating the gourd and the bones. I'm going to ask Eddie."

"Who is—"

"A curator at the museum in Victoria," Muriel said.

"Which is on the other side of the continent."

"It's right here for me, and she's the closest mask expert I know."

"Mask expert. Why do you say mask? I don't want this to end up in a museum, Muriel."

"What, you going to keep it?"

"No, I want to give it back. To whoever's family might want it. I don't feel like it's mine. Mask or gourd or whatever it is."

"Eddie can help. She's genuine. She'll understand. And I do think, in the photos you sent, it looks like a mask, don't you?"

Mildred went to the table where she had the pieces of paper laid out. Such a long trail, and no closer to an answer. Something would have to budge. And the only thing she could think of to shift was herself. "I'm going to the Met."

Before she organized to go, she drafted an email and read aloud as she typed.

"Slavery and You: How History and Future Possibilities Define Us. All Welcome. Mercy Church, Saturday Panel Discussion. P.S. Bring Cookies."

~ 67 ~

Apartment Living

"This is where I feel my most juicy," Amalia said.

"Be careful who you say that to!" Jen stood beside the tall canvas, which stretched from one countertop edge to another, in the Brooklyn apartment.

"Not what I meant. Just, I feel like I could paint here. I get the feeling here."

"When you said you'd got a big canvas," Jen said, "I thought it sounded like a good idea. But it's not for me. I'm too busy since I decided to jump back in." She hesitated. "You haven't painted anything. I mean, beyond where you've penciled this in overtop of what you started."

"It's charcoal," Amalia said.

"It's very light."

"It used to be darker. It brushed off a little."

Jen opened her mouth to speak and leaned back and crossed her arms, looking into the center of the white, rectangular stretched canvas. "If you want to know."

"I do." Amalia did want to know, but. But. But. "I don't know if it will make any difference. I have to do this myself."

"That's what I was going to say. Why are you doing this? Who are you doing it for? Do it for yourself. Because you enjoy it. I assume you do? Enjoy it?"

"Of course," Amalia said. "At least, I did. Now it feels like something I have to finish, to get it out of the way. I think that's why I wanted to try it on your canvas."

"In my apartment."

"I thought it might help. To be in this space."

"Where you feel juicy!"

"Something like that."

"And why do you want to finish it?"

Amalia felt a rise of energy within her. "Because there's something else I want to paint after. I have to get this one done first. I feel like I do." She fingered the line where it had smudged on the canvas. "I kind of lost my focus on this but I've been thinking about another." It was a little like how she felt about Mark. His things were still in her apartment—their apartment. With his frequent trips back and forth to Iceland and Wales for work, to Quebec to visit his grandmother, and with their lack of options for new apartment living, moving on had become a deferred decision. They were not in each other's hair. They were not in each other's lives. It made her a little sad.

"Do you still like this one?"

"I definitely do!"

"You could do both. Start the new one and come back to the first one."

Amalia frowned. She would not do that. It had to be one or the other. "No, I need to keep my focus."

"But if your focus has already changed, then why not go with it? See where it leads? It might lead you back, you never know."

Amalia shook her head. "No, I can't do that. I'm a one painting at a time kind of gal."

~ 68 ~

American and Canadian

Amalia let the deliciousness of the day overtake her thoughts.

There was much to appreciate about the day spent with her parents—their combined force of will overtook any hanging doubts she had about having made the trip to Scranton.

"He's a wonderful person, we agree," her mom said, "but if the timing wasn't right, then the timing wasn't right."

"You can't rush love," her dad said.

"Do you think you might get back together?" Her mom stirred as she spoke, and Amalia feared the pudding would take on the texture of the conversation. Artificially sweet. "Is he open to talking?"

The desire of her parents to steer the conversation was oddly comforting to her. They meant well. There was nothing to be done about her situation, and she was for the most part happy, if nothing else, to be with her parents at home. Not her home-home, of course. Scranton was her high school home. Vancouver was her childhood home. But still, it was home enough, and the roots they'd put down after her dad's transfer to the University of Scranton sustained the three of them, their little tribe, extended overseas by cousins and aunties and uncles in England and India.

"How are the Klauses doing?" The kids next door, her former babysitting charges, were in their teens, and the parents were visible from kitchen window to kitchen window, the houses mirrored in plan across the property line. They observed a discreet and unspoken veil of privacy and did not wave to one another.

Her mom stopped stirring and poured the custard into bowls. "Republicans. I can't get over their love for the party. All these years you think you know someone, and then they'll support a party like that?"

"You knew they were Republicans. And you had a Republican sign out last time, too."

"That was just to mix it up. You know we can't vote. We just like to provoke people to consider their options."

It was no secret in the neighborhood that her parents Soumya and Joe, as visa-holding Canadians, did not vote. The political signs always amused Amalia. "I grew up in a crazy political household," she said. "And I'm the only one of us who can vote here."

"Being born while we were on vacation had its benefits," her mother said. "I never did regret that trip we took when I was pregnant with you."

"And I never regretted taking out extra travel health insurance on that weekend's vacation, either," said her dad. "Who knew that a quick trip across the border from Vancouver would result in you being born an American citizen in the San Juan Islands."

"I'm happy I'm American and Canadian."

"We're happy to have you home, Amalia; don't let the neighbors bother you." He picked up his pudding and took a dip with a spoon. "Yum!" He put the bowl down and brought Sou and Amalia in for a hug. "With you women in my life, I am wanting for nothing."

He was sweet to the extreme. Amalia smiled a curling interior smile to herself, feeling the warmth of her parents, the potential of the weekend ahead, and the knowing that even in a world with political differences with the neighbors, there was still pudding. Warm, sweet, custardy pudding.

Mark, her favorite Libertarian, favorite even after all that had fallen away between them, called the next day after she'd returned to Brooklyn. He had spread out with ease in their old one-bedroom apartment as soon as Amalia announced she was turning it over to him, but said it was temporary. He planned to go to Quebec.

He'd become more chatty, in their parting, and the call that afternoon was a good example. "You know when you said that I'm not even Indian?"

"I never," Amalia said.

"You did, and you were right," Mark said.

"I mean you're not South Asian. I didn't mean you're not Native."

"Turns out I'm not really Abenaki after all," he said.

"What are you, then?"

"I'm French."

"But you're brown like me," she said.

"Lots of people are brown, doesn't mean they're native."

"Wait, how do you know this?" Amalia felt a confusion descend over her eyelids, fog-like and thick.

"I read it. I'm descended from this woman who—"

"Where did you read it?"

"Online."

"You're kidding me, you of all people are getting hooked by something you read online?" The fog was turning thicker and settled in her cheekbones. Her tongue started to feel sluggish. "I need to make coffee."

"Doesn't matter where I read it," Mark said. "The genealogy isn't there. They did DNA tests."

Amalia ran water into the little saucepan. "Sorry, noisy." Turned on the gas to boil the water. "They did DNA tests on who? On you?" The irony of natural gas struck her for the first time: here she was, counseling the gas man himself, while draining the same source of fuel for her own purposes. Didn't know what to make of it. She adjusted the pot to be more centered on the flame.

"No! But I'm descended from her. The tests were on the other ancestors."

"And so—" Amalia took a coffee mug from the open shelf in front of her and scooped in some instant espresso. The smell of it gave her a little rise of energy.

"I'm not Abenaki."

"You're French. Brown and French."

"Yes."

"What else are you? Are you only descended from that French woman?"

"No, of course not." He had that plaintive tone she associated with his feelings of loss, loss of family, loss of connection. He sounded lost. Amalia lifted the cup of dry, instant espresso to her nose and inhaled.

"You could have other Abenaki in you. Or other something else."

"It doesn't matter, Amalia."

"It matters who you are. Of course it does! You've identified Abenaki your whole life. Your mom even wrote that book."

"What book? She never wrote a book."

"The one I saw after the fire, in your house in Quakertown, the binder. The Abenaki quilts. Her manuscript." She found a pot lid that covered the open water, but it wasn't a tight fit. It would do. She inhaled the dry coffee powder again. Crispness would return soon enough. She felt less sluggish in her face. Was she having a stroke? It was more a feeling of being overcome.

"No idea what you're talking about."

"I'm sure you have it packed up with your things," she said. "It was on the shelf."

"I didn't keep the books on the shelf. They got all charred, remember?"

"The quilt binder—"

"The quilt we scattered in New Hampshire two years ago. The quilt part that your mom remade for Tim and Candace's baby."

The baby. "Did they come into the city for that appointment? You never told me. How's the baby?"

"You never asked."

Amalia couldn't jump down that hole with him. She'd find out about the baby another time. If anything had gone wrong, he'd have told her. "Your mom wrote a whole book about Abenaki quilts. I guess she meant to publish later."

"But she died."

"Yeah." Amalia didn't know how to translate the feeling she held inside into words. "I'm sorry."

"I'll ask my Grand-mère."

"Good idea. But the binder?"

"I didn't save anything. I told you. The baby is fine."

"Thank god." It wasn't that she hadn't cared, and it wasn't that she'd forgotten. It had been too tender, to similar, too familiar, and too painful.

"If you want, you can ask my Grand-mère yourself. About the quilt book. The research. I'm spending more time up there."

"You're inviting me to meet her? You never did before when we were living together." Amalia jiggled the pot on the stove and the too-big lid slid off. The water was tepid. It would do; she poured it over the instant espresso. Even lukewarm instant espresso would be better than the feeling that had moved down into her shoulders and collarbone. Lukewarm instant espresso, she mused, was a cultural insult to one, if not many, cultures from around the world.

"There's nothing to hide, she's my grandmother, and you wanted to have a chat about stuff. Why don't you come up for a long weekend? When you have some time off. Rent a car. It's beautiful up there. I'll be going back in a few days. To be honest, I'm more there than here in New York."

"How long are you going to be there?"

"My work is remote, it's okay, I fly out from Montréal when I need. It's pretty good."

"You're staying."

"For now. Amalia, if you come out for a weekend, we could chat. That would be good. And it seems like you're interested to know about this quilt stuff and Grand-mère is a quilter, too. She might know some more. And you'd like her. And it's a good break. We could chat."

"Chatting would be good. And it would be good to get away. I bet fall is beautiful there."

"A lot like New Hampshire, gets colder earlier, darker earlier. Just let me know when. I'll be there."

"Okay, Mark, I will take that as an invitation."

"Helene might be there."

Amalia remembered the ex-girlfriend more as a fresh face of New Hampshire than of Quebec. Not that they'd ever met in person; Mark had discarded a photo of her, to be found as if by chance, or was it on purpose she wondered, by Amalia herself. If Helene was there, so what. So what.

When the call ended. Amalia was stumped. Was his invitation a proposition or a resolution? She couldn't read Mark's tone. She took one sip of the strong, black, culturally challenged espresso and shuddered. The feeling of suffocation lifted a little. She took another sip and searched for some shelf-stable milk in the back of the cupboard. He had more of a tone of proposition. Hers was a feeling of resolution. She'd accept the invitation and find out what was up with Mark in the mountains outside Montréal. The milk, once opened and poured, formed a silky ribbon of dark, lighter, and lighter still, snaking through the oily surface of the instant coffee. Amalia poured it down the drain, shoved her unsocked feet into her tall fall boots, grabbed her tote back and scarf, and headed for the door. Coffee shop coffee would suit her mood better. She flipped the scarf around her neck and shoulders and slammed the apartment door behind her.

~ 69 ~

To The Field

Amalia laid both hands straight out across the fence rail in front of her and stared down the horse across the way. It seemed to ignore her; she knew better. Its stomping and head shake told her something was amiss. "I'm ready, you big bully," she said, then caught herself. "I mean, nice horse. Gentle horse." The beast bent its head down and nuzzled toward its forelegs, then raised its head, flicked its tail, and turned and trotted to the far corner of the field, away from Amalia, without a look back. "Fine, have it your way." She pulled herself up on the top of the rail near where it connected to the post and felt for steadiness beneath her. Swung a leg overtop of the rail and held the post behind her, opened her throat and chest to the evening air of Quebec in autumn, and exhaled. Being friends with a horse didn't matter. And it wasn't why she'd come.

Mark's grandmother—his grand-mère—had inherited farmland by treaty, off-reserve although ancestrally connected to the Abenaki, and kept for generations in the family due to a peculiarity of French and English settlement. There was no way of telling—short of DNA testing—whether Mark's genealogical hunch was true. Regardless, it provided a beautiful respite for Amalia from New York. Amalia hoped she and Mark might reconcile there, or at least make love and then part with that as a sweet memory, but when she'd arrived, she found not Mark and his grandmother in the gravel driveway of the semirural Lac Mégantic farmhouse, but Mark, Helene, Mark's grandmother, and the little blue Saab Mark and Helene had bought together long before Amalia and Mark had ever met. Amalia parked her rental between Mark's car and Grand-mère's grey pickup truck.

It was in this ancient landscape of trees and stumps and open farmland, bones, ancestors, and wars fought for what, that she found herself confronting a horse, a disinterested horse, and exhaling into a wide, blue sky above.

"Salut," she heard from behind. Helene approached from the farmhouse, palms open to Amalia at her sides, as if feeling the vibration of sunset, docile to the breeze and unprotesting of its power. Helene walked as if she was part of the land. And then, Amalia knew. It was over. Helene put her hands on the fence post near Amalia. "It's a beautiful evening. You came for some quiet?"

"To the field? Or to see Mark?"

"I meant to the field." Helene looked toward where the horse had gone and clicked her tongue.

From the far side, the horse returned, and when it neared the fence, Amalia saw the connection, as bright as a sun streak across a table set for a happy luncheon, to which she was not invited.

Helene pulled a carrot from her pocket and fed it, open-palmed, to the horse. "She is docile," she said, and smoothed a hand down the horse's forehead. "If you approach with grace, she will meet you with grace."

Amalia felt her stomach gurgle. Hungry after a long drive north. "I didn't know for sure you were going to be here."

"Why would I not be here? It is the best time of day for this field!"

"When I planned to come up to visit Mark."

"Why would I not be here?"

"I don't understand." Amalia had a sudden feeling she'd been played, but how?

"I've been living here, helping Mémé for ages. Didn't he tell you?"

Amalia looked at Helene's hands on the fence post. Strong hands. Capable. "No, he did not."

"Amalie, can I ask you something? I hate to ask. But I have to know." Helene looked a mite concerned and continued. "Do you like Mark? I mean, do you have a thing for him? I'm sorry. I know it's silly. I'm sure I'm just being jealous for no reason." Helene patted the mane of the horse. "Bibi knows, don't you Bibi?"

Amalia's face felt hot. "No, wait. I'm sorry. Mark didn't tell you about us?"

"What do you mean, 'us'?" Helene pulled the horse to her, and Bibi nuzzled back.

"He never told you?" Amalia jumped down from the fence and landed with two feet on the farmhouse side of things. "What did he tell you?"

"That his roommate was coming for a visit—but Amalie, are you not only roommates? I am an idiot! How did I not realize?" Helene clung to Bibi and almost lost her balance off the fence, into the field. Amalia caught a whiff of skunky marijuana around her. Could not be someone Mark was associated with.

"How long have you two—I thought you broke up?" Amalia's heart pounded. When had Mark said they were broken up? Had he, indeed, clarified that? Amalia was stupid to have never probed further. She'd seen Mark as fragile around the issue, too tied up with the death of his parents and the subsequent guardianship of Timmy. Timothy. Tim. Did Helene know about Tim and Candace and the baby? Her thoughts raced. Helene was silent, her eyes closed as she caressed Bibi's forelocks. It was all not making sense.

"Amalie, I don't find you at fault." Helene turned to Amalia, smiling. "I like you. I can see why Mark might like you. It is he who has been dishonest. Not you. We have been deceived. It is he who must answer. Not you. You, Amalie, I embrace you. You are a beautiful woman." Helene let go of Bibi, jumped to the ground, and reached out a hand. "Let's go together. It is time truths were told aloud."

"We were living together," Amalia whispered. She took Helene's hand, and giving Bibi a backwards glance, looked toward the farmhouse where Mark and Grand-mère were preparing supper. Stepping forward, she felt the cool breeze that came with the onset of autumn dark bring a salve of calm to her overheated self.

"I didn't lie," said Mark when they confronted him. "I was completely honest with both of you!"

"And you thought we'd never figure it out?" Amalia heard the timbre of her voice become unsteady. She wasn't going to mention the smell of pot that clung to Helene. Perhaps he had not noticed. Was that even possible? He would have been outraged with Amalia. Perhaps he was a different person with

Helene. That could be. Why could he not have been a different person sooner? Had she done something wrong? Amalia stared at the worn linoleum floor tile in an attempt to silence her self-critical voice rattling inside.

"There was nothing to figure out. I wasn't with you both at the same time. I was faithful." He looked like a cornered cat who had broken a favored family heirloom; Amalia felt a little sorry for him despite her anger. Maybe it was no one's fault. One of those things that happens when people look away. She herself was guilty of that. She looked up from the floor toward the window. The brightness of golden hour, end of a beautiful day, shone through. There was that to appreciate at least. She tried to focus on it. Mark's grandmother glowed in the rays that backed her.

"We should confess," Helene said, "hearts have been broken wide, and it is time to choose." She looked at Mark with something akin to the docility Amalia had seen before, but it was nothing like passivity; it was like a full-bodied knowing that she was the victor, with complete and quiet confidence. The sun moved behind a cloud, letting fall Amalia's temporary feeling of appreciation.

"I think I should go," Amalia said. "I'm going to pack my bag. I'll see if there's a hotel I can get tonight." Heat arrived at her midsection, a sudden and unwelcome guest that made her feel nauseous. Neither Mark nor Helene protested; instead, they looked at one another and Mark stood a little closer to Helene. As Amalia backed out of the room, her face aflame and heart pounding, he put his arm around Helene's shoulders and kissed the top of her head.

Amalia stuffed the few things she'd brought and unpacked, back into her bag. Grand-mère's dinner was smelling good and ready. Could she leave without saying goodbye? It would be rude. She didn't think she could face the woman without bursting into tears. She would go in silence to her car and find a hotel. If there was no hotel, she'd sleep in her car. How cold could it get overnight in Quebec in fall? It would serve Mark right if she froze to death. That'd show him. She laughed out loud to the room. Show him what? She'd only be showing him her foolishness. And she was done with that. She'd say goodbye to Grand-mère. To hell with tears. Let them fall. If she wanted, she'd cry.

They were all gathered in the kitchen when she entered the room. Grand-mère had an outside coat on. "I'll walk you out to your car, Amalia. If you leave now, you'll settle in a hotel before it gets too dark." There was no emoting. No explanation.

Helene reached out to hug her. "I wish you strength and grace, my friend." Amalia returned the gesture with a polite squeeze. "You, too. Keep searching for your truth." Where had that come from? She felt high, out of her body. Helene let go and looked at Mark. "What have you got to say?"

"I'll walk you to your car," he said.

"I'll meet you there," Grand-mère said. "You'll have to be quick, so she gets there before dark."

Mark pushed past his grand-mère to the kitchen door and addressed her as he pushed the door open. "Mémé," he said, "please pack a bowl of stew for Amalia to take." To Amalia, he said, "after you."

Amalia's skin tingled all over. Didn't know what to say. Felt not even present. At her car, Mark said, "I'm sorry," and then Grand-mère, Mémé to Helene and Mark, she supposed, passed her a plastic tub of stew with a spoon and a paper napkin on the top. Amalia was starting the engine. Mark was in the driveway. Waving. Turning back to the farmhouse with Mémé.

Out of sight from the farmhouse, still in the rural zone beyond the town limits, she pulled over to find a cell phone signal to search for hotels. Fortune was with her, and she had a full range of signal bars appearing to power her cell phone. She found two nearby motels that were promising: Hotel Motel Le Château and Motel Le Quiet. Either would do. She trundled along the dirt road until she met pavement and followed the chirping of her map app south on Rue Laval. This was the location of the horrid fire. The disastrous wreck. Where had it been, among these roads? Didn't matter. It was a wreck enough of a night as it was, and she could not take on another emotional burden like contemplating the train derailment. The more she tried to not-think of it, though, the more she did, and when she crossed the train tracks on her way into town, she felt a shimmer along her forearms that told her she'd connected to a profound moment in the history of the township. She crossed train tracks again farther down the road and her heart raced. The confluence of energy and memory felt too strong for her to resist.

Where were the motels? Had she missed them on the darkening road? It was a quiet town with houses set back a bit, businesses attended by car. Her normal interest in all things new felt silent within her. The shimmer up her forearms turned to a shiver. She saw the Motel Le Quiet on the opposite side of the road but missed the turn. She saw another sign, marked with clarity as MOTEL on her side of the road, and peeled off into its gravel parking lot.

She would steady herself before she went in. Remembered the stew in the plastic pot, and when she took off the lid, the smell made her mouth water. Grand-mère was a good cook, Amalia reckoned, and with one taste of the hot mélange, it was confirmed. There was love in the food. The thought of it made her queasy again; she was hungry right down to the pit of her stomach. She ate. When she was done, she put the pot and the spoon with the napkin on the backseat floor and opened her driver's side door. The cold air outside came as a shock after the warming meal. She leaned with her back against the side of the car and cried. Her tears were hot on her face and her ears burned with anger and frustration and a feeling of shame and grief and inner berating. She cried until she had no more tears, and shuddering one last time in the cold, got back into the car, set her map app for Brooklyn, and drove, looking ahead at the sunset-darkening tree crown of rural Quebec.

She drove until she reached the American border with Canada and met car-side with the passport control agent. She had to go to the bathroom but said nothing. Amalia drove with only a short break at a rest stop in Vermont to pee. Long after midnight and, she was quite certain, nearing dawn, she arrived at her Warren Street home in Brooklyn, numb and yet in a satisfying way, resolute. She was home. Exhausted, and home, and too tired to process. Too pissed off to utter words.

Nothing had gone wrong, had it? Everyone had told their version of the truth, hadn't they? Still, it hurt, and she felt confused, and it was more than a normal, moral confusion. Amalia felt split at her core. It was a complete bifurcation of the self: what she'd thought was, versus what she'd found to be true. She could not reconcile the two.

In the blankness of this grief and shuttering of self, she could think to reach only for one thing. The great, unfinished canvas stood propped up in the kitchen. She laid it flat on the floor, found the paint she'd purchased but never opened, and squeezed globs of it all over the stretched fabric on the frame of the piece she'd felt to be called Odin's Wind. She took a kitchen knife, the biggest one she could find, and scraped the globs of color flat against the canvas in long, swooping and swirling arcs, colors blending, knife edge scraping the fibers of the base, and with all the care and delicacy she could balance on the knife's edge, she meted out dose after dose of the exact words she wanted to say, in feeling-tones, in color-hues, and without the need for verbal articulation, she was at once expressive and empty, soundless and at peace.

"Holy shit," she said to the room. The work was done. It was still wet, but it was done. How had she completed it then, after such a long time coming? She giggled, then laughed, and pushed her paint-smeared hands up into her hair, knowing color would rein through her strands of blackness, then scratched her scalp with her painty fingernails, and danced. Danced to no audible music, through the fatigue of the early morning hours and the fading memory of two days' driving up north then back again. Danced out the gunk that had come before. Danced until, in her exhaustion, she flopped down on the floor next to the canvas and let her body rest with a deep satisfaction that was sustaining, life-affirming, and sound.

~ 70 ~

Catskills

An opportunity presented itself, well into her exam preparations, to get clear on where she was headed in work. It would take longer to figure out where she was going in her love life. She needed to figure it out, the work part at least. Amalia would hike it out with Jen.

Amalia drove up in a rental through late season tree colors, to meet her for a morning hike, later in the hiking season than she'd ever hiked before—but not icy. She rattled around the thought that once upon a time, she and Mark would have argued about global warming being the cause of the temperature, and she shook it off. Didn't need to bring him into her thought-space.

She wanted to talk to Jen about love and architecture. They'd had an expansive talk on their last hike at Bear Mountain. She wanted that again. She'd loved that. A smile grew within her and came out the cracks of her mouth, and as she turned off the highway onto the local roads Jen had indicated the last time, Amalia realized she was profoundly happy.

Maybe it didn't matter that she didn't know ahead of time how the whole love-and-architecture thing was going to work out for her.

Jen had made it work. She'd decided to move out to the Catskills, a sad moment of conversation for Amalia, but happy, too, because Jen was so happy. Jen would work from home; Jen would come into the city once a week for meetings. She'd stay at the apartment she was turning over to Amalia, rental lease transferred and all. In the Catskills, Jen said, she would have time and space to express everything she desired in love and in her design career.

Jen would have some perspective to share. But would the guidance be relevant to Amalia? And then, Amalia realized it was not someone else's guidance she was needing at all. It was connection: some time spent with a loved one, sharing something beautiful, outdoors, and laughing in the goodness that surrounded them.

Its relevance did not need to be justified, just enjoyed.

~ 71 ~
Stops

On the drive down from Binghamton—a four-hour drive with additional stops—Mildred patted the gourd-without-bones in the bag next to her on the seat. "We'll get you sorted," she said. She didn't have an appointment at the museum.

Lost her nerve. Turned right around and back down those wide stone steps. She'd have to rethink. Her head was buzzy and spinny from all the driving. She needed a rest. She needed a friend. She called Amalia, whose cell phone went to voice mail.

"Leave a message!" said Amalia's much happier-sounding voice.

"Amalia, I may have got in over my head. I have driven to Manhattan, and I am at the Metropolitan Museum of Art. I would be happy to meet with you while I am here." She hung up. That was satisfying to a small degree. More pieces would fall into place. She called Mark.

"It's Mark. Leave a message." Her boy Mark sounded good. Were he and Amalia better off apart? From the tone of both their voices, they sounded so. Maybe she'd called that wrong.

She'd need to clear her head. It was grey. The park was right there.

A day of grey and lovely, Mildred thought. Never mind about the gourd, or mask, or whatever it was. She patted her bag at her hip. "We'll go for a little walk and have another think about what to do." The pathways of Central Park opened behind the museum, and Mildred struck out to walk them.

A few people were out, not many on that day of grey and lovely. She went off a bit into a rockier area, a bit slippery in the mist. Didn't seem like a good idea for her to continue that alone; she went back down to where she might find other people, and soon found herself lost in smaller pathways and nearer trees.

"Never mind. We'll find a nice place to sit until someone comes along to guide us." She patted the bag at her hip, a move that reassured both her and, she hoped, the gourd.

Further down the trail—for it was no longer a path, nor something one would call a walkway, in Mildred's eyes, being roughed out on the edges and muddy with puddles untended— she saw a boulder near the side. It would do for a rest stop since there were no park benches there. It would be wet, but she needed to sit. With care, she took the gourd and her wallet out of her bag and laid them on the rock, the gourd still bubble-wrapped as she'd done it on her table at home, the wallet resting atop it. With her bag empty of everything but her keys, she smoothed its fabric out and laid it on the boulder as a sit-upon square. It worked quite well, except for the keys, which she shuffled out and put into her coat pocket. She should have brought a second bag. Maybe she'd get a new one. A city one.

She turned her face into the bubble-wrapped mask, gourd, whatever it was she didn't know, and felt a little wiggly joy bubble up from within her, and she giggled to it, to the gourd-mask. "This is fun," she said to it. "Look at us, lying down in Central Park, all John Lennon and Yoko Ono like!" They were two to be remembered. She'd liked them together. Felt them together still.

After some time she became a little sleepy, and so she curled into the boulder, hip on the square, and laid her head on the bubble-wrapped gourd-mask, took the wallet in her hands. She giggled at her form on this great boulder, supported by this cushioned mask, and in that moment realized she'd lost her phone. She hadn't seen it when she stopped. She hadn't noticed it before when she'd entered the park. In fact, she was not sure she had seen it since she'd left a voice message for Mark.

The phone could be replaced. It was not worth worrying. Her mind was already wandering into the interesting nooks and crannies in the park around her, and with the mask, she was safe. The park brought her a great sense of calm, and the mask, too. She only wished she'd had the sense to call Muriel before she'd lost her phone. No matter. As her mind traveled around the park, she felt her body's temperature cool where it met the cold stone, and she smiled as she settled into a nap. There would be ample time for other things, other times.

~ 72 ~

A Day of Grey and Lovely

A day of grey and lovely, Amalia thought. She smiled. The papers before her lay in preparation for the meeting, completed except for Betsy's last blessing. Betsy would return to the office within a few minutes. Jen came over with the presentation drawings.

"What are you noodling over? Smiling to yourself?"

"I was just thinking how sometimes someone can seem close, even when they're far away."

"Your grandfather? Or someone far away? Here you go with the drawings." Jen stuck the tube out.

"Maybe both." Amalia took the tube and picked up the papers from her desk. "I'm ready, let's go."

"Betsy still needs to see the set," Jen said. "We should wait."

"We can catch her on the way down, wait in the lobby for her. We'll need to move fast if we're going to get to Landmarks on time for the meeting. We can save five minutes at least. I'll call and tell her." Amalia put down the papers and roll of drawings to fish for her phone in the depths of her tote bag. "I missed a call from Mildred."

"You need a new bag!"

"Mark called, I should call him back, he's left three messages. Besides, you gave me this bag!

"Call him. And you can't have too many bags!

"I don't want to."

"Get a new bag?"

"No! I don't want to call him."

"What would your beloved Mildred say?"

"Call him. Of course." Amalia sighed. "I'll step outside." She saved the work on her computer, grabbed her tote bag, and went out to the elevator. Betsy would be back. Amalia would go get coffee for everyone from the Starbucks on the corner and call Mark at the same time. She didn't care to hear his voice; an inner

315

tugging at her gut told her to check her voice mail. She listened to all three, his tone more insistent with each message.

~ 73 ~

Easier and Easier ~ November

The next weekend, Amalia sat with her notebook and noodled.

today is a blank canvas
I can draw and paint anything I want—and maybe there is
yet another painting in me after all—
take over the Hungarian Pastry Shop with my sketchbook, or
a corner of it
sketch
Figure out the next step in painting
no
figure out the next step in the sketchbook
painting will come later

Amalia closed the cover on the pencil, packed it all into her
tote bag, and headed for the subway. Her phone buzzed with an
incoming text. She'd ignore it. What if—? She checked in case—
in case what?
It was Jen.

I'm coming into the city, want to meet later this morning?
For yoga?

No, going sketching, but happy to see you!

cool, but not yoga.

meet me later, will show you what I did
what did you do?

No I mean what I'm doing today sketching!

ok cool, you're good.

We'll see

you totally are.

Well thank you, we'll see

you got this! you sketch like nobody can.

I guess?

You got this!

thank you

what are you doing it for, a project?

No just for me

that's the best.

gets easier and easier

<3

Back at the office on Monday, Amalia considered the email from Sunil.

Meet me.
Happy to talk about whatever, geothermal or ganja or whatever!

She smiled and hit 'Reply.'

Amalia waited for Sunil at the front door of her newish apartment; over the weekend she'd moved from the lower garden suite to the upper half of the brownstone, after the tenants moved out. The couple had left a beautiful credenza of a Dutch modern style, saying it was their parting gift to her for having been a good and companionable neighbor. She felt they must have meant "quiet" and that in fact they didn't want to haul the huge wooden thing down the stairs. They'd done the move themselves; boxes and bedding only, they said, for their cross-country U-Haul move. Among other things they left were a king-sized bed, a 1950s Formica dining set, and a long, lumpy, and oh-so-comfy old sofa. "It just needs a new cover," they'd said. They would take no money for the items, but gladly accepted the bottle of Prosecco Amalia had in her fridge.

She'd been out for bedding for the very large bed. Was glad to have left Mark with the mattress she'd bought with him, back in Hamilton Heights. Brought up the dishes she'd inherited after Jen's move out of the apartment. Dragged up her computer and art canvases, and her clothes in suitcases. Left the old sofa that practically came with the garden suite, having been there before Jen had moved in with a previous girlfriend. As far as moves went, the move upstairs was Amalia's easiest. The only thing she was unsure about was the old quilt belonging to Sandra's Great Aunt Joan—she'd hang onto it until either Sandra or Joan returned from Europe. Amalia had thrown it over the top of the credenza. It reminded her of Mark, and she didn't want it in the new bedroom. Somehow, though, it seemed to belong where she'd laid it out, folded length-ways, covering the mars and dents in the varnish of the old piece of furniture. Maybe one day she'd get the credenza refinished. The Saraswati wall hanging was pinned above it with two clear plastic pushpins. Mark had not wanted it in the end, and she could not part with it once he'd discounted it as important to him. Maybe it had been more hers, all along. It felt right at home where it was, on the wall, over the old credenza and borrowed quilt. She studied the montage as if she'd come across it in a museum, and felt a shimmer of happy, improbable happy, rise from within.

Sunil was not arriving. He had only a short walk from the F-train, and he'd texted before he left home. He was on his way. She went back inside. His train ride would be a long one.

Why had she invited him? He'd wanted to talk. Didn't she know better?

Amalia's belly radiated an unfamiliar warmth. Wonderful warmth. Wonderful new apartment, with its rooftop access and views of the boroughs. Wonderful in her skin, tight and taut from the running she'd taken up after she and Mark had split. Wonderful, with Sunil a friend. A true, decent, supportive friend.

Which was why, when the bell rang and she answered it, she greeted him with a beaming smile, a warm hug, and a gracious kiss on the cheek.

"It's good to see you, Amalia. Wow, you look great. This new life, it suits you." He radiated brightness that hit her at her midsection.

"Thank you." Complimented to her core. "I'll show you in," she said. She felt her cheeks warm. "You're the first visitor, my first visitor." She smiled and turned, seeing him looking up, not at her.

"Good bones," he said. "Great structure." Sunil caught her glance. "Sorry. Can't help myself." He beamed. "Let's see more."

His face was lit up. Amalia felt it too; their mutual arrival at this point of contentedness, easiness, and eagerness in each other's presence. "I'm happy to see you," she said, and then, "that sounds dumb. Of course, I'm happy to see you." She'd censor the babble. No need for her to run on and on, giving away how giddy she now realized she'd become. "Let it build its own momentum," she heard inside, in Mildred's kind voice. Mildred had begun to appear in her thoughts with an accuracy of timing and appropriateness of guidance that gave Amalia a little shiver.

"Okay?"

"I'm great. This way," she said, and led him up the stairs.

It was two o'clock before they realized they were hungry; chatted all the way through the visit, fell silent at other times, Amalia heeding Mildred's guidance. It was good, natural, and easy between them. Sunil felt like an old friend. He understood her, and she, him. It went beyond their Indian connection. He sat next to her on the sofa in the living room and she received his right hand between her two. The contact between their eyes was warm, warming—it made a poignant moment. It became something clearer, but the words escaped her, words on a runaway train with a load lightened and without cargo. Inhale, exhale, she heard in her temples. She held his gaze and inhaled, exhaled. They breathed together like that with eyes locked, until she realized they were surrounded by a grand energy that was both palpable and invisible, and where did it come from? Within them? Within her? Was he feeling the same, in the moment? She smiled, and inhaled a question, breathing it out in a whisper. "May I put my hand here, on your neck, on the side like this?"

"Here?" He leaned into her a little.

"Yes, just there." She smiled and curled toward him.

"Yes,"

She put her fingers alongside his neck, softly, and stroked the tip of his ear. "Inhale. Exhale."

He closed his eyes and said, "Divine." Moved his head a little to the side as she stroked.

The energy, now apparent to them both, built a momentum that encircled the pair where they stayed locked on the sofa, expanding into the room beyond.

Had they known each other like this before, in another life? Did he wonder it, too? "He does," she heard in Mildred's voice, deep within her, somewhere between her head and her heart.

Strong morning light came in with a directness through the unshielded window, as if to say, you sleep, we'll keep playing out here. Catch you on the bright side. She rolled over and squinted, moved an arm across her eyes. He slept, breathing gently on his side, away from the light. He seemed to have that figured out even in sleep. Amalia pushed off the warm covers, shivered in the morning cold, and reached for sweatpants and a top from her pile of clean laundry, still not put away. Mildred's old Greenham Common t-shirt, borrowed. She smiled when putting it on. Tiptoed into the bathroom avoiding the creaky board, and puttered around in her morning routine, to which she added a wide smile to herself in the mirror. Tiptoed back out, hitting the creaky board, and danced away to the kitchen to make coffee. Coffee, strong, aromatic and all pervasive in its delightful scent.

He was up soon after. Greeted her with a kiss.

The coffee was consumed in appreciative gulps in the morning light that filtered through the branched trees where leaves remained to fall.

Amalia fiddled with the gemstone bracelet on her wrist while the phone call connected to Sandra. Their weekly call schedule had been interrupted by sleeping in with Sunil, who'd left with kisses and promises to return in the evening. The bracelet stones, smooth pink quartz, were cool on her wrist, warming between her fingers, and the feeling transported her to the sensations of the night before. When Sandra picked up, Amalia was already daydreaming of Sunil's return.

~ 74 ~

Emergence

In the weeks that followed in the last of the year, Amalia's focus came to be set with certainty on the completion of her architectural licensing exams. Their sole and all-encompassing essence of "completion" drove her inner engines with a ferocity she had not felt, if ever, then at least not in a long time. Odin's Wind sat propped in the corner of her apartment. Fall colors had turned to the whiteness of snow and the crisp blueness of the East Coast winter. She took exams one after another and by springtime, she was done. As she emerged from the haze of study-and-work, work-and-study, and as spring turned to summer, Amalia found a new element had emerged up and around the media and the country, although less in her neighborhood: signs pointing to a challenge to the Democrats' leadership, and signs that their leader's probable replacement would face a challenge as well.

It seemed an odd emergence to Amalia—her own emergence from the cross-border parting from Mark (and Helene and Grand-mère), to the dancing completion of Odin's Wind, through the dark tunnel of architecture registration, seeming to never end, then with a sudden, bright and unwavering light before her, a beacon of hope and possibility.

If only she could find a way to blend her love of architecture with her thoughts about policy and environmentalism. Maybe her dad would know. A chemist at the university, and a professor. She'd ask him.

Sunil had dismantled the entire ecology of the kitchen worm bin and put it back together. He put the soil, worms, and compost into another container and replaced the rotted wood, reinforced the edges with caulking, and polyurethaned the outside, giving it a new copper rim where the lid sat tight over the top.

"You added copper flashing to the worm bin. Unbelievable!"

"It was already a good piece of construction. I added my own design feature. Does the architect approve?"

"The architect," she smiled, feeling the wave of happiness and relief at being able to call herself that after having passed all her registration exam sections and completed all of her requirements, "this architect does approve." Sunil's arrival at the brownstone was a welcome one, worm bin and all. "We should celebrate your moving in downstairs."

"I feel we should wait until Jen gets the rest of her things out. Then it will feel like mine."

"Next weekend," Amalia said. "She promised to drive down from the Catskills. She has some things to drop off at Paige's place, too."

"They seemed solid," Sunil said. "But then, so did she and Suky."

"Solid doesn't have to mean forever. Look at me and Mark. We affected each other. In a good way. I think we are better for having known each other and been together, even if it didn't last."

"About that," he said. "About us, I mean."

Amalia felt a force of unspoken thoughts emerge in the room.

The apartment house was up for sale, but it had not sold, not yet. Amalia loved the old brownstone and appealed to the owners for more time. She wanted more than anything to buy it. By then, the old debts to boyfriends past (Nadel, Mark) had been repaid; student loans had not. She reached out to her parents. They would help her with the cosigning of a mortgage. But no, they could not help her with the down payment. She reached out to Betsy. The firm, while solvent, could not help her fund a transaction with a loan. Sunil, living downstairs, was a happy neighbor-lover, but did not have money for a down payment. Amalia wasn't ready to buy a place with him in any case. It was enough that he was subletting from her.

She came to a dead end there, a drawbridge across the moat, her on one side, the brownstone on the other. She called the Reverend Mildred on the phone, first her cell phone (which elicited no answer) and then her land line (which rang as expected). Numbers dialed and phone ringing, Amalia realized it had been ages since they'd spoken. How could she have neglected Mildred for so long? Her own selfish distraction kept her from calling. Truth was, she didn't want to know any more about the crazy gourd saga, or the drugs she'd come to associate with it. Amalia tried to recall when they'd last spoken. Mark would have spoken to her in the more recent past.

"Hello?" A chipper voice answered the phone.

"Hello, Mildred?" Amalia's heart pounded.

"This is Muriel, Mildred's sister." There was a pause on the line. "I'm sorry, dear."

"Have I called at a bad time?"

"You haven't heard."

It wasn't a question. "Has something happened to Mildred? Is she okay?" The gourd may have brought no good. Amalia had hated to say to Mildred that she suspected it was cursed. Mildred would never have believed it.

"Mildred went out in her own joyful way, wouldn't you know," Muriel said. "Dramatically, quietly, and on her own terms."

"She went out?" Amalia knew, didn't need to ask. There had been no illness Amalia knew of, save the eye troubles that Mildred self-medicated with marijuana and then Reiki. Had there been more?

"She died, dear. Her light went out. But it shines on, you know? She's not really gone." Muriel paused. "I'm sorry. We couldn't reach everyone. We didn't know how. Just the congregation and Raymond's faculty. Did you know Raymond, too?"

"I didn't," Amalia said. A wavering feeling of loss flooded her shoulders and midsection. She looked toward the windows, and as she looked up, she saw a streak of light enter the room as if through the solid space between the windows. It passed with a speed and momentum that shocked her.

"What is your name, dear?"

"Amalia. Amalia Sengupta Erenwine."

"Oh! Amalia! You're the one I've been trying to reach. You don't have a listed phone number."

"I have a cell phone," she said. "I'm in New York City. I must have been in Mildred's cell phone?"

"We never did find her cell phone. She was found with just herself."

"Found?"

"Found, when she died. But you're the one!"

"Mildred and I did have a lot of fun together," she said. Amalia didn't like to ask how she'd died. The thought made her feel guilty for not having been there. "Fun, we had fun." She realized the repeating was not going to bring her back.

"Dear, we know you had fun, because she's left you some money!"

No. "What? Why not Father Jasper, or Frankie?"

"Dear—you know of them?"

"I think I know more than most," Amalia said. Her teeth chittered a little and she felt very cold. "Why me?" And why did Mildred have to go—or was she there, in the room?

"She left the house in Maine to Jasper and Frankie."

"She didn't own it."

"We did. Both of us. I found the deed when I was cleaning up a while back, and I signed it over to her before she died. Because I have a house, back on Salt Spring Island."

"But your girls?"

"You know of my girls," she said. "They received their grandmother's condominium on Salt Spring.

"And you?"

"I'm at Mildred's in Binghamton. I have two houses, back on Salt Spring where I live, and on the mainland. I have more houses than I know what to do with! Our father built them all over, his demonstration houses, and he didn't sell them all. He wasn't much in sales; his downfall, but our windfall."

"I have to go," she said, "I'll call you back." Amalia hung up. She teetered between shock and a brightness for which there was no comparison; the combined sensations threatened to knock her off her living room sofa to the floor. She stabilized on the armrest. "Mildred," she whispered to the room, shaky from both fear and excitement at a response.

"Yes, Amalia," she heard back.

~ 75 ~

A New Creation

Amalia picked up the paintbrush the day after learning of Mildred's passing and danced a new creation into being. It had all the color and exuberance of Mildred, and all the sorrow at the loss of her friend. For indeed, she was a friend, the Reverend Mildred, and although more than fifty years separated them by age, the connection felt timeless, more sister-like than anything definable by the society around them. The painting held the tenderness and appreciation of this sister-love, and at its edges, Amalia painted a little ode to sisters everywhere: those of kin, those of circumstance, and those of choice. She inked the words into three corners of the painting, leaving the fourth corner blank. For what?

"Mildred?" She questioned the room. There was no answer. She'd imagined it before. Perhaps she'd connected enough and, in the process, rediscovered her inner spark. The painting lay on the floor before her, wet and colorful, complete in its imperfection, and in that moment, Amalia realized she was happy.

She took her happiness to Scranton, where she sat with her dad and a cup of tea one weekend, her mother out shopping. "Hedging his bets against an uncertain future," he said. "Sounds like Mark's not sure things will stabilize here in the natural gas industry and so he's pitching his tent in Iceland."

"Not really," she said. "He's not much of a camper. Hiker, yes."

"You know what I mean, Amalia. He does not see potential expansion for his career here in North America. He's spreading his wings."

"Around his tent."

"What?"

"Pitching his tent and spreading his wings around it. That's what you're saying he's doing."

"Something like that. My point is, Pumpkin, it had nothing to do with you. He's career focused. He's looking toward where he can make the biggest difference."

"And it wasn't with me." She sighed, squidged up her cheeks. "Not my tent."

"You had wings together, for a while. But don't you see, love, you're still soaring. You still have all the potential in the world."

"Just not with him."

"No, not with him. But it has nothing to do with you, is what I'm saying. I see this all the time with my students. They get in a head over heels relationship, and then as soon as a good post-doc comes along, there goes the relationship in favor of the post-doc."

"I can't tell if you're saying that's a good thing or a bad thing."

"It's neither, I'm saying it's human nature."

"I don't think it's natural to be so focused on work."

"It's natural here in the US, for sure," he said.

"But maybe not in Iceland. Maybe he's looking for something I could not give him. We argued over so many things. Medical marijuana. I mean, who argues over medical marijuana?"

Her dad shifted fast in his seat, as if she'd flicked something toward him. "You're just going to have to stop beating yourself up over this, Amalia. And one day, you will. This is not about you. I mean, it is about you, but it's not only about you. You're half the relationship. You do your half. He'll do his half. And there will be another one for you. You're young. Be responsible for your own feelings. That's your powerful starting point." His face clouded, despite the certainty in his words.

"I have a life in New York. I had it before Mark, and I have it now. It's something I need to figure out." She hadn't spoken of Sunil. Her parents loved Mark, still. It was complicated having Sunil shift from being neighbor lover to tenant-lover, and when he began paying her rent, it felt odd. They became on-again off-again. Nadel had visited from Vancouver, and the spark reignited. Mark came with a small box of Amalia's things—an excuse for a visit, really—and ended up sleeping over on the sofa. The intimacy of feeling was still apparent between them, in spite of all that had transpired. Amalia was not one to hold onto hurts. It was for these and many other reasons that she had not told her parents about Sunil. Or Nadel's visit, or Mark's appearance. Too complicated for her, and too complicated to explain.

He sat back on the old couch. "You're thinking of leaving? Taking a break?"

"Mildred, you know, the Reverend Mildred? She left me some money. Her nieces were upset about it, apparently, but they got to share the family's condominium in Canada. Did you know Mildred was from BC? I don't think I ever told you that."

He sat forward, intent. "Amalia. That is amazing. This Mildred—you mentioned her, but not that. And the money?" He looked more furrowed than she would have expected given the windfall she'd just announced.

"Actually, I'm thinking I might buy the brownstone. You and Mom said you could cosign if I came up with the down payment."

"Good." He relaxed a little, but his voice sounded flat, unenthused for a man whose daughter had just announced she would buy a house. "Ever have any desire to go back to school?"

"I've thought about it. To dive deeper into some of the aspects of the environmental research side of things. I'm pretty satisfied with what I'm doing in design. It wouldn't be for that."

"Something with green buildings. You always had that focus."

She nodded. "Buying a house seems more important. And, doing a green building renovation of my own would be a great thing for me."

"You could be right."

~ 76 ~
Driftwood

It almost looked like any other piece of driftwood or debris, but its unique wrapping and waxy coat made evident to the girl that this was not an ordinary piece of driftwood at all.

She fetched a stick to pull it toward her—she didn't want to get too cold or wet—and she pulled it out and removed a piece of green seaweed from it.

She turned it over to face its frontside, for it had a very clear frontside. It said, "I am Otter." She screamed, dropping the mask at the water's edge. She ran back toward the woodsy shore, determined to tell no one. What wonder had occurred, she did not know.

~ The End ~

Read the next in the Erenwine Series
Rail: A High Speed Adventure
~ 1 ~
Old Things and New Things

Binghamton, New York, was beautiful on any given day, but that late fall afternoon, as Amalia Sengupta Erenwine sat at the old wooden table on the back porch of the Reverend Mildred's house, it was spectacular.

The old table sat solid beneath her forearms, paint-streaked, worn through in spots where years had left their trace. Before her, Odin's Wind. She had started the painting before her architectural exams, before she imagined selling the rowhouse in Brooklyn, inheriting Mildred's house, digging roots into Binghamton's slow rhythm. Mildred's sister Muriel arranged the transfer.

The leaves had already passed their peak since her thirty-second equinox birthday, colors rich, deep, scattered in crisp piles across the lawn. Some hung mid-fall, caught between branch and ground, twisting in the breeze. Each gust lifted them in swells, tumbling, skimming the deck with a dry hiss.

The painting was almost finished—its blues and golds threading together, the brushstrokes shaping wind into form, movement locked into canvas. She dipped her brush, dragged deep indigo into the texture, watched the pigment spread like dusk over sky, swallowing the layer beneath it. The porch creaked. Wind needled through the screens. She paused, tracked the wind across the yard; it tugged at the clothesline, and another flurry of leaves broke loose from the high branches and scattered to ground.

She thought about the wind not as weather, but as a force that could be harnessed, redirected, translated into motion. She'd been sketching and painting for years. Not for clients. For continuity. For survival. She hadn't come to Binghamton just to inherit a house. She didn't want to preserve the past. She wanted to prototype the future, one painting at a time.

Her phone rang; it was Jen, friend and colleague in the architectural firm. She wiped her hands on a rag. She stepped inside, the screen door clicking shut behind her. The air was warmer, scented faintly with pie and old wood. She crossed to the sink, turned on the tap, and let the water run cool over her fingers. The brushstrokes lingered in her muscles, but the shift in light—porch to kitchen—made everything feel slightly reframed.

Jen's voice came through the phone, steady and familiar.

"Hey, Catskills. How's your side of the world?" Amalia dried her hands on a towel, one of Mildred's, faded but soft, and leaned against the counter. Outside, the wind kept moving. Inside, the house held its own quiet. She'd inherited the structure, but she was still figuring out how to live in it. The kitchen felt like a pause in the day, a place between decisions. She wasn't sure what she was becoming, only that something was unfolding.

"Cold," Jen said. "Pretty, though. The trees are hanging onto the last of the leaves. Everything smells like woodsmoke."

"Same here. Minus the woodsmoke."

"Betsy says New Jersey is the same as ever," Jen said.

"She's got ideas brewing. Says we should start pitching more aggressively. Get jobs on the books." A gust of wind pushed through the yard, rattling the branches, pushing through the open back door. Papers rustled and rushed in the wind to the floor. She glanced at the documents Muriel had sent, unclipped and fallen to the old linoleum tile. The house transfer papers, the note in Muriel's looping script. "Muriel thinks I've landed," Amalia said, picking up the papers. "Like this house is the final piece."

"Isn't it?" Jen asked.

"It's a canvas," Amalia said. "But I haven't chosen the palette." She stared at Muriel's note, the signature. It felt like someone else's composition—balanced, finished, but not hers.

She tore a corner from the envelope, took it back outside, and set it into the wet paint. The paper curled slightly, resisting.

She dipped her brush, dragged a streak of indigo across the edge, sealing it in. The wind caught the scent of pigment and paper and floated it up. "I need movement," she said. "Not just shelter. Not just a place to be."

She needed systems that moved with the world. Not static structures, but living ones. Infrastructure that didn't just hold people—that connected them, protected them. The kind of design that didn't wait for crisis to prove its worth. Where would she connect with that kind of design?

Projects that once took months to plan vanished before the first sketch dried. Developers scaled back. Budgets froze. Timelines thinned into static. One by one, firms vanished under the drag of their own weight. Proposals dissolved mid-draft. She wondered about quitting, temp work, teaching. New York design studios hollowed out. Betsy said they were fine. Amalia heard tension between the words. Work had become like the wind: everywhere, invisible, hard to hold. Clients nodded, smiled, promised follow-ups that never came. "We should talk. Soon. You, me, Betsy. Get a plan."

"Are you finishing Odin's Wind right now?"

"I thought I finished it years ago, but little did I know."

"Send me pictures when you do."

The wind folded into the quiet. Road noise hummed behind it. The season changed in her bones. She dipped her brush again, pressed it to the canvas, watched the blue stretch across the surface.

It would be finished. But first, there would be Thanksgiving at her dad's. The pie was cooling inside, ready to be strapped into its container and hauled by bus to Pennsylvania.

~ 2 ~
Betsy's World

Betsy Mei Polson, born in the 1960s and with looks no worse off than if she'd been born twenty years later (according to her mother), stood at the kitchen counter, arranging sweet potato slices in concentric rings like she was drafting a roofline. The twins, Jacob and Jonathan, were sprawled on the living room floor, building a Lego duplex with solar panels and a suspiciously oversized hot tub.

Her mother sat at the dining table folding napkins. "You're making too much," she said, without looking up. Her mum's face, unlike Betsy's, showed the lines of time.

"It's Thanksgiving," Betsy replied. "Too much is tradition."

She glanced at the fridge. Ben's handwriting was on the calendar—a note about a Cambridge conference circled twice. He hadn't erased himself. Just... relocated.

"Hey guys," she called. "Quick break from construction?"

Jacob looked up. "Is this about Dad?"

Jonathan didn't look up. "He's not coming, right?"

Betsy nodded. "He's working in Cambridge. We're figuring things out. It's not about you. It's about grown-ups needing space to think clearly."

Jacob shrugged. "Okay. Can we do the scavenger hunt later?"

"Of course," she said. "And you get to pick the movie tonight."

They went back to their Lego city. Betsy turned back to the pie, slicing thinner now. She didn't cry. She didn't even flinch. She just felt the quiet rest like fog.

Her phone buzzed. A video call. Jen and Amalia, already mid-laugh, mid-chaos.

"Happy Thanksgiving!" Jen shouted, her background a blur of Catskills woodgrain.

Amalia leaned into frame. "We started without you. Sorry!"

Betsy smiled. "I was wrangling pie and children."

"Who's coming over?" Amalia asked.

"My mum and the kids," Betsy said, keeping her tone light. "Small crew. Cozy chaos."

Jen raised an eyebrow. "No Ben?"

"Cambridge," Betsy said. "Orbiting."

Amalia nodded, not pressing. "Tell the twins we expect a full report on pie quality."

"I'll have them draft a memo," Betsy said.

Jen grinned. "Speaking of memos—we need to talk about our first quarter of next year. FEMA's steady, but the theater project is frozen. The Jersey Shore retrofit's dragging."

Amalia leaned into the screen. "We need something to build on. Something that matters."

Betsy took a sip of her tea. "We need something that pays."

"What about that Flatbush walk-through? Mold," Jen said, "cracked foundation, no insulation."

Amalia nodded. "It's a mess. But it's ours."

"Then let's make it beautiful," Betsy said.

The call rolled on—laughter, updates, a brief debate about whether solar panels should be standard in every design. But after it ended, Betsy stood alone in the kitchen, the scent of cinnamon and quiet settling around her. She didn't feel broken, but ... paused.

Around the corner, the twins were arguing about whether their Lego city needed a rooftop garden. Betsy stepped into the room.

"Rooftop garden's a yes!"

~ End of Bonus Chapters ~

Acknowledgements

I would like to thank many key people who contributed to the flow and creation of this story:

my family: sister Cass Chowdhury who provided a huge amount of archeological information and input, not to mention comic relief in many years' worth of 'bones' jokes (errors are mine, not hers), parents Sheila Chowdhury and Dev Chowdhury who maintained a steady interest in my progress with the work, and of course Tom, James, and Chris Gilman, who were part of the initial inspiration of this series of Erenwine books;

my stellar editor, Jillian Magalaner Stone, without whom this story would not have structure, and Jane Collins-Colding, who contributed to much discussion of the novel over the last many years;

my beta reader, Deidre D'Entremont, who gave me hope early on that this story could, indeed, have structure, and was worth pursuing;

my shamanic somatic group of friends who've supported me on retreats through this process, led by Lori Dalvi (also book designer!) and Gena Rho, at Dharmakaya Center for Wellbeing, a Buddhist retreat in Cragsmoor, New York;

my oldest sister-friends, Alison Bain and Pamela Costanzo, who never doubt me;

my newer sister-friends, Lucia Vaca-Izurieta and Smitha Murthy, who support me;

my newest sister-friends, Kerry Cordero and Julie Perlow-Greene, who help me to amplify who I am inside.

Countless others have influenced the weave of this story, and I thank you, too.

—Maia